SHAZAM! THUNDERCRACK

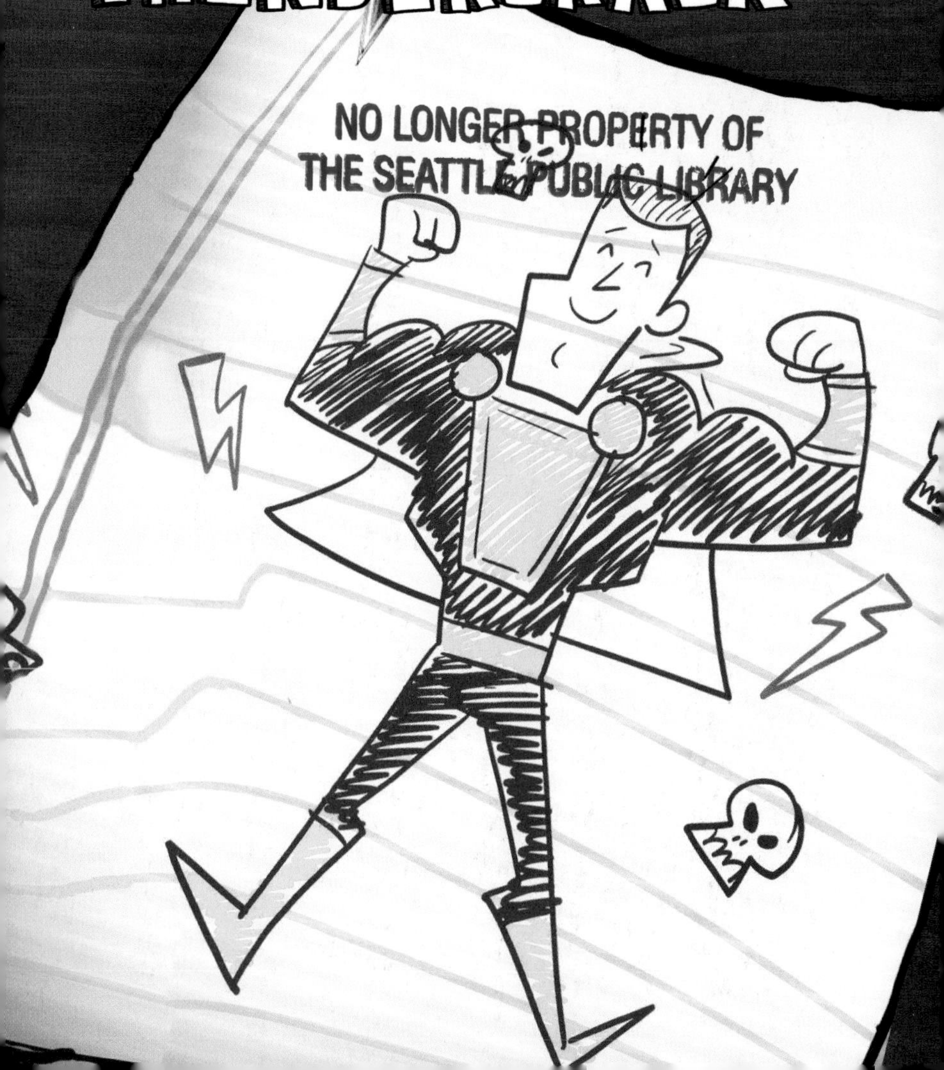

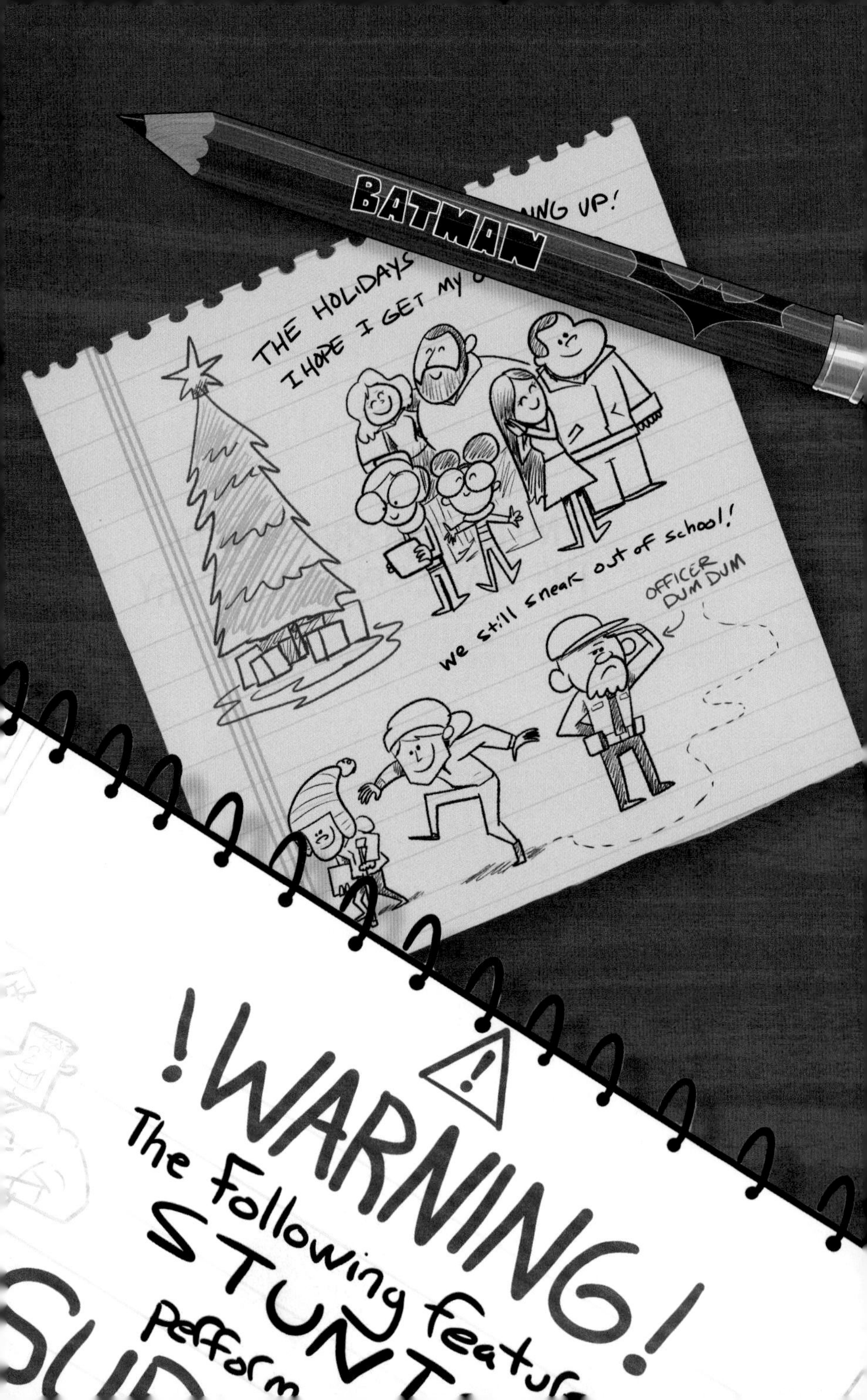

BATMAN
NG UP!
THE HOLIDAYS
I HOPE I GET MY
we still sneak out of school!
OFFICER DUM DUM
!WARNING!
The following featu
STUNT
Perform

SHAZAM! THUNDERCRACK

Written, drawn, and colored by Yehudi Mercado

Lettered by Saida Temofonte

Cover by Yehudi Mercado

Superman created by Jerry Siegel and Joe Shuster.

By special arrangement with the

Jerry Siegel family

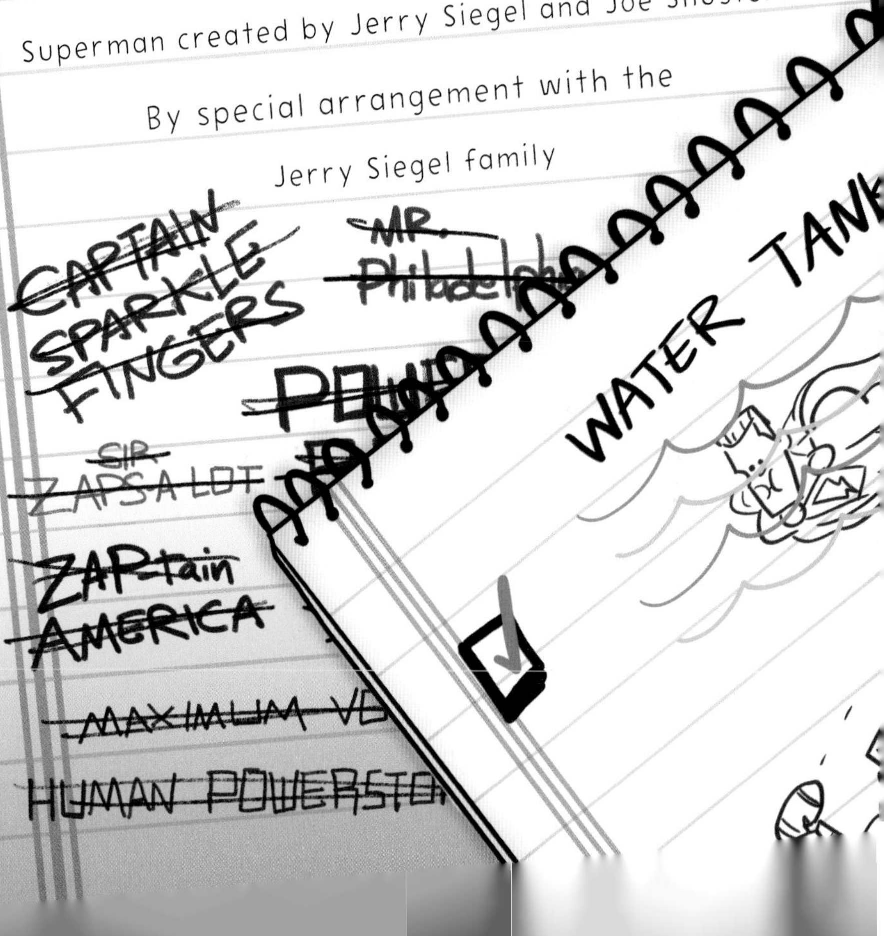

~~CAPTAIN SPARKLE FINGERS~~ ~~MR. Philadelphia~~

~~SIR ZAPSALOT~~ ~~PEW~~

~~ZAPtain AMERICA~~

~~MAXIMUM V8~~

~~HUMAN POWERSTO~~

WATER TANK

KRISTY QUINN   Editor
STEVE COOK   Design Director – Books
SYDNEY LEE + AMIE BROCKWAY-METCALF   Publication Design
SANDY ALONZO   Publication Production

MARIE JAVINS   Editor-in-Chief, DC Comics

ANNE DePIES   Senior VP – General Manager
JIM LEE   Publisher & Chief Creative Officer
DON FALLETTI   VP – Manufacturing Operations & Workflow Management
LAWRENCE GANEM   VP – Talent Services
ALISON GILL   Senior VP – Manufacturing & Operations
JEFFREY KAUFMAN   VP – Editorial Strategy & Programming
NICK J. NAPOLITANO   VP – Manufacturing Administration & Design
NANCY SPEARS   VP – Revenue

SHAZAM! THUNDERCRACK

Published by DC Comics. Copyright © 2023 DC Comics. All Rights
Reserved. All characters, their distinctive likenesses, and related
elements featured in this publication are trademarks of DC Comics.
The DC logo is a trademark of DC Comics. The stories, characters, and
incidents featured in this publication are entirely fictional. DC Comics does
not read or accept unsolicited submissions of ideas, stories, or artwork.

DC Comics, 4000 Warner Blvd., Bldg. 700, 2nd Floor, Burbank, CA 91522
Printed by Worzalla, Stevens Point, WI, USA. 1/13/23.
First Printing.
ISBN: 978-1-77950-502-6

MIX
Paper from
responsible sources
FSC® C002589

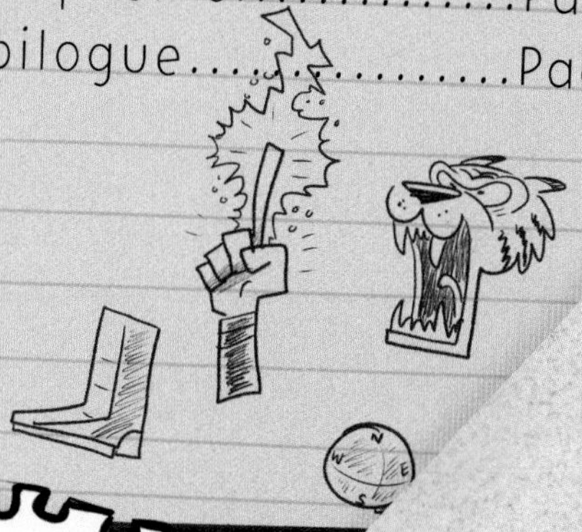

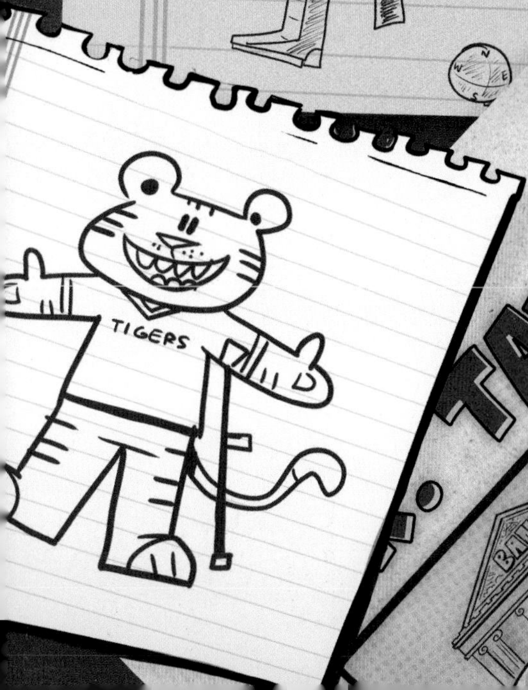
TIGERS

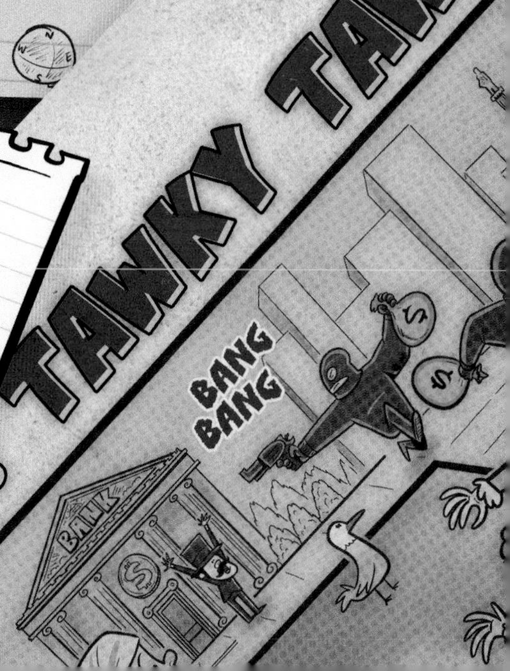
TAWKY
BANG BANG
BANK

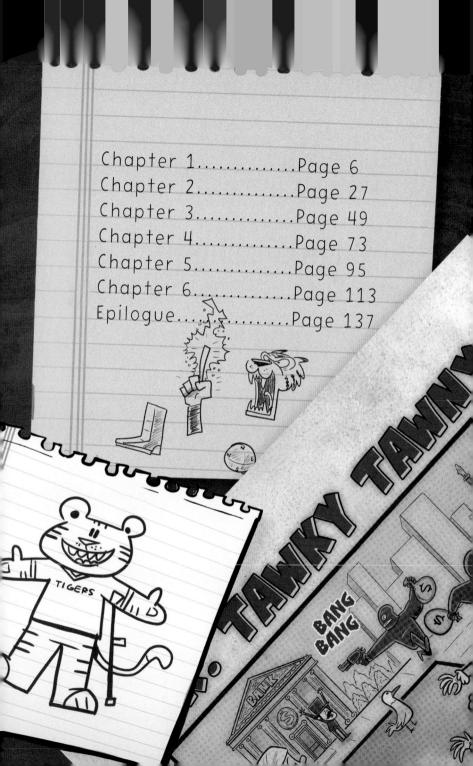

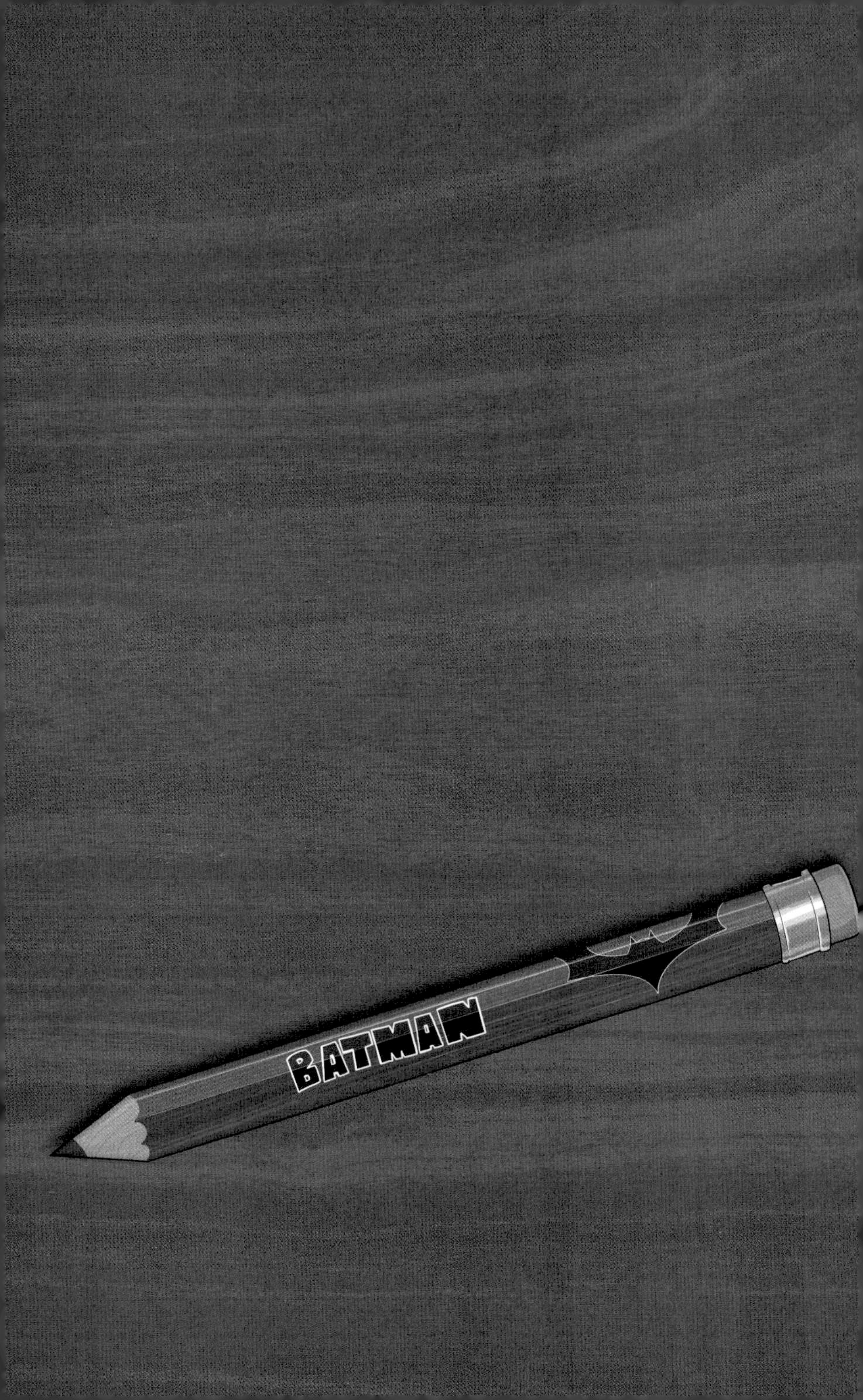
BATMAN

CHAPTER 1

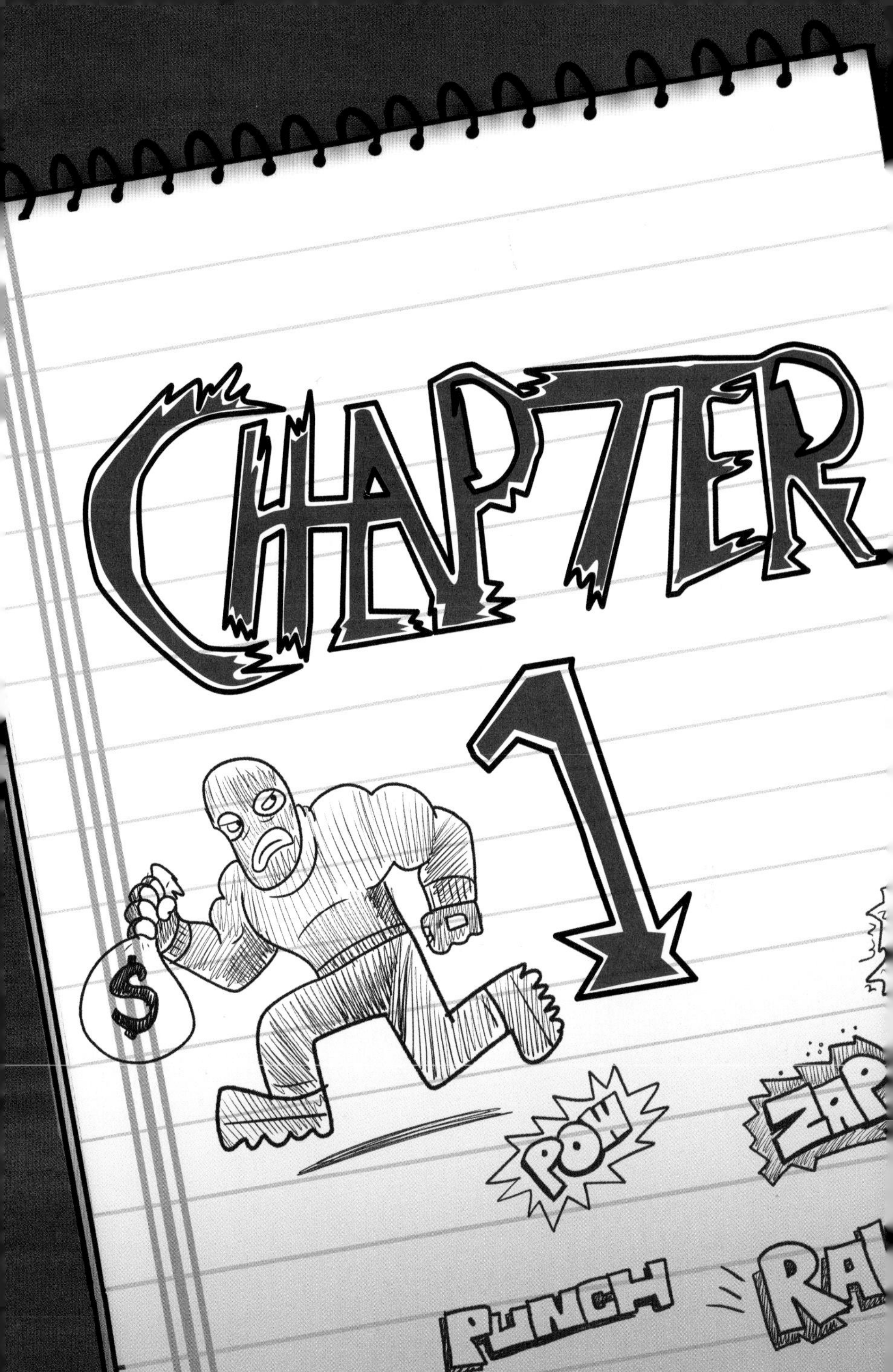

POW
PUNCH

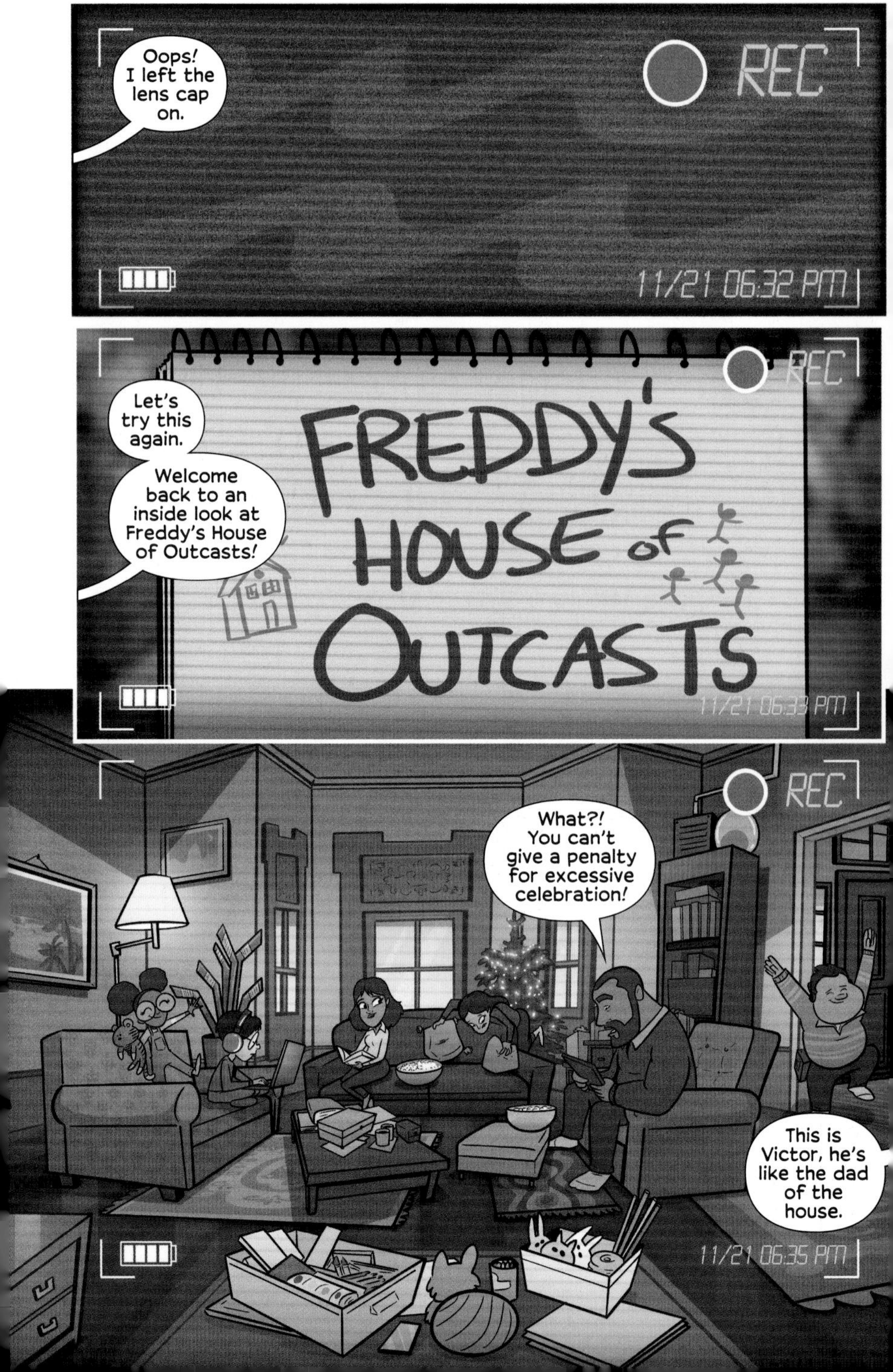
Oops! I left the lens cap on.
REC
11/21 06:32 PM
Let's try this again.
Welcome back to an inside look at Freddy's House of Outcasts!
FREDDY'S HOUSE of OUTCASTS
REC
11/21 06:33 PM
What?! You can't give a penalty for excessive celebration!
This is Victor, he's like the dad of the house.
REC
11/21 06:35 PM

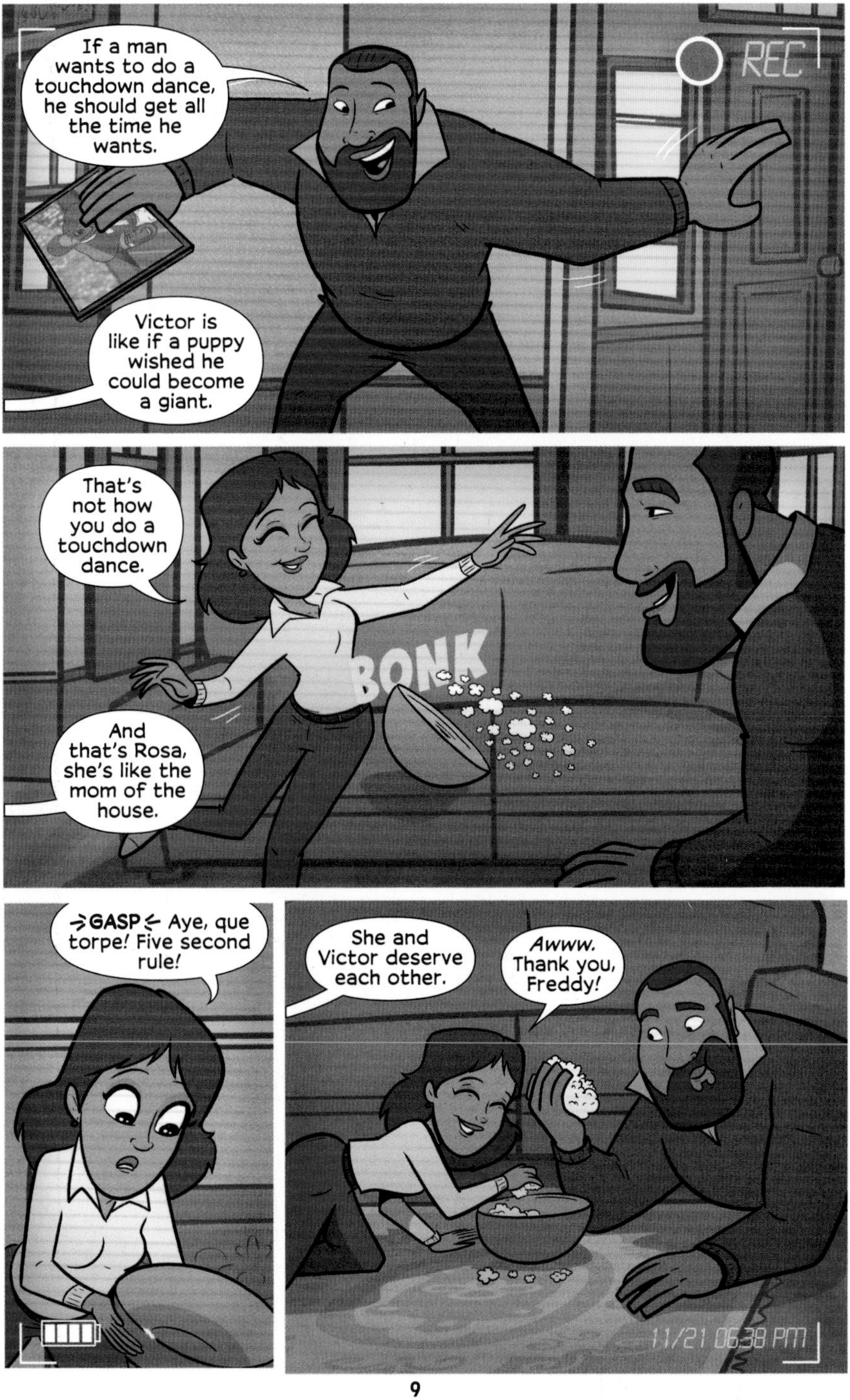
REC
If a man wants to do a touchdown dance, he should get all the time he wants.
Victor is like if a puppy wished he could become a giant.
That's not how you do a touchdown dance.
BONK
And that's Rosa, she's like the mom of the house.
GASP Aye, que torpe! Five second rule!
She and Victor deserve each other.
Awww. Thank you, Freddy!
11/21 06:38 PM

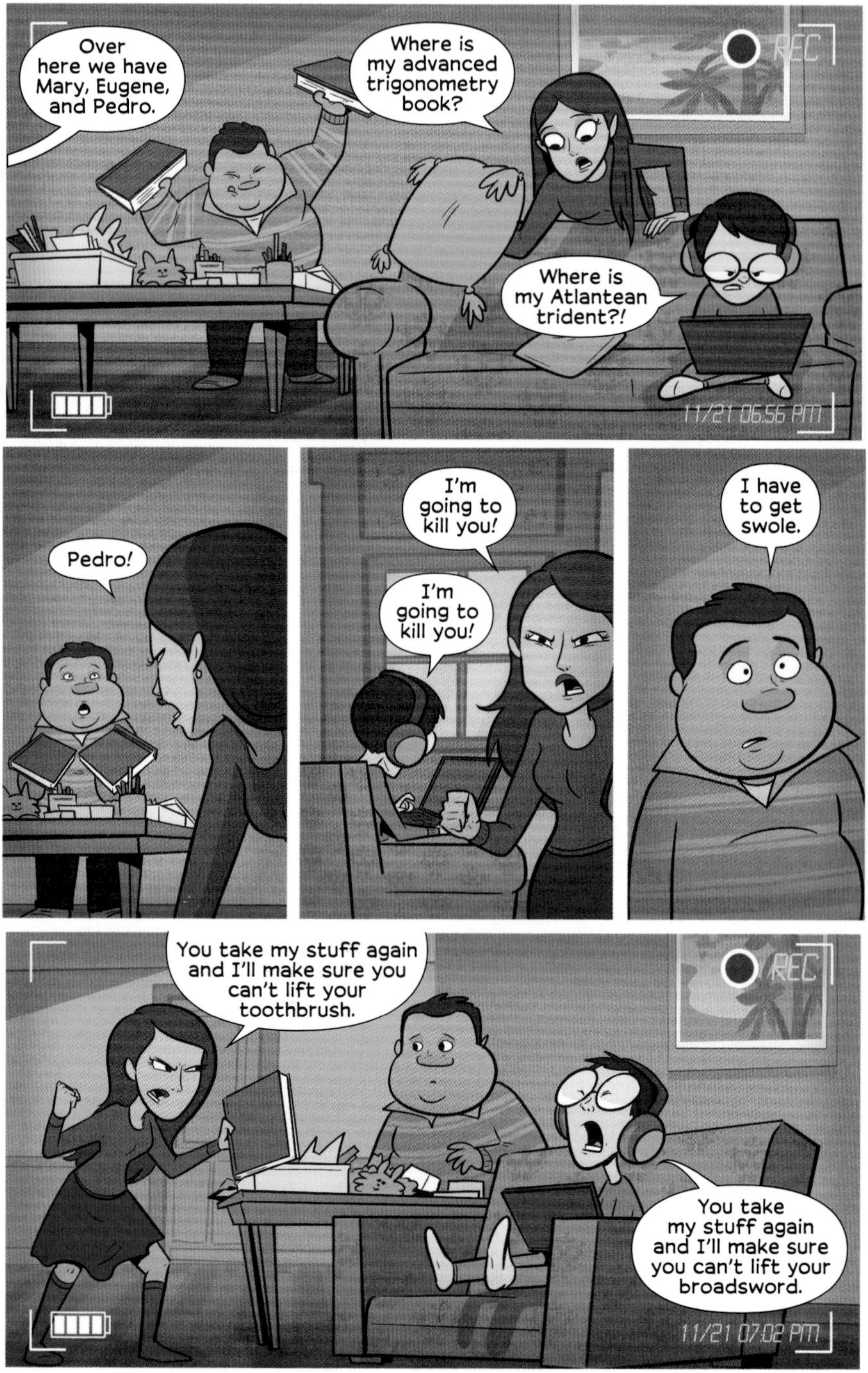
Over here we have Mary, Eugene, and Pedro.
Where is my advanced trigonometry book?
REC
Where is my Atlantean trident?!
11/21 06:56 PM
Pedro!
I'm going to kill you!
I'm going to kill you!
I have to get swole.
You take my stuff again and I'll make sure you can't lift your toothbrush.
REC
You take my stuff again and I'll make sure you can't lift your broadsword.
11/21 07:02 PM

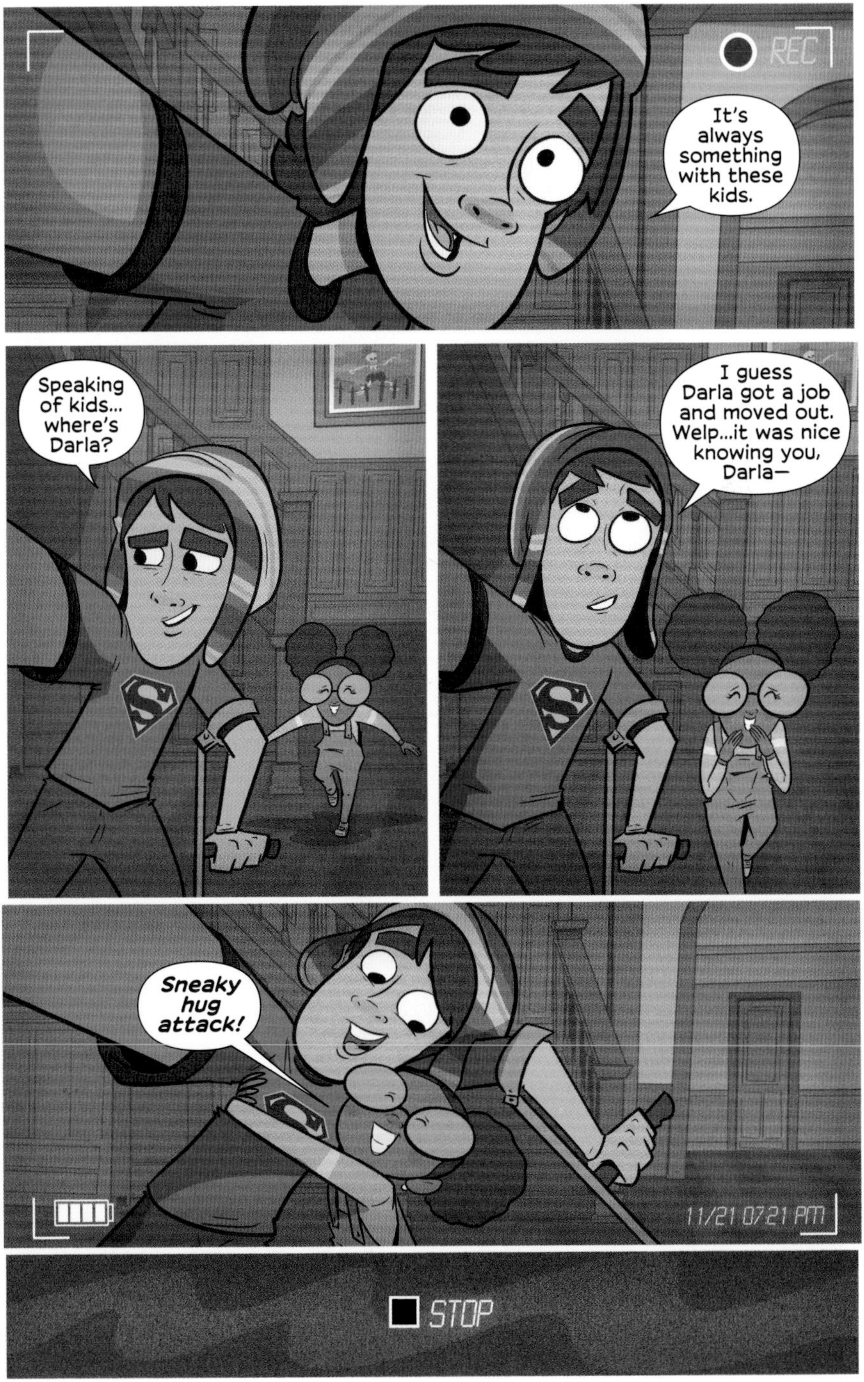
REC
It's always something with these kids.
Speaking of kids... where's Darla?
I guess Darla got a job and moved out. Welp...it was nice knowing you, Darla—
Sneaky hug attack!
11/21 07:21 PM
STOP

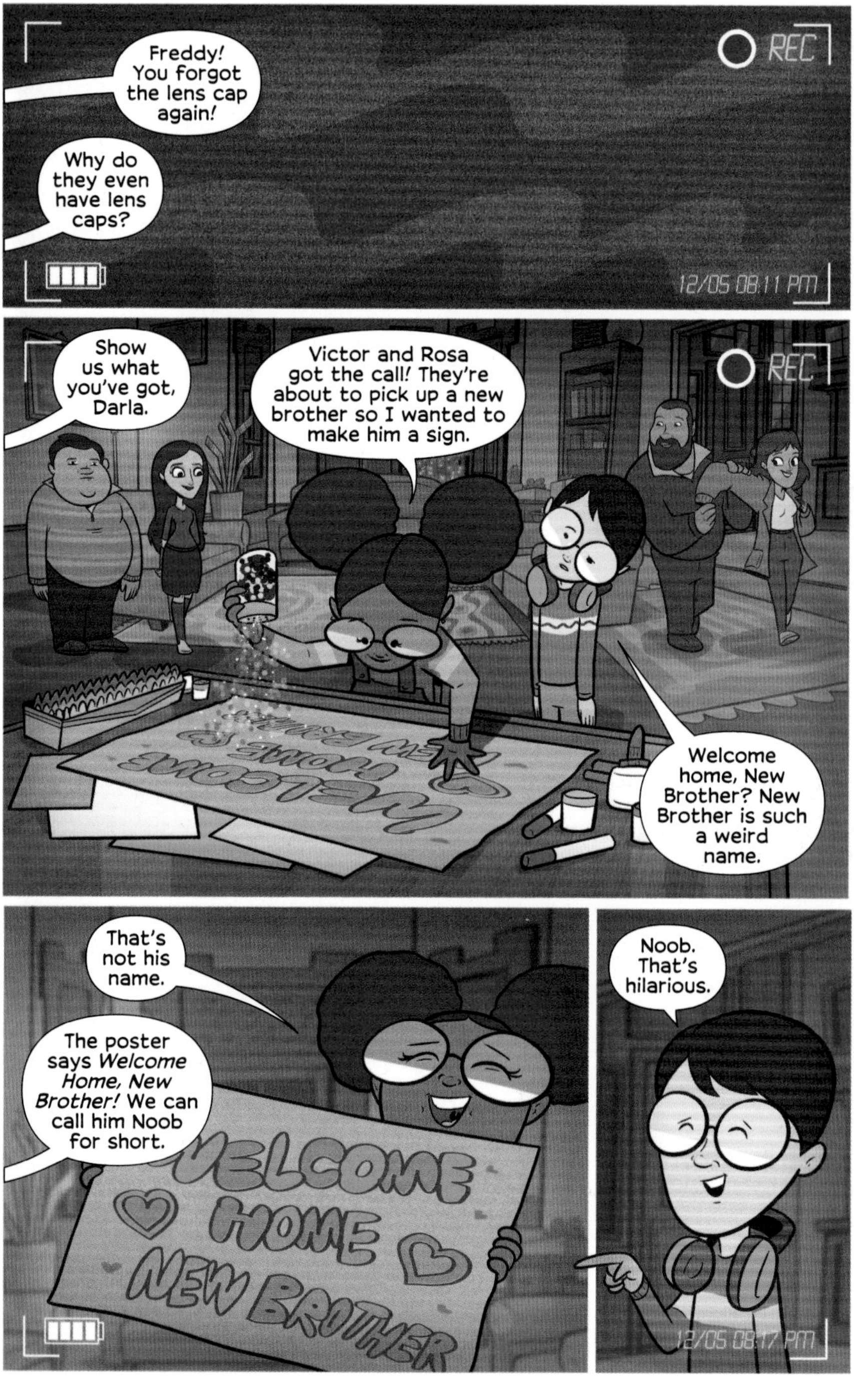
REC
Freddy! You forgot the lens cap again!
Why do they even have lens caps?
12/05 08:11 PM
REC
Show us what you've got, Darla.
Victor and Rosa got the call! They're about to pick up a new brother so I wanted to make him a sign.
Welcome home, New Brother? New Brother is such a weird name.
That's not his name.
The poster says *Welcome Home, New Brother!* We can call him Noob for short.
WELCOME HOME NEW BROTHER
Noob. That's hilarious.
12/05 08:17 PM

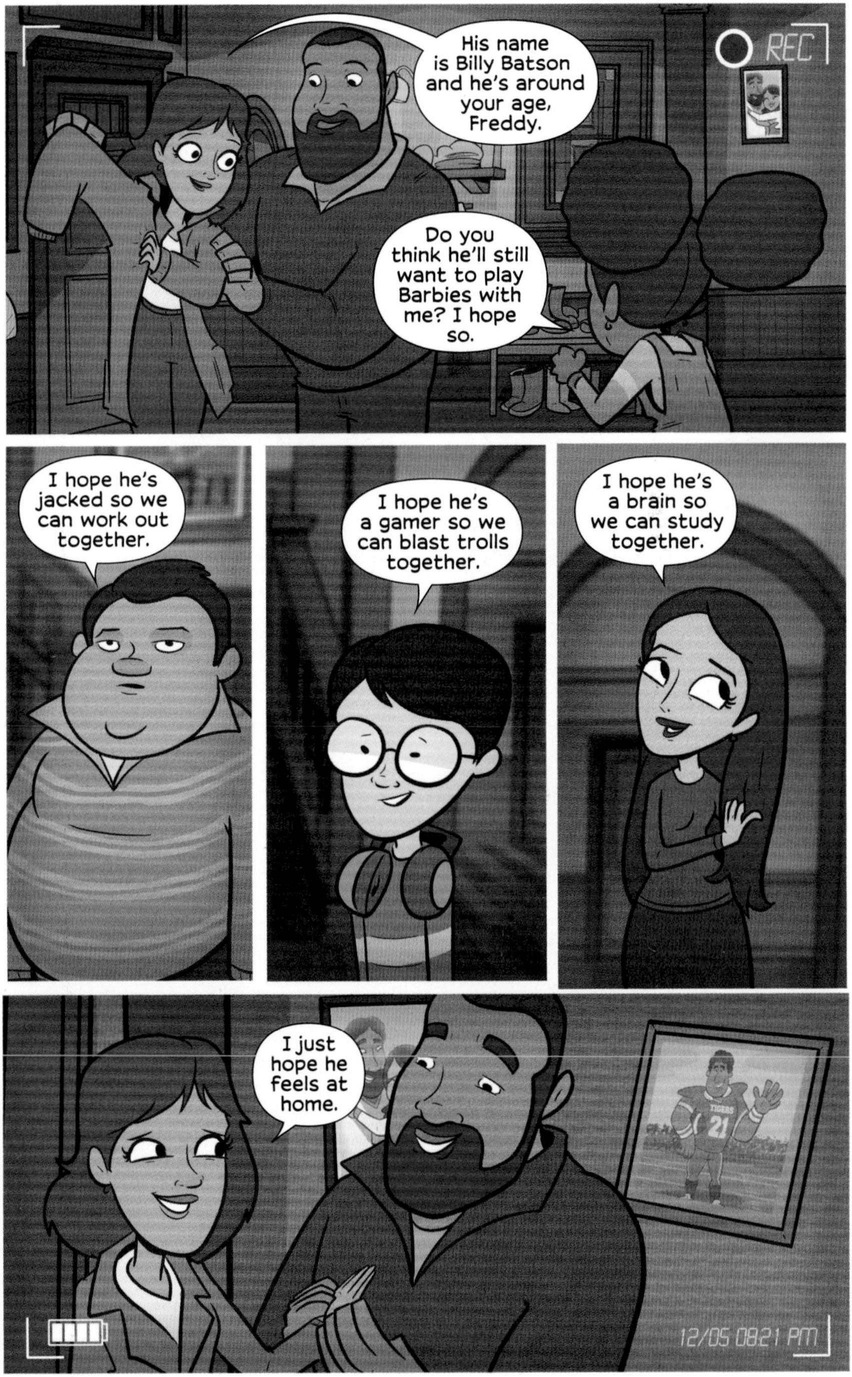
REC
His name is Billy Batson and he's around your age, Freddy.
Do you think he'll still want to play Barbies with me? I hope so.
I hope he's jacked so we can work out together.
I hope he's a gamer so we can blast trolls together.
I hope he's a brain so we can study together.
I just hope he feels at home.
TIGERS
21
12/05 08:21 PM

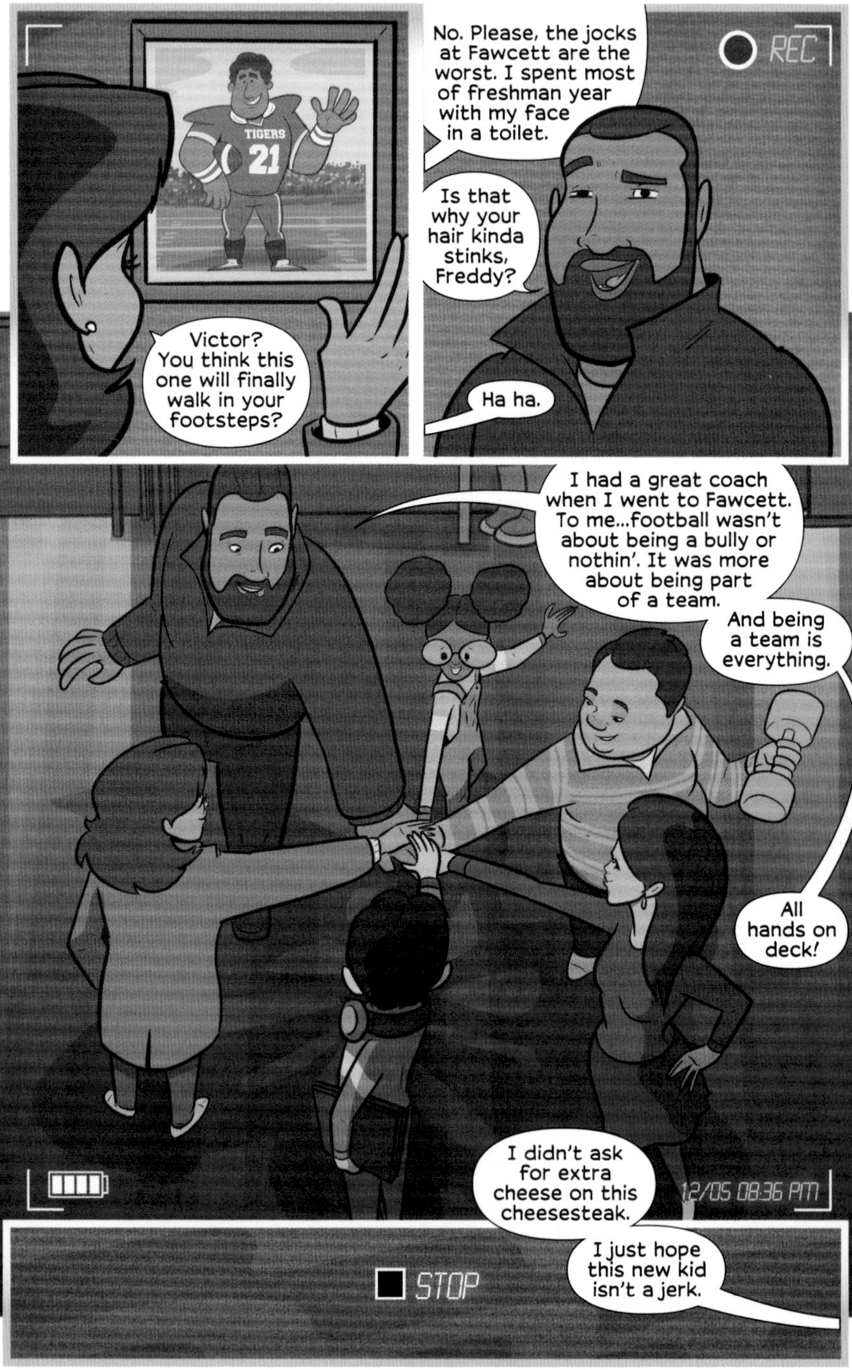
REC
Victor? You think this one will finally walk in your footsteps?
No. Please, the jocks at Fawcett are the worst. I spent most of freshman year with my face in a toilet.
Is that why your hair kinda stinks, Freddy?
Ha ha.
I had a great coach when I went to Fawcett. To me...football wasn't about being a bully or nothin'. It was more about being part of a team.
And being a team is everything.
All hands on deck!
I didn't ask for extra cheese on this cheesesteak.
12/05 08:36 PM
I just hope this new kid isn't a jerk.
STOP

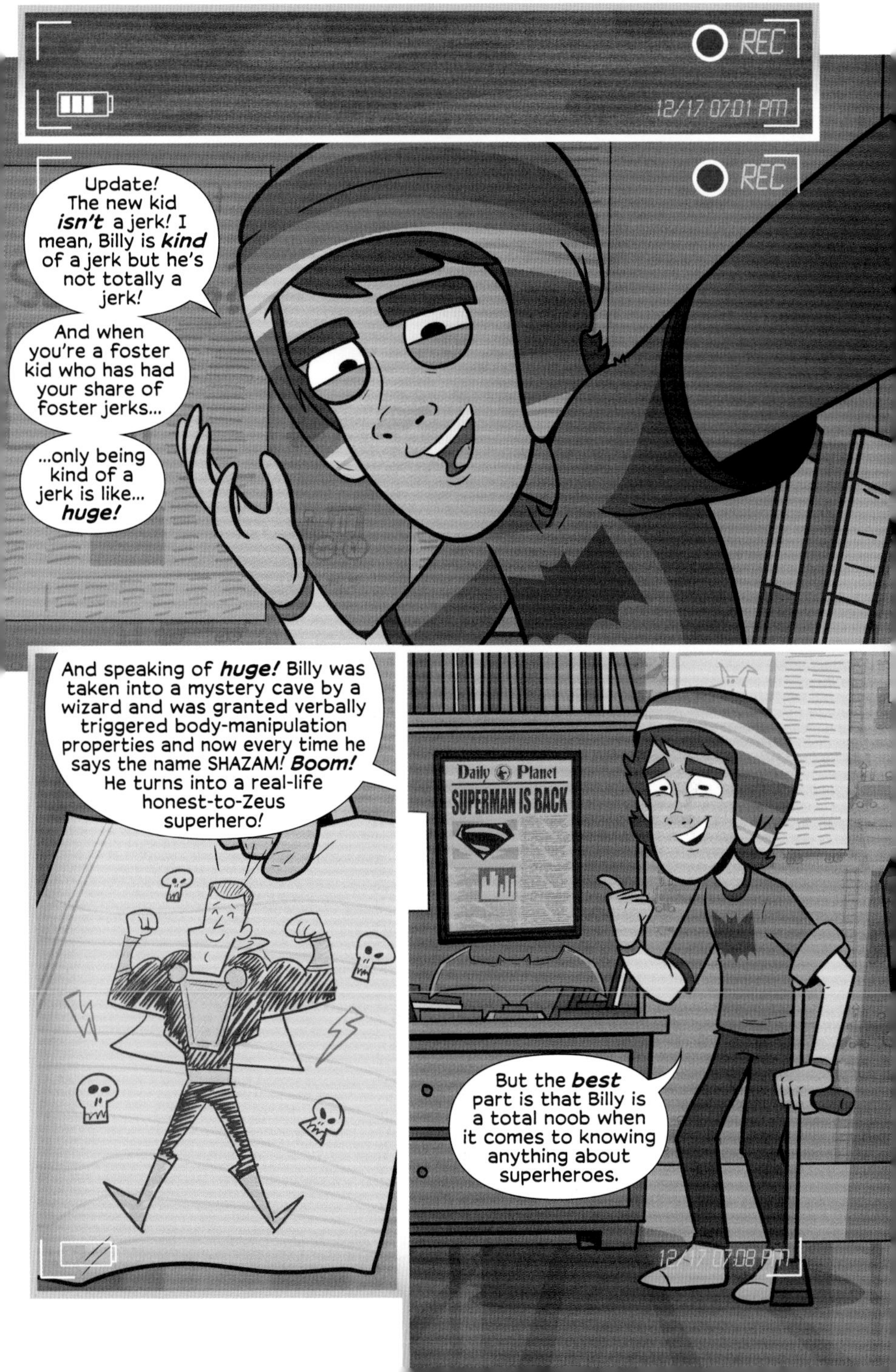
REC
12/17 07:01 PM
REC
Update! The new kid *isn't* a jerk! I mean, Billy is *kind* of a jerk but he's not totally a jerk!
And when you're a foster kid who has had your share of foster jerks...
...only being kind of a jerk is like... *huge!*
And speaking of *huge!* Billy was taken into a mystery cave by a wizard and was granted verbally triggered body-manipulation properties and now every time he says the name SHAZAM! *Boom!* He turns into a real-life honest-to-Zeus superhero!
Daily Planet
SUPERMAN IS BACK
But the *best* part is that Billy is a total noob when it comes to knowing anything about superheroes.
12/17 07:08 PM

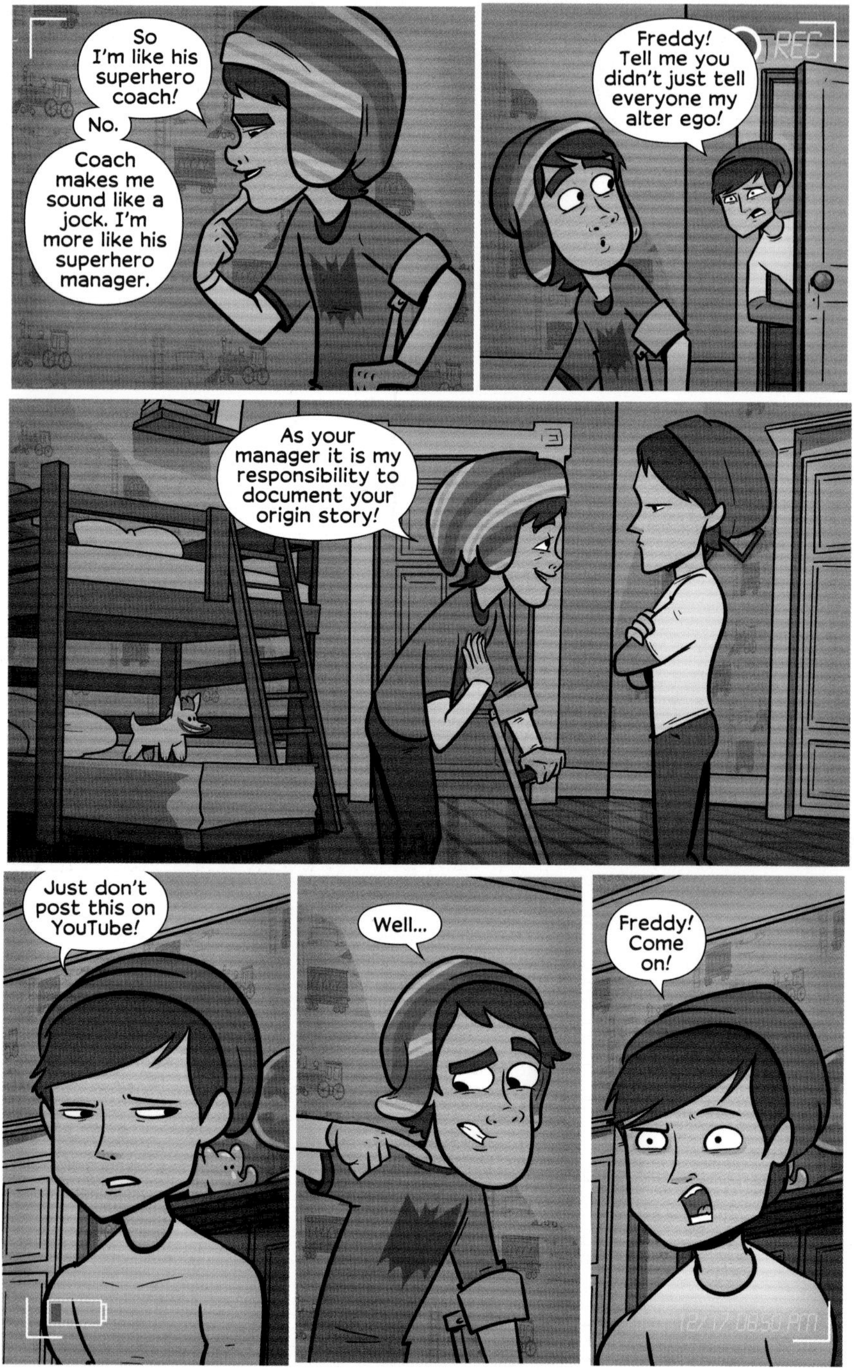

REC
So I'm like his superhero coach!
No.
Coach makes me sound like a jock. I'm more like his superhero manager.
Freddy! Tell me you didn't just tell everyone my alter ego!
As your manager it is my responsibility to document your origin story!
Just don't post this on YouTube!
Well...
Freddy! Come on!

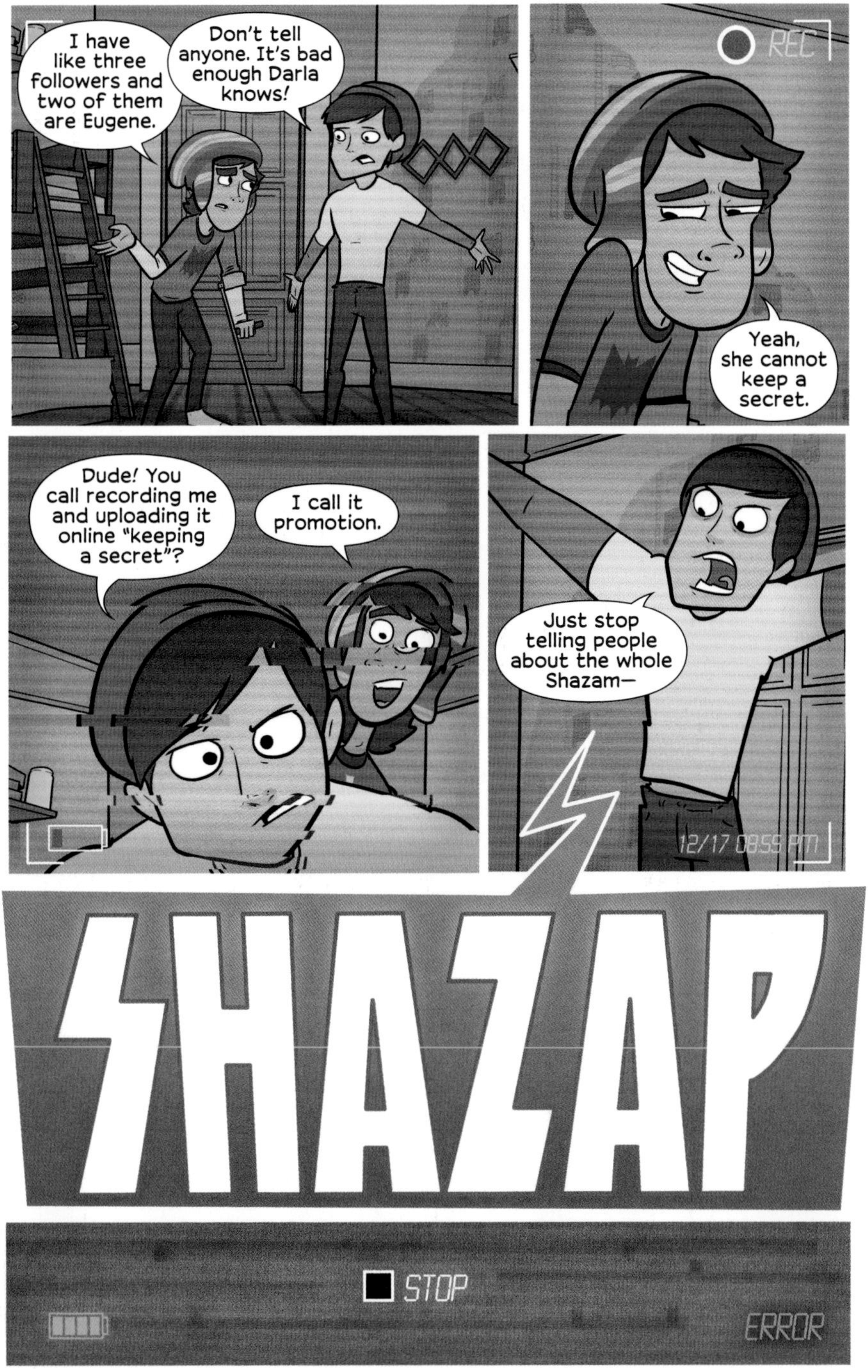
I have like three followers and two of them are Eugene.
Don't tell anyone. It's bad enough Darla knows!
REC
Yeah, she cannot keep a secret.
Dude! You call recording me and uploading it online "keeping a secret"?
I call it promotion.
Just stop telling people about the whole Shazam—
12/17 08:55 PM
SHAZAP
STOP
ERROR

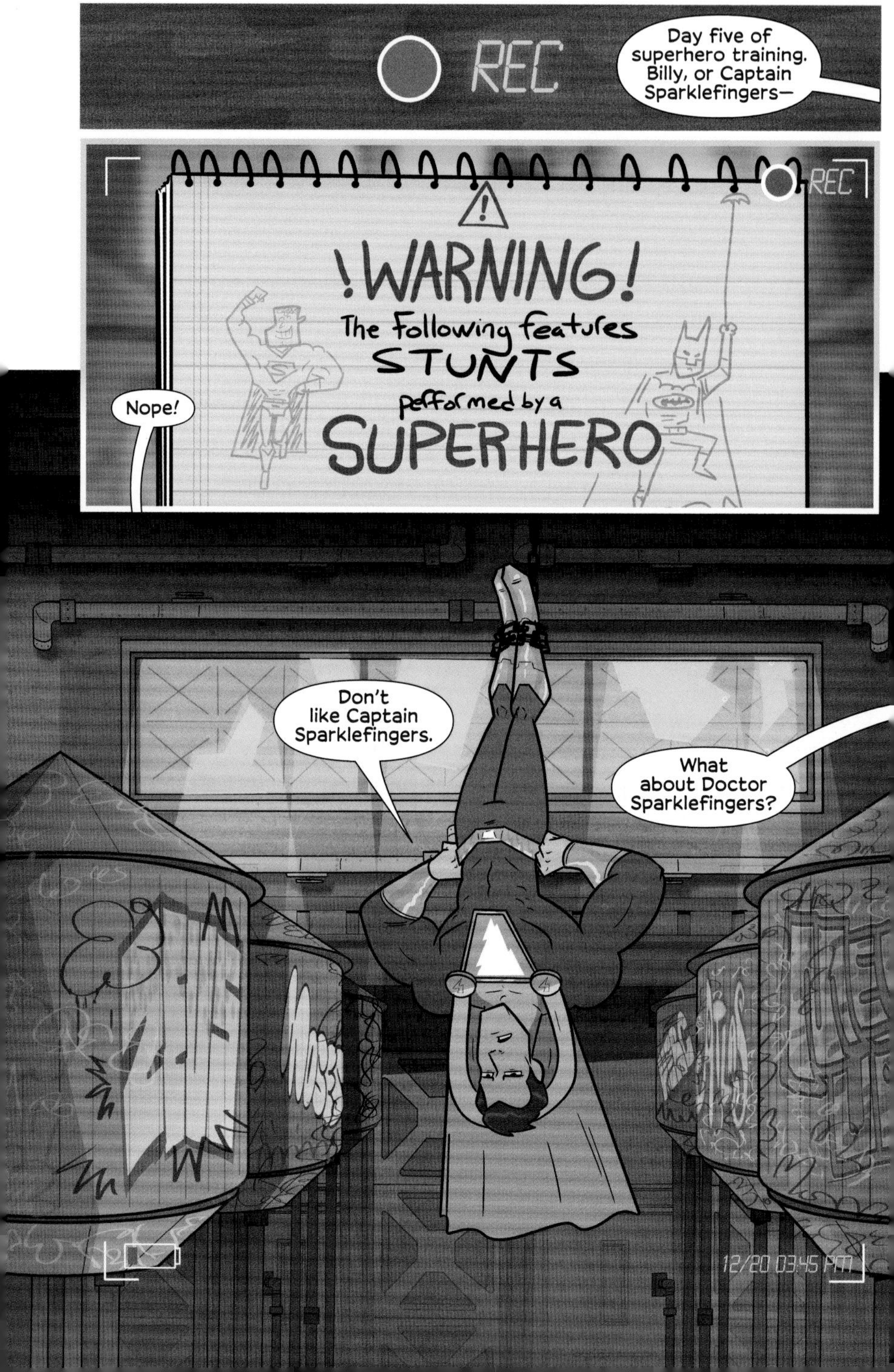
REC
Day five of superhero training. Billy, or Captain Sparklefingers—
REC
!WARNING!
The following features STUNTS performed by a SUPERHERO
Nope!
Don't like Captain Sparklefingers.
What about Doctor Sparklefingers?
12/20 03:45 PM

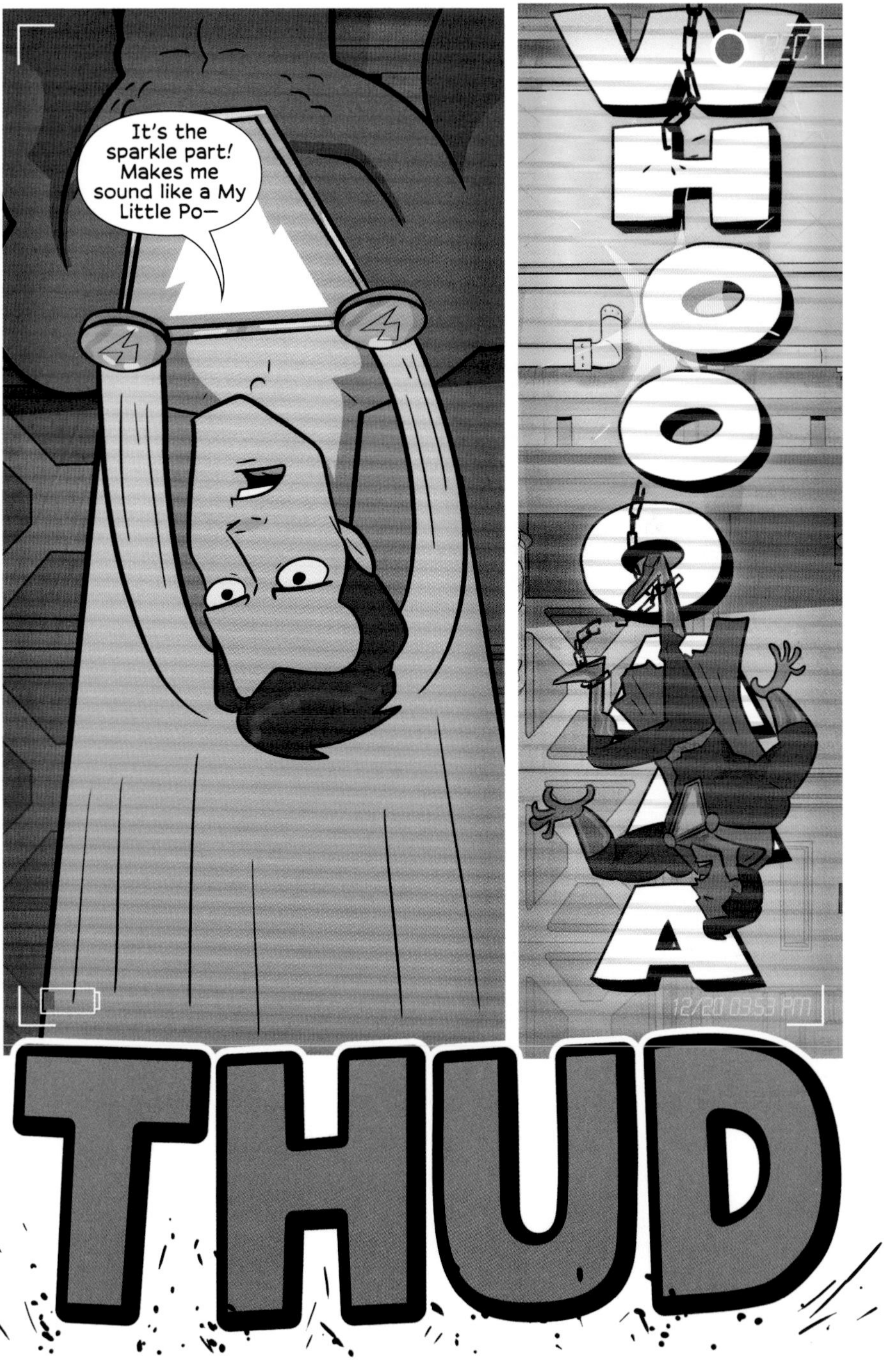
It's the sparkle part! Makes me sound like a My Little Po—
REC
WHOOOA
12/20 03:53 PM
THUD

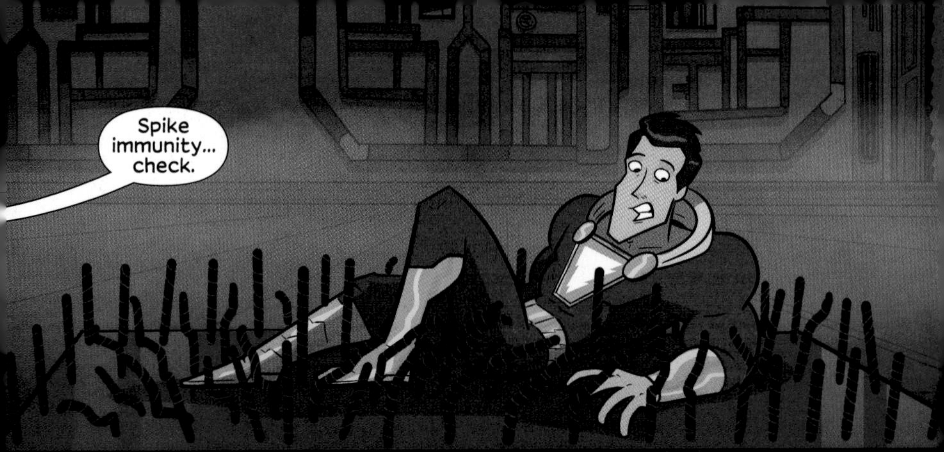
Spike immunity... check.

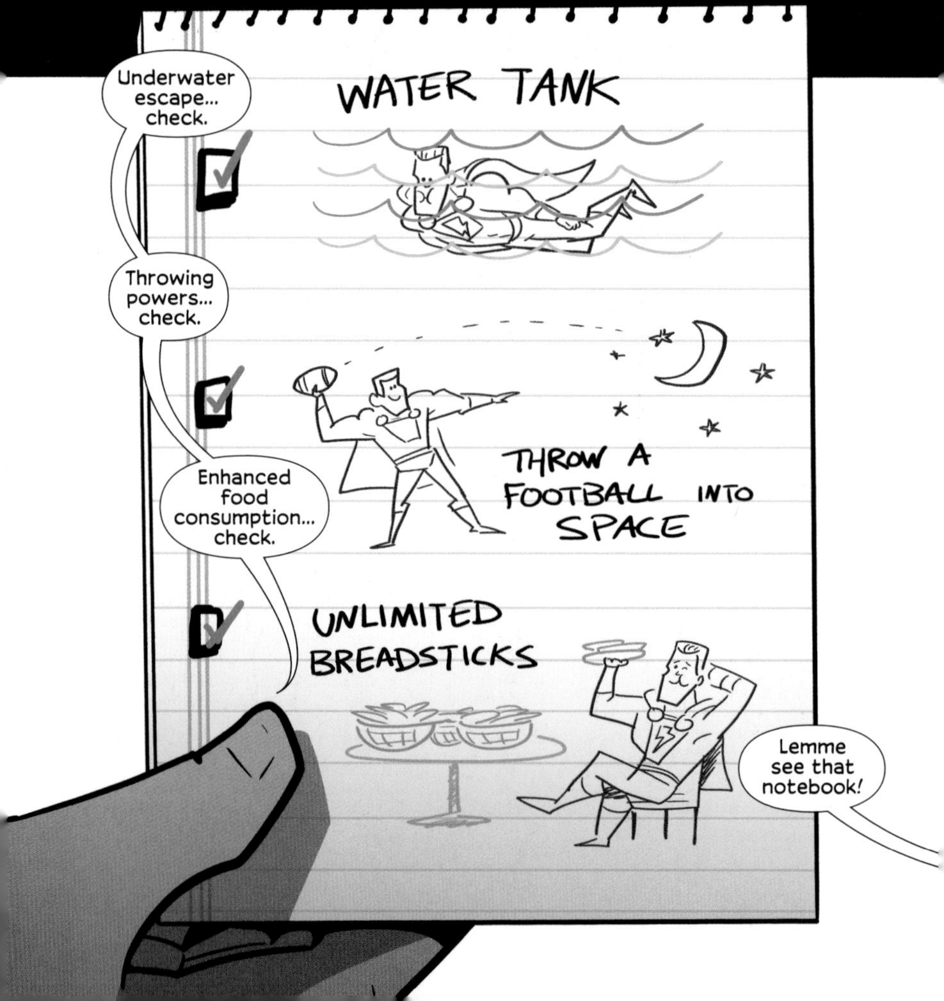
Underwater escape... check.
WATER TANK
Throwing powers... check.
THROW A FOOTBALL INTO SPACE
Enhanced food consumption... check.
UNLIMITED BREADSTICKS
Lemme see that notebook!

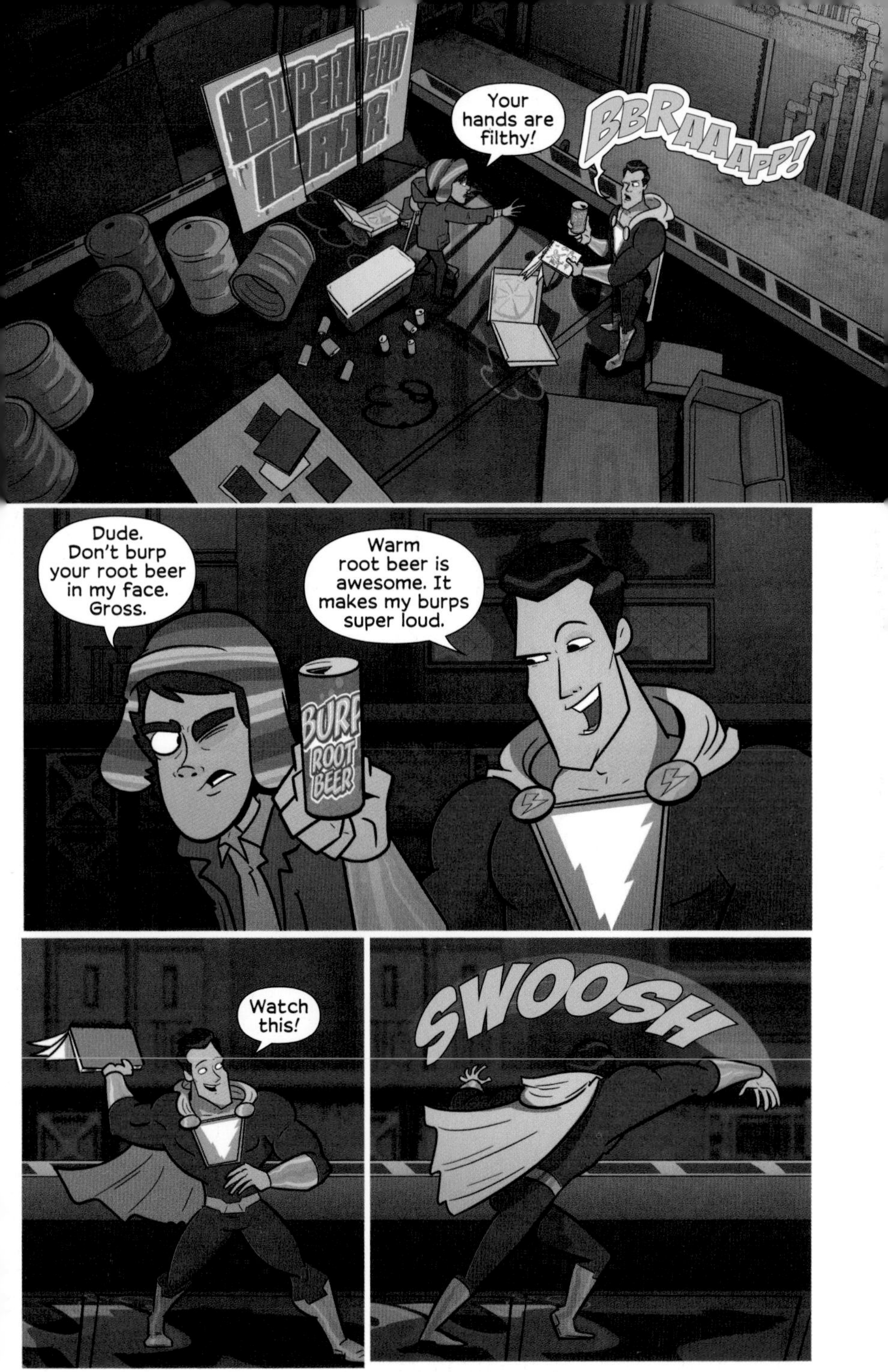
Your hands are filthy!
BBRAAAAPP!
Dude. Don't burp your root beer in my face. Gross.
Warm root beer is awesome. It makes my burps super loud.
BURP ROOT BEER
Watch this!
SWOOSH

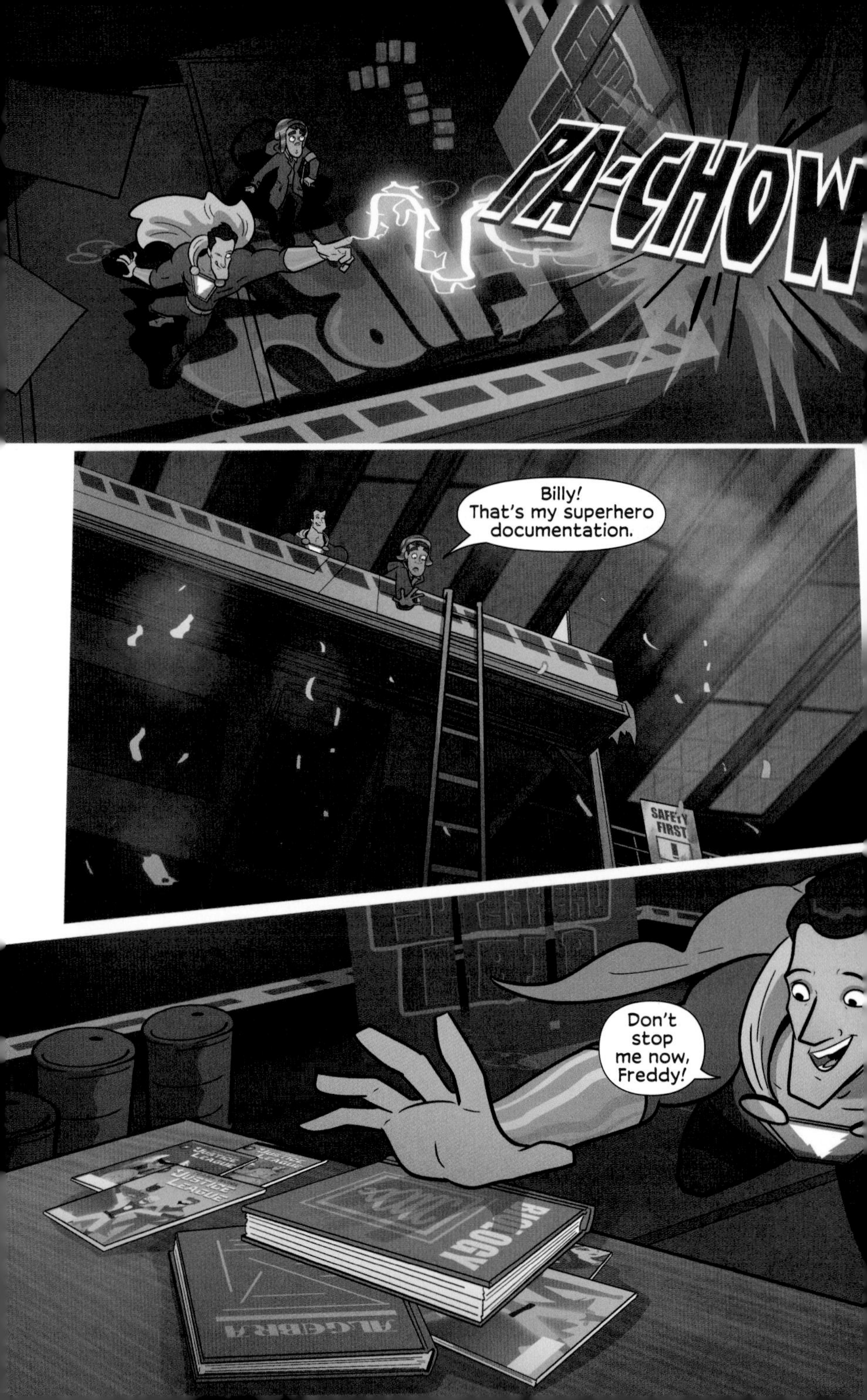
PA-CHOW
Billy! That's my superhero documentation.
SAFETY FIRST
Don't stop me now, Freddy!
JUSTICE LEAGUE
JUSTICE LEAGUE
JUSTICE LEAGUE
BIOLOGY
ALGEBRA

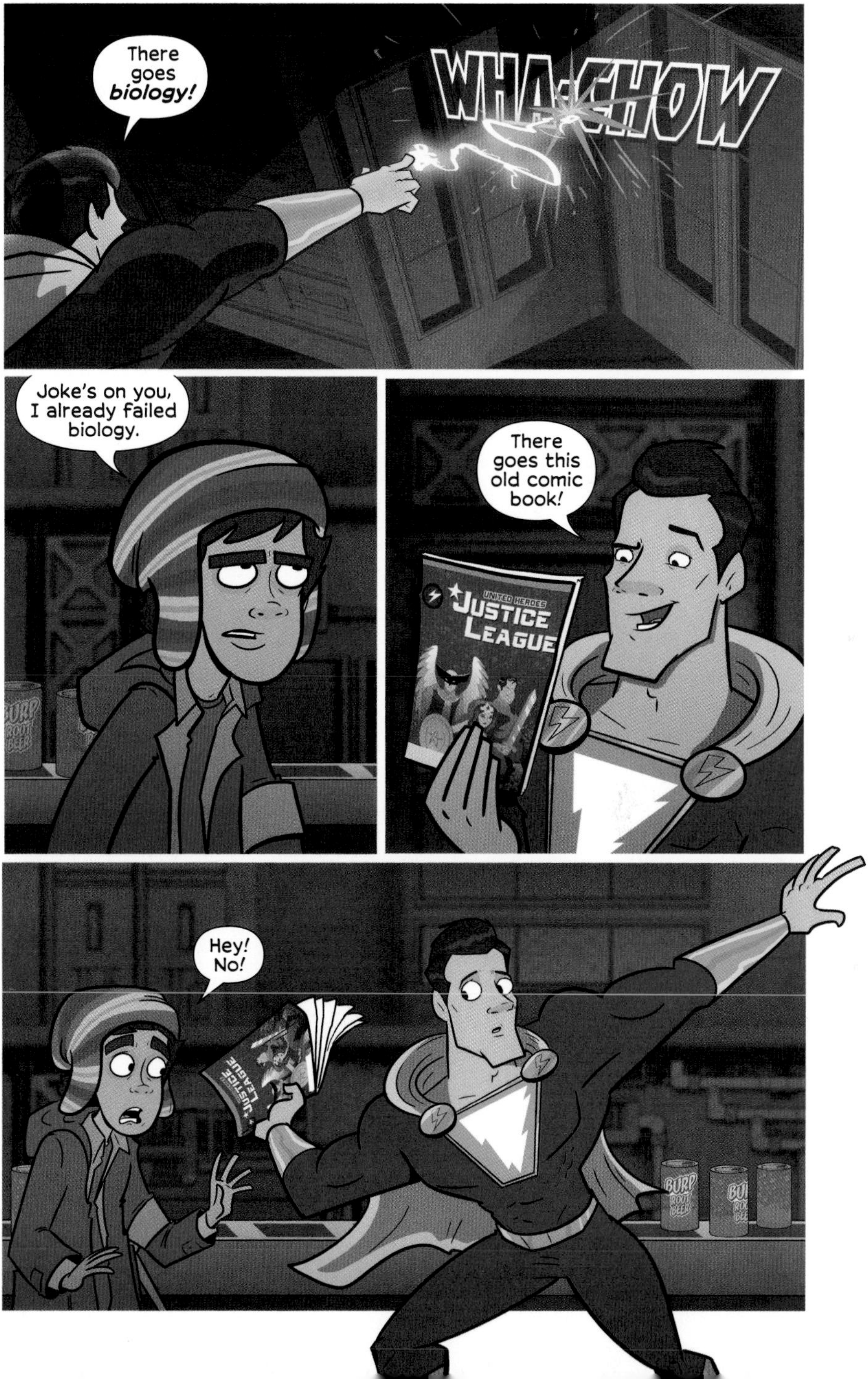
There goes *biology!*
WHA-CHOW
Joke's on you, I already failed biology.
There goes this old comic book!
UNITED HEROES
JUSTICE LEAGUE
BURP ROOT BEER
Hey! No!
BURP ROOT BEER

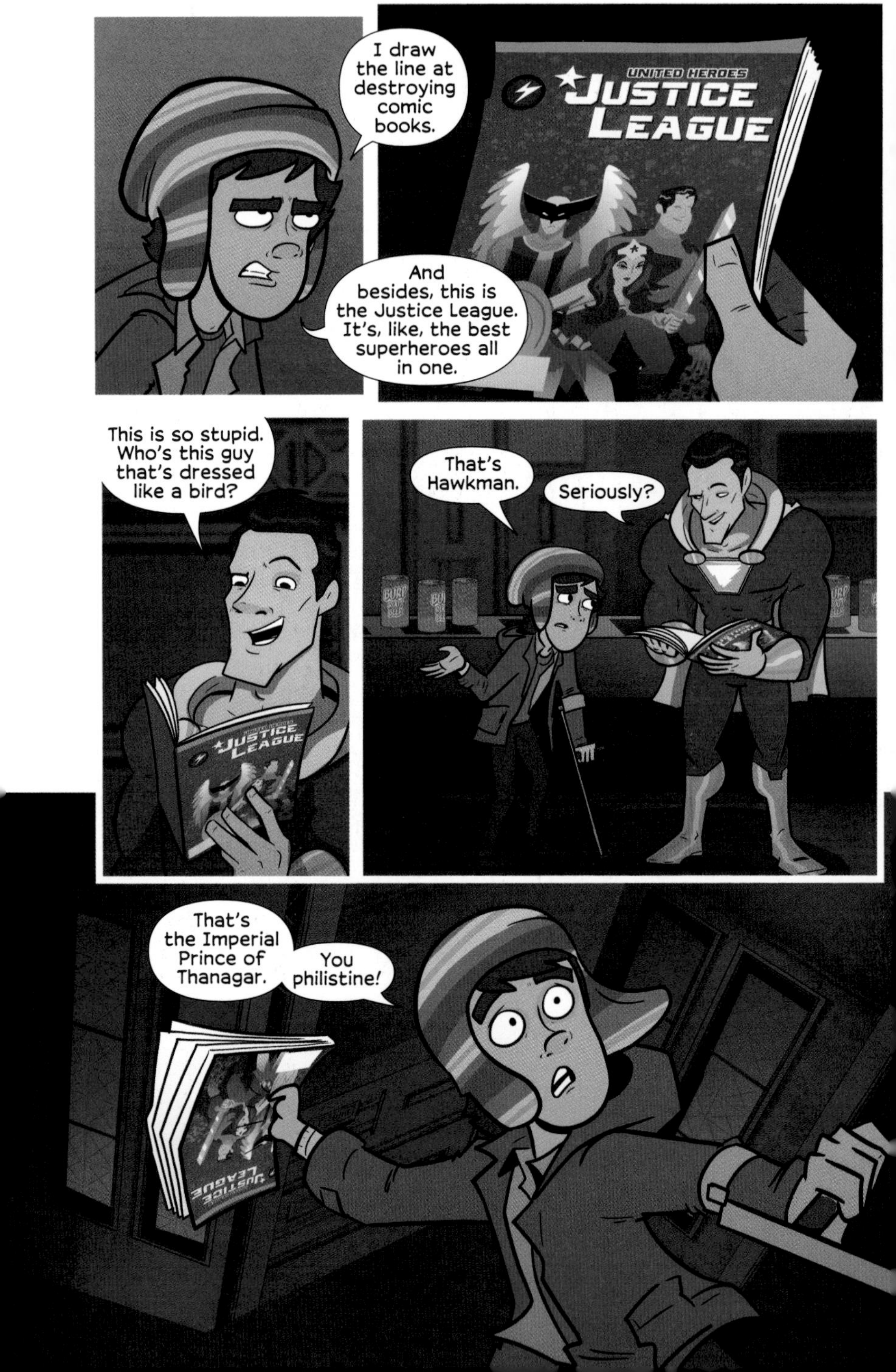
I draw the line at destroying comic books.
UNITED HEROES
JUSTICE LEAGUE
And besides, this is the Justice League. It's, like, the best superheroes all in one.
This is so stupid. Who's this guy that's dressed like a bird?
JUSTICE LEAGUE
That's Hawkman.
Seriously?
That's the Imperial Prince of Thanagar.
You philistine!

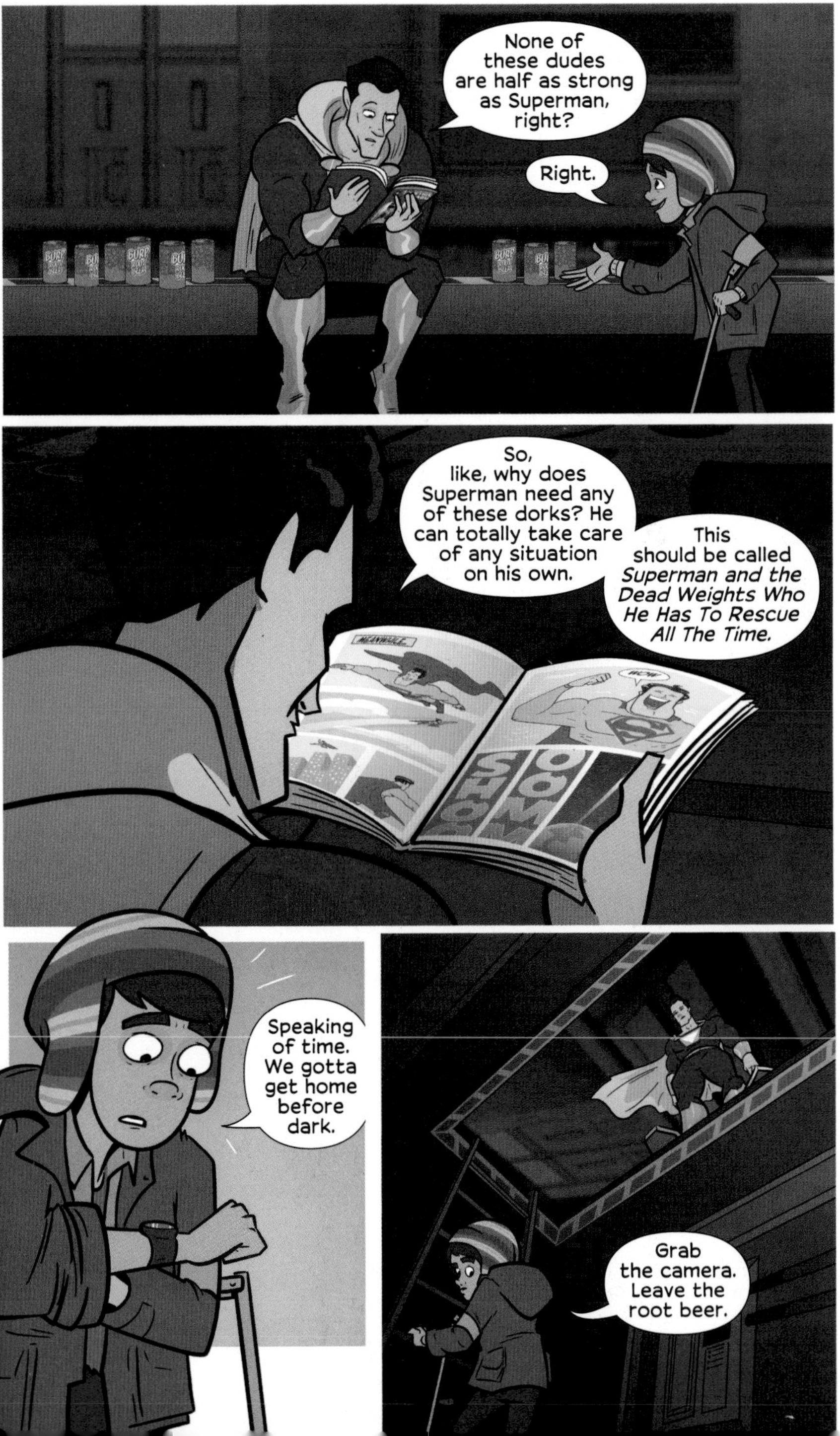
None of these dudes are half as strong as Superman, right?
Right.
So, like, why does Superman need any of these dorks? He can totally take care of any situation on his own.
This should be called *Superman and the Dead Weights Who He Has To Rescue All The Time.*
Speaking of time. We gotta get home before dark.
Grab the camera. Leave the root beer.

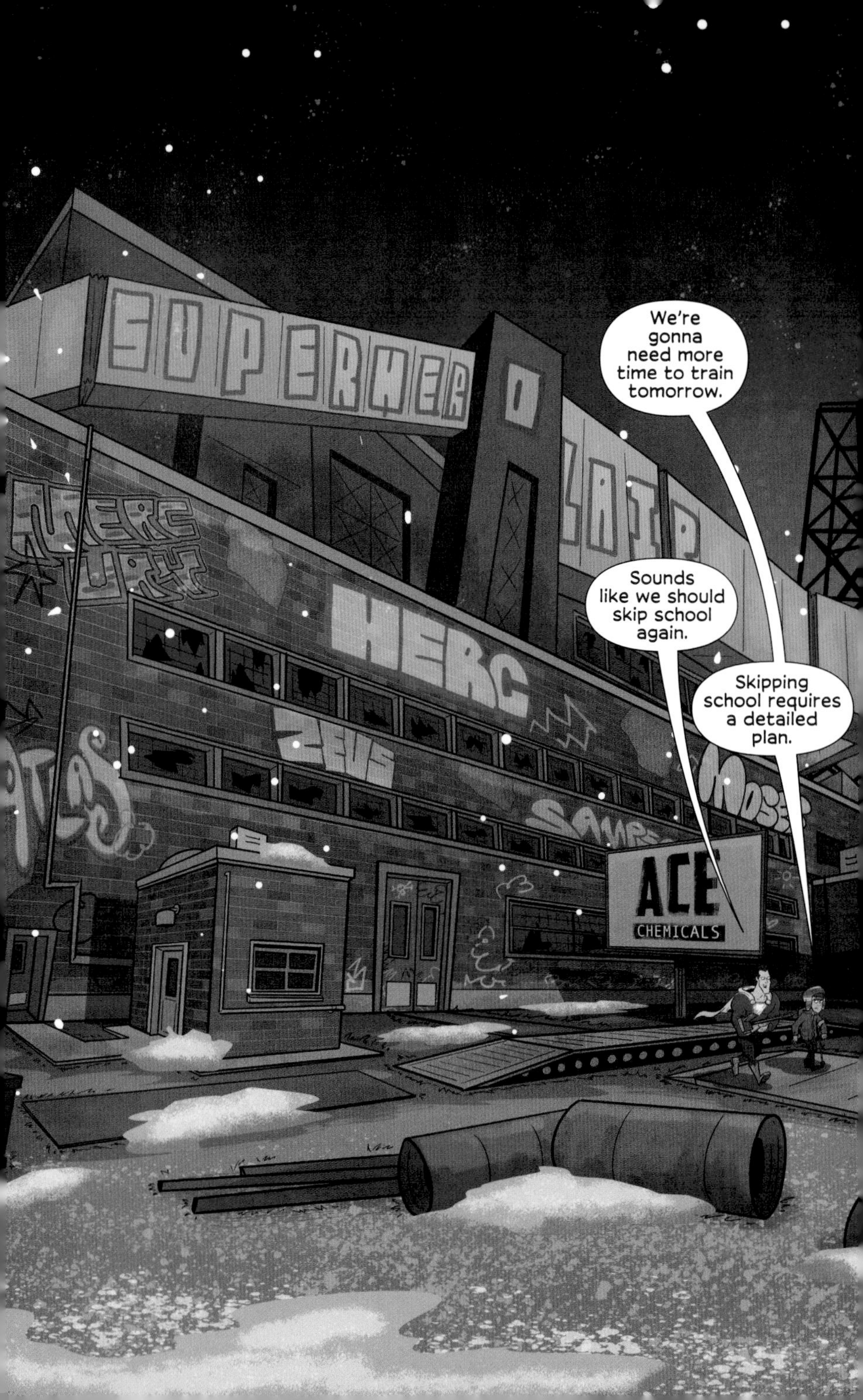
We're gonna need more time to train tomorrow.
Sounds like we should skip school again.
Skipping school requires a detailed plan.
HERC
ZEUS
ACE
CHEMICALS

CHAPTER 2

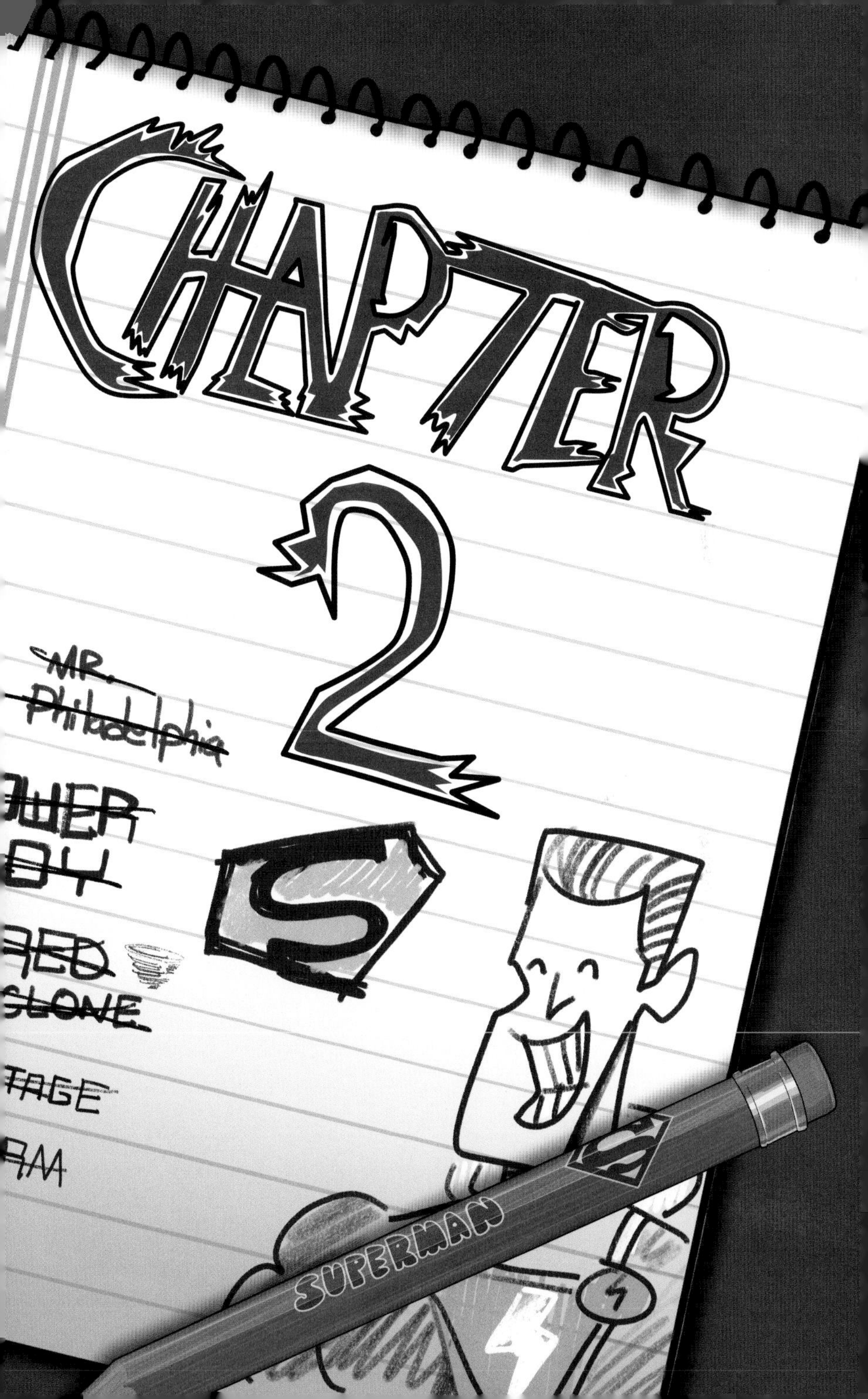
MR.
Philadelphia
SUPERMAN

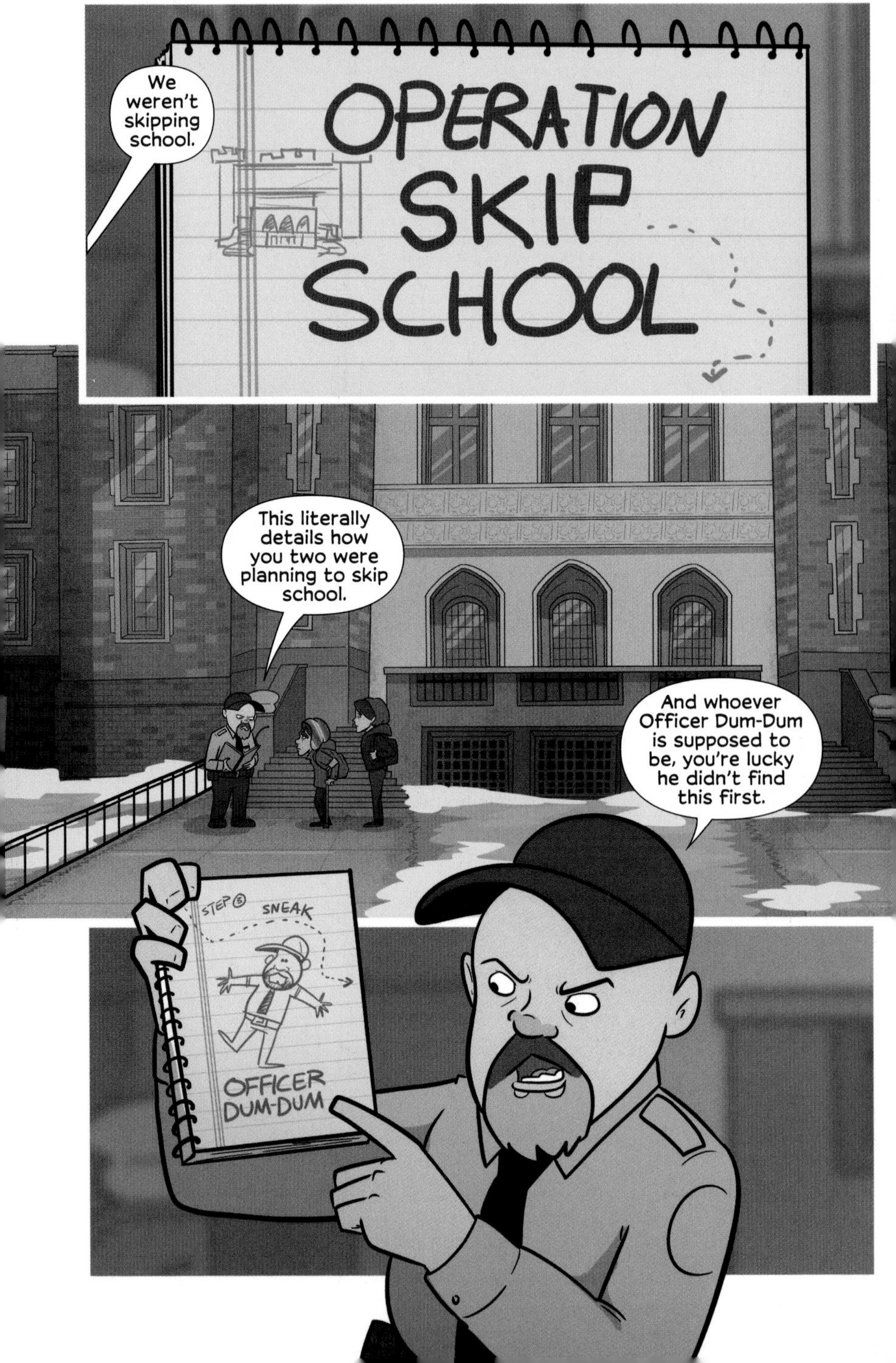
We weren't skipping school.
OPERATION SKIP SCHOOL
This literally details how you two were planning to skip school.
And whoever Officer Dum-Dum is supposed to be, you're lucky he didn't find this first.
STEP 5
SNEAK
OFFICER DUM-DUM

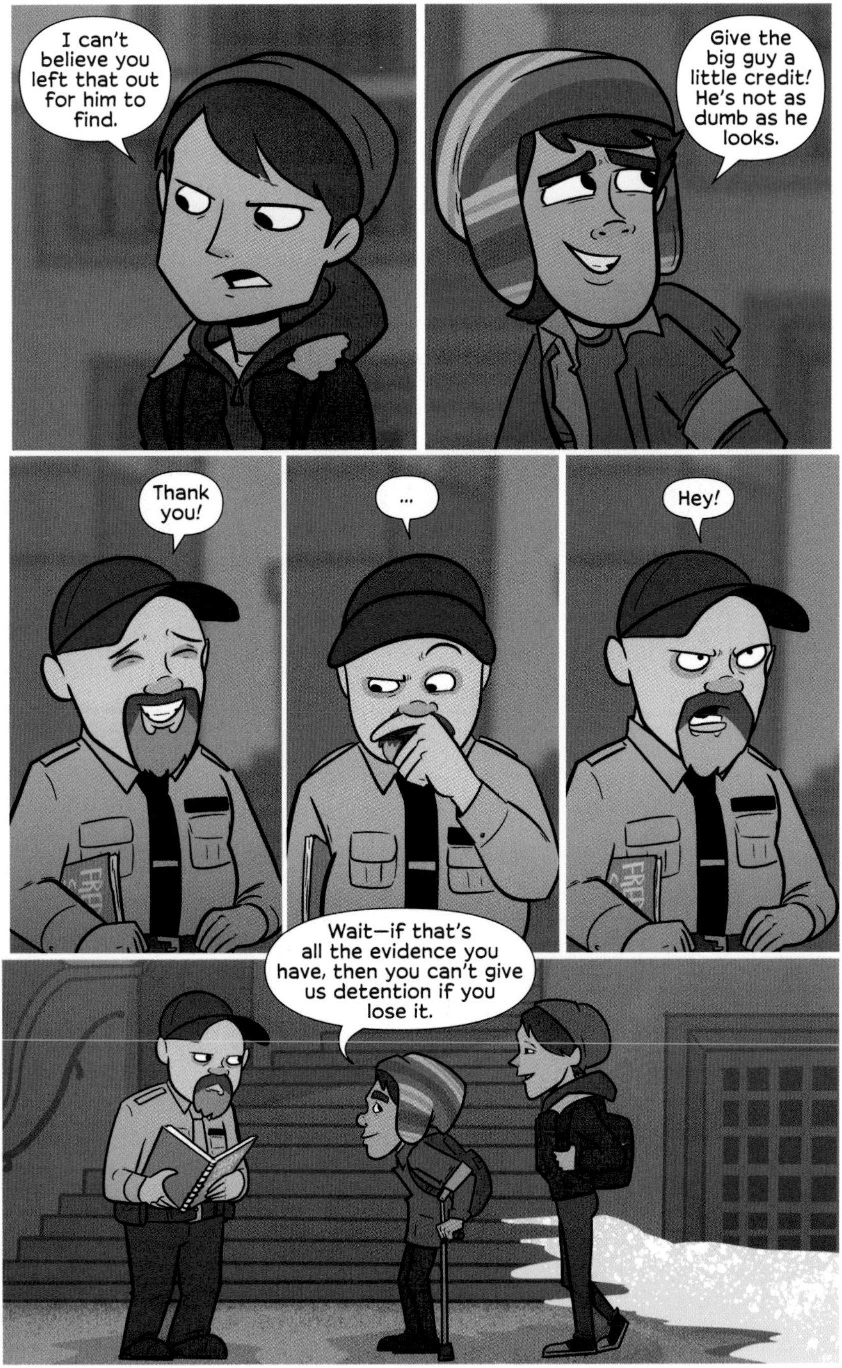
I can't believe you left that out for him to find.
Give the big guy a little credit! He's not as dumb as he looks.
Thank you!
...
Hey!
Wait—if that's all the evidence you have, then you can't give us detention if you lose it.

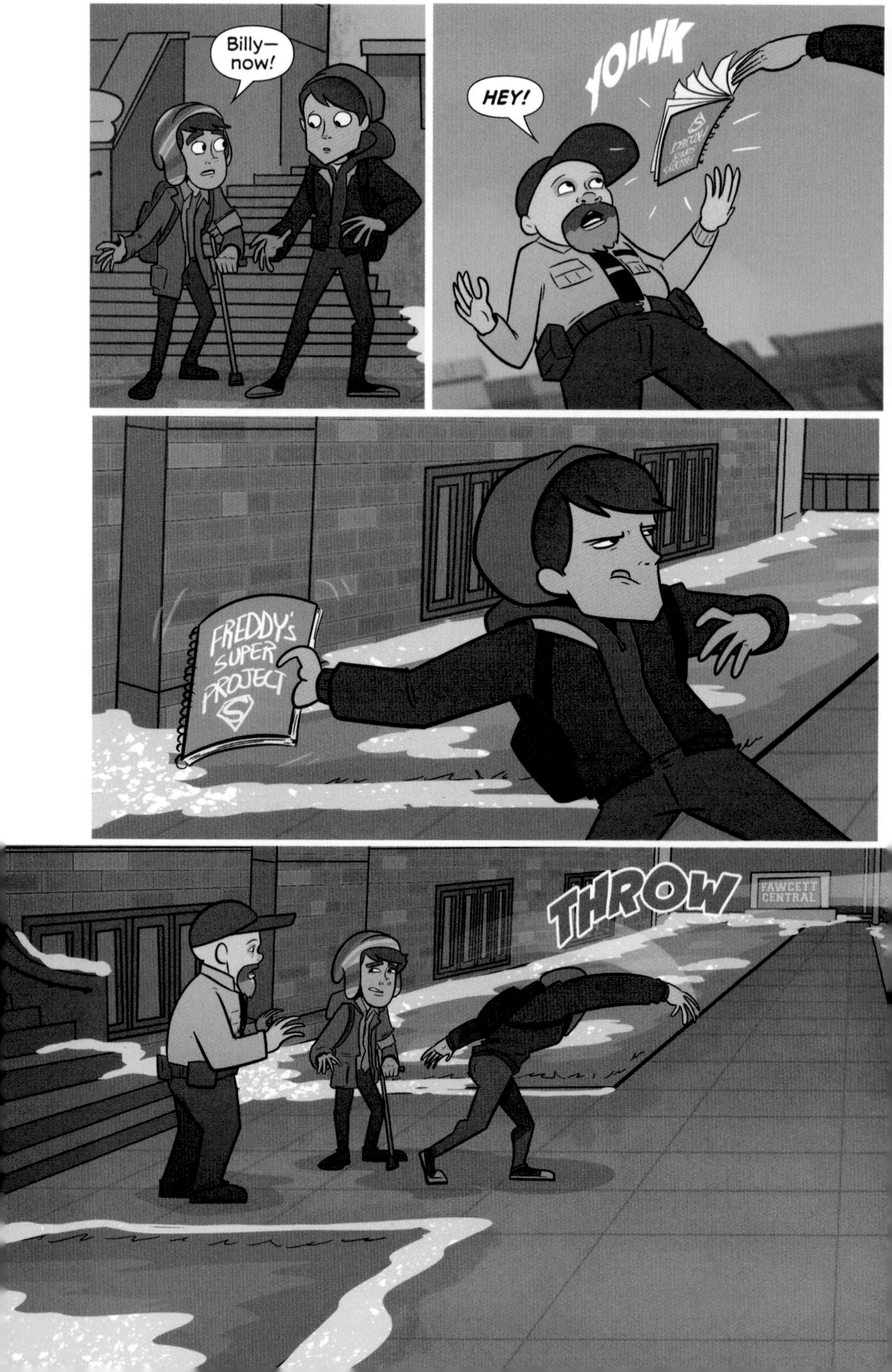
Billy—
now!
HEY!
YOINK
FREDDY's
SUPER
PROJECT
THROW
FAWCETT
CENTRAL

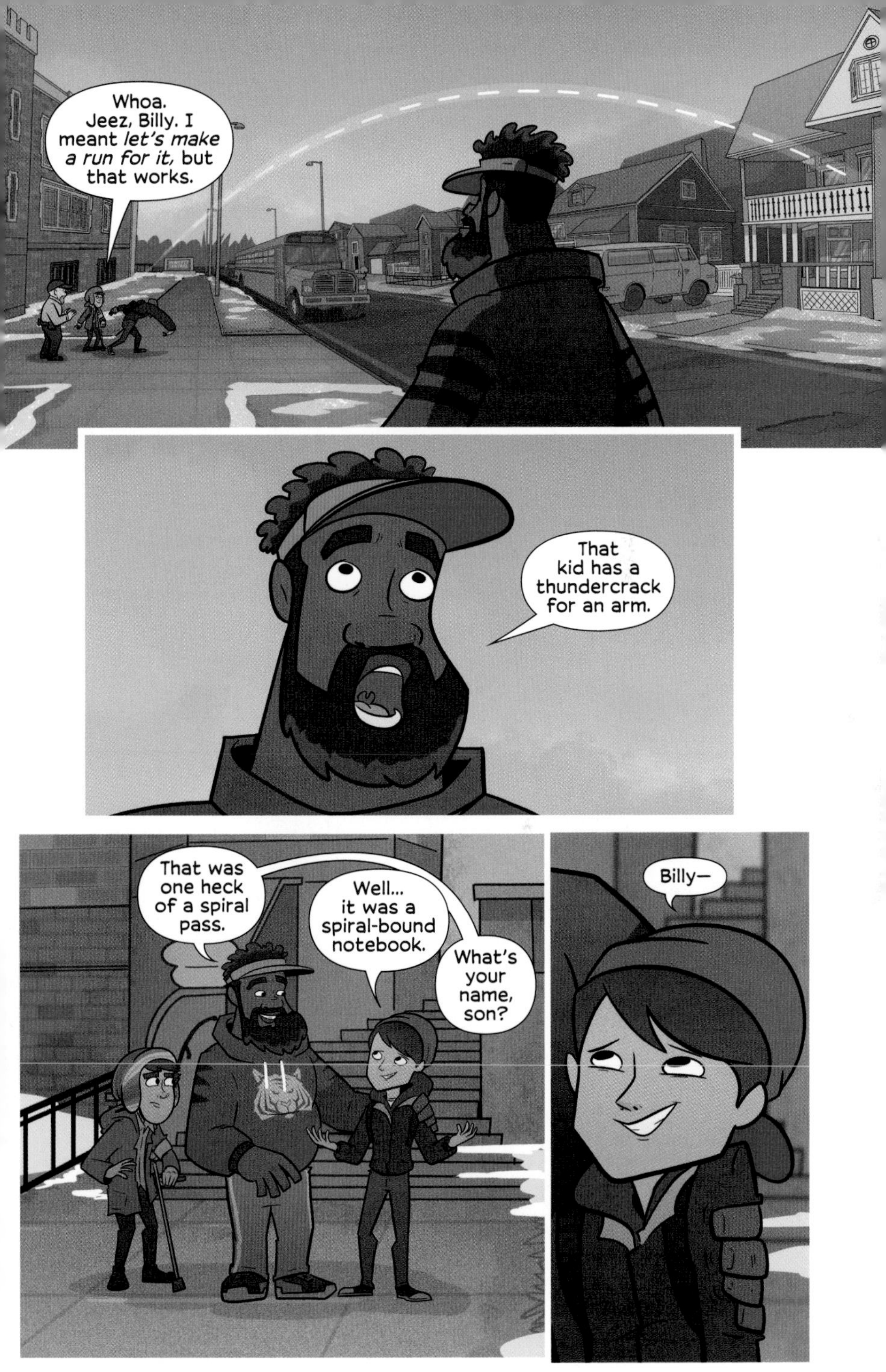
Whoa. Jeez, Billy. I meant *let's make a run for it,* but that works.
That kid has a thundercrack for an arm.
That was one heck of a spiral pass.
Well... it was a spiral-bound notebook.
What's your name, son?
Billy—

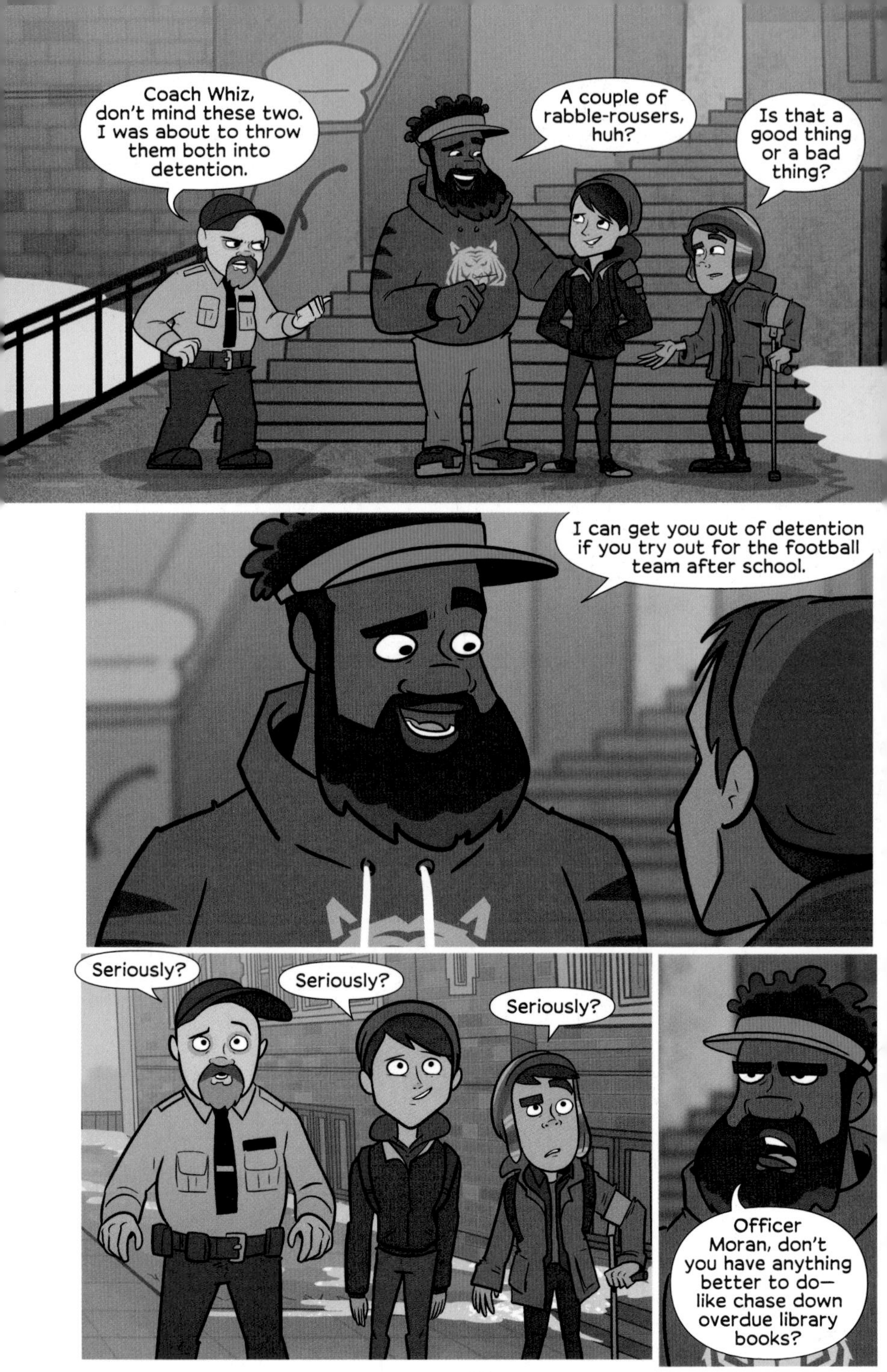
Coach Whiz, don't mind these two. I was about to throw them both into detention.
A couple of rabble-rousers, huh?
Is that a good thing or a bad thing?
I can get you out of detention if you try out for the football team after school.
Seriously?
Seriously?
Seriously?
Officer Moran, don't you have anything better to do—like chase down overdue library books?

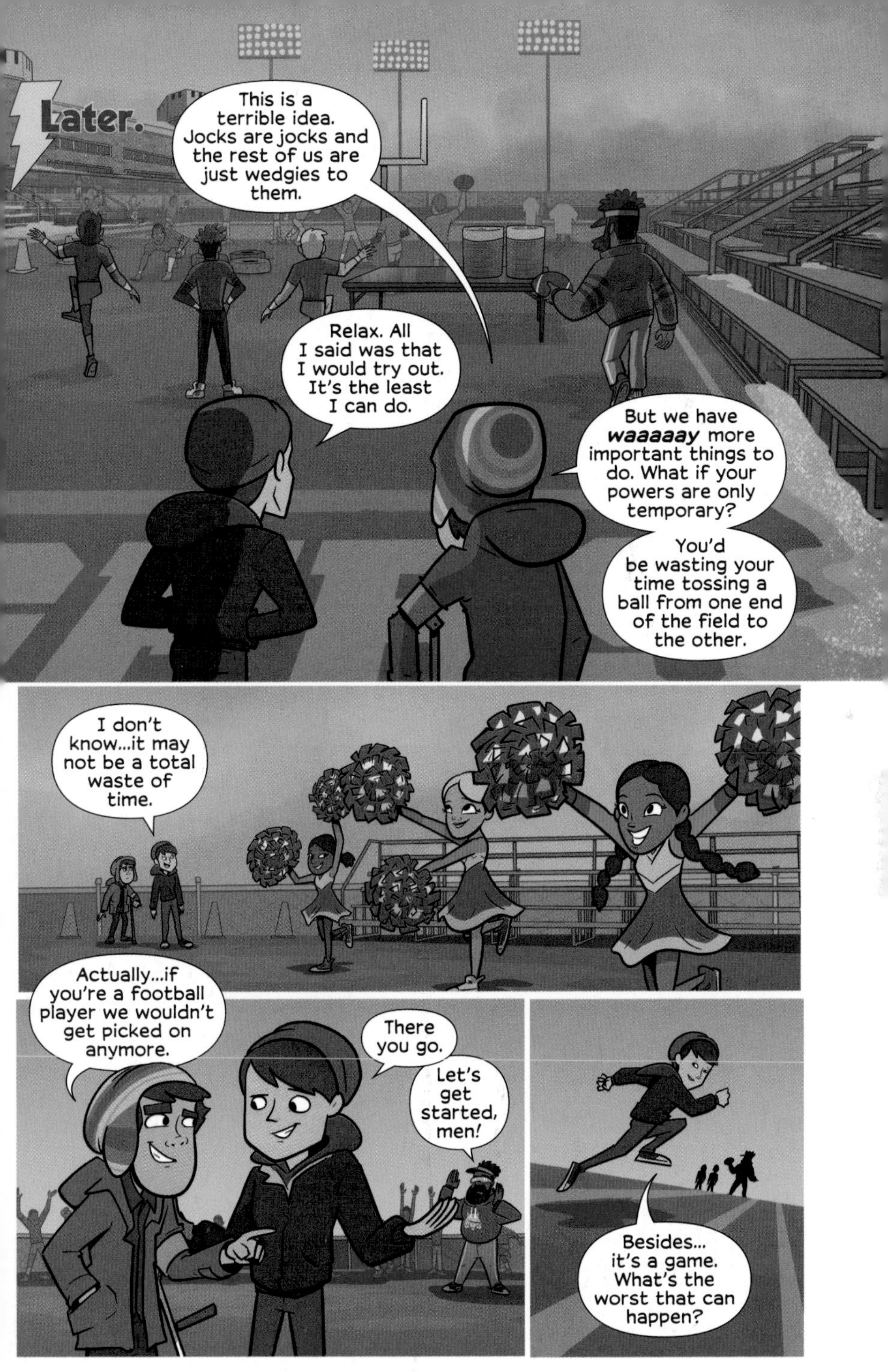
Later.
This is a terrible idea. Jocks are jocks and the rest of us are just wedgies to them.
Relax. All I said was that I would try out. It's the least I can do.
But we have ***waaaaay*** more important things to do. What if your powers are only temporary?
You'd be wasting your time tossing a ball from one end of the field to the other.
I don't know...it may not be a total waste of time.
Actually...if you're a football player we wouldn't get picked on anymore.
There you go.
Let's get started, men!
Besides... it's a game. What's the worst that can happen?

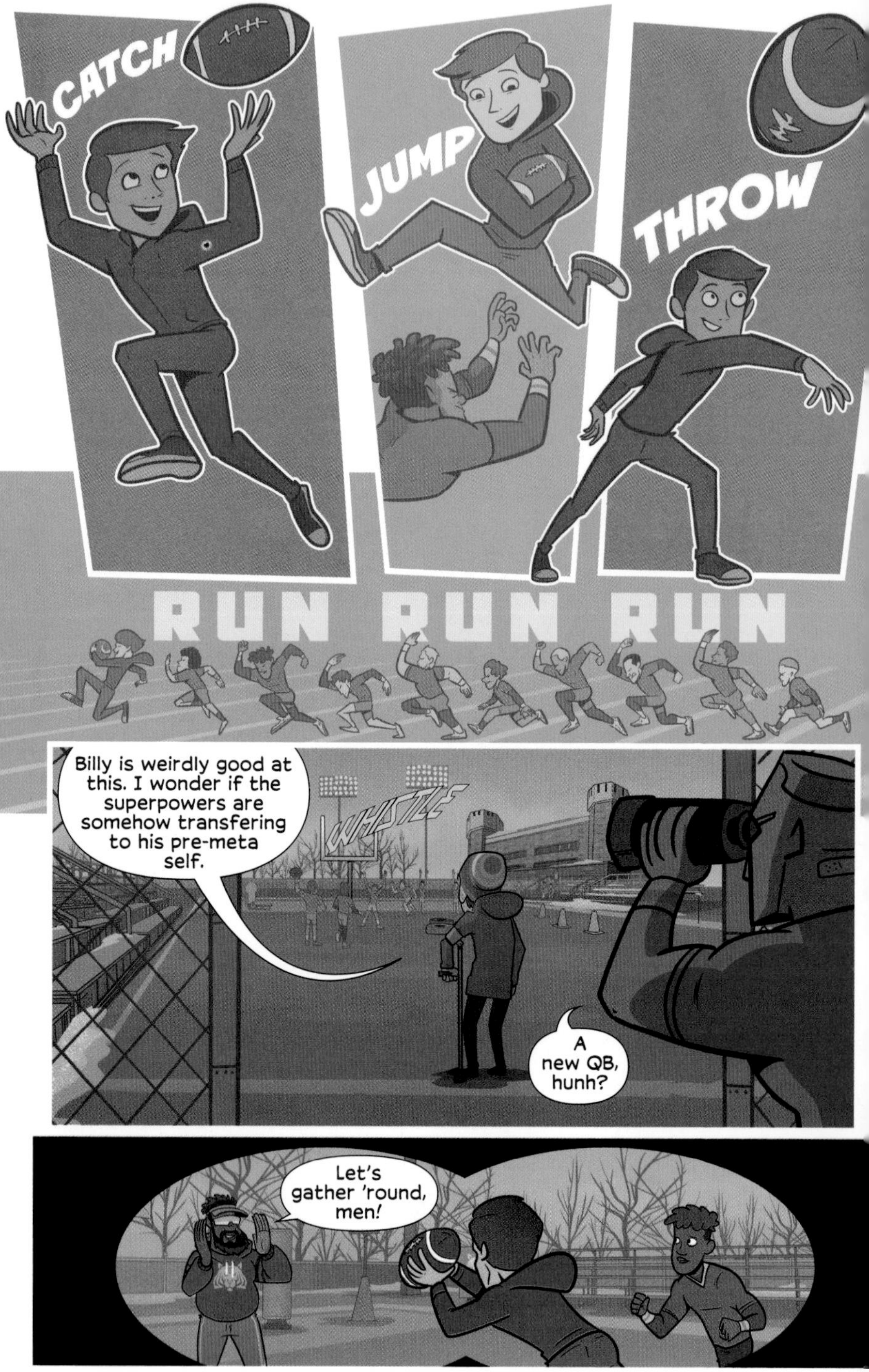
CATCH
JUMP
THROW
RUN RUN RUN
Billy is weirdly good at this. I wonder if the superpowers are somehow transfering to his pre-meta self.
WHISTLE
A new QB, hunh?
Let's gather 'round, men!

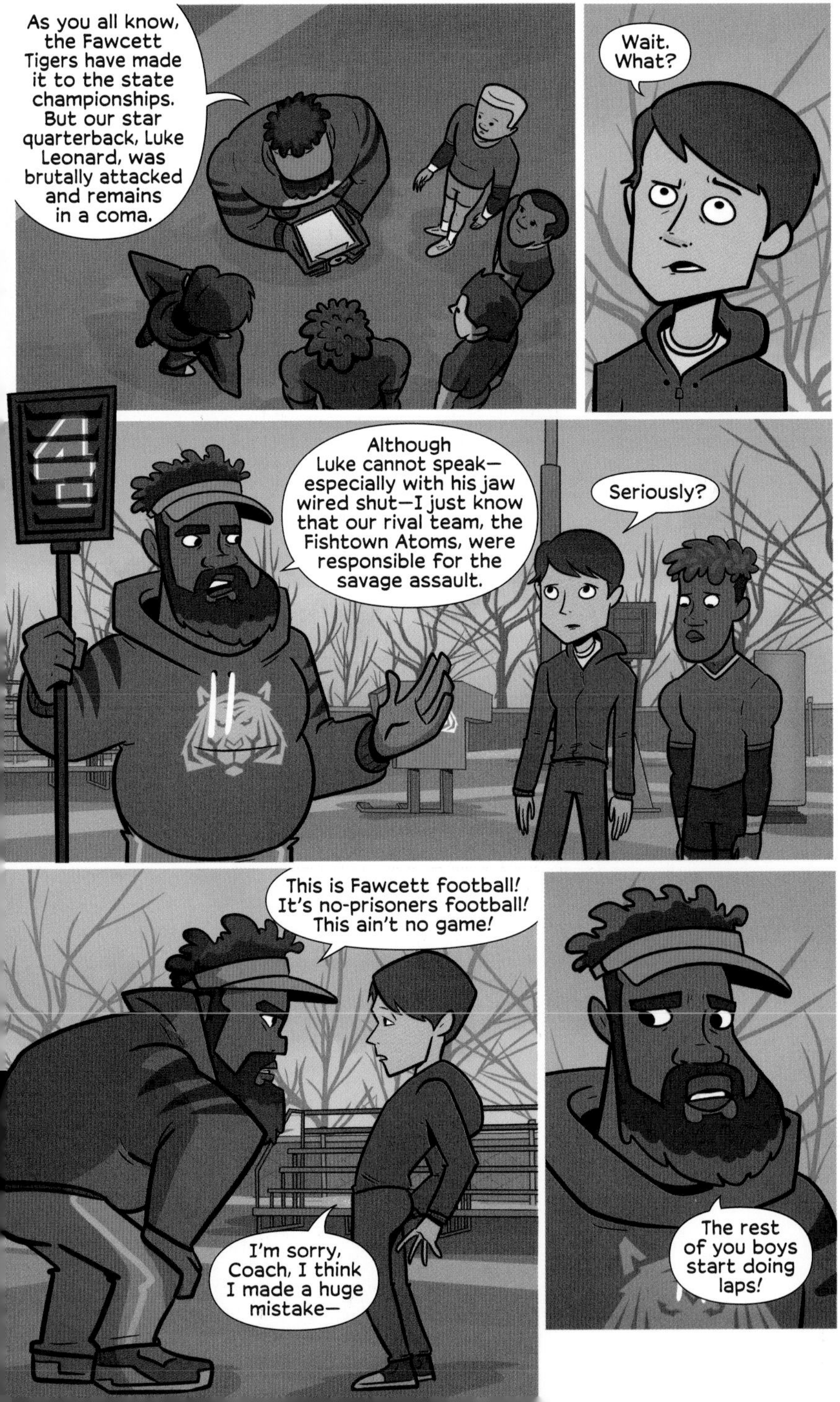
As you all know, the Fawcett Tigers have made it to the state championships. But our star quarterback, Luke Leonard, was brutally attacked and remains in a coma.
Wait. What?
Although Luke cannot speak—especially with his jaw wired shut—I just know that our rival team, the Fishtown Atoms, were responsible for the savage assault.
Seriously?
This is Fawcett football! It's no-prisoners football! This ain't no game!
I'm sorry, Coach, I think I made a huge mistake—
The rest of you boys start doing laps!

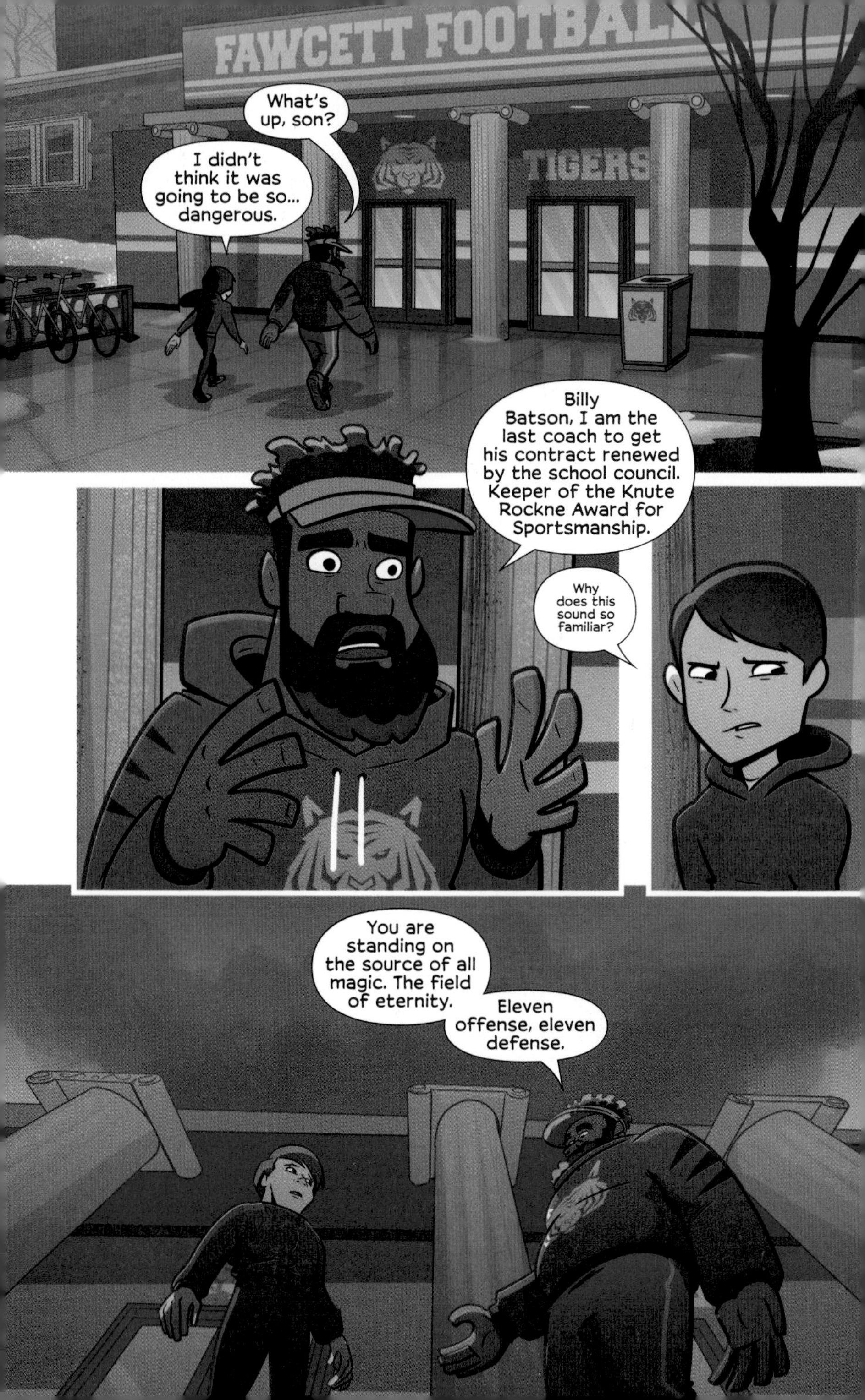
FAWCETT FOOTBALL
TIGERS
What's up, son?
I didn't think it was going to be so... dangerous.
Billy Batson, I am the last coach to get his contract renewed by the school council. Keeper of the Knute Rockne Award for Sportsmanship.
Why does this sound so familiar?
You are standing on the source of all magic. The field of eternity.
Eleven offense, eleven defense.

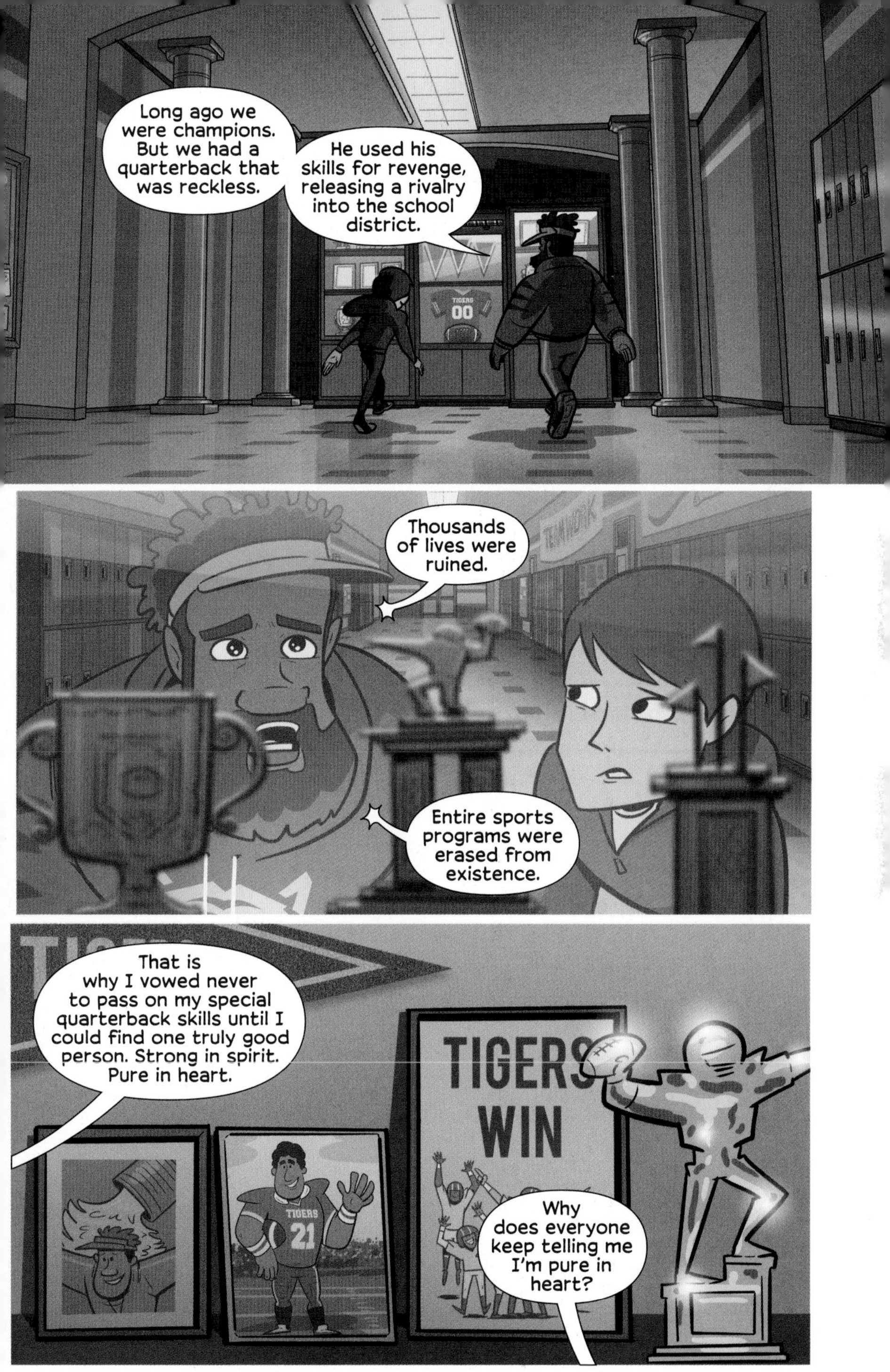
Long ago we were champions. But we had a quarterback that was reckless.
He used his skills for revenge, releasing a rivalry into the school district.
Thousands of lives were ruined.
Entire sports programs were erased from existence.
That is why I vowed never to pass on my special quarterback skills until I could find one truly good person. Strong in spirit. Pure in heart.
TIGERS WIN
TIGERS 21
Why does everyone keep telling me I'm pure in heart?

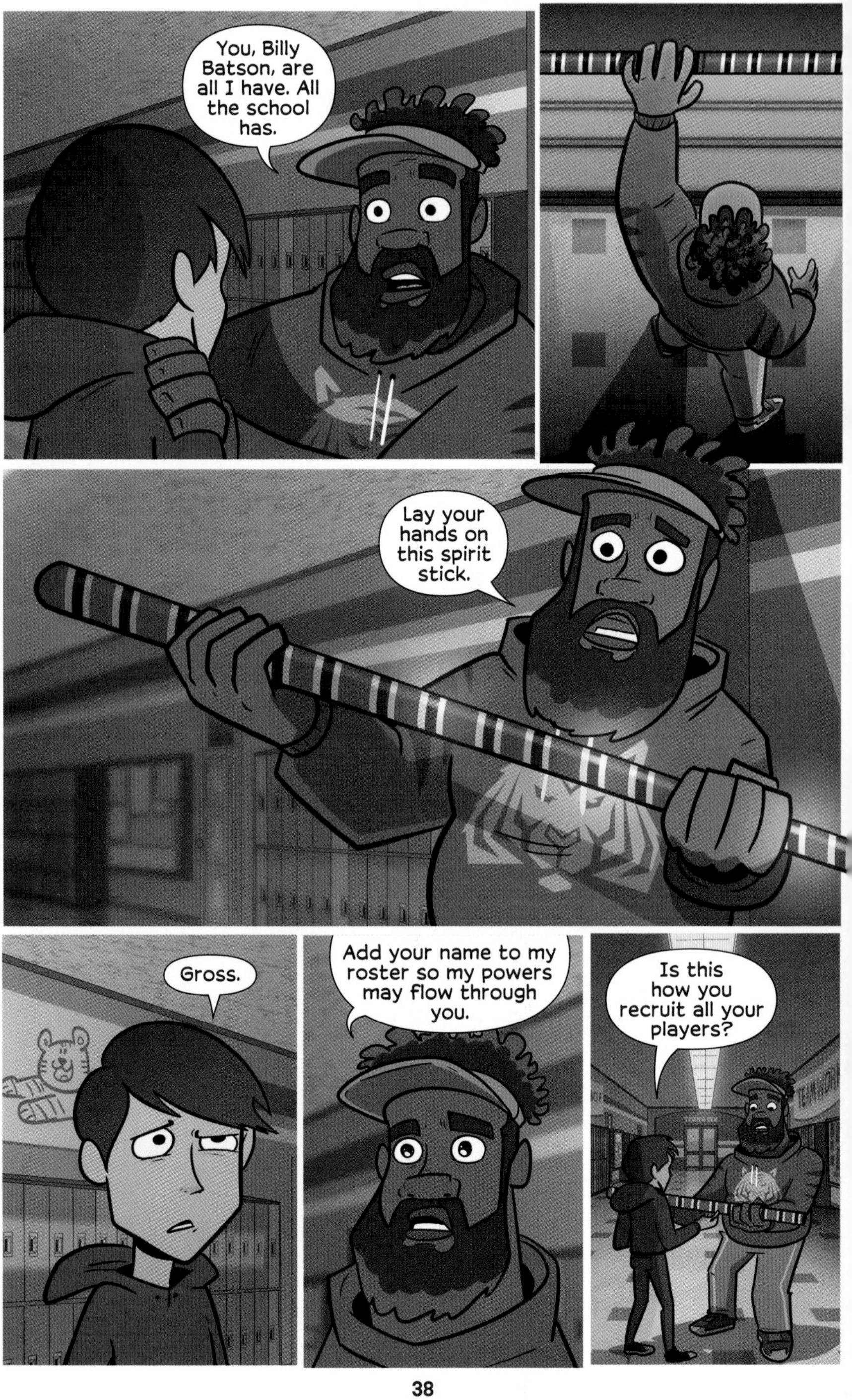
You, Billy Batson, are all I have. All the school has.
Lay your hands on this spirit stick.
Gross.
Add your name to my roster so my powers may flow through you.
Is this how you recruit all your players?

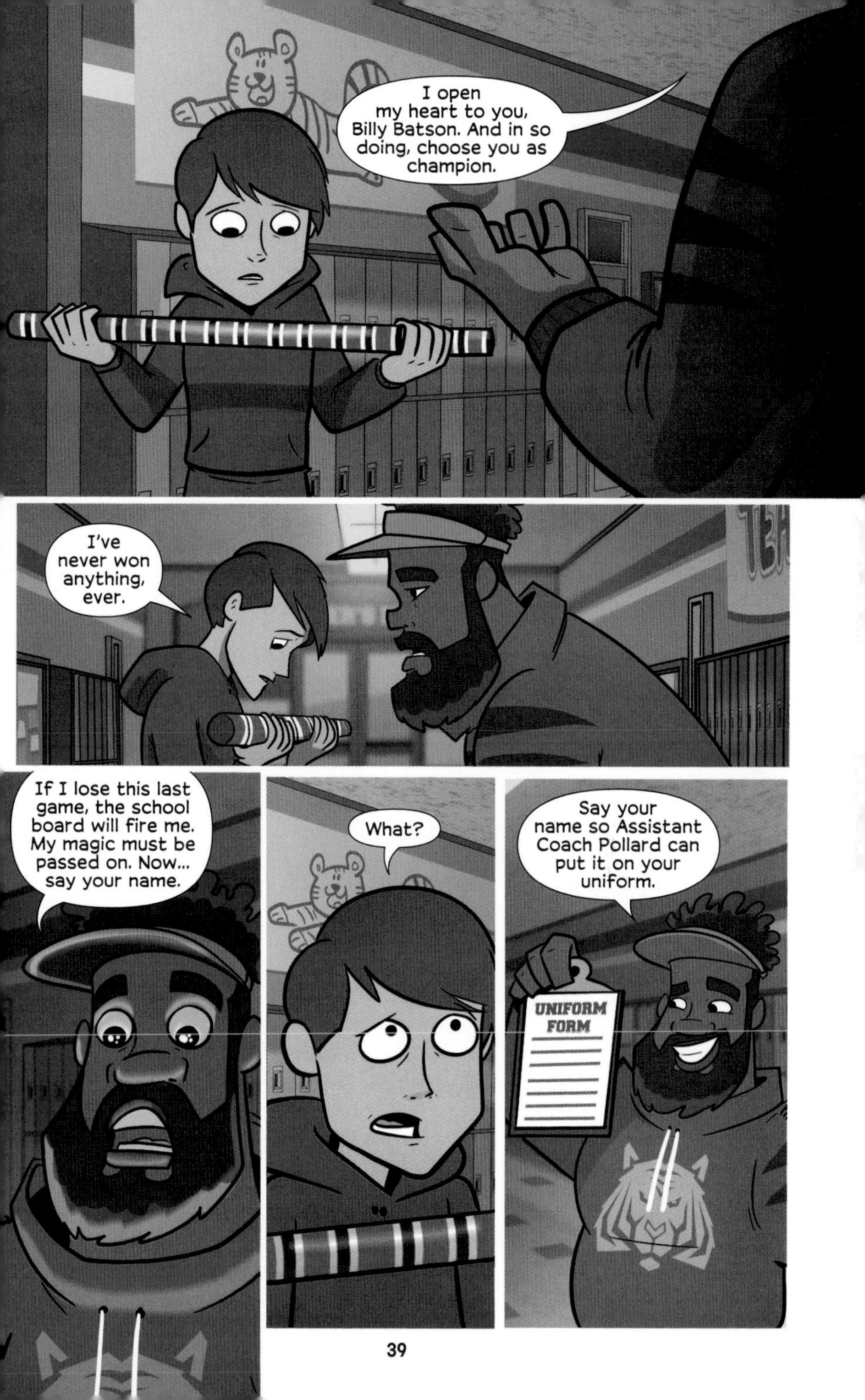
I open my heart to you, Billy Batson. And in so doing, choose you as champion.
I've never won anything, ever.
If I lose this last game, the school board will fire me. My magic must be passed on. Now... say your name.
What?
Say your name so Assistant Coach Pollard can put it on your uniform.
UNIFORM FORM

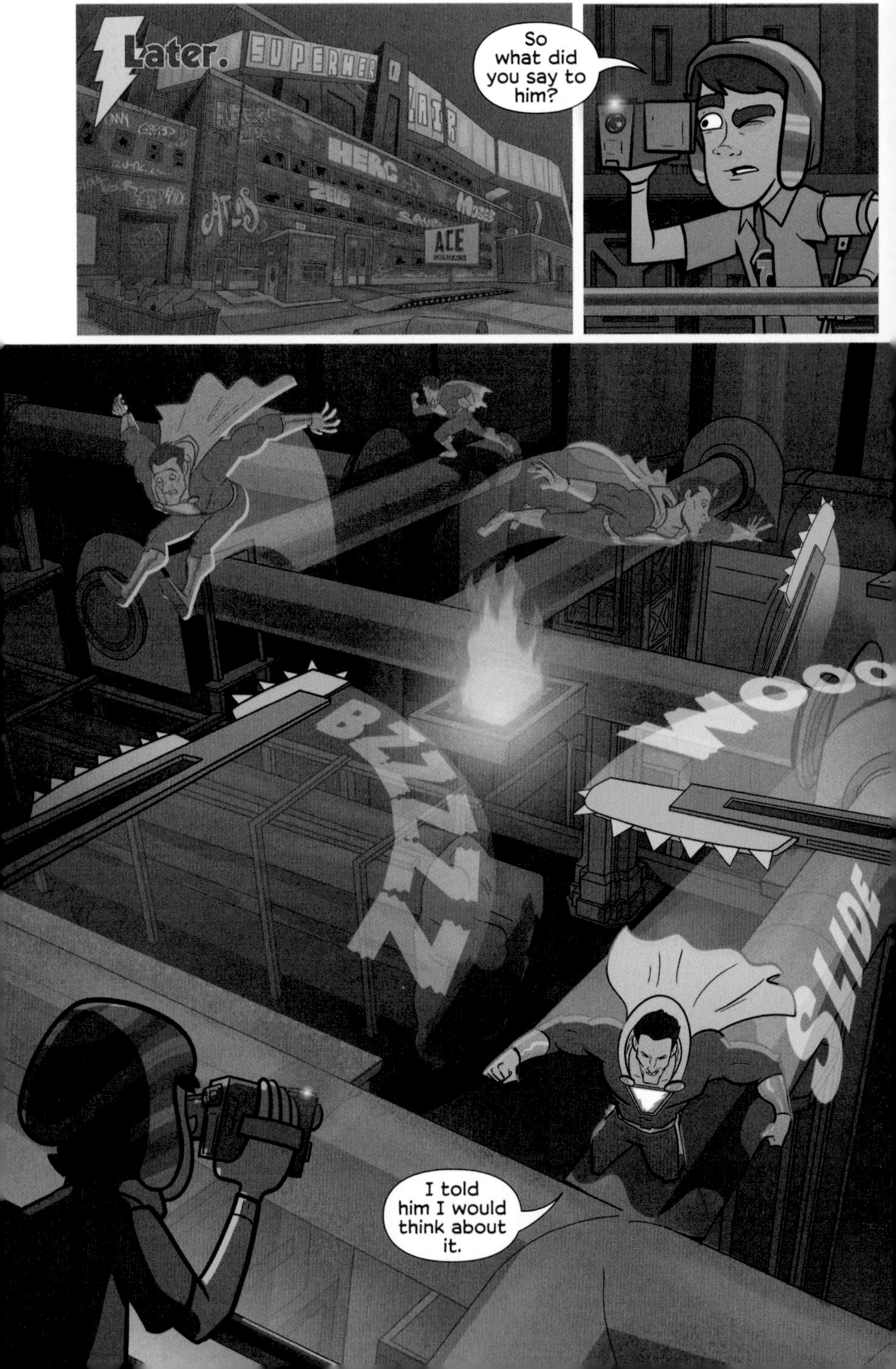
Later.
HERC
ACE
So what did you say to him?
BZZZZ
WOOO
SLIDE
I told him I would think about it.

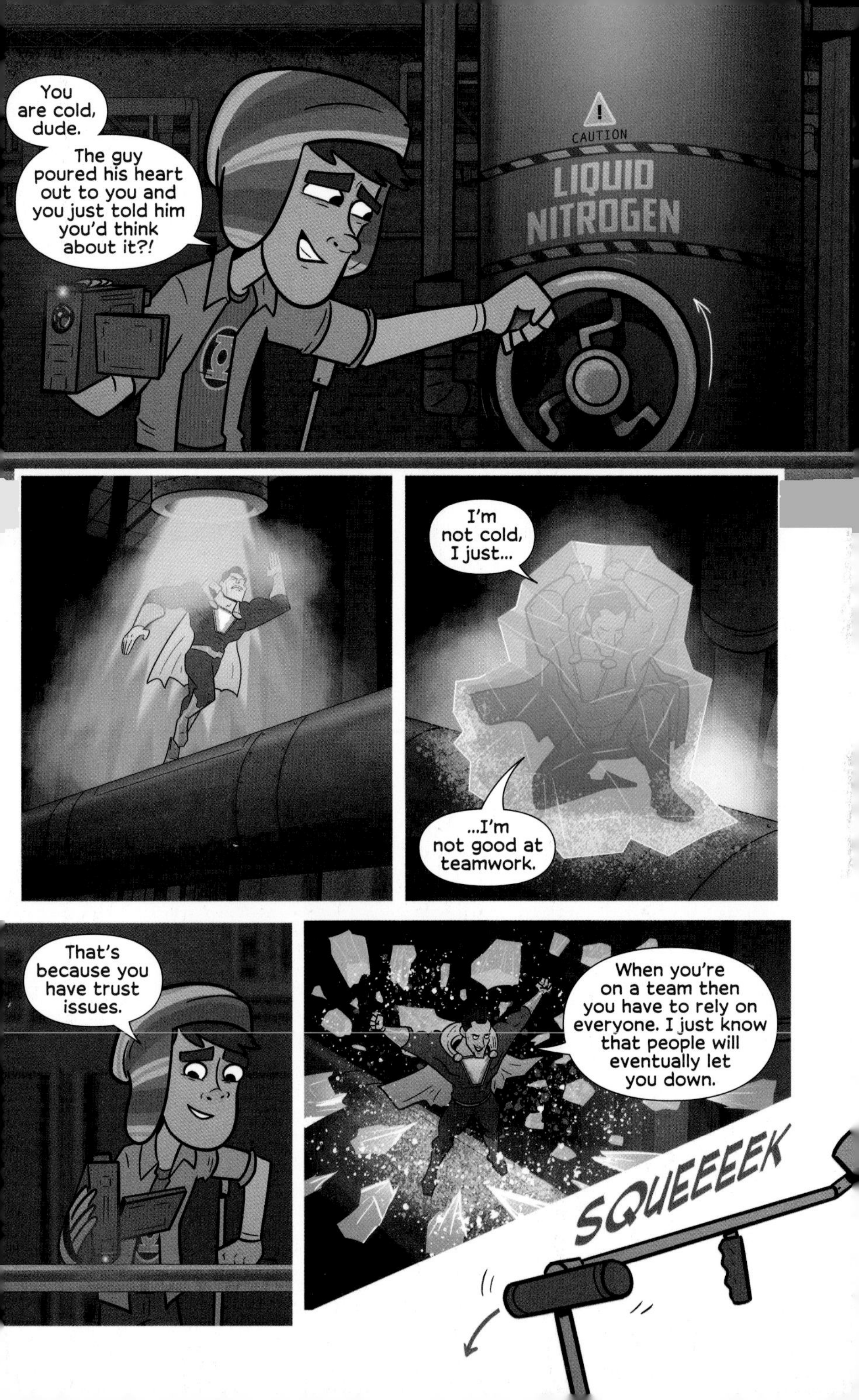
You are cold, dude.
The guy poured his heart out to you and you just told him you'd think about it?!
CAUTION
LIQUID NITROGEN
I'm not cold, I just...
...I'm not good at teamwork.
That's because you have trust issues.
When you're on a team then you have to rely on everyone. I just know that people will eventually let you down.
SQUEEEEK

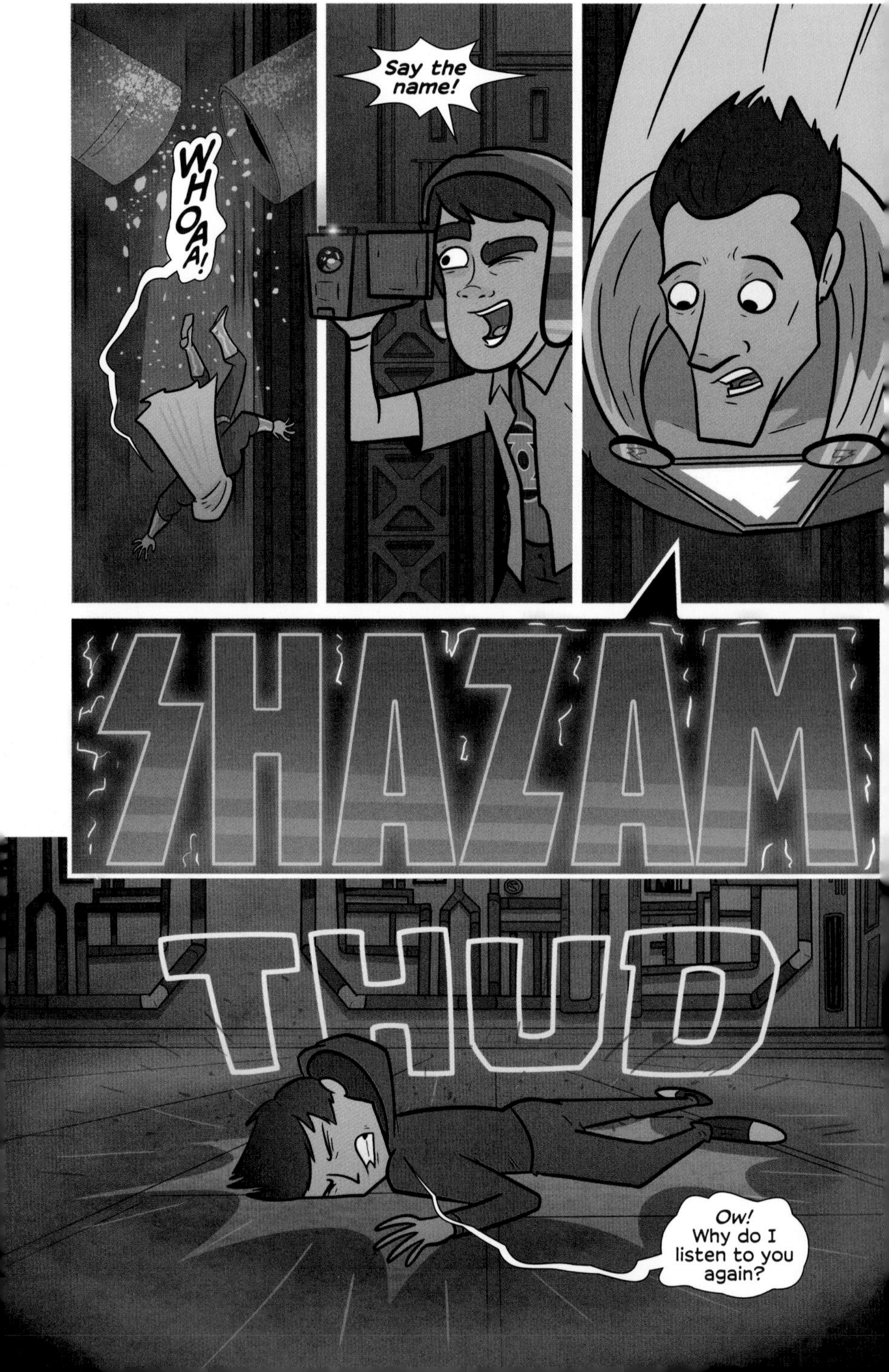
WHOAA!
Say the name!
SHAZAM
THUD
Ow! Why do I listen to you again?

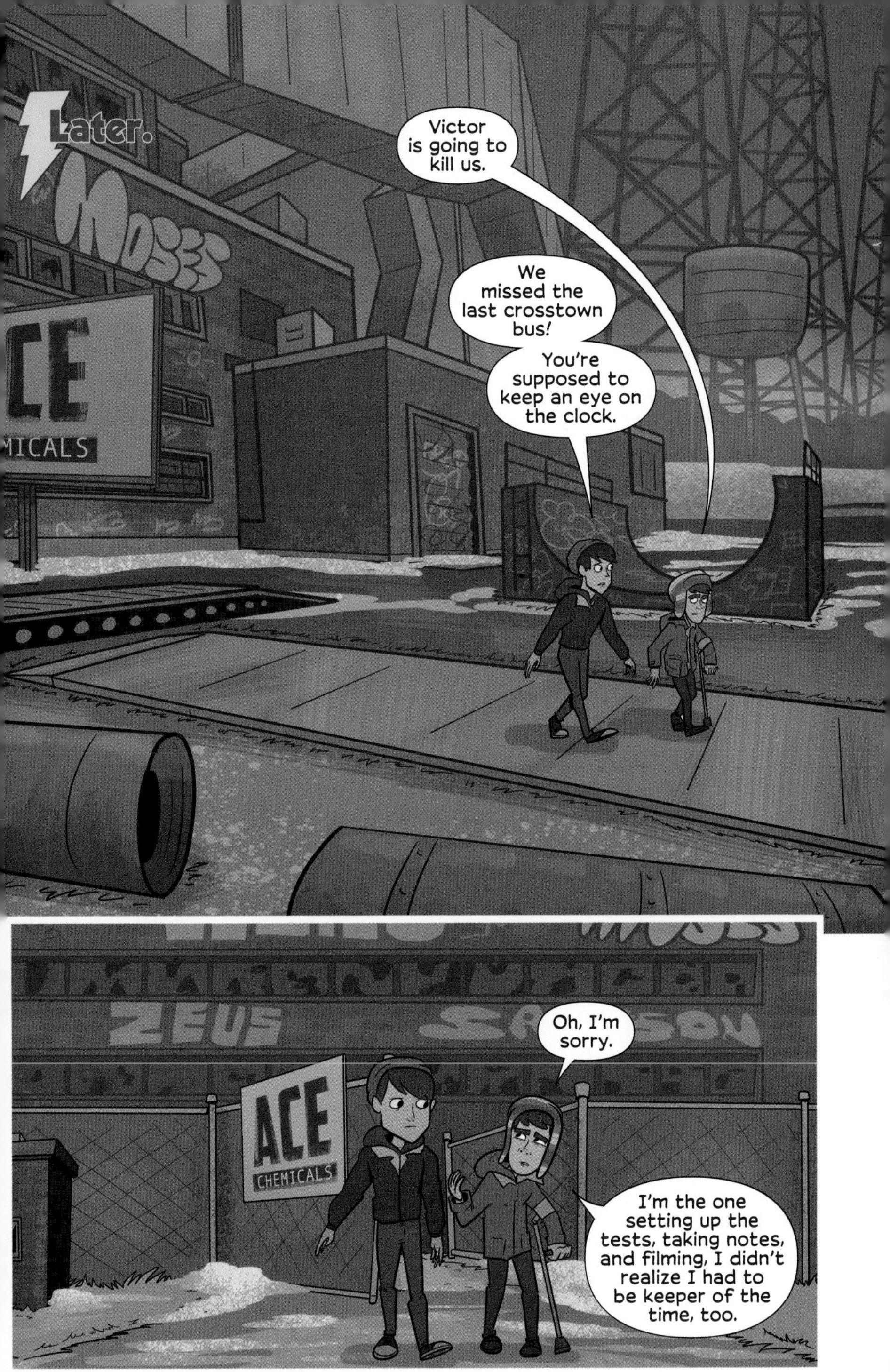
Later.
MOSES
ICALS
Victor is going to kill us.
We missed the last crosstown bus!
You're supposed to keep an eye on the clock.
ZEUS
ACE
CHEMICALS
Oh, I'm sorry.
I'm the one setting up the tests, taking notes, and filming, I didn't realize I had to be keeper of the time, too.

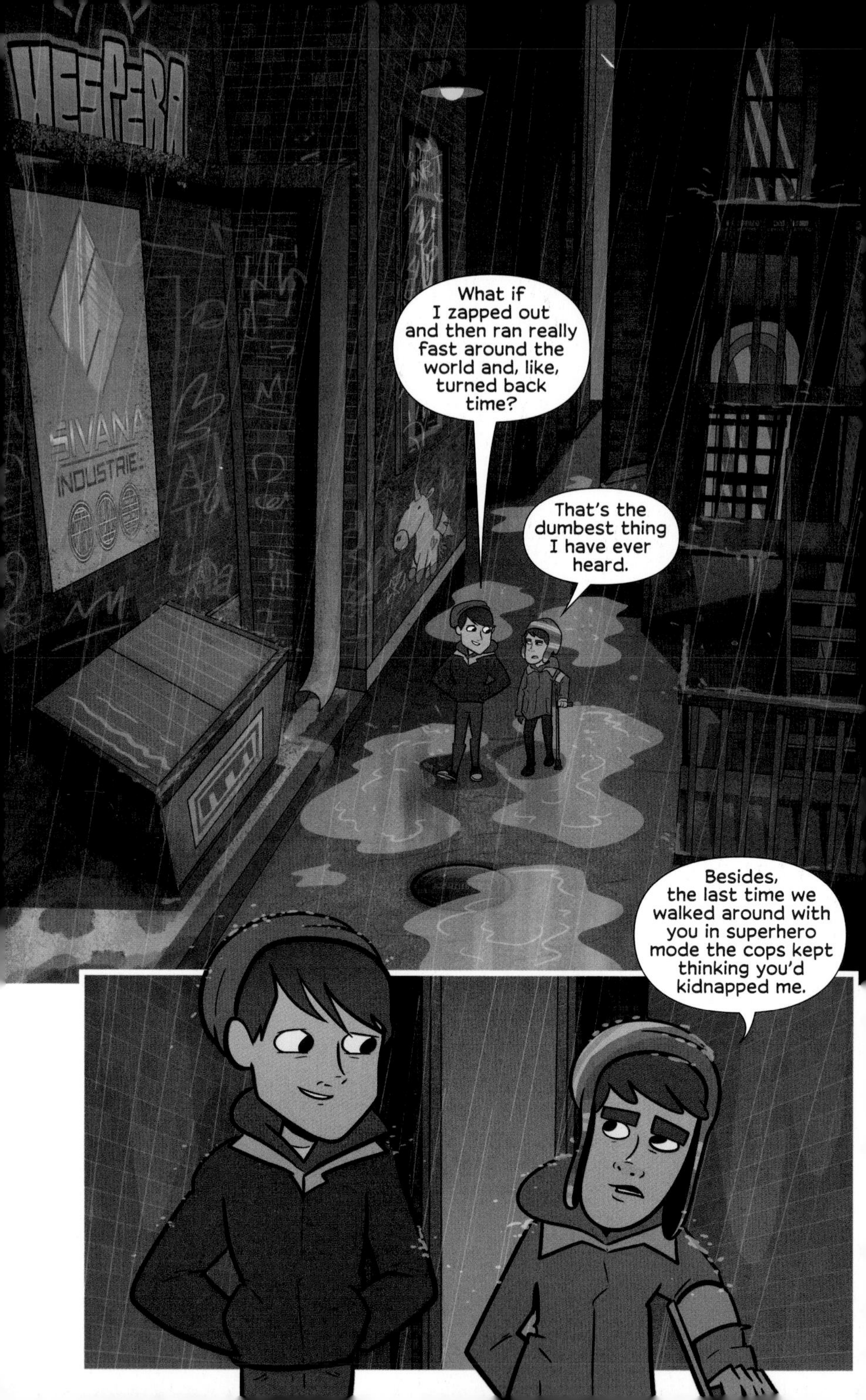

HESPERA
SIVANA INDUSTRIES
What if I zapped out and then ran really fast around the world and, like, turned back time?
That's the dumbest thing I have ever heard.
Besides, the last time we walked around with you in superhero mode the cops kept thinking you'd kidnapped me.

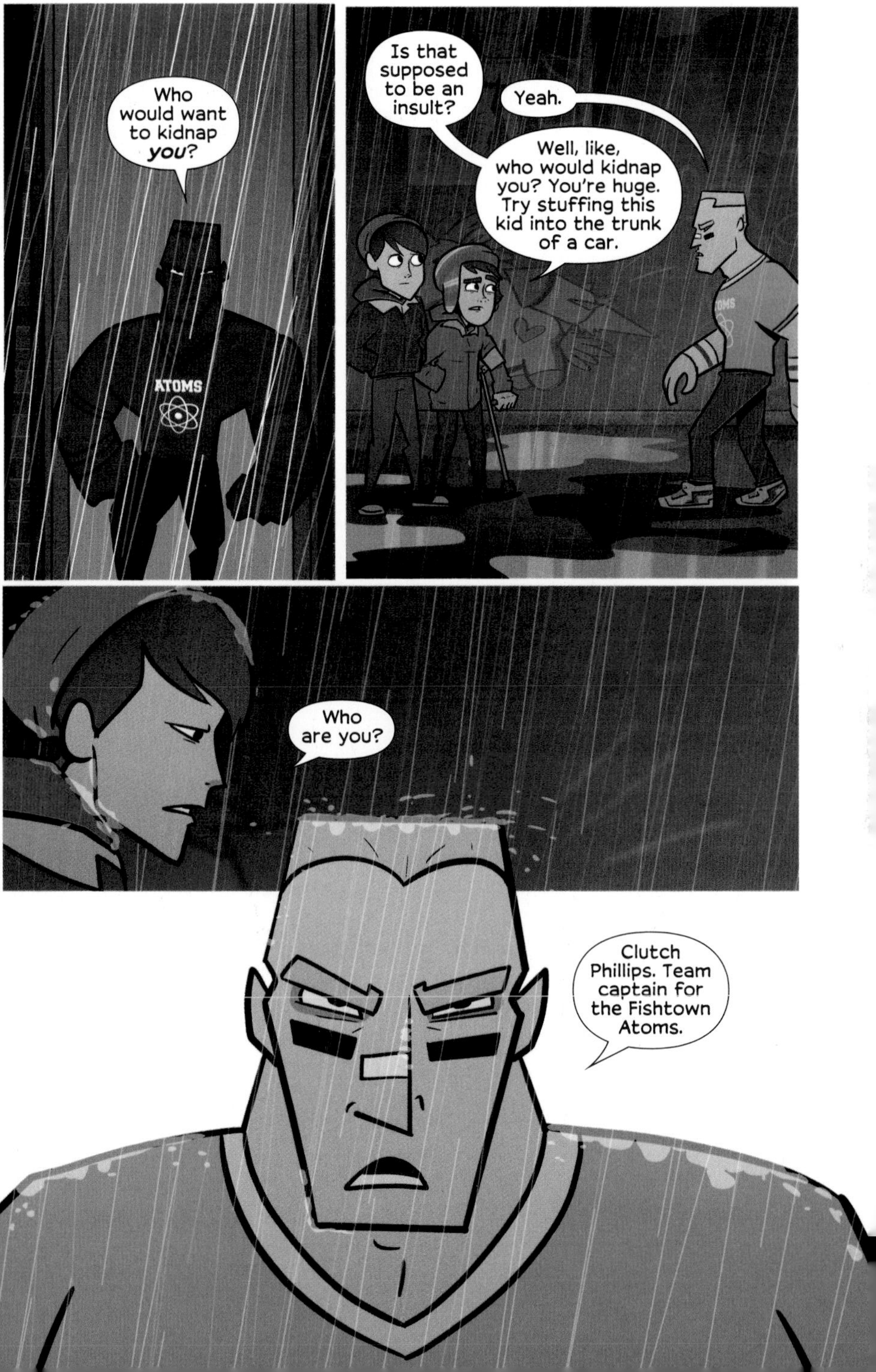
Who would want to kidnap *you*?
Is that supposed to be an insult?
Yeah.
Well, like, who would kidnap you? You're huge. Try stuffing this kid into the trunk of a car.
Who are you?
Clutch Phillips. Team captain for the Fishtown Atoms.

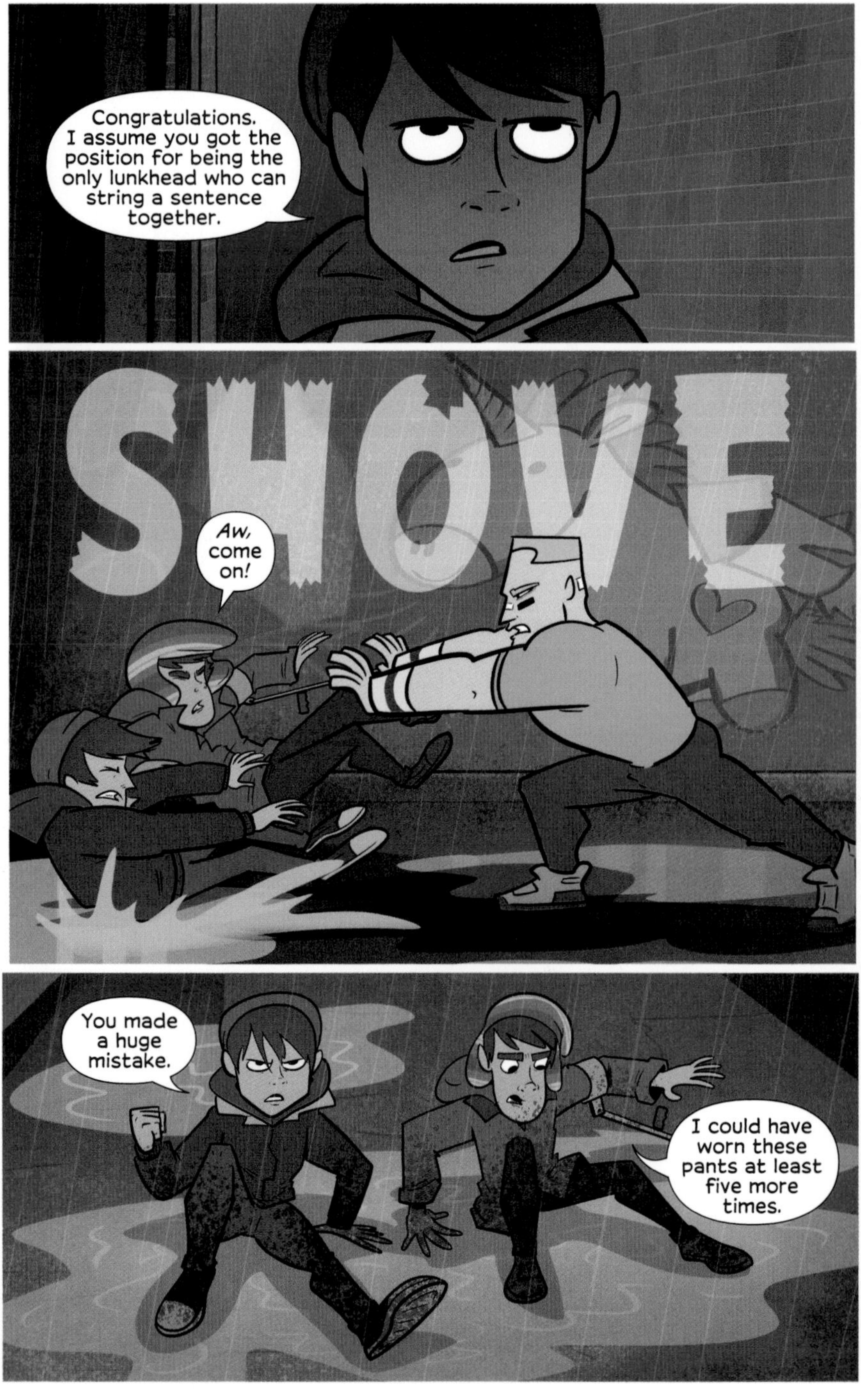
Congratulations. I assume you got the position for being the only lunkhead who can string a sentence together.
SHOVE
Aw, come on!
You made a huge mistake.
I could have worn these pants at least five more times.

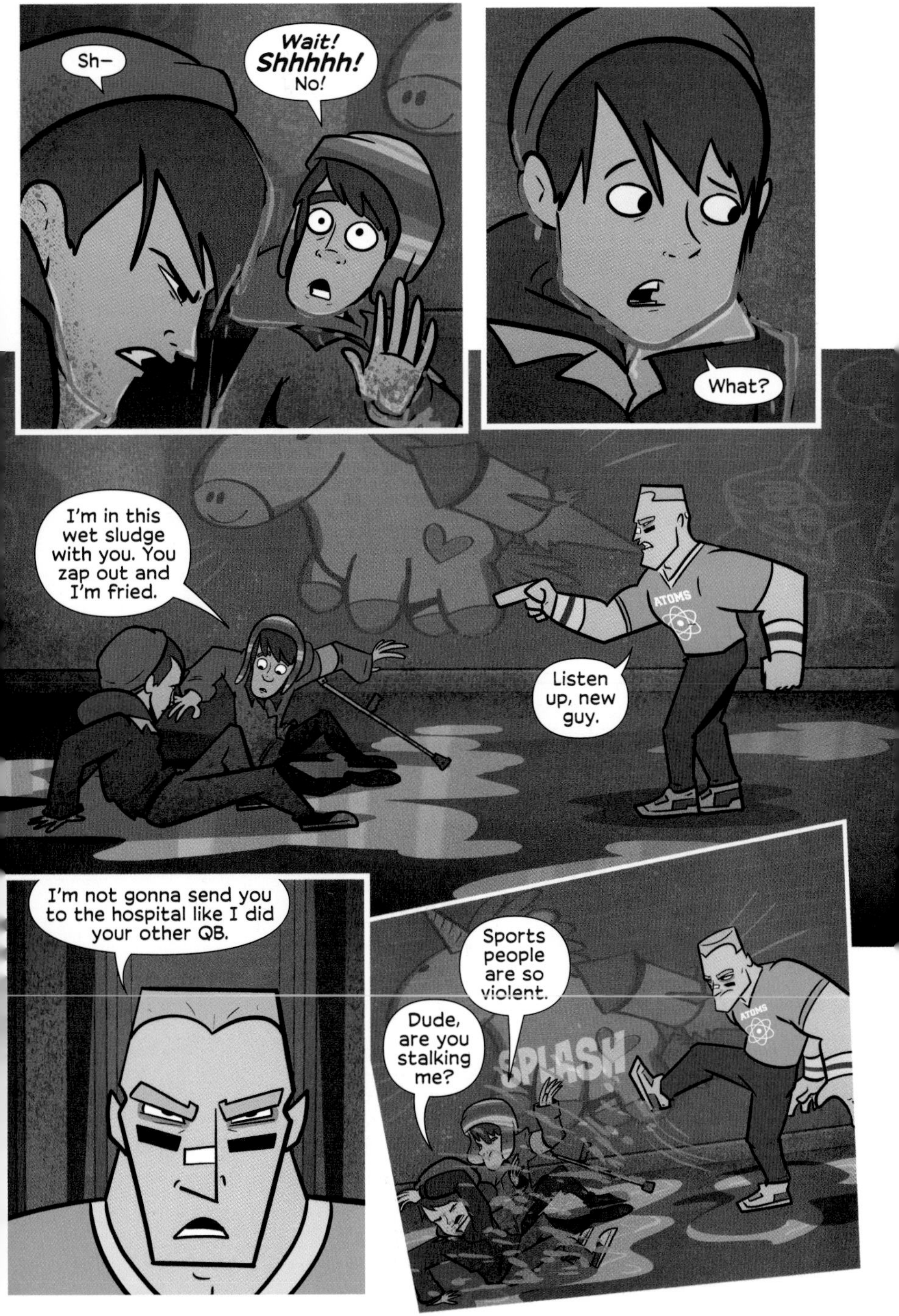
Sh–
Wait! Shhhhh! No!
What?
I'm in this wet sludge with you. You zap out and I'm fried.
Listen up, new guy.
ATOMS
I'm not gonna send you to the hospital like I did your other QB.
Sports people are so violent.
Dude, are you stalking me?
SPLASH
ATOMS

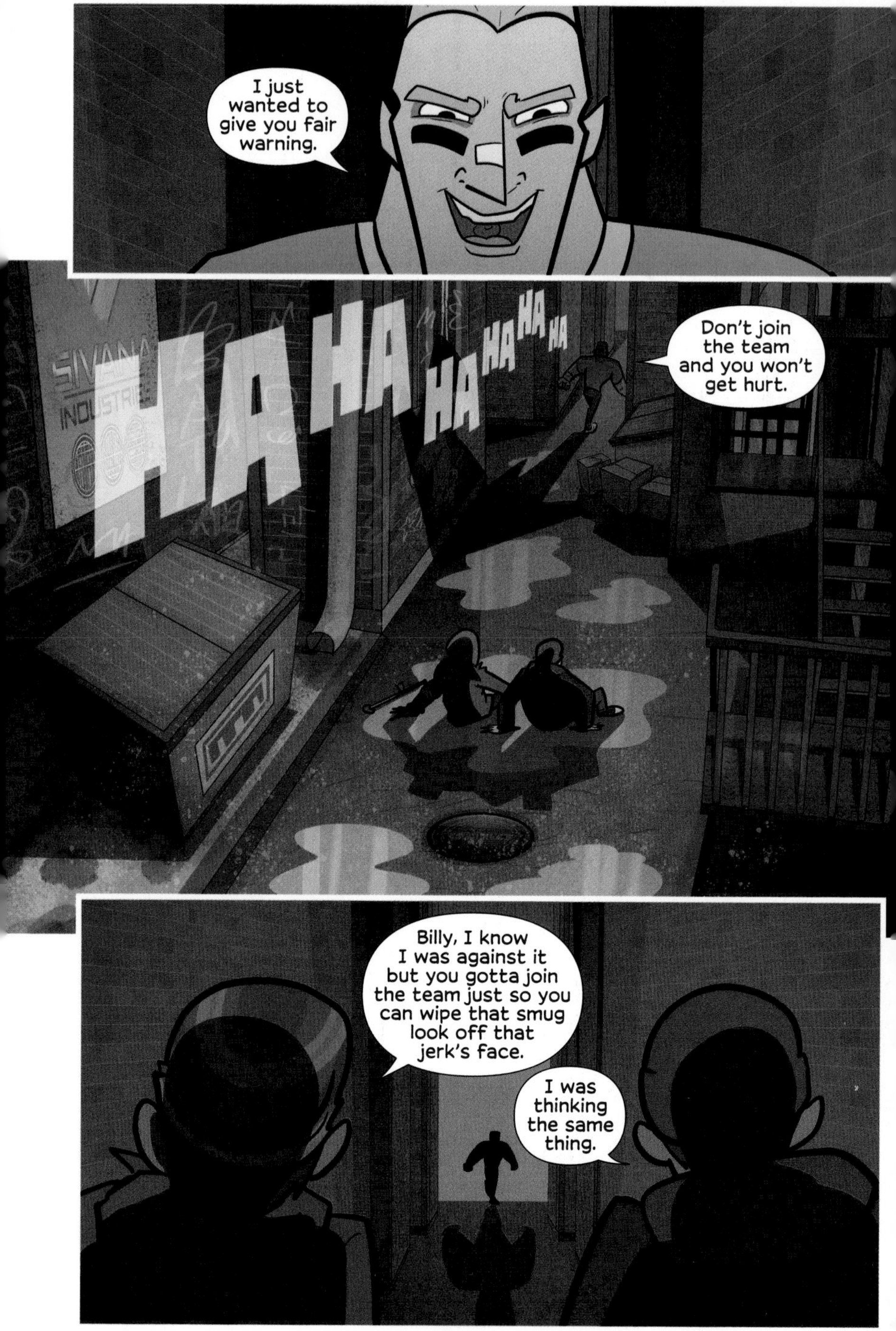
I just wanted to give you fair warning.
HA HA HA HA HA HA HA
SIVANA INDUSTRIES
Don't join the team and you won't get hurt.
Billy, I know I was against it but you gotta join the team just so you can wipe that smug look off that jerk's face.
I was thinking the same thing.

CHAPTER 3

FREDDY

BILLY

FAWCETT

WONDER WOMAN

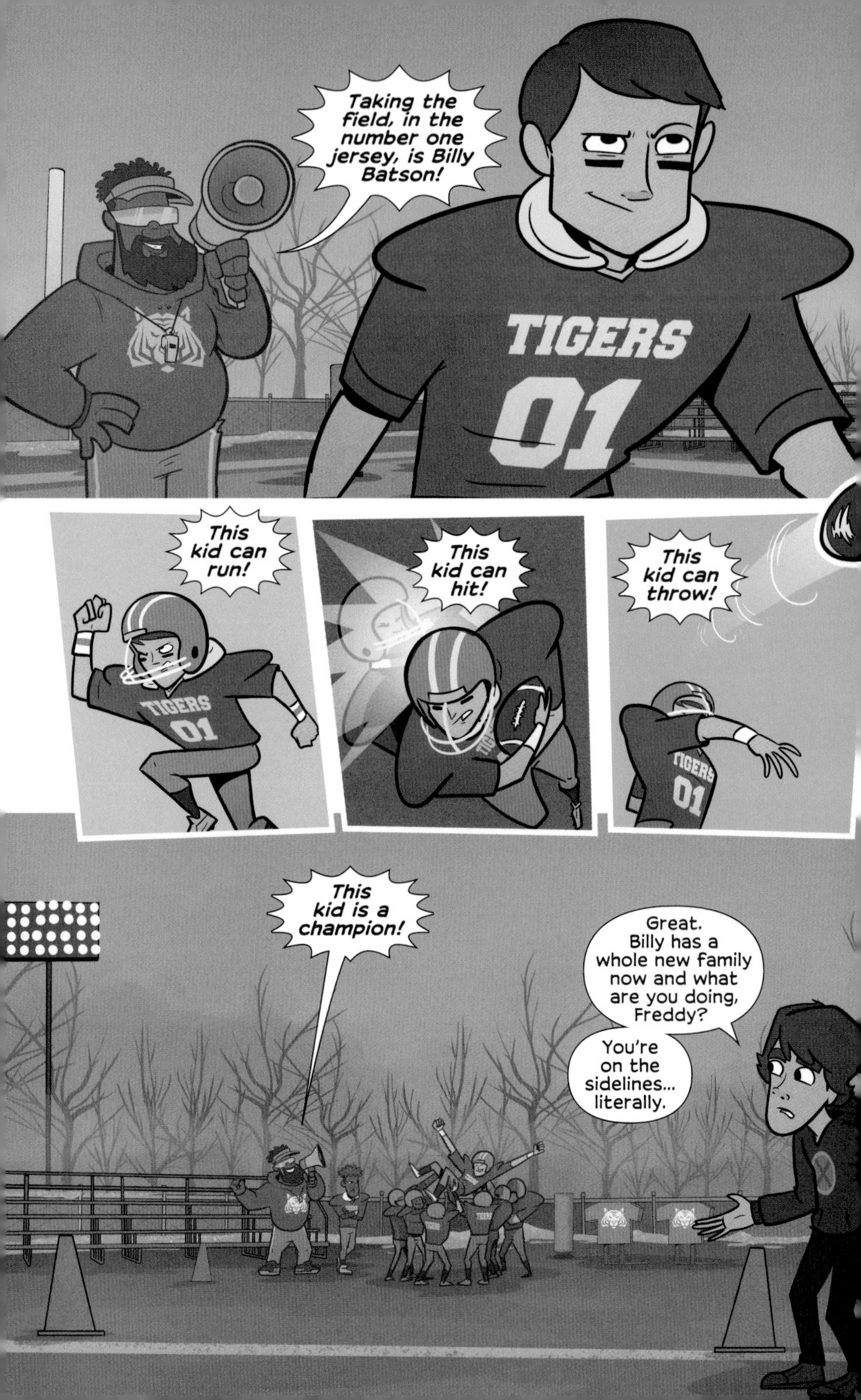
Taking the field, in the number one jersey, is Billy Batson!
TIGERS 01
This kid can run!
This kid can hit!
This kid can throw!
This kid is a champion!
Great. Billy has a whole new family now and what are you doing, Freddy?
You're on the sidelines... literally.

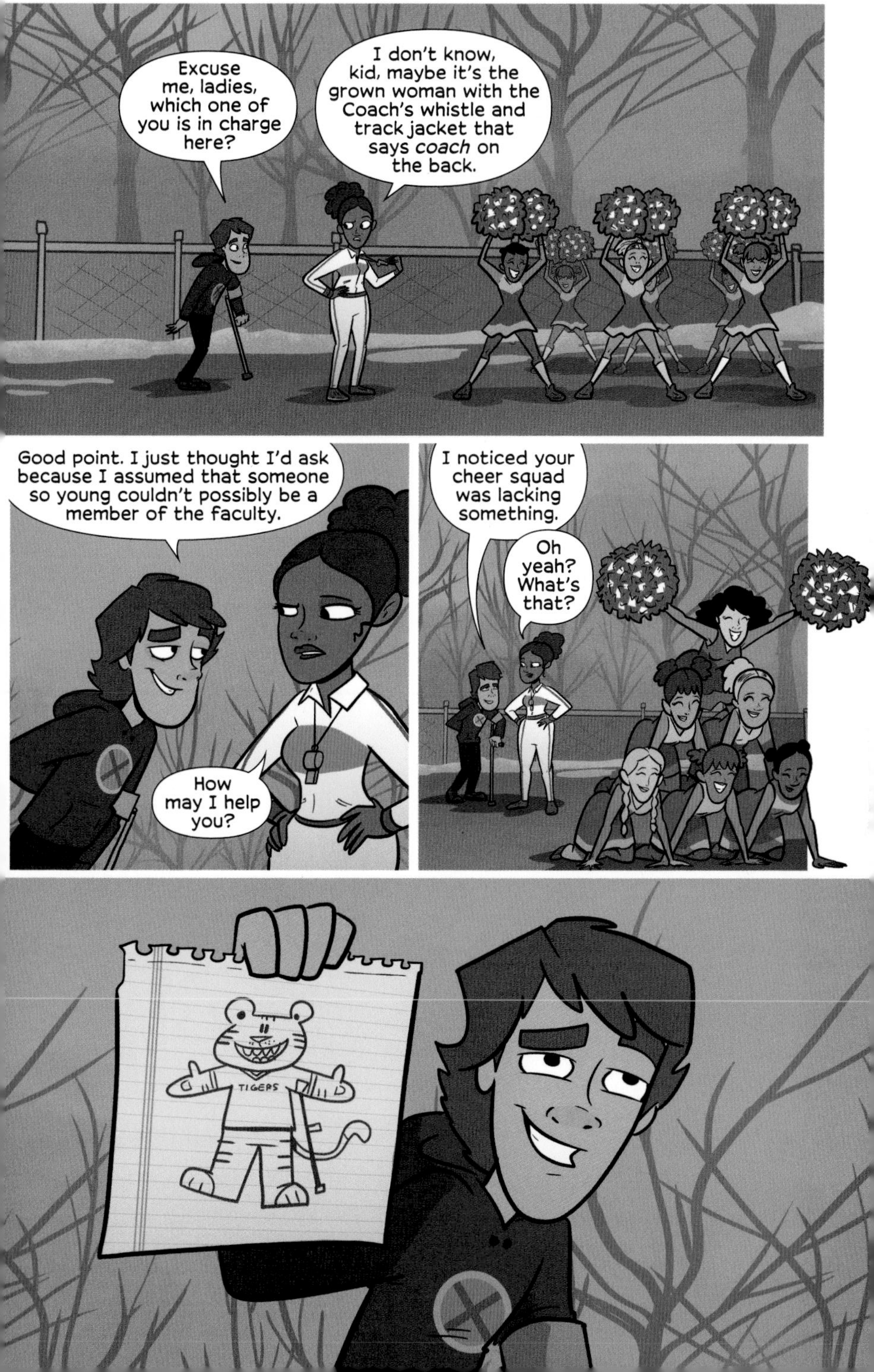
Excuse me, ladies, which one of you is in charge here?
I don't know, kid, maybe it's the grown woman with the Coach's whistle and track jacket that says *coach* on the back.
Good point. I just thought I'd ask because I assumed that someone so young couldn't possibly be a member of the faculty.
How may I help you?
I noticed your cheer squad was lacking something.
Oh yeah? What's that?
TIGERS

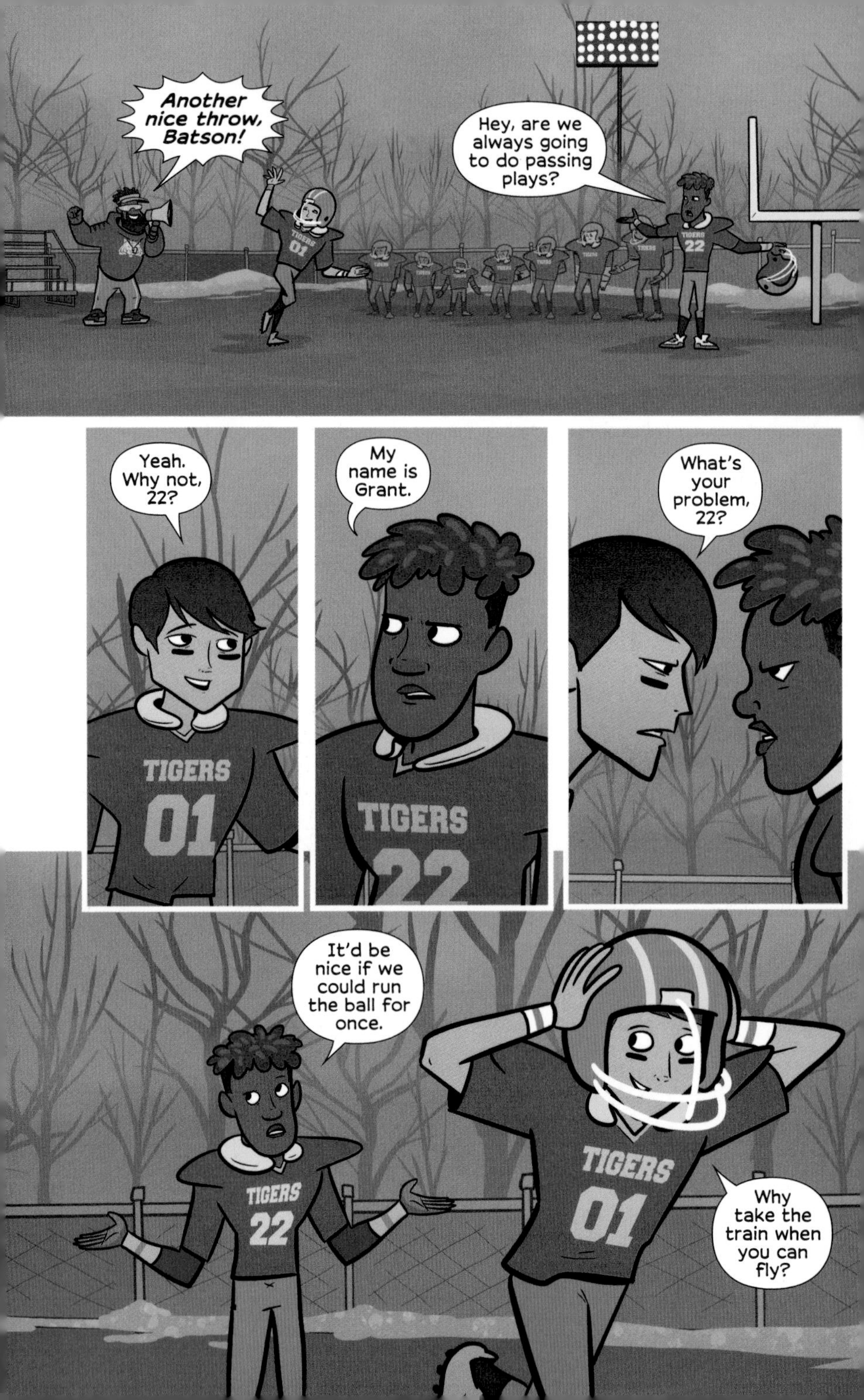
Another nice throw, Batson!
Hey, are we always going to do passing plays?
TIGERS 01
TIGERS 22
Yeah. Why not, 22?
My name is Grant.
What's your problem, 22?
It'd be nice if we could run the ball for once.
Why take the train when you can fly?

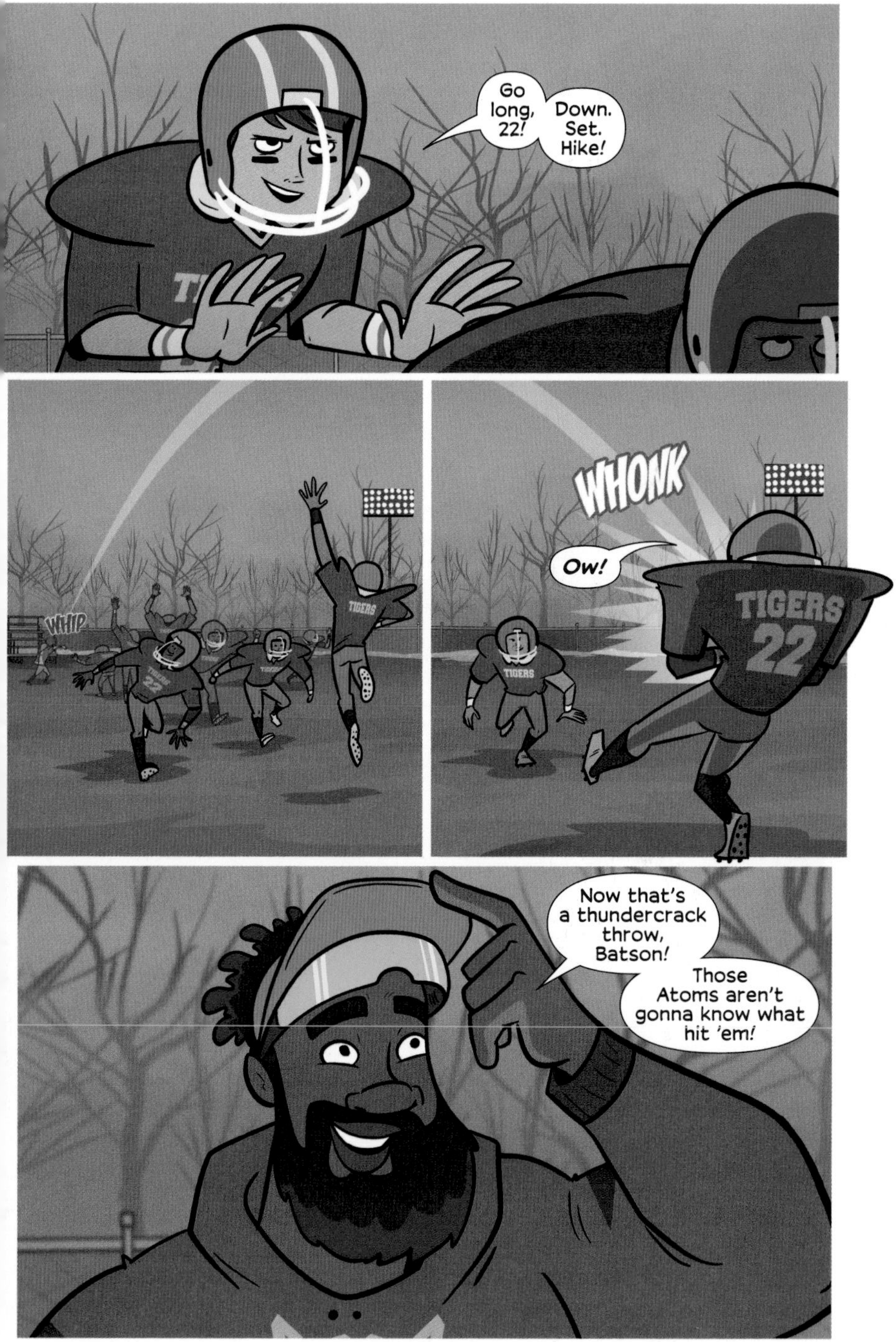
Go long, 22!
Down. Set. Hike!
WHIP
WHONK
Ow!
TIGERS 22
Now that's a thundercrack throw, Batson!
Those Atoms aren't gonna know what hit 'em!

Those Atoms aren't gonna know what hit 'em!

That Batson guy is good.

Batson is good?

So, Clutch, what you're telling me is that all this next-generation equipment was just a waste of money.

No, coach, that's not what I said—

WIN POWER

LEADERBOARD

CLUTCH 89557
BOSCO 79737
BUCKY 69737
FINSTER 59737
TEX 43737
ROCKET 32737
BUSTER
BIFF
QUIMBY
RENATO
RALPH

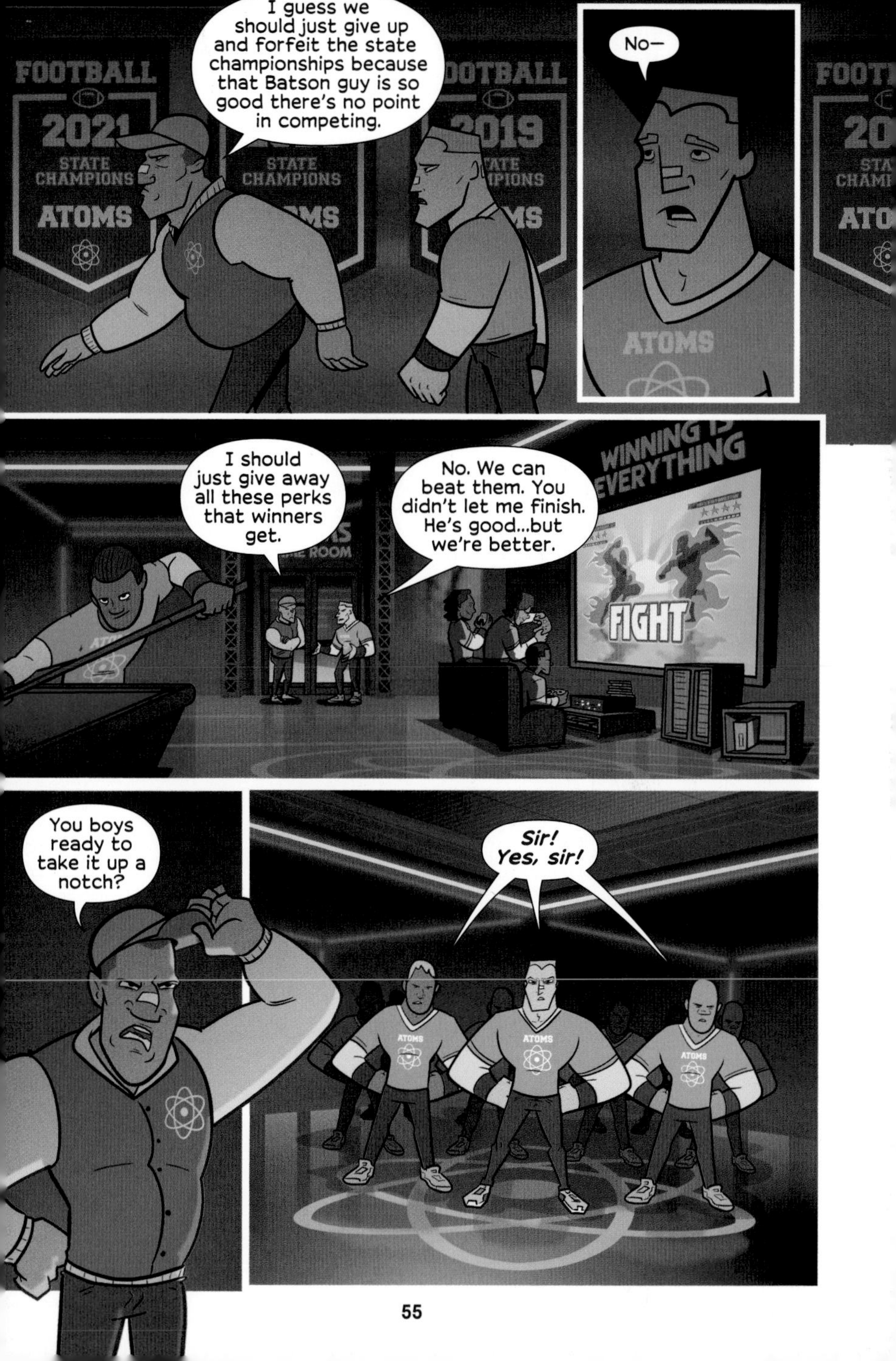
FOOTBALL 2021 STATE CHAMPIONS ATOMS
I guess we should just give up and forfeit the state championships because that Batson guy is so good there's no point in competing.
No—
WINNING IS EVERYTHING
FIGHT
I should just give away all these perks that winners get.
No. We can beat them. You didn't let me finish. He's good...but we're better.
You boys ready to take it up a notch?
Sir! Yes, sir!

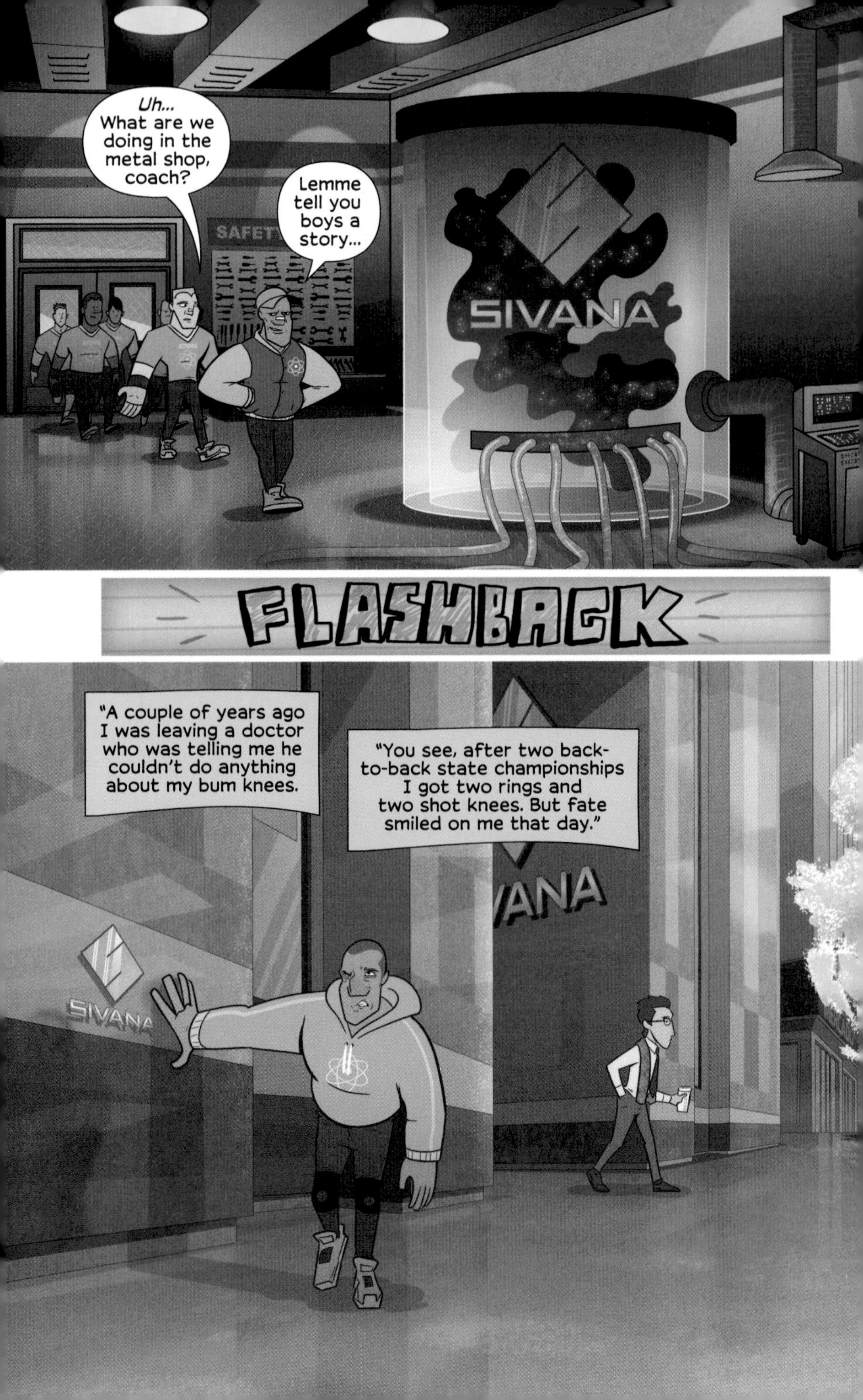
Uh... What are we doing in the metal shop, coach?
Lemme tell you boys a story...
SAFETY
SIVANA
FLASHBACK
"A couple of years ago I was leaving a doctor who was telling me he couldn't do anything about my bum knees.
"You see, after two back-to-back state championships I got two rings and two shot knees. But fate smiled on me that day."
SIVANA
VANA

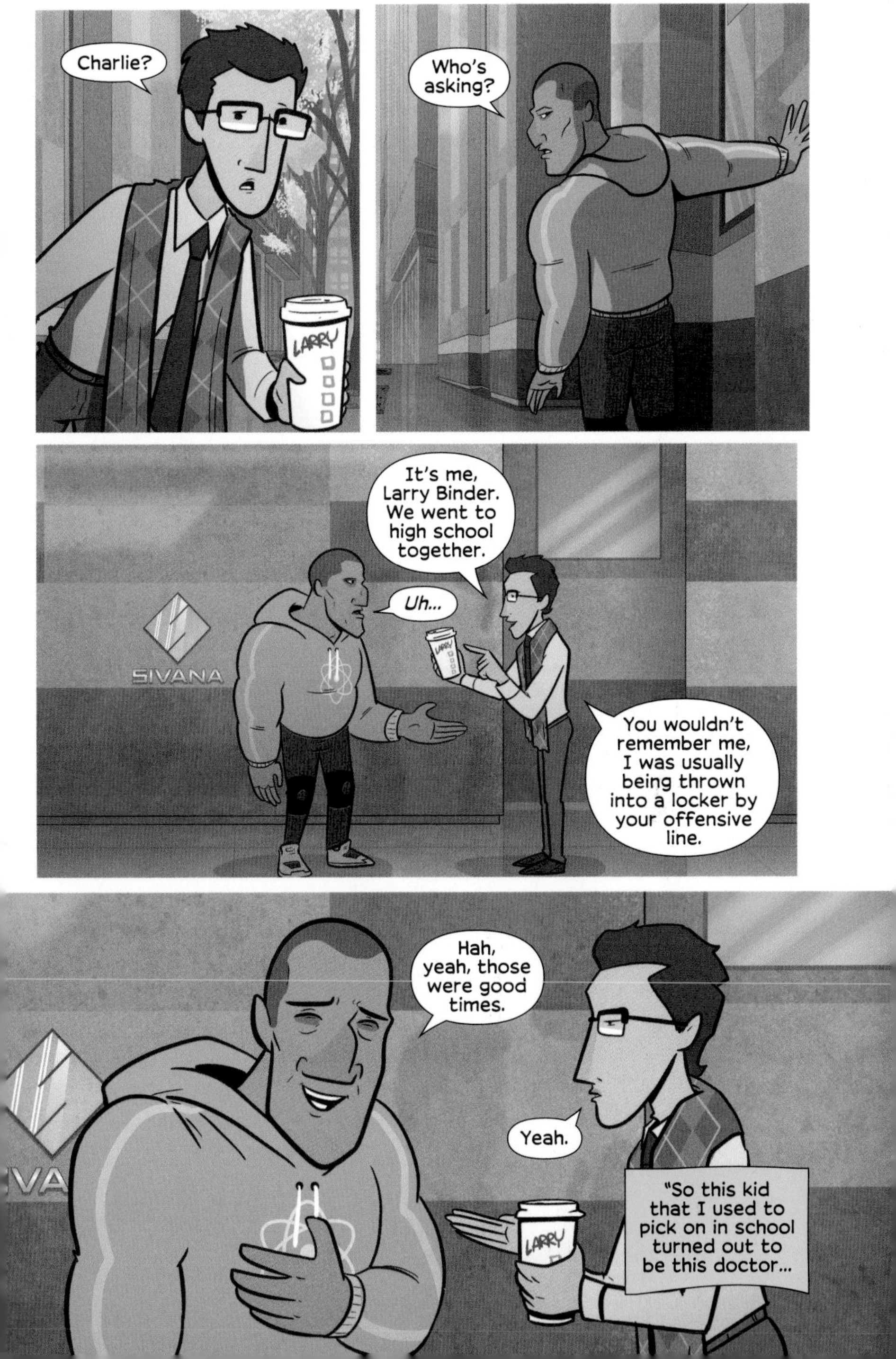
Charlie?
Who's asking?
It's me, Larry Binder. We went to high school together.
Uh...
SIVANA
You wouldn't remember me, I was usually being thrown into a locker by your offensive line.
Hah, yeah, those were good times.
Yeah.
"So this kid that I used to pick on in school turned out to be this doctor...

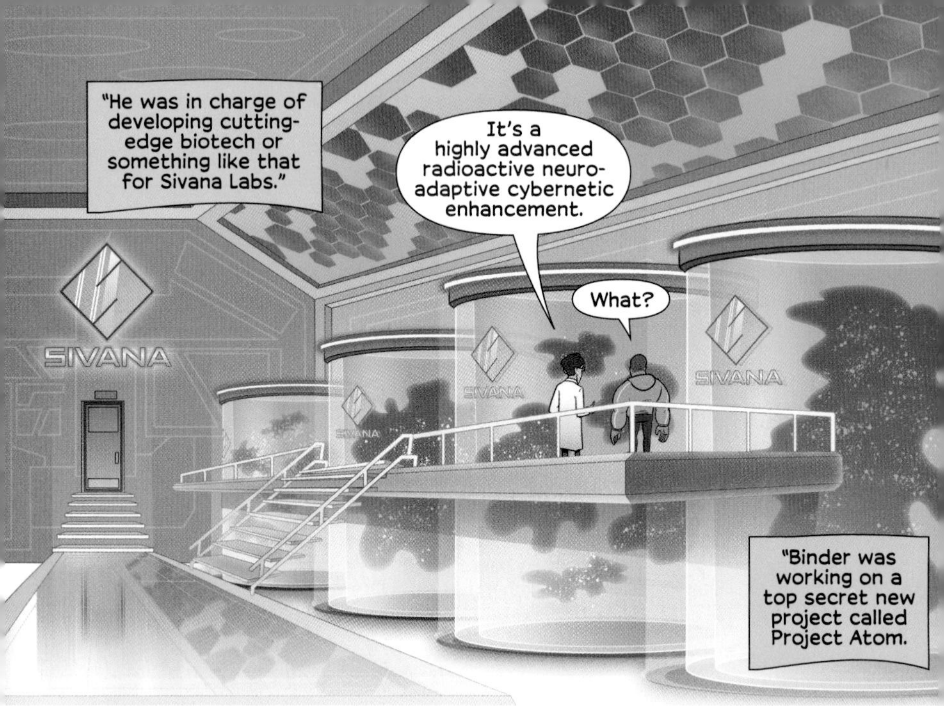
"He was in charge of developing cutting-edge biotech or something like that for Sivana Labs."
It's a highly advanced radioactive neuro-adaptive cybernetic enhancement.
What?
"Binder was working on a top secret new project called Project Atom.
SIVANA

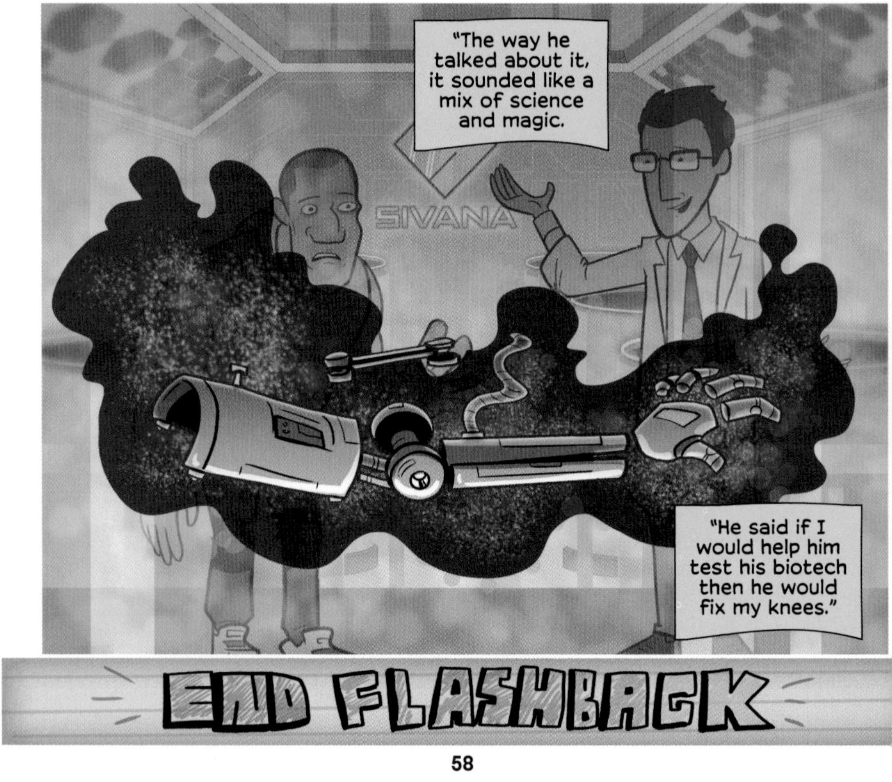
"The way he talked about it, it sounded like a mix of science and magic.
SIVANA
"He said if I would help him test his biotech then he would fix my knees."
END FLASHBACK

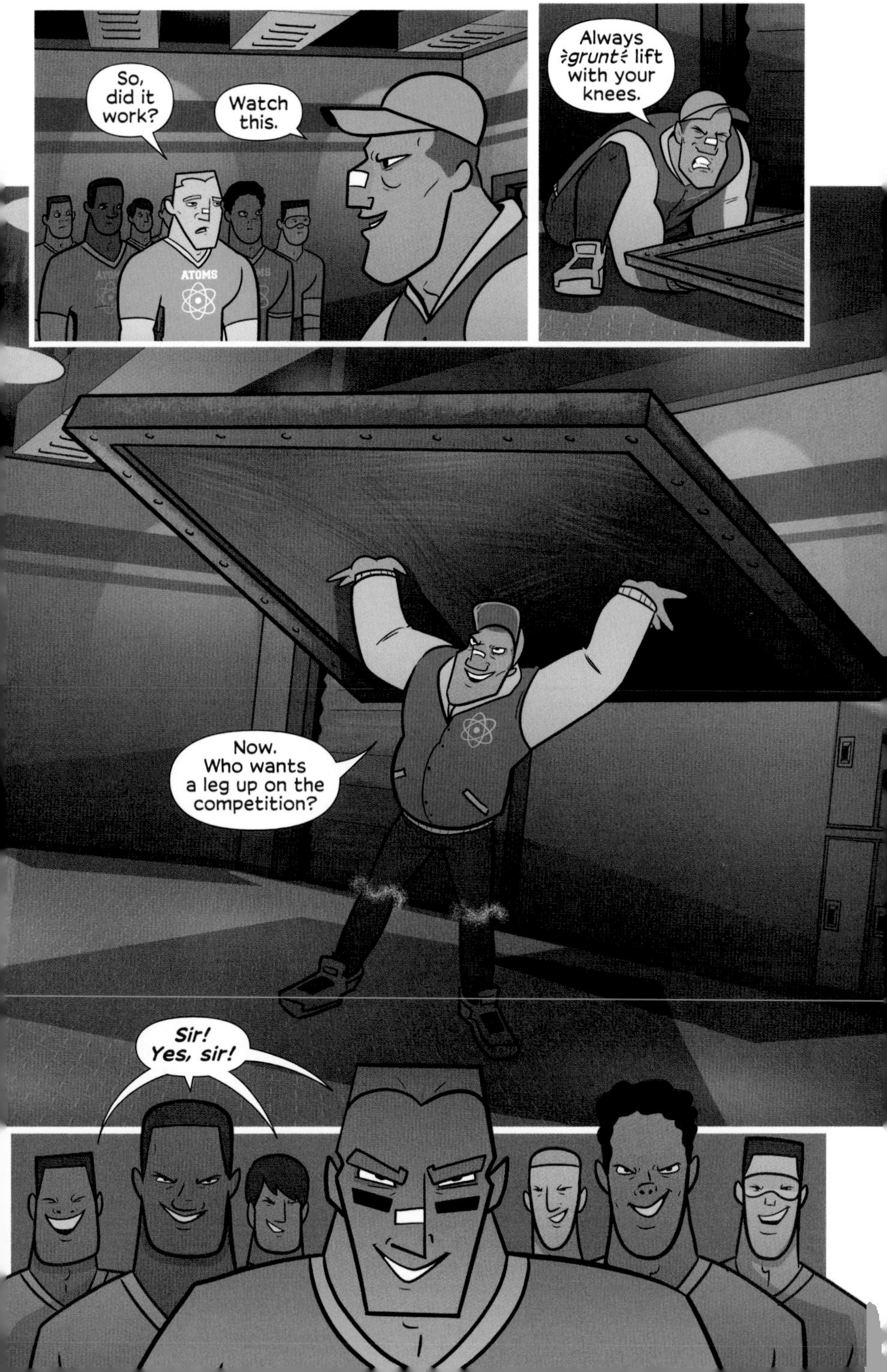
So, did it work?
Watch this.
Always ⸗grunt⸗ lift with your knees.
ATOMS
Now. Who wants a leg up on the competition?
Sir! Yes, sir!

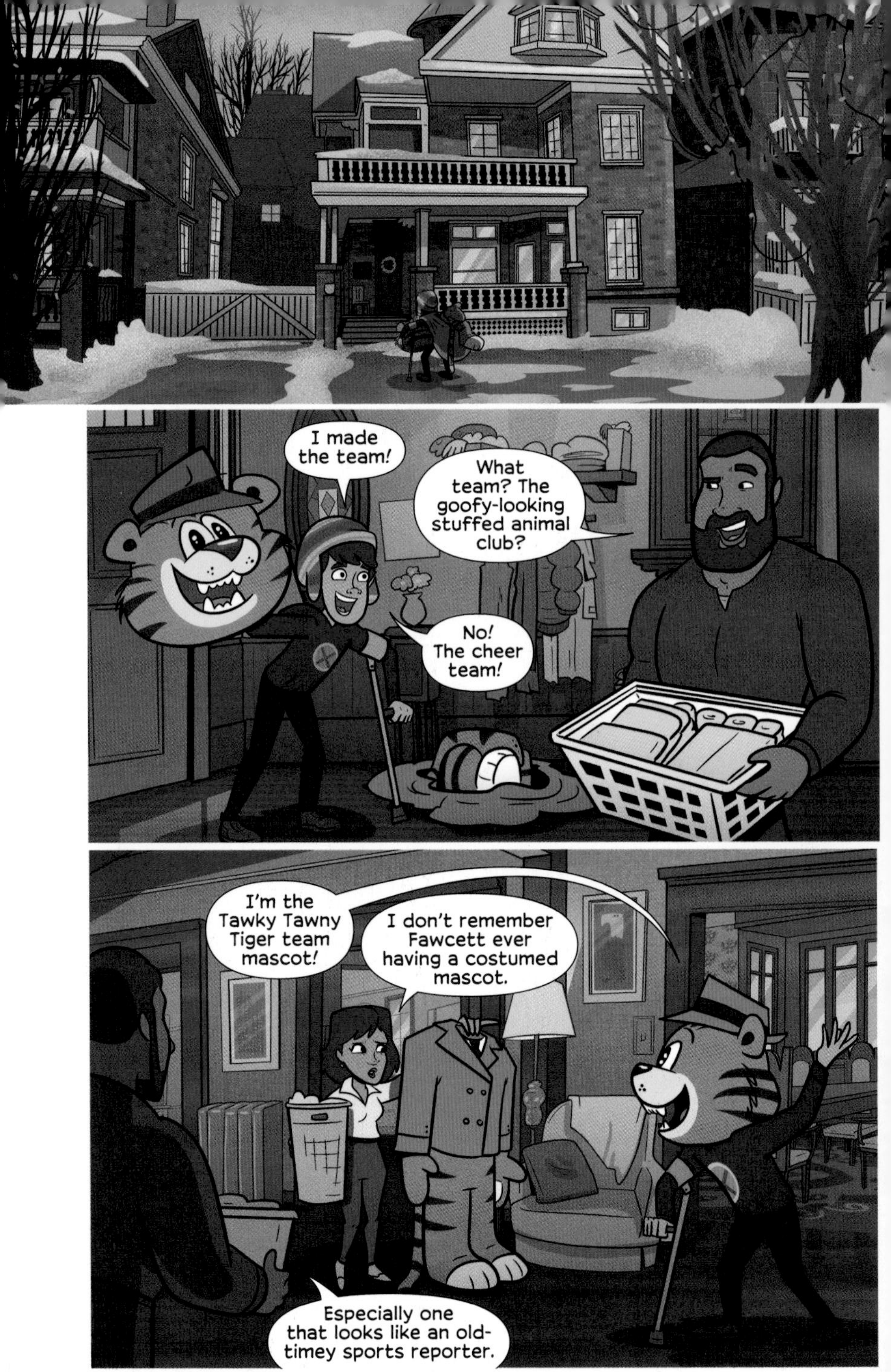
I made the team!
What team? The goofy-looking stuffed animal club?
No! The cheer team!
I'm the Tawky Tawny Tiger team mascot!
I don't remember Fawcett ever having a costumed mascot.
Especially one that looks like an old-timey sports reporter.

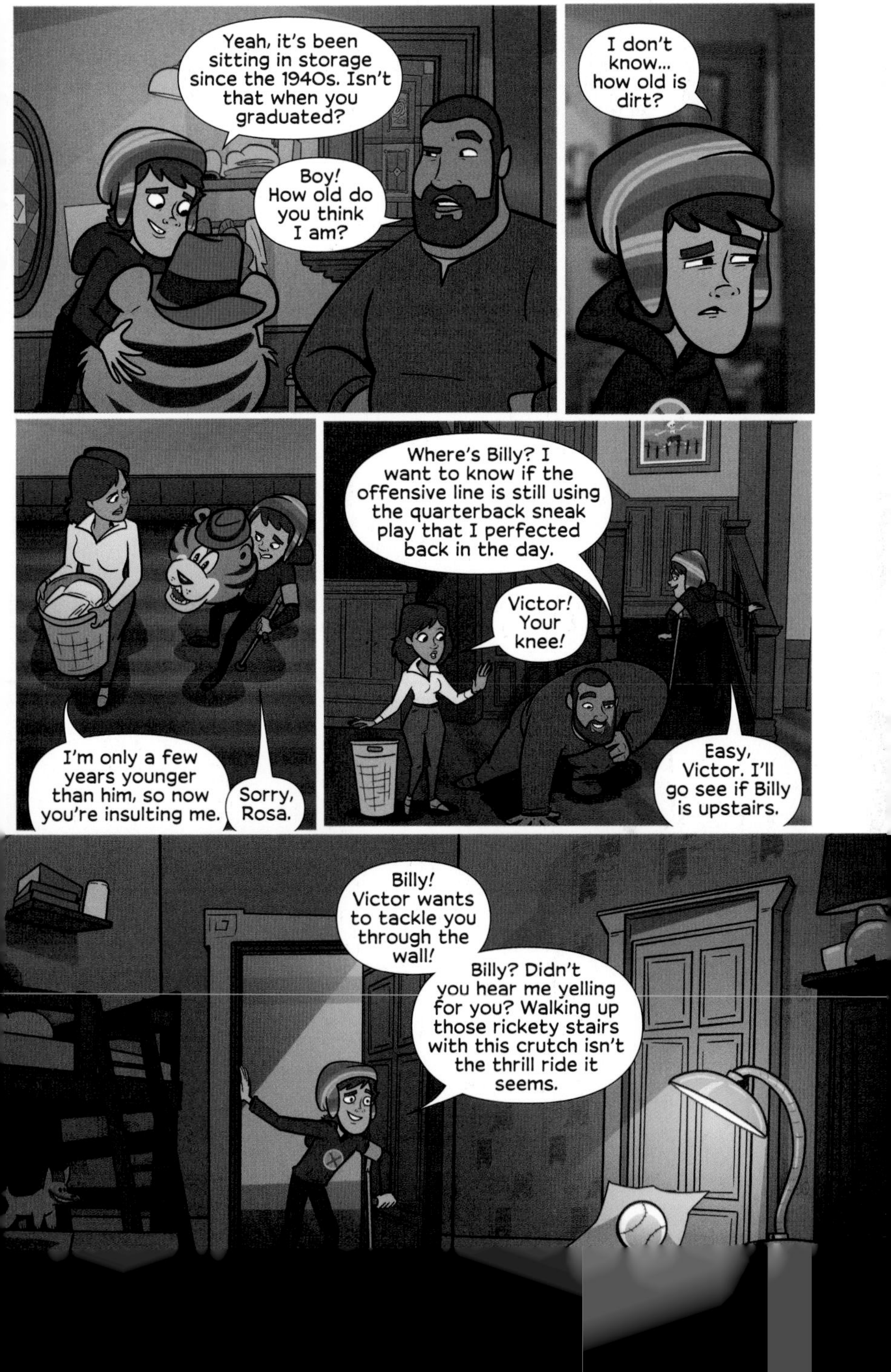
Yeah, it's been sitting in storage since the 1940s. Isn't that when you graduated?
Boy! How old do you think I am?
I don't know... how old is dirt?
I'm only a few years younger than him, so now you're insulting me.
Sorry, Rosa.
Where's Billy? I want to know if the offensive line is still using the quarterback sneak play that I perfected back in the day.
Victor! Your knee!
Easy, Victor. I'll go see if Billy is upstairs.
Billy! Victor wants to tackle you through the wall!
Billy? Didn't you hear me yelling for you? Walking up those rickety stairs with this crutch isn't the thrill ride it seems.

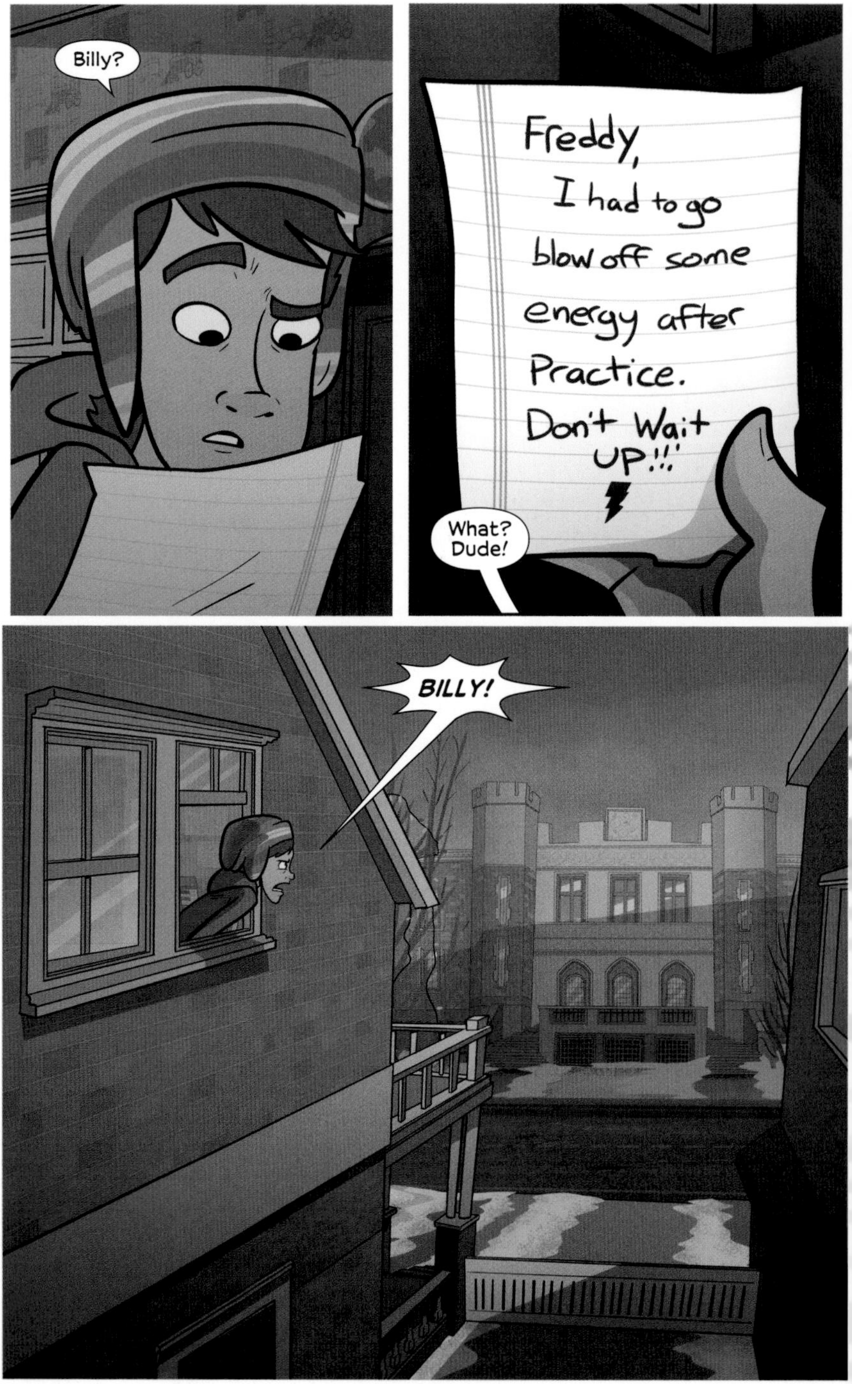
Billy?
Freddy,
I had to go
blow off some
energy after
Practice.
Don't Wait
UP!!!
What?
Dude!
BILLY!

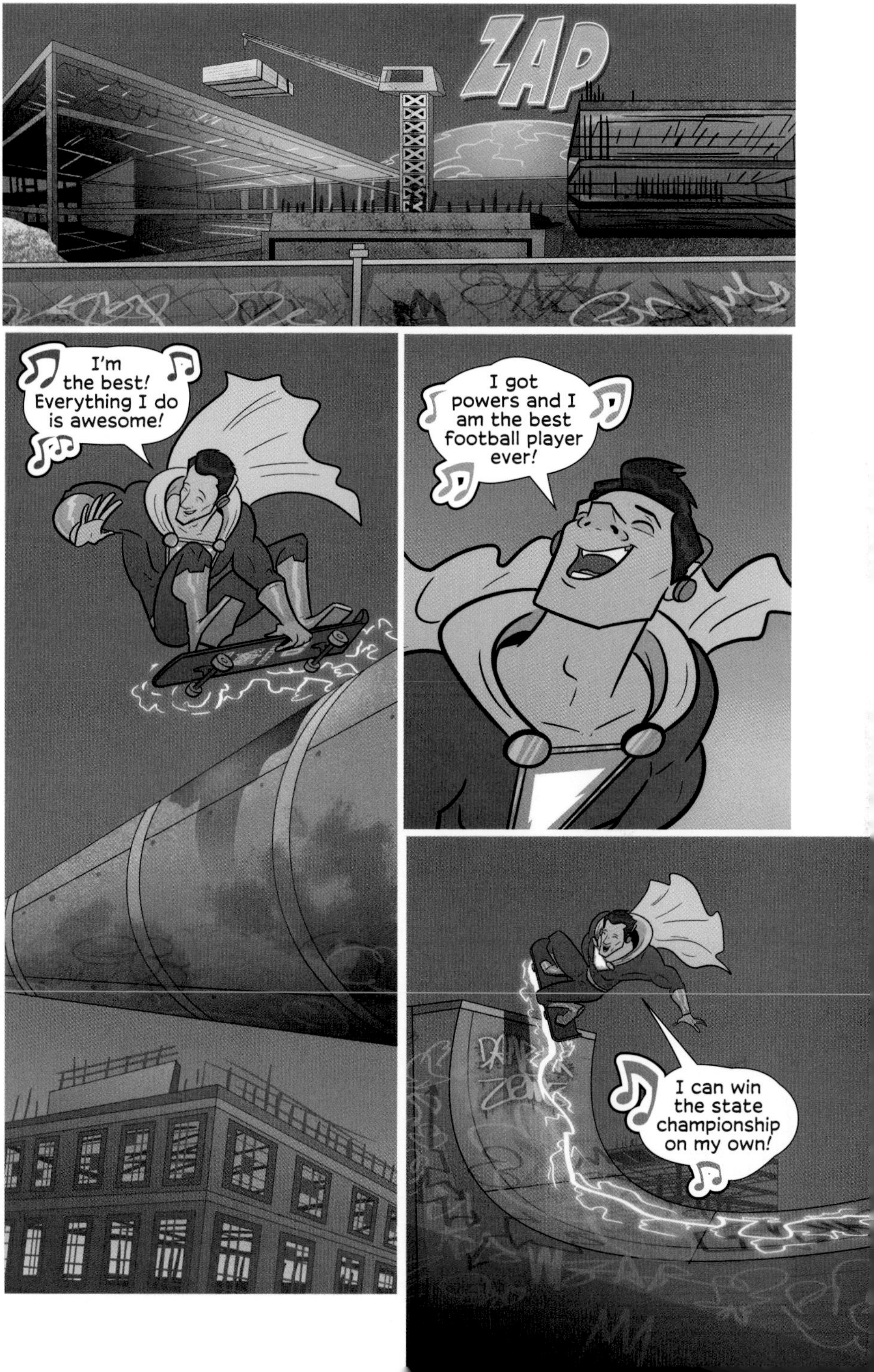
ZAP
I'm the best! Everything I do is awesome!
I got powers and I am the best football player ever!
I can win the state championship on my own!

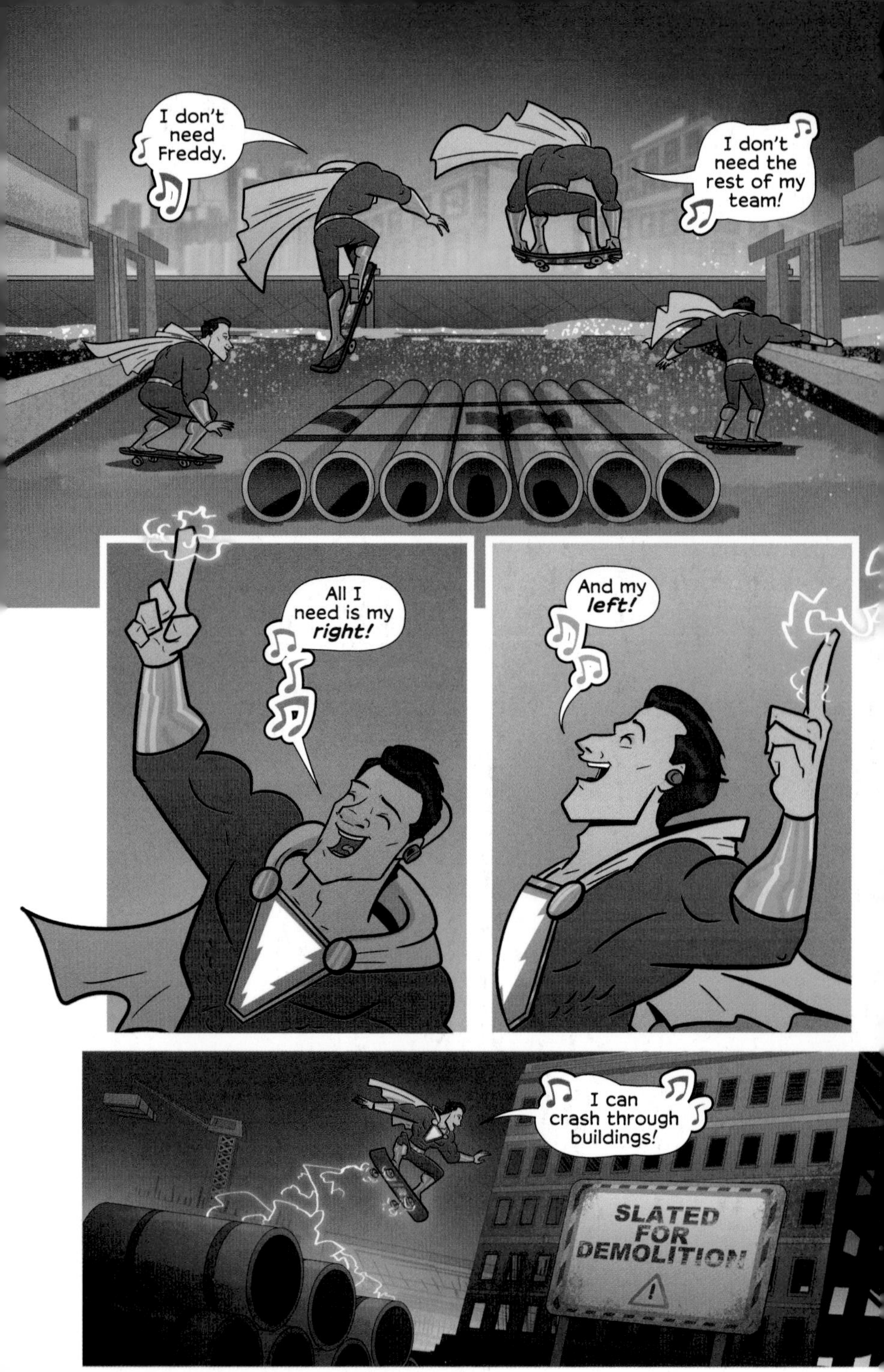

I don't need Freddy.
I don't need the rest of my team!
All I need is my right!
And my left!
I can crash through buildings!
SLATED FOR DEMOLITION

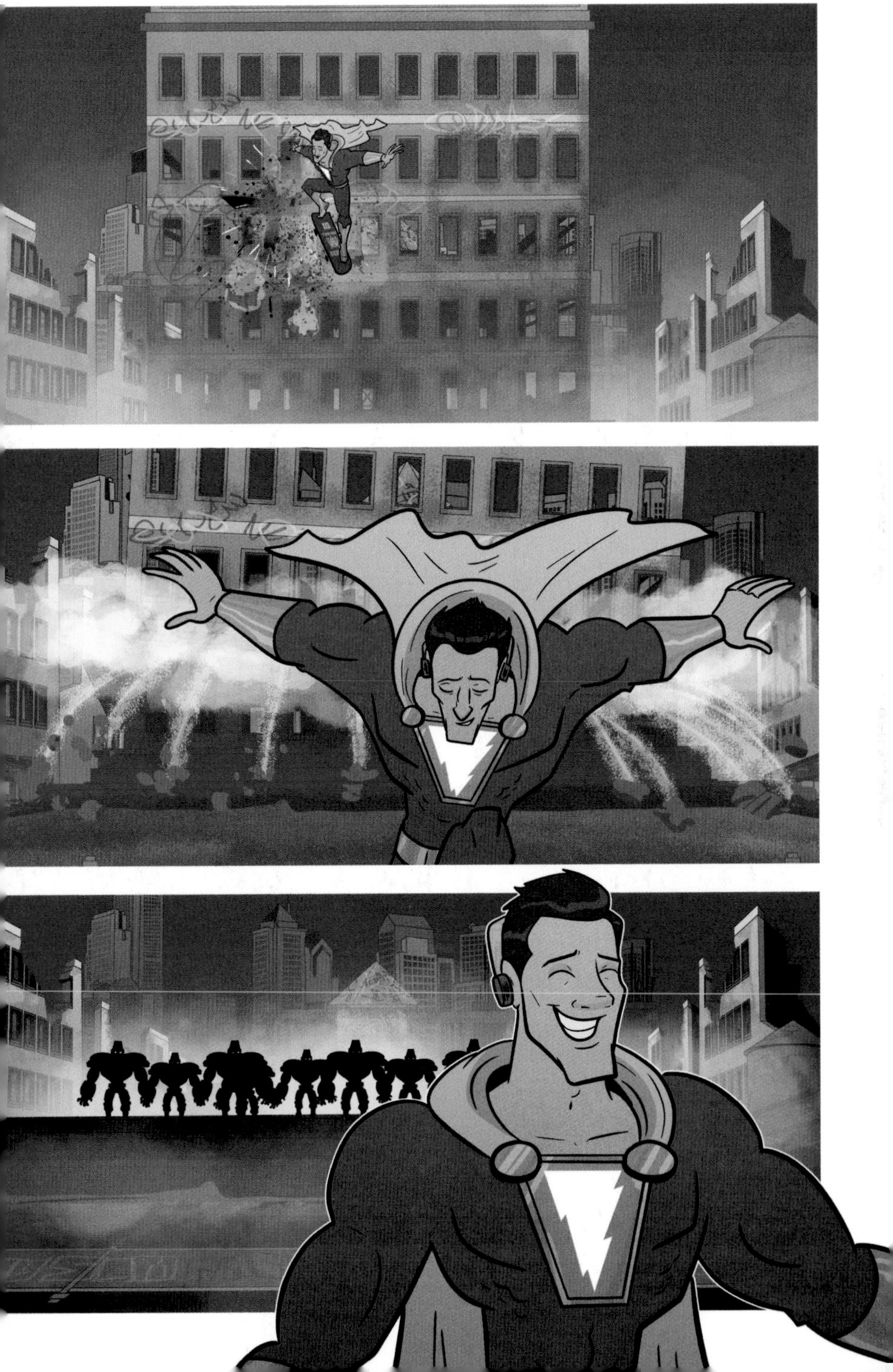

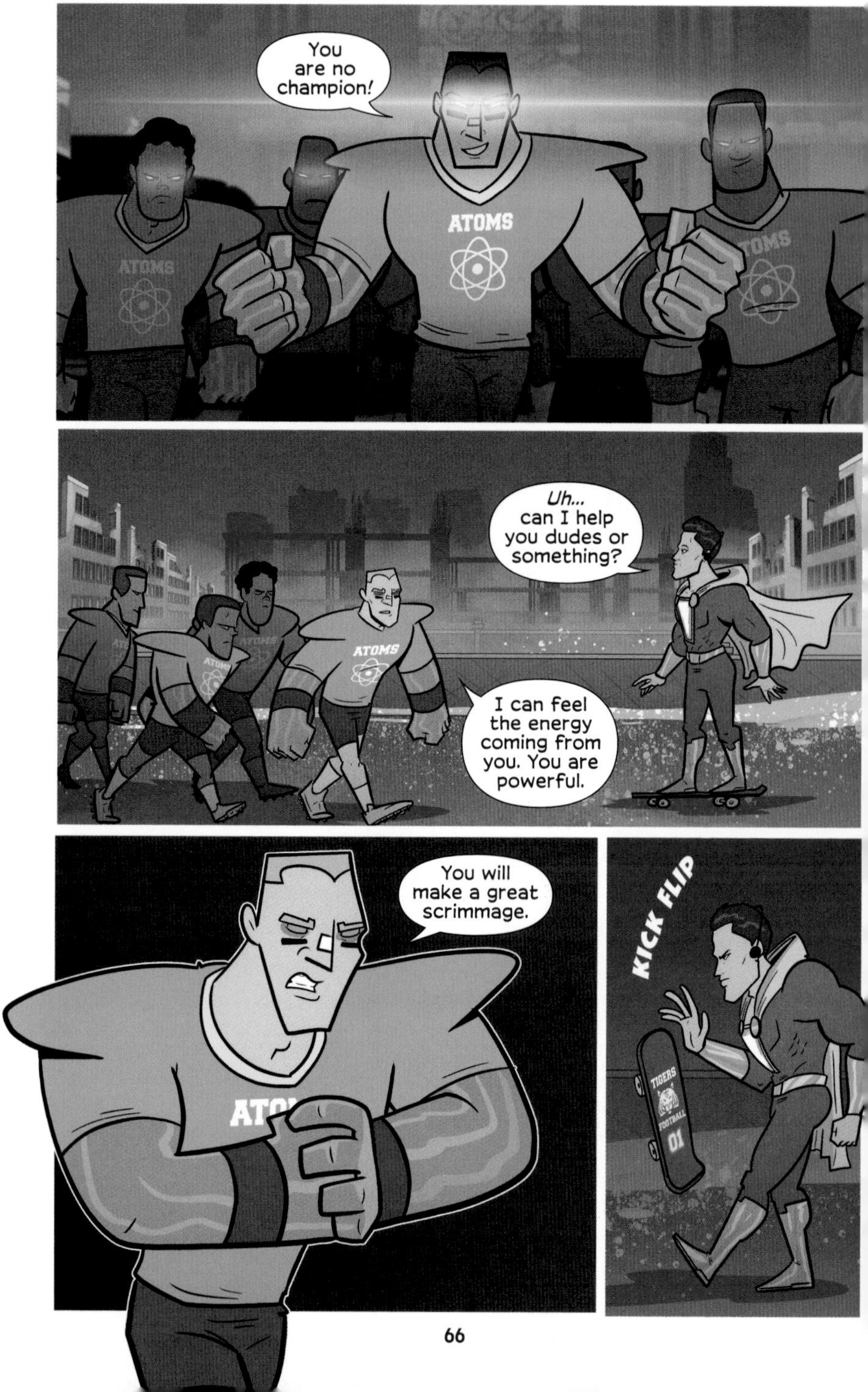
You are no champion!
ATOMS
ATOMS
ATOMS
Uh... can I help you dudes or something?
ATOMS
ATOMS
I can feel the energy coming from you. You are powerful.
You will make a great scrimmage.
ATO
KICK FLIP
TIGERS
FOOTBALL
01

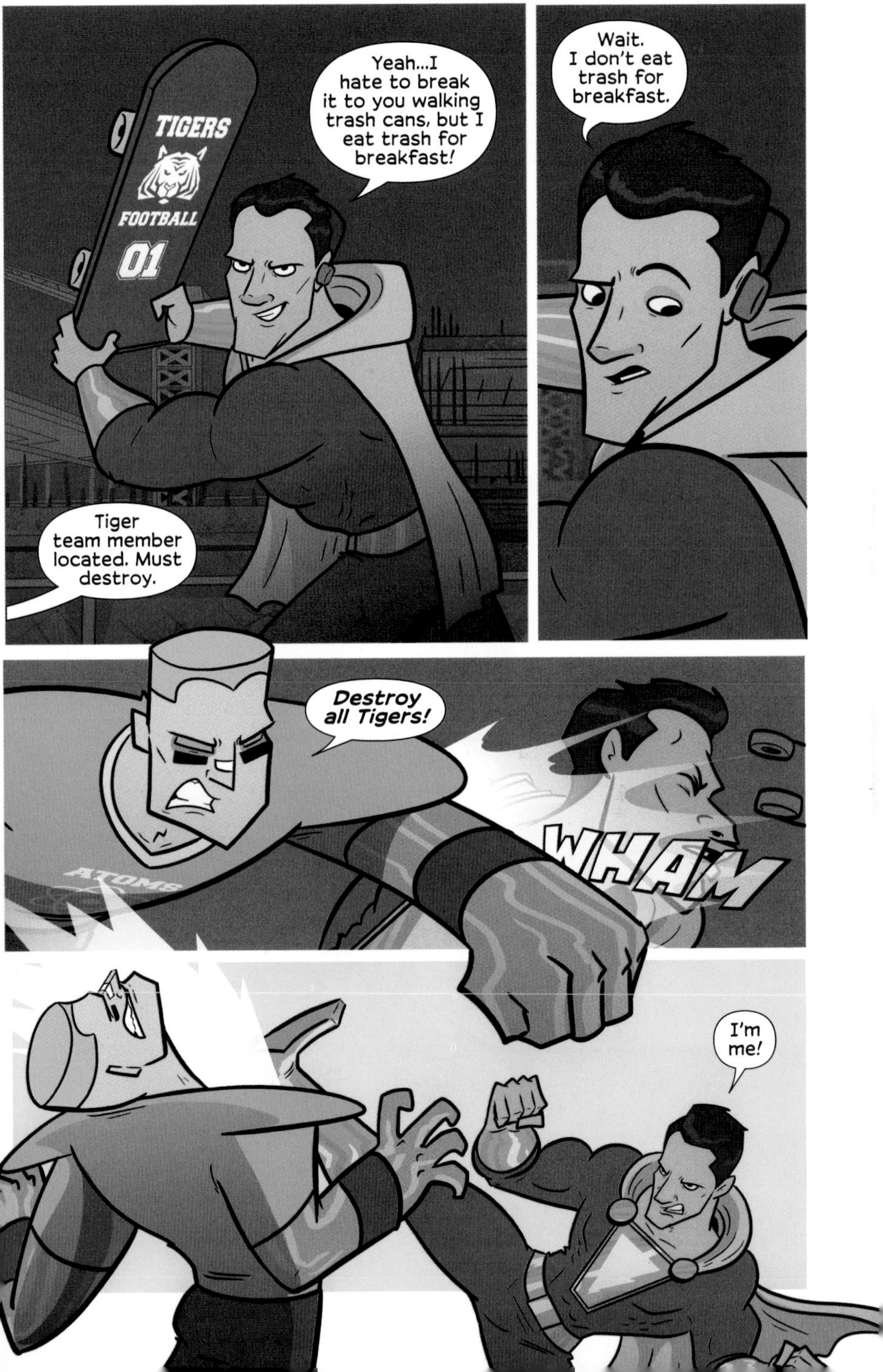
TIGERS
FOOTBALL
01
Yeah...I hate to break it to you walking trash cans, but I eat trash for breakfast!
Tiger team member located. Must destroy.
Wait. I don't eat trash for breakfast.
Destroy all Tigers!
ATOMS
WHAM
I'm me!

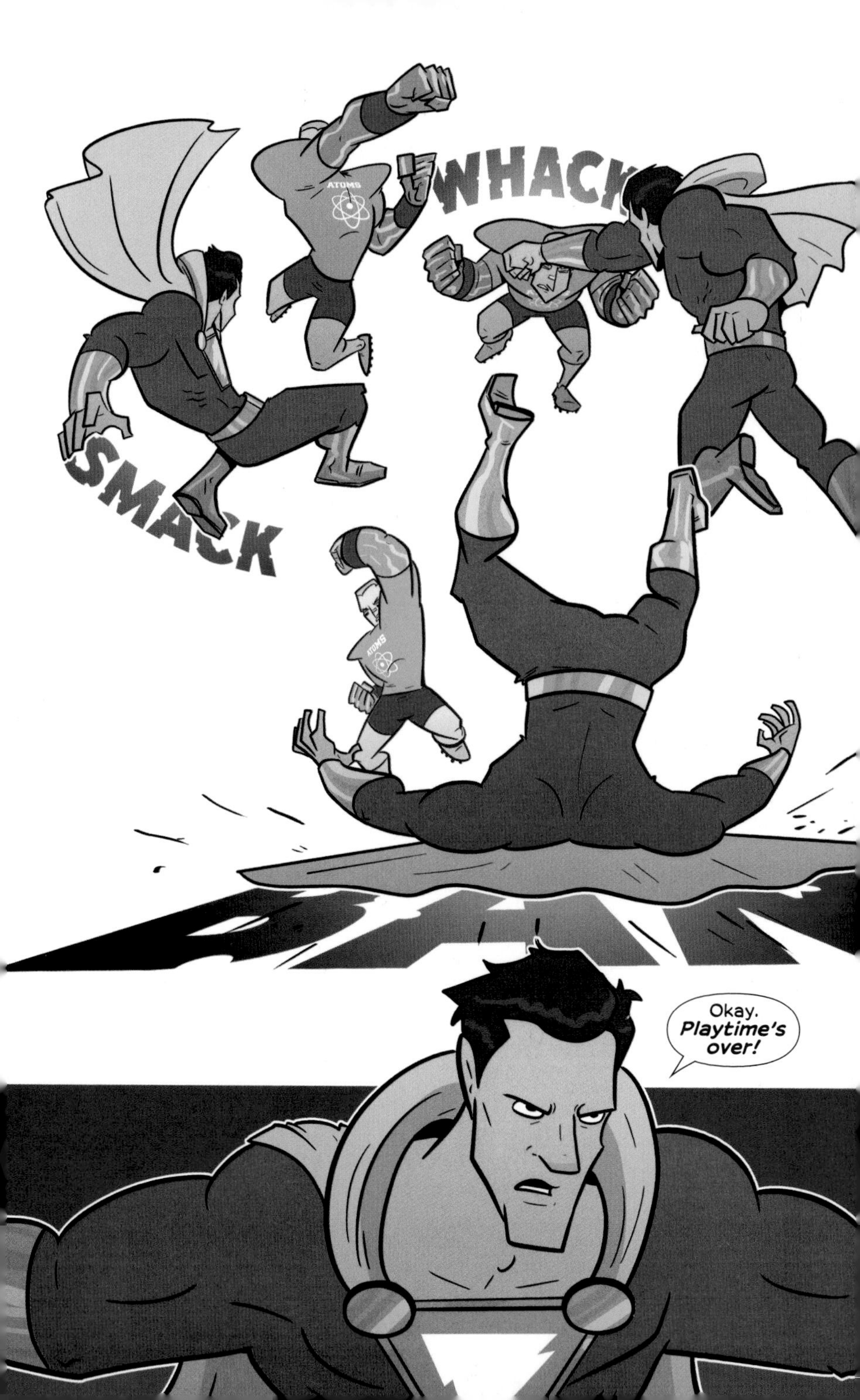
WHACK
SMACK
Okay. Playtime's over!

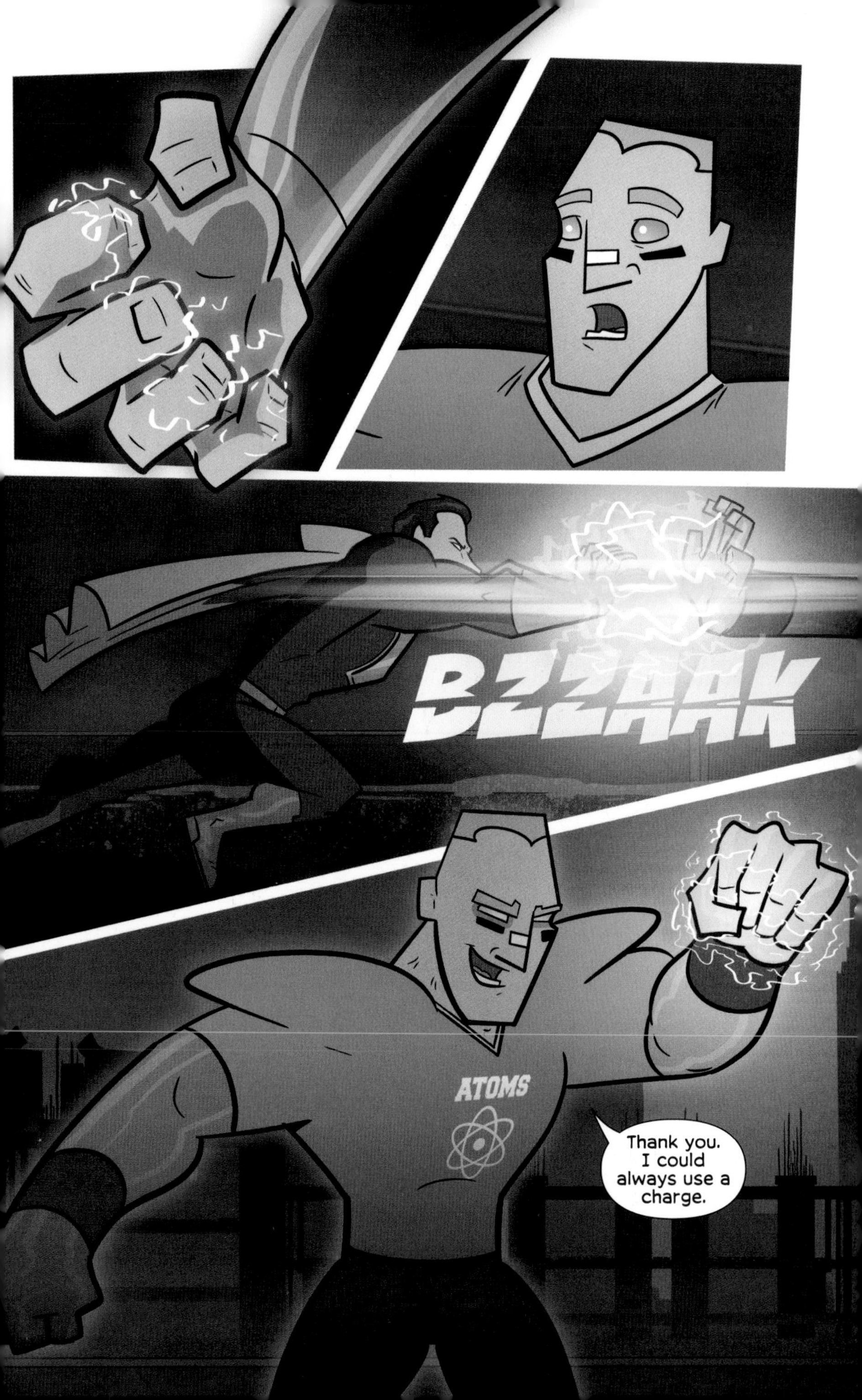
BZZAAK
ATOMS
Thank you.
I could
always use a
charge.

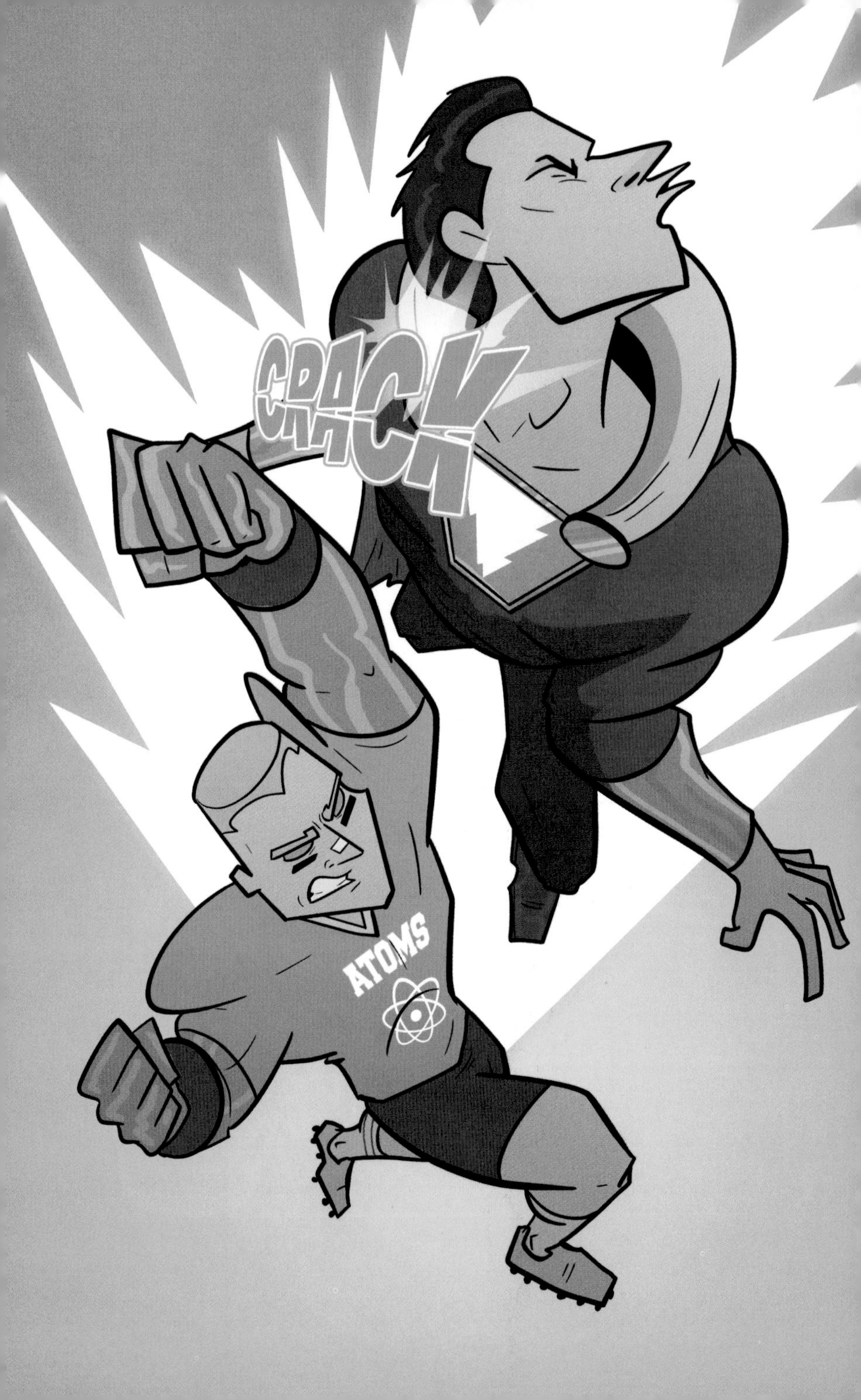
CRACK
ATOMS

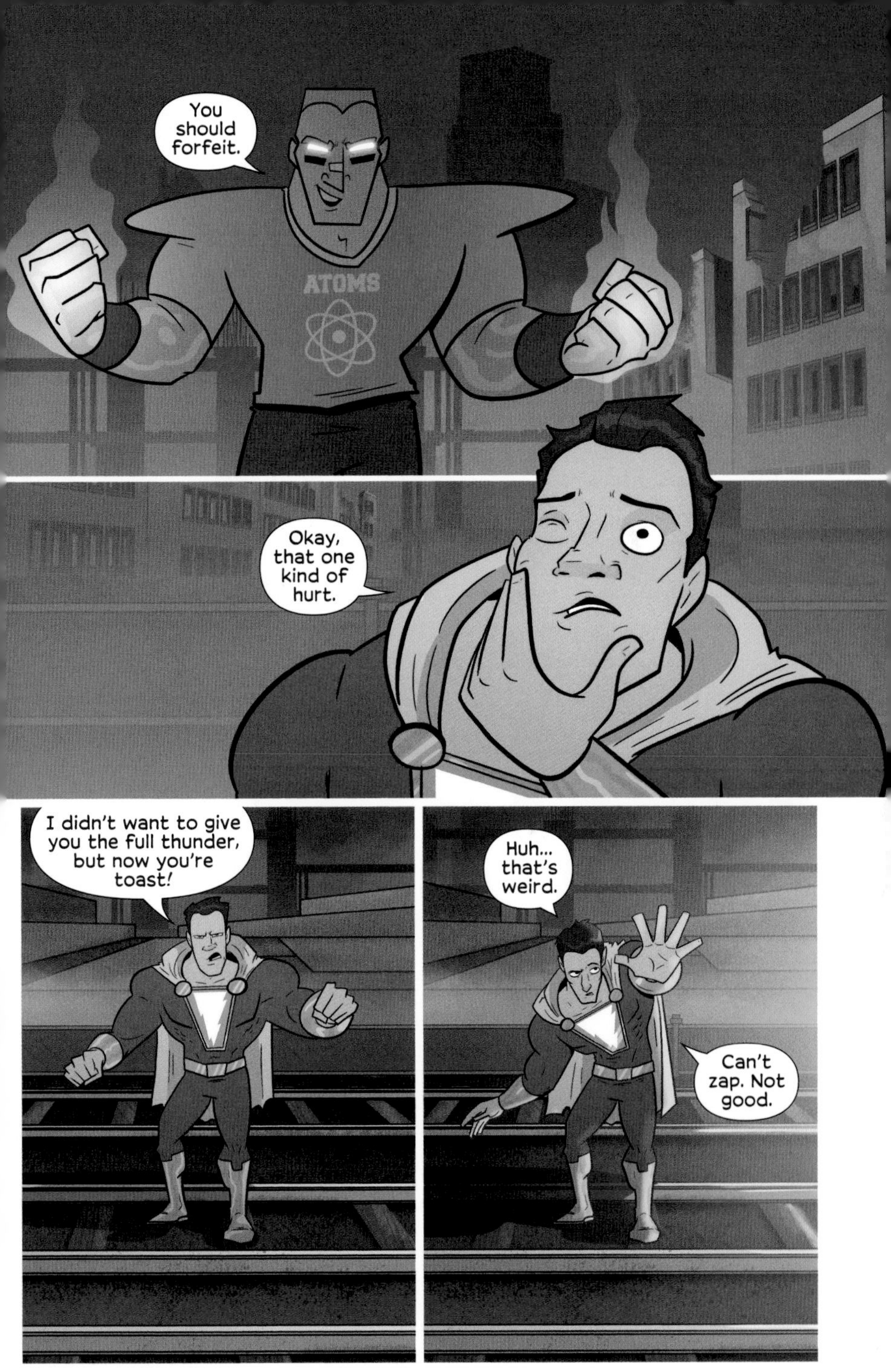
You should forfeit.
Okay, that one kind of hurt.
I didn't want to give you the full thunder, but now you're toast!
Huh... that's weird.
Can't zap. Not good.

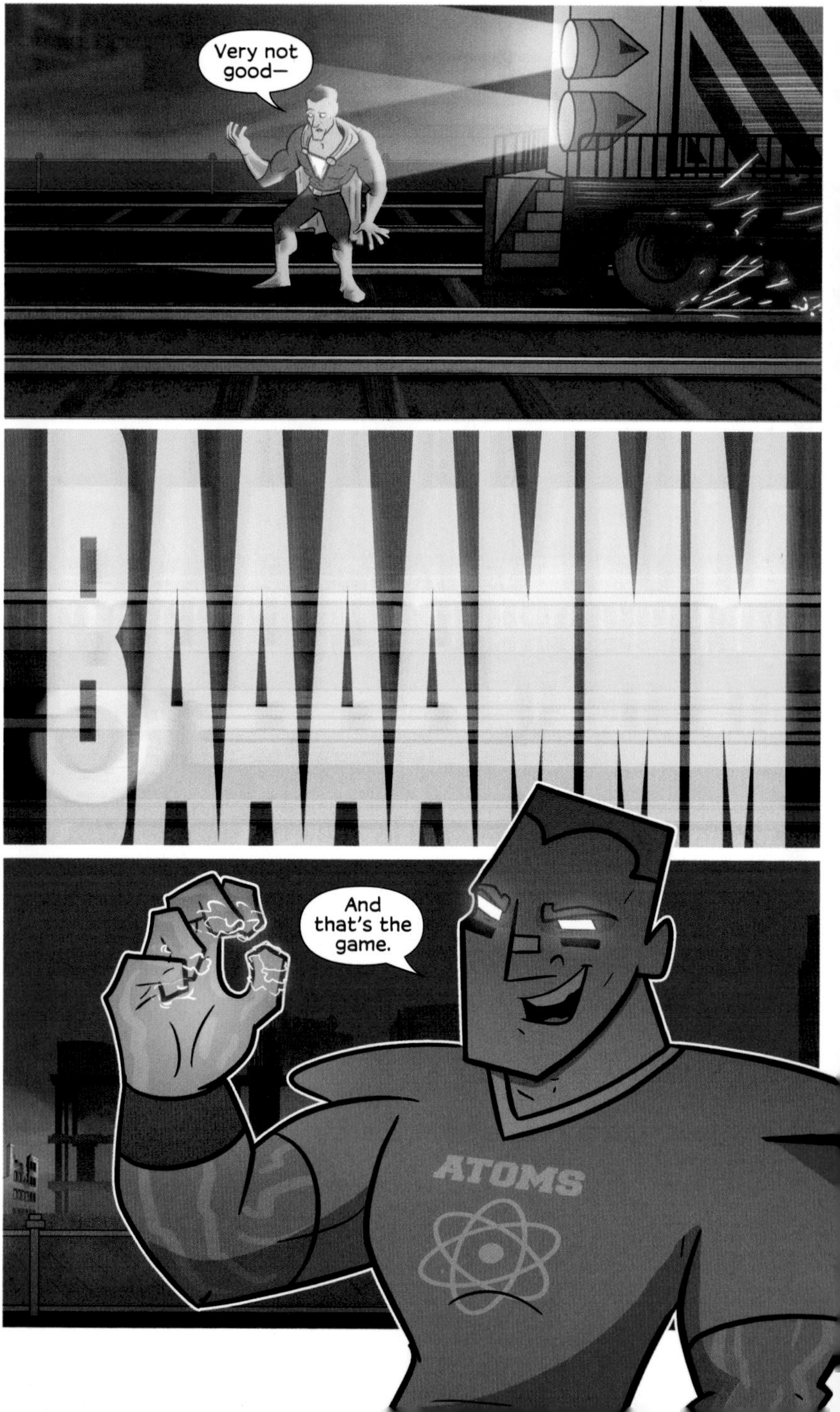

Very not good—
BAAAMMM
And that's the game.
ATOMS

CHAPTER

4

BATMAN

SUPERMAN

WONDER WOMAN

AQUAMAN

AMAN

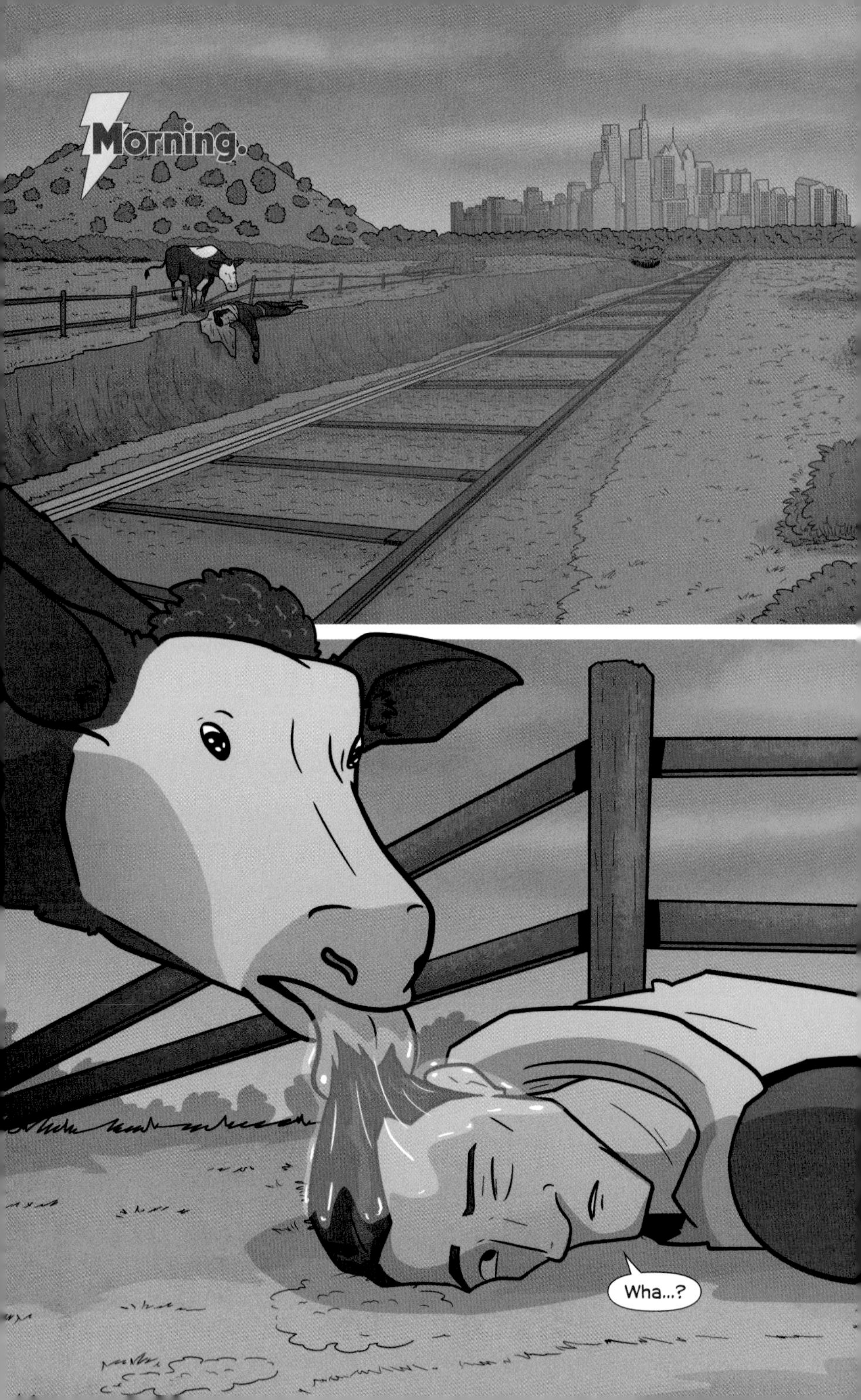
Morning.
Wha...?

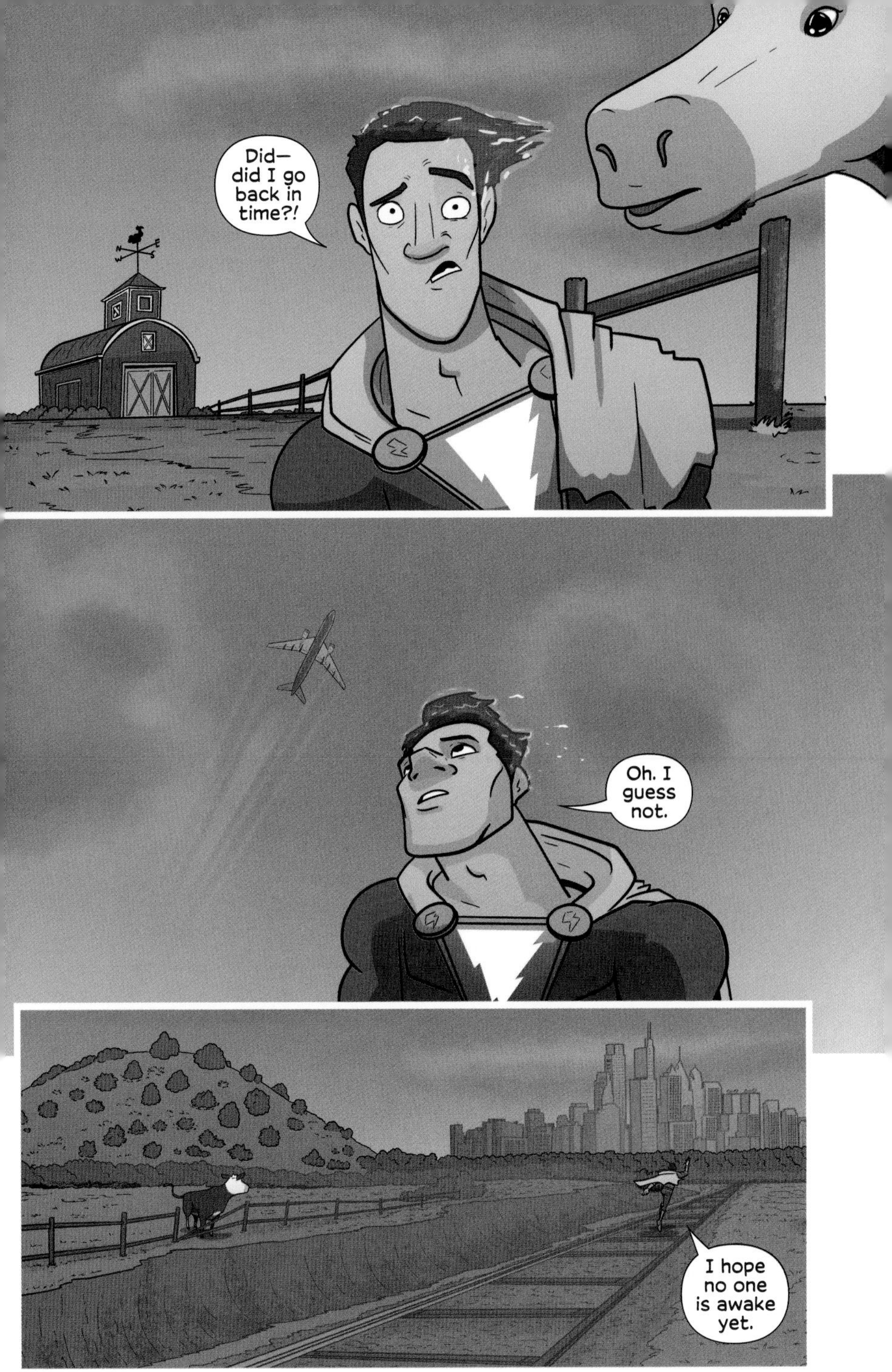
Did—
did I go
back in
time?!
Oh. I
guess
not.
I hope
no one
is awake
yet.

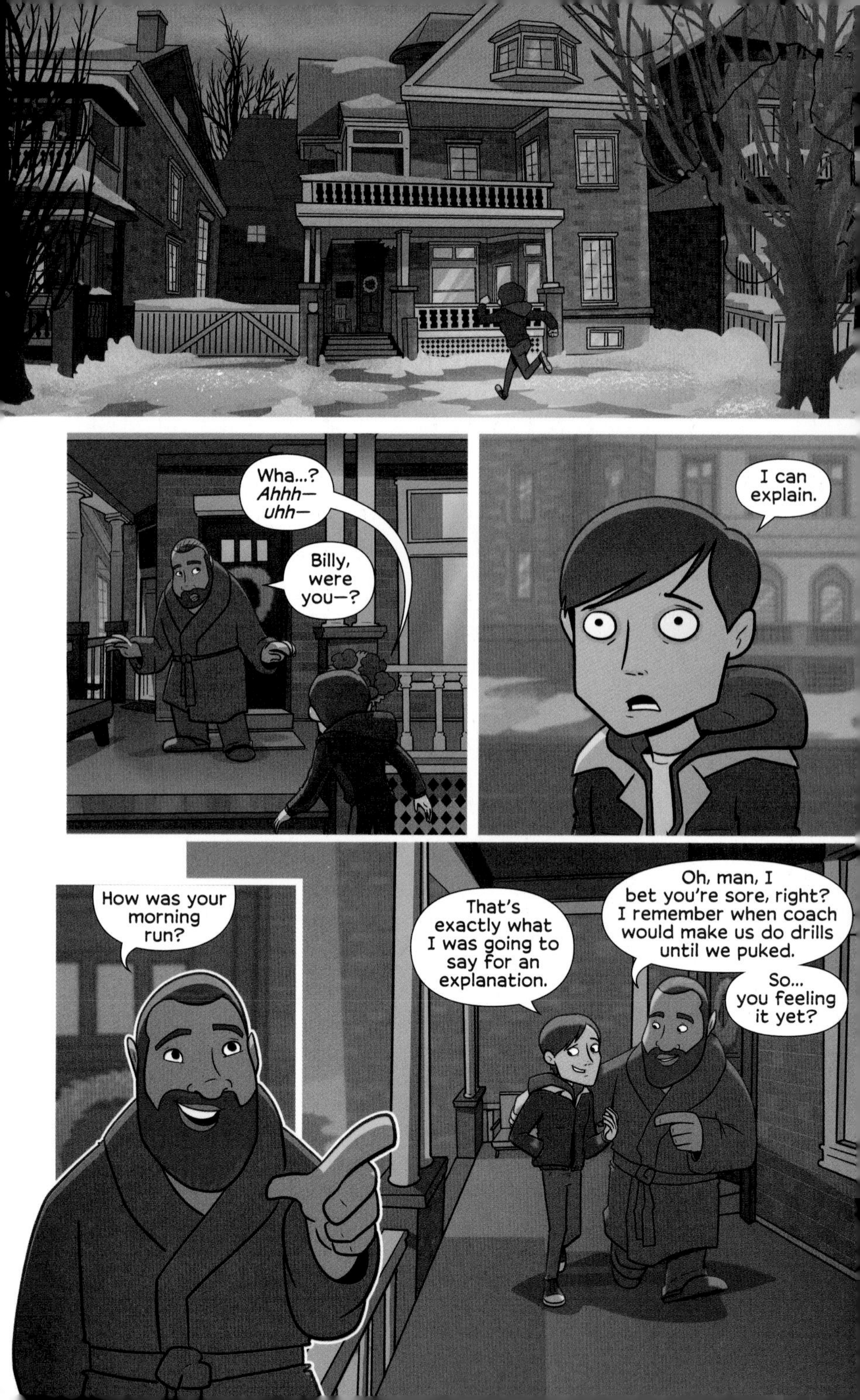
Wha...?
Ahhh—
uhh—
Billy, were you—?
I can explain.
How was your morning run?
That's exactly what I was going to say for an explanation.
Oh, man, I bet you're sore, right? I remember when coach would make us do drills until we puked.
So... you feeling it yet?

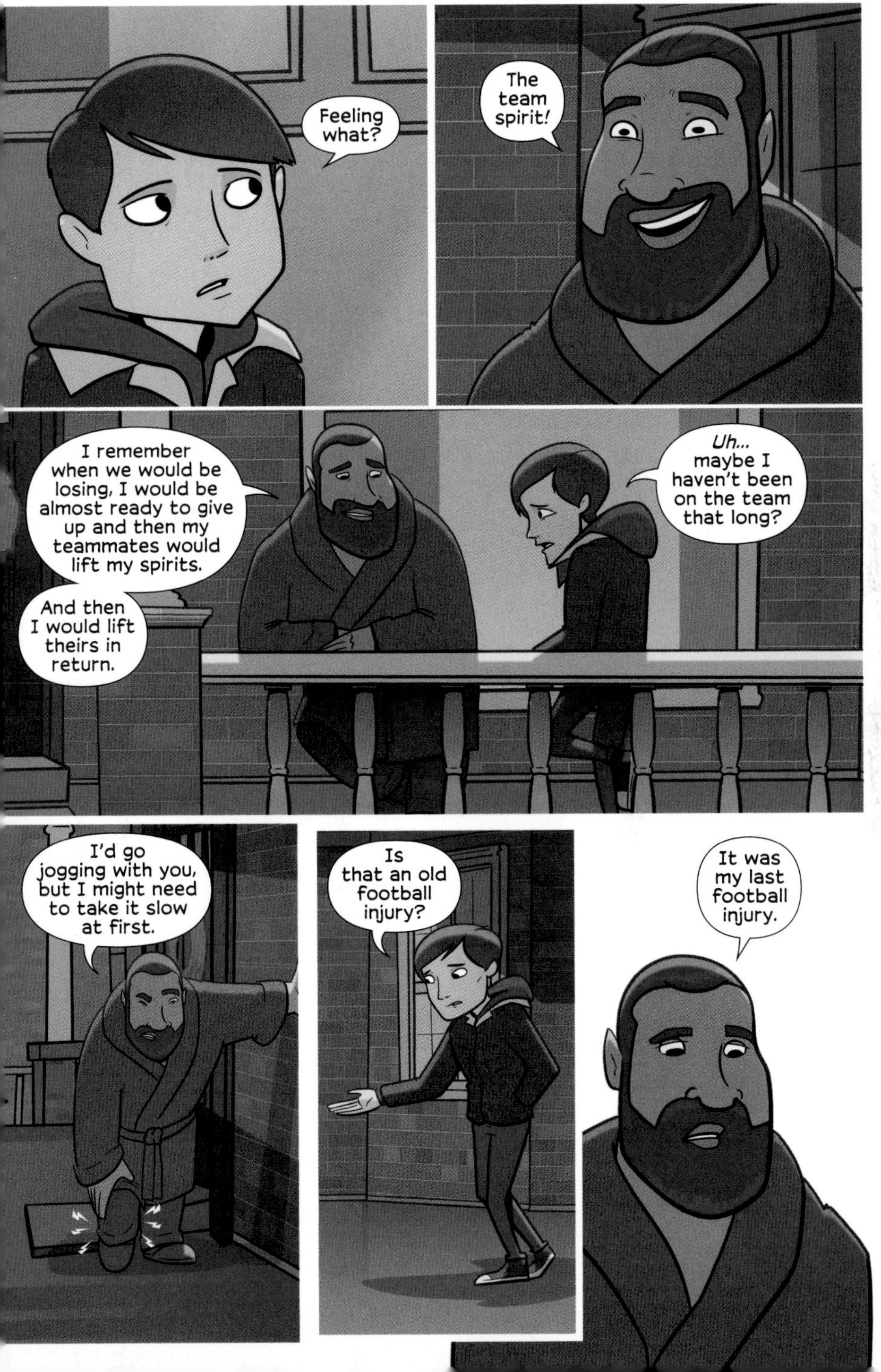
Feeling what?
The team spirit!
I remember when we would be losing, I would be almost ready to give up and then my teammates would lift my spirits.
And then I would lift theirs in return.
Uh... maybe I haven't been on the team that long?
I'd go jogging with you, but I might need to take it slow at first.
Is that an old football injury?
It was my last football injury.

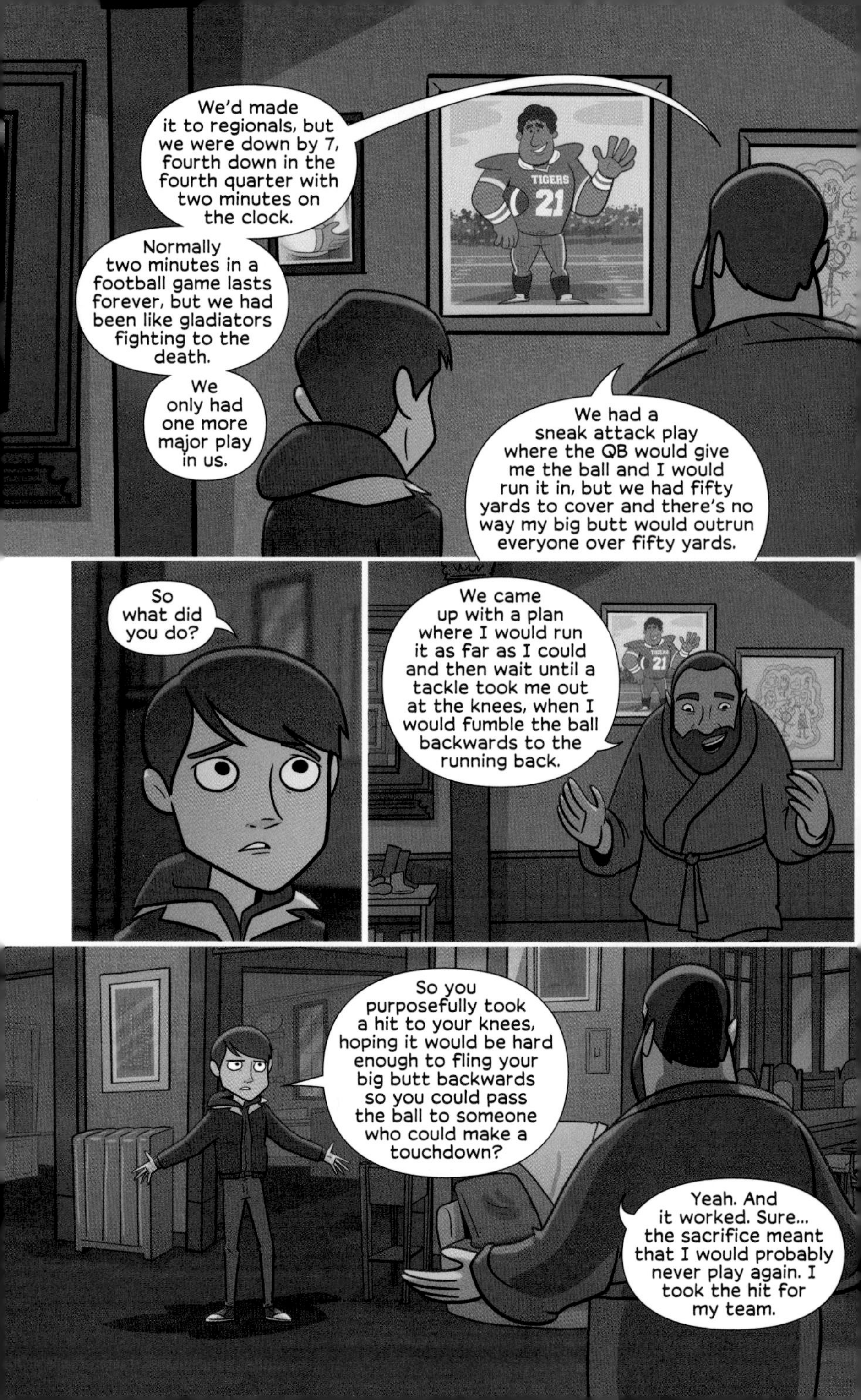
We'd made it to regionals, but we were down by 7, fourth down in the fourth quarter with two minutes on the clock.
Normally two minutes in a football game lasts forever, but we had been like gladiators fighting to the death.
We only had one more major play in us.
We had a sneak attack play where the QB would give me the ball and I would run it in, but we had fifty yards to cover and there's no way my big butt would outrun everyone over fifty yards.
So what did you do?
We came up with a plan where I would run it as far as I could and then wait until a tackle took me out at the knees, when I would fumble the ball backwards to the running back.
So you purposefully took a hit to your knees, hoping it would be hard enough to fling your big butt backwards so you could pass the ball to someone who could make a touchdown?
Yeah. And it worked. Sure... the sacrifice meant that I would probably never play again. I took the hit for my team.

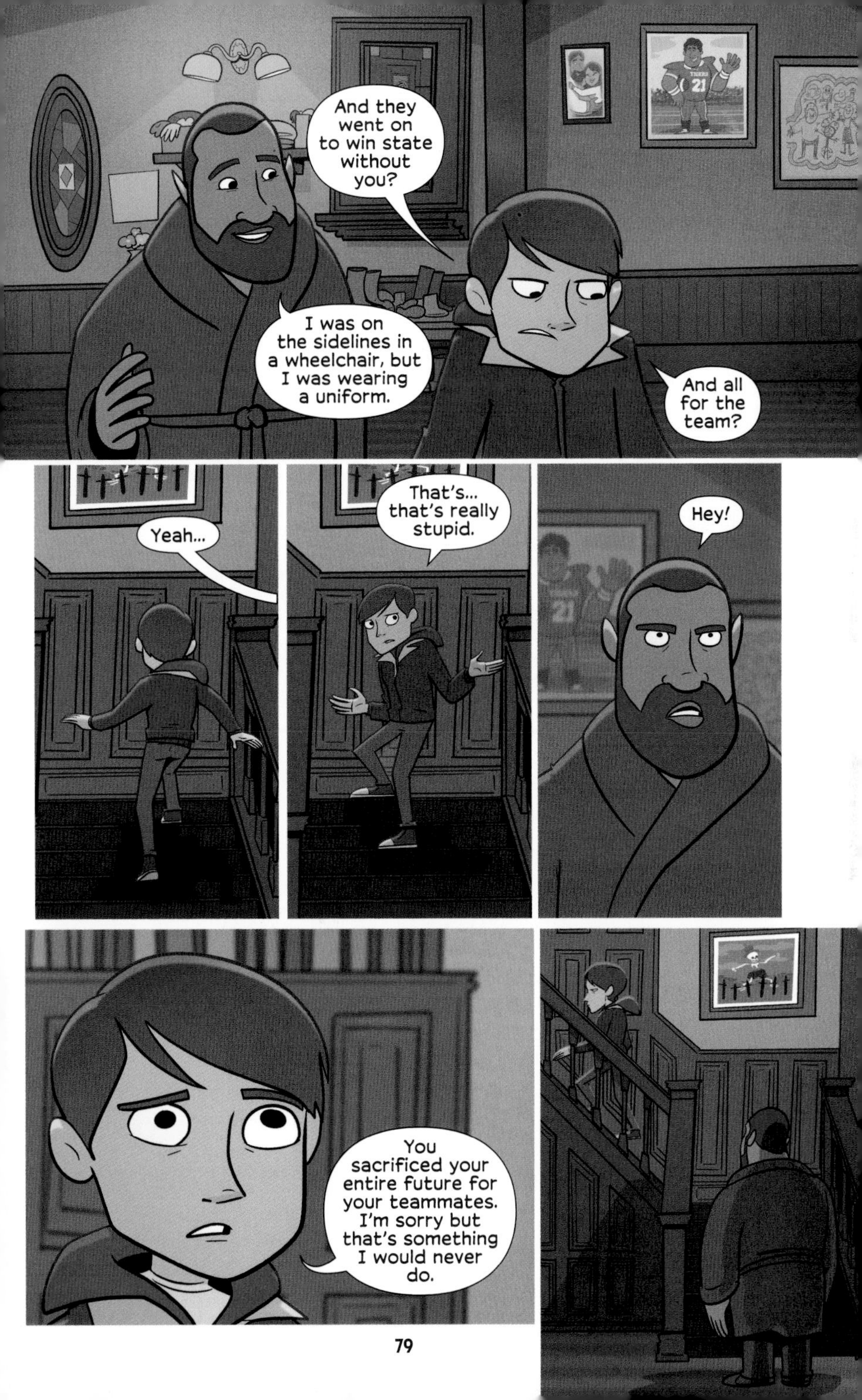
And they went on to win state without you?
I was on the sidelines in a wheelchair, but I was wearing a uniform.
And all for the team?
Yeah...
That's... that's really stupid.
Hey!
You sacrificed your entire future for your teammates. I'm sorry but that's something I would never do.

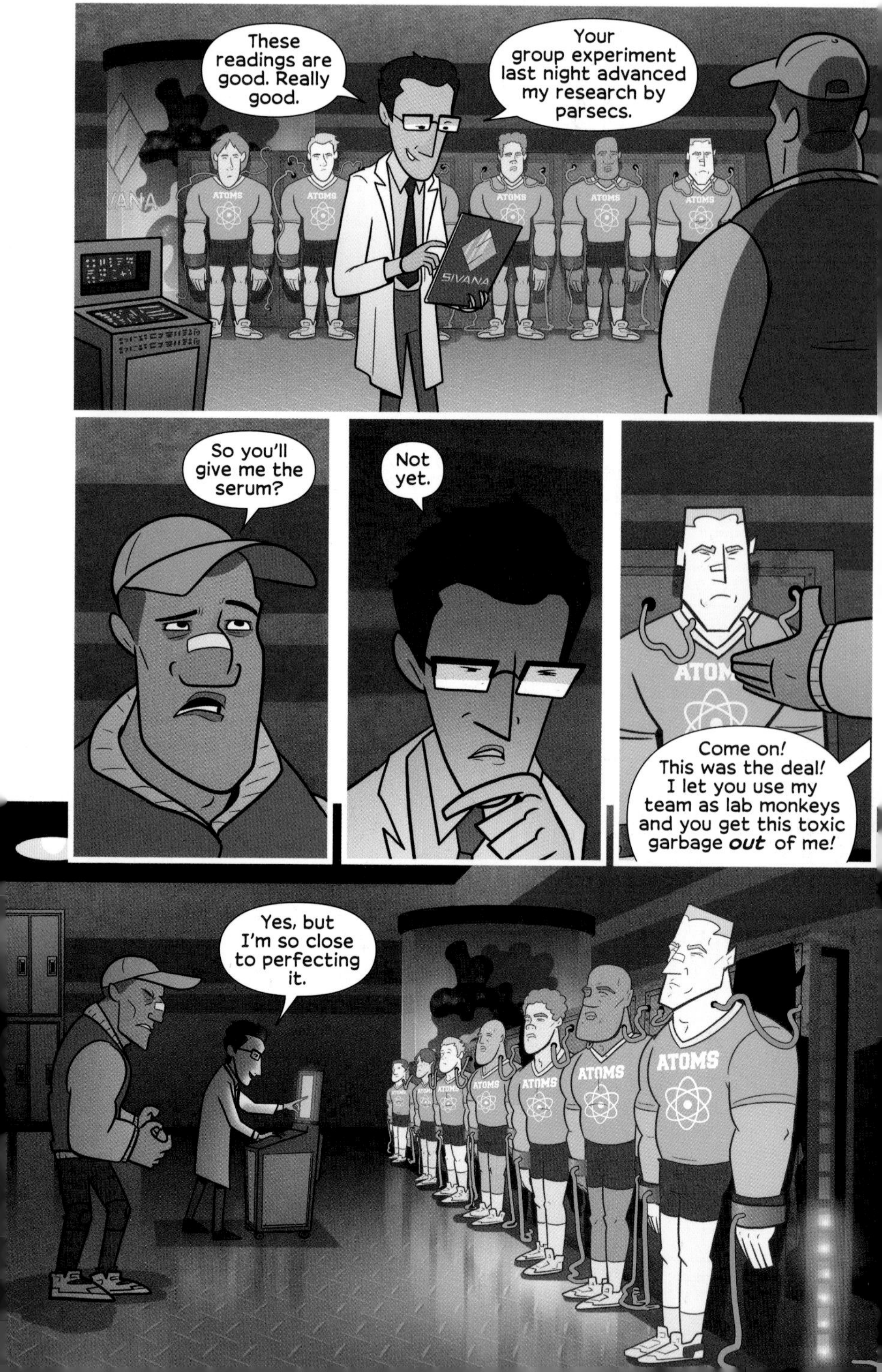
These readings are good. Really good.
Your group experiment last night advanced my research by parsecs.
SIVANA
ATOMS
So you'll give me the serum?
Not yet.
Come on! This was the deal! I let you use my team as lab monkeys and you get this toxic garbage *out* of me!
Yes, but I'm so close to perfecting it.

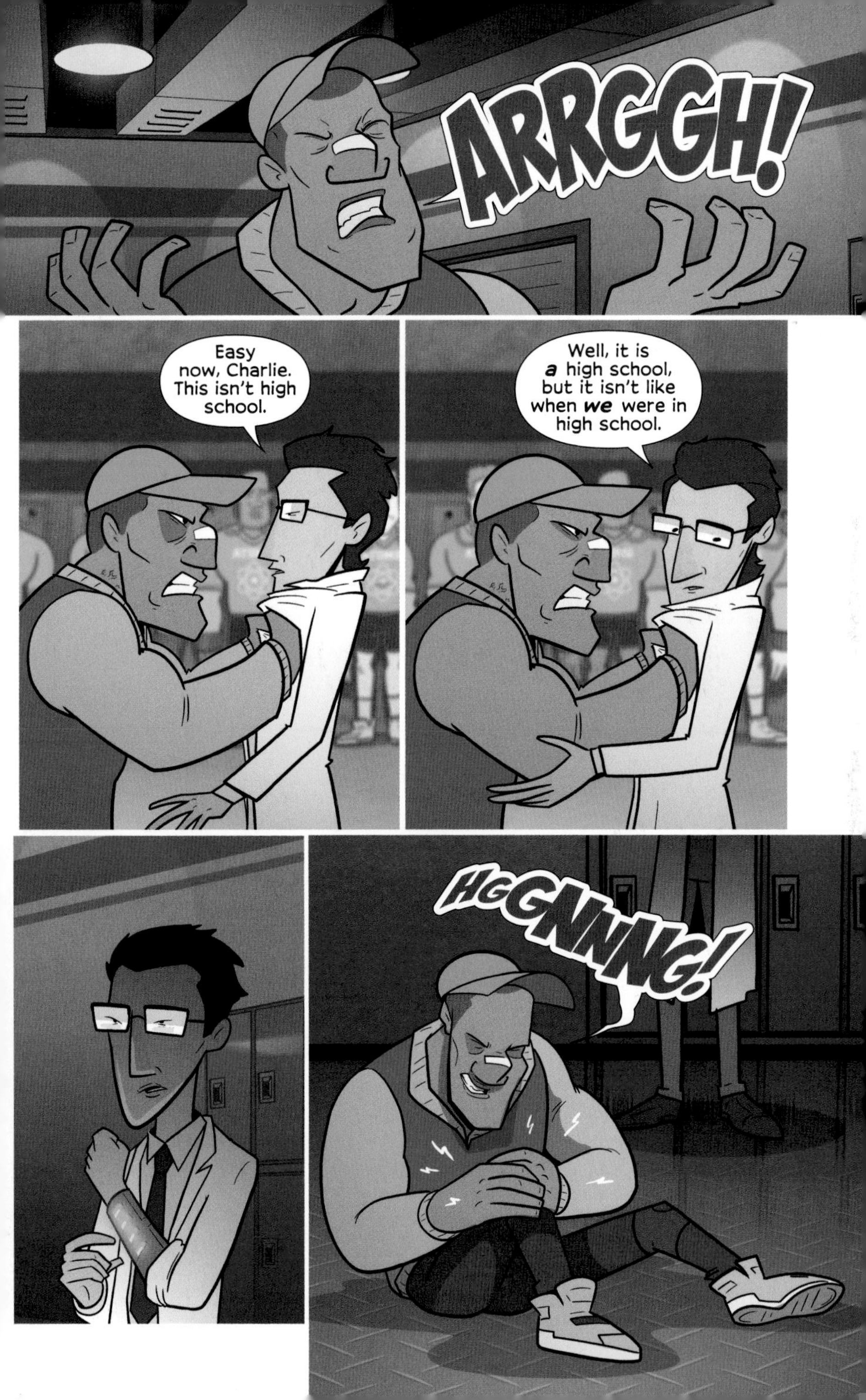
ARRGGH!
Easy now, Charlie. This isn't high school.
Well, it is *a* high school, but it isn't like when *we* were in high school.
HGGNNNG!

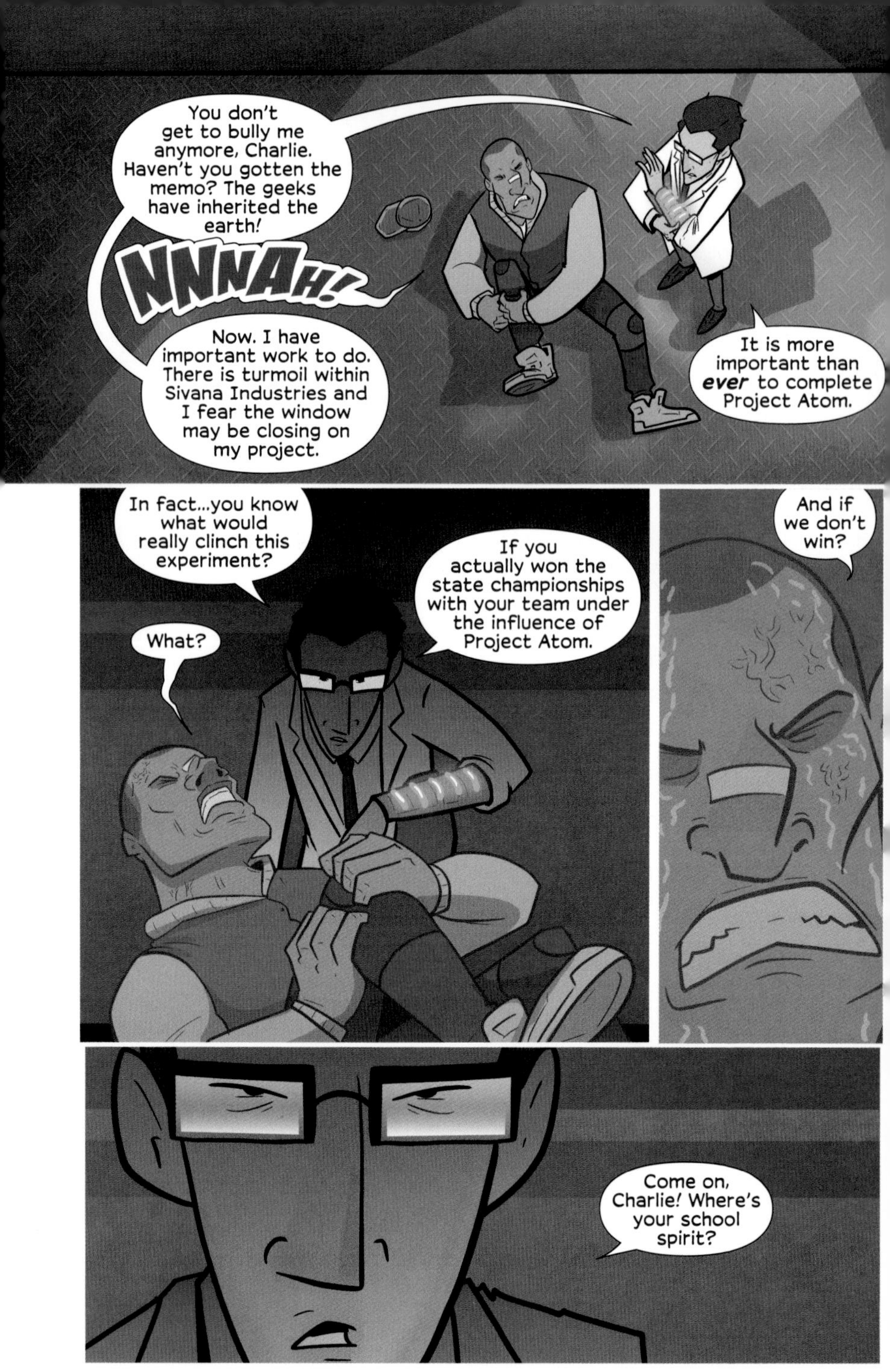
You don't get to bully me anymore, Charlie. Haven't you gotten the memo? The geeks have inherited the earth!
NNNAH!
Now. I have important work to do. There is turmoil within Sivana Industries and I fear the window may be closing on my project.
It is more important than *ever* to complete Project Atom.
In fact...you know what would really clinch this experiment?
What?
If you actually won the state championships with your team under the influence of Project Atom.
And if we don't win?
Come on, Charlie! Where's your school spirit?

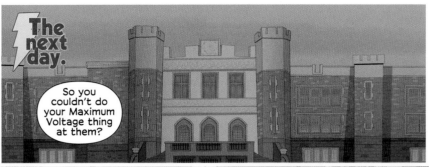

The next day.

So you couldn't do your Maximum Voltage thing at them?

No. It was really strange. Maybe I'm losing it.

You see, I was worried that the powers might be degenerative.

Let's duck out early and go do some tests.

Can't.

What do you mean you can't?

I can't let the team down.

What team?

Aaah! What the heck is that?

I'm the team mascot.

Come on. What happened to the superhero team thing?

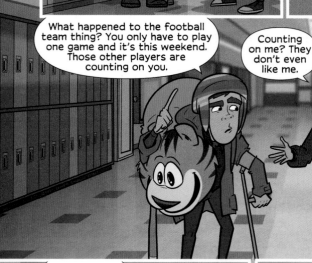

What happened to the football team thing? You only have to play one game and it's this weekend. Those other players are counting on you.

Counting on me? They don't even like me.

They see me as a show-off who swooped in and stole their spotlight because I'm so good.

Wow. Did you get a super-sized ego when you got super-powers?

I am the best.

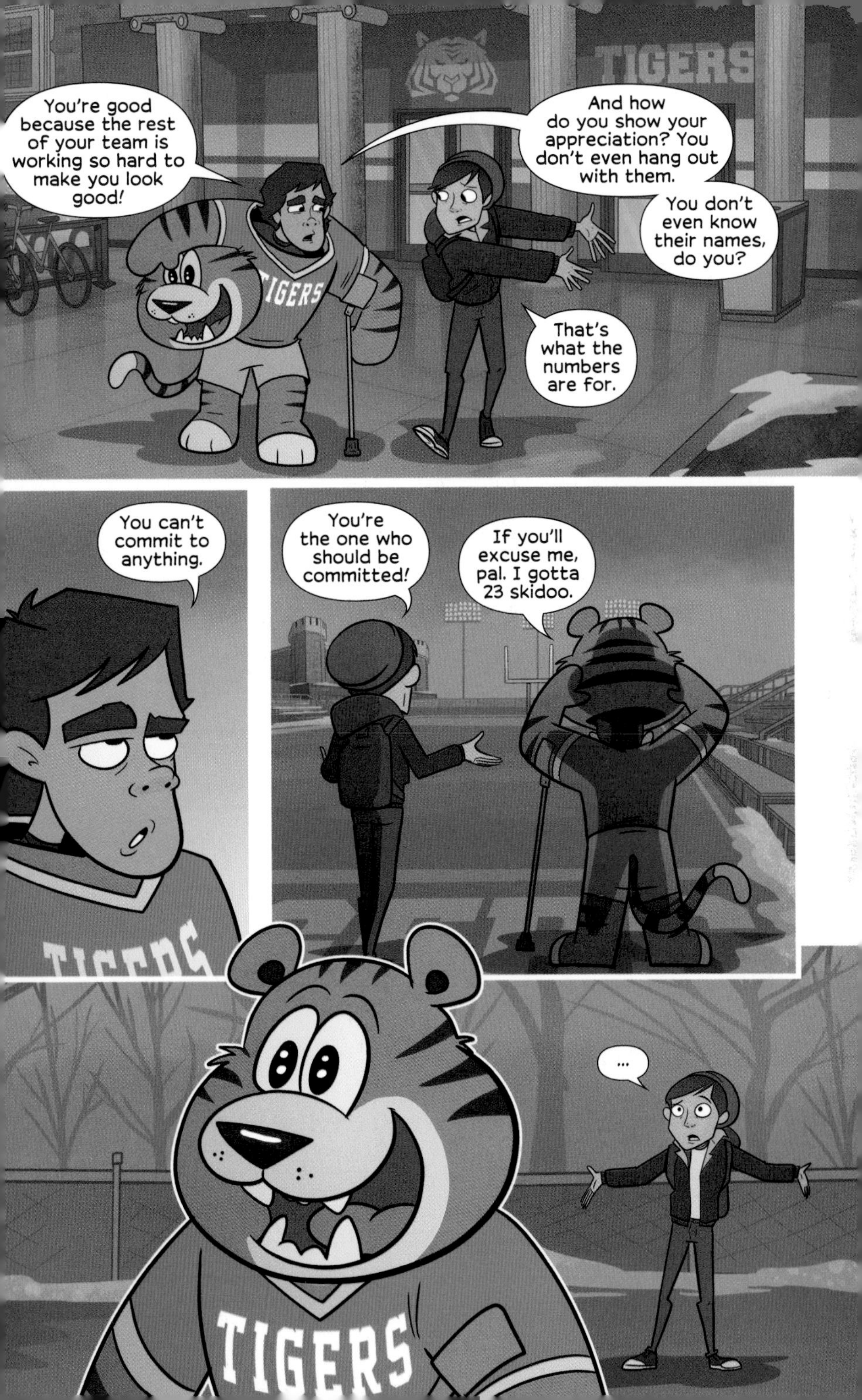

TIGERS
You're good because the rest of your team is working so hard to make you look good!
And how do you show your appreciation? You don't even hang out with them.
You don't even know their names, do you?
That's what the numbers are for.
You can't commit to anything.
You're the one who should be committed!
If you'll excuse me, pal. I gotta 23 skidoo.
...
TIGERS

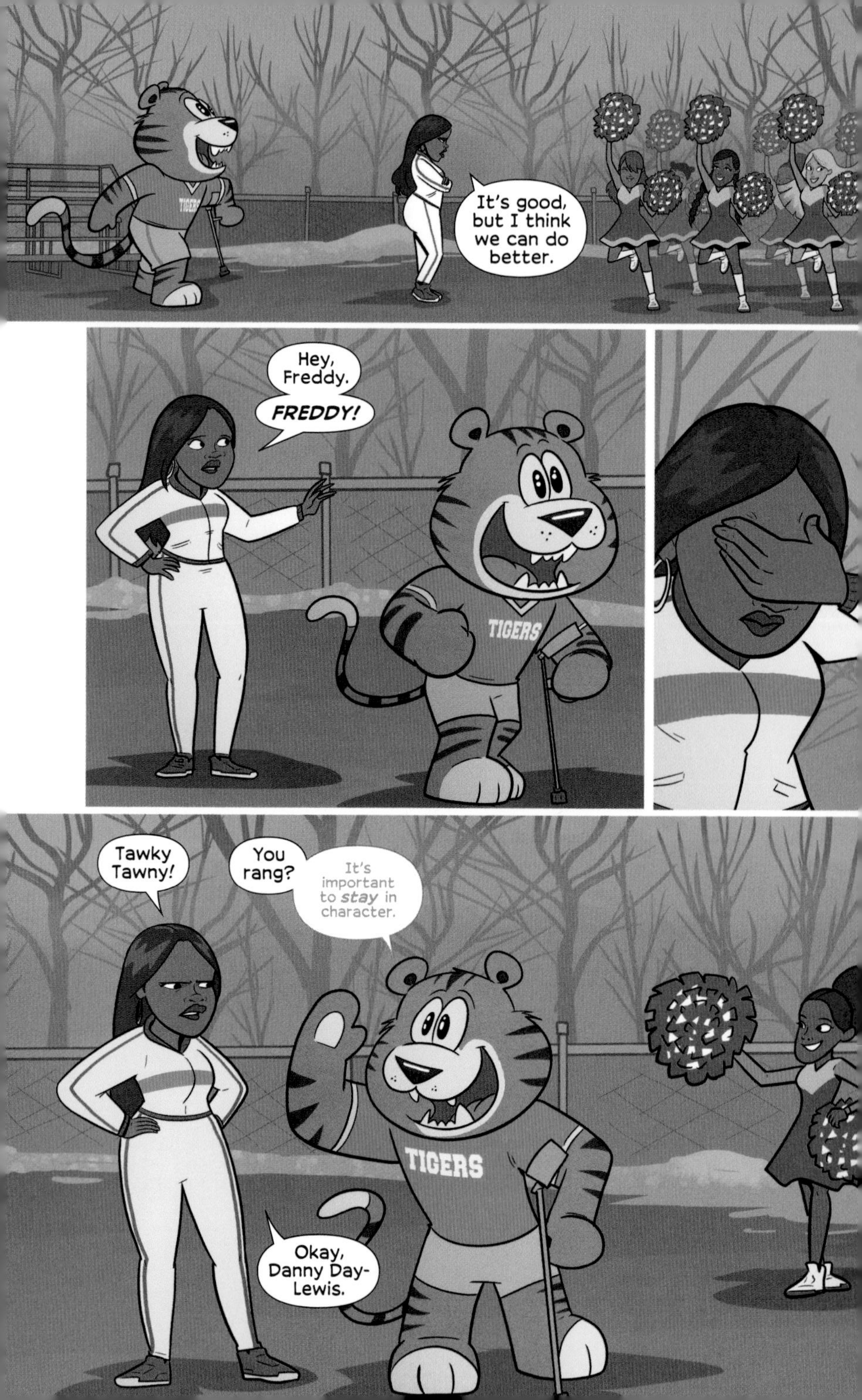
It's good, but I think we can do better.
Hey, Freddy.
FREDDY!
Tawky Tawny!
You rang?
It's important to *stay* in character.
Okay, Danny Day-Lewis.

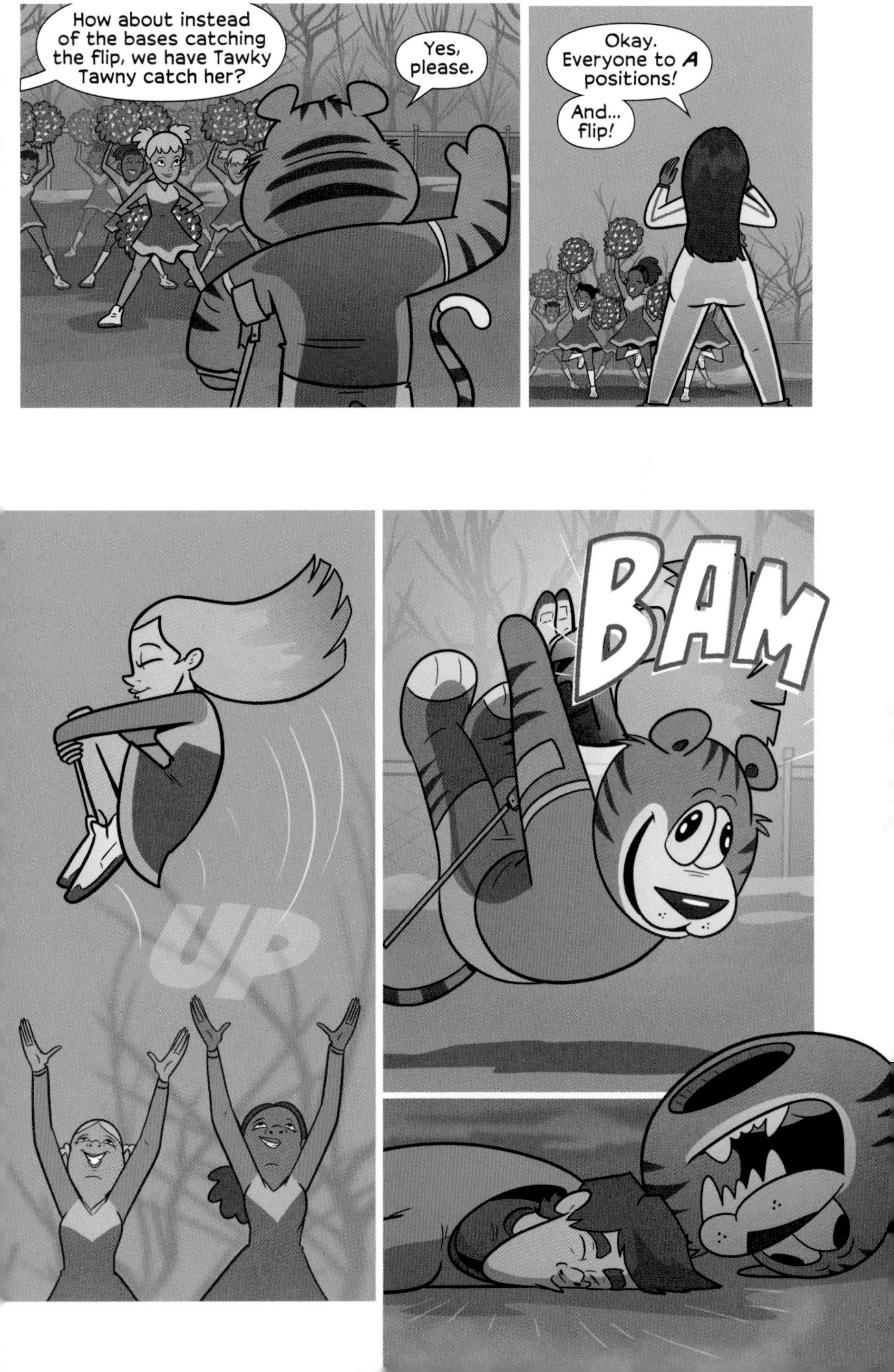
How about instead of the bases catching the flip, we have Tawky Tawny catch her?
Yes, please.
Okay. Everyone to A positions!
And... flip!
UP
BAM

MR. TAWKY TAWNY

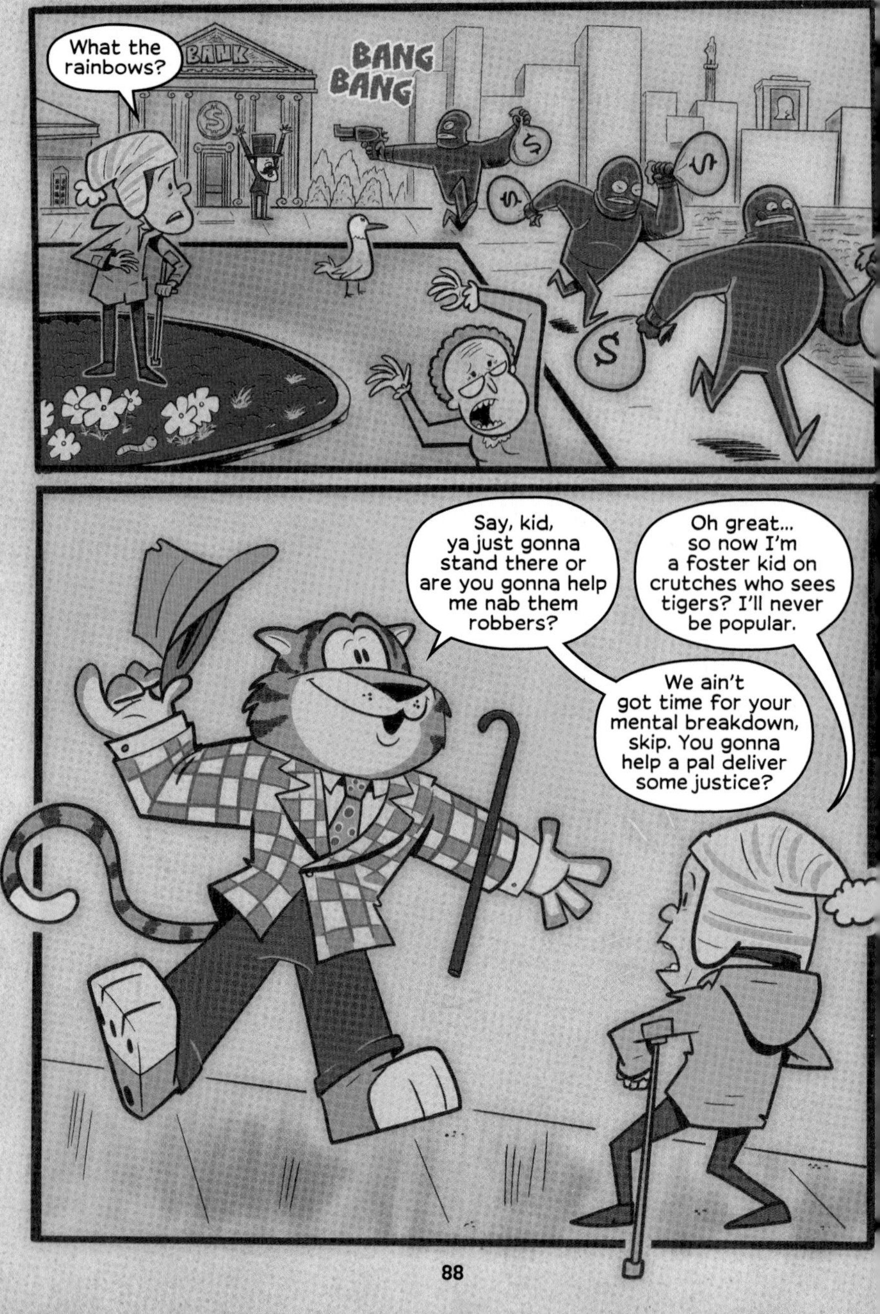
What the rainbows?
BANK
BANG BANG
Say, kid, ya just gonna stand there or are you gonna help me nab them robbers?
Oh great... so now I'm a foster kid on crutches who sees tigers? I'll never be popular.
We ain't got time for your mental breakdown, skip. You gonna help a pal deliver some justice?

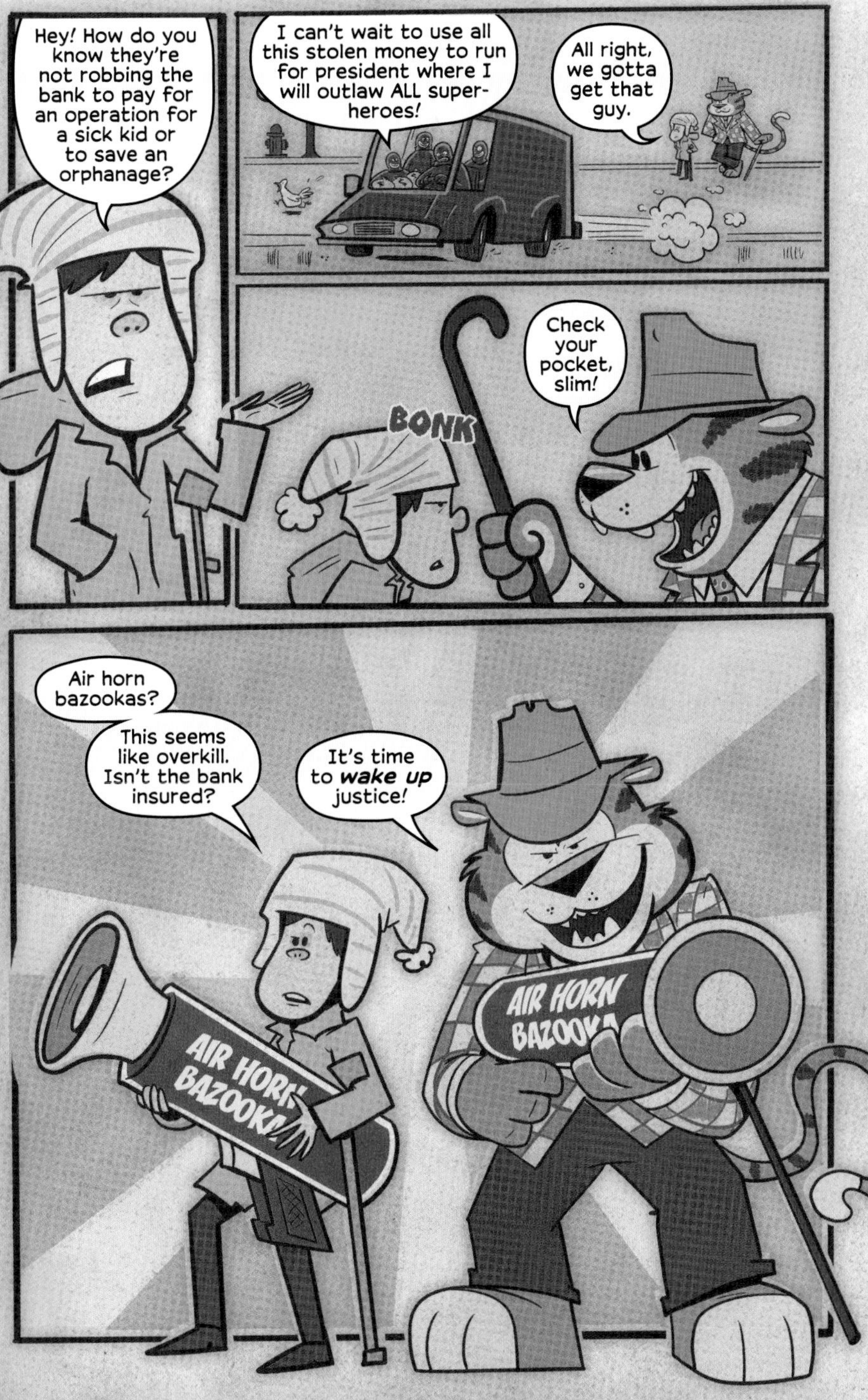
Hey! How do you know they're not robbing the bank to pay for an operation for a sick kid or to save an orphanage?
I can't wait to use all this stolen money to run for president where I will outlaw ALL super-heroes!
All right, we gotta get that guy.
BONK
Check your pocket, slim!
Air horn bazookas?
This seems like overkill. Isn't the bank insured?
It's time to *wake up* justice!
AIR HORN BAZOOKA
AIR HORN BAZOOKA

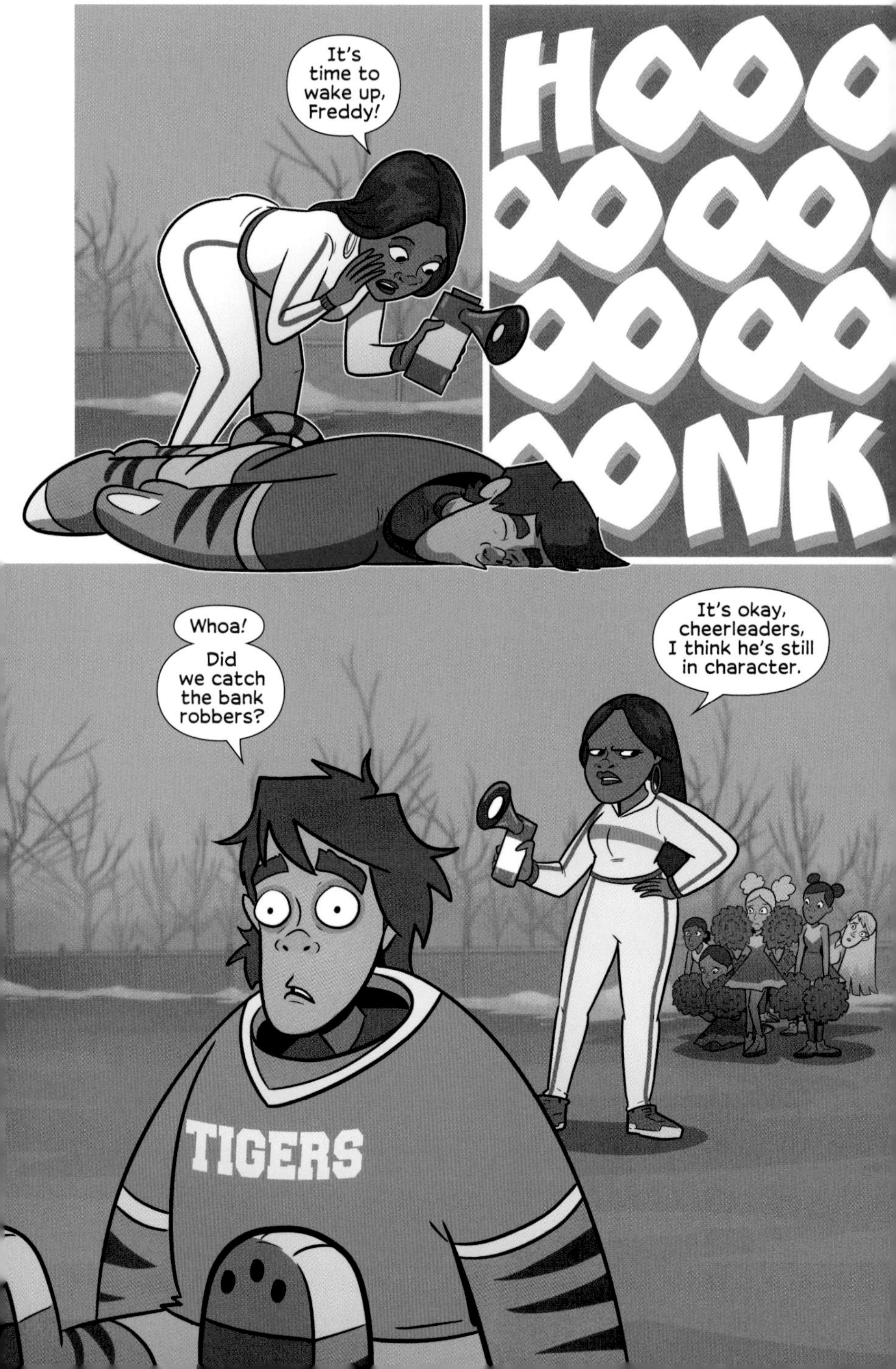
It's time to wake up, Freddy!
HOOOOOOOOOOOOOOOONK
Whoa!
Did we catch the bank robbers?
It's okay, cheerleaders, I think he's still in character.
TIGERS

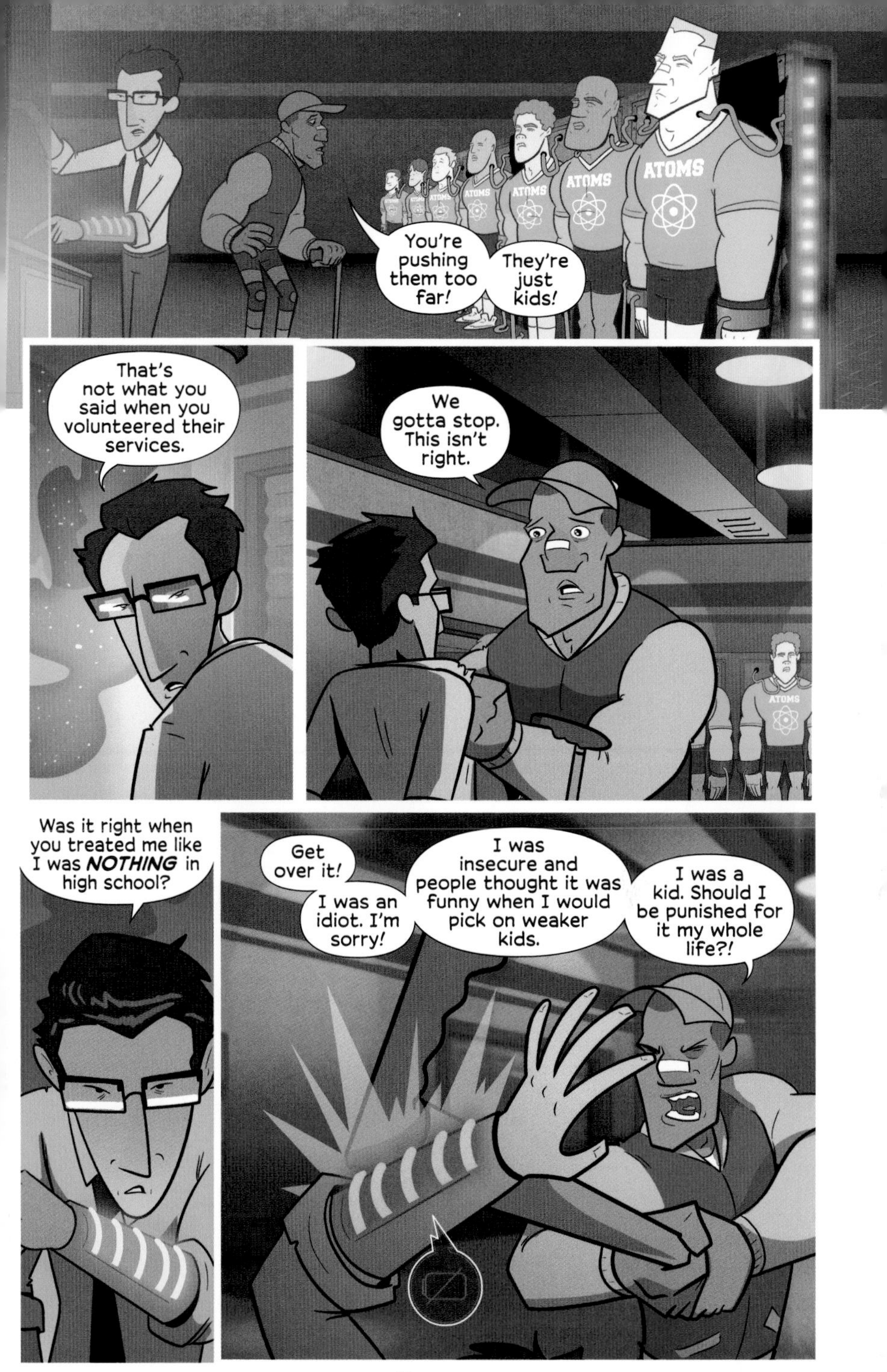
You're pushing them too far!
They're just kids!
That's not what you said when you volunteered their services.
We gotta stop. This isn't right.
Was it right when you treated me like I was *NOTHING* in high school?
Get over it!
I was an idiot. I'm sorry!
I was insecure and people thought it was funny when I would pick on weaker kids.
I was a kid. Should I be punished for it my whole life?!

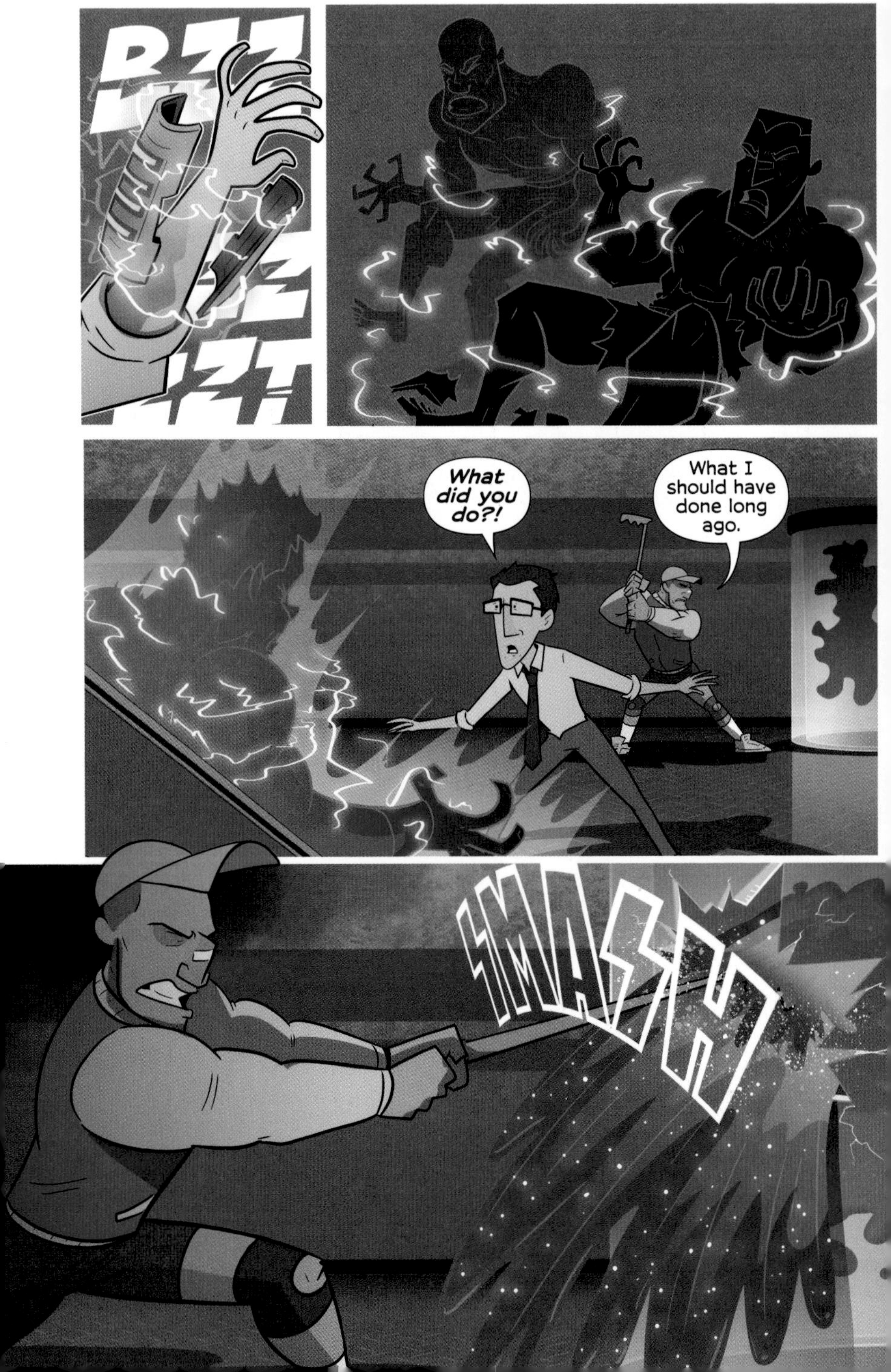
What did you do?!
What I should have done long ago.
SMASH

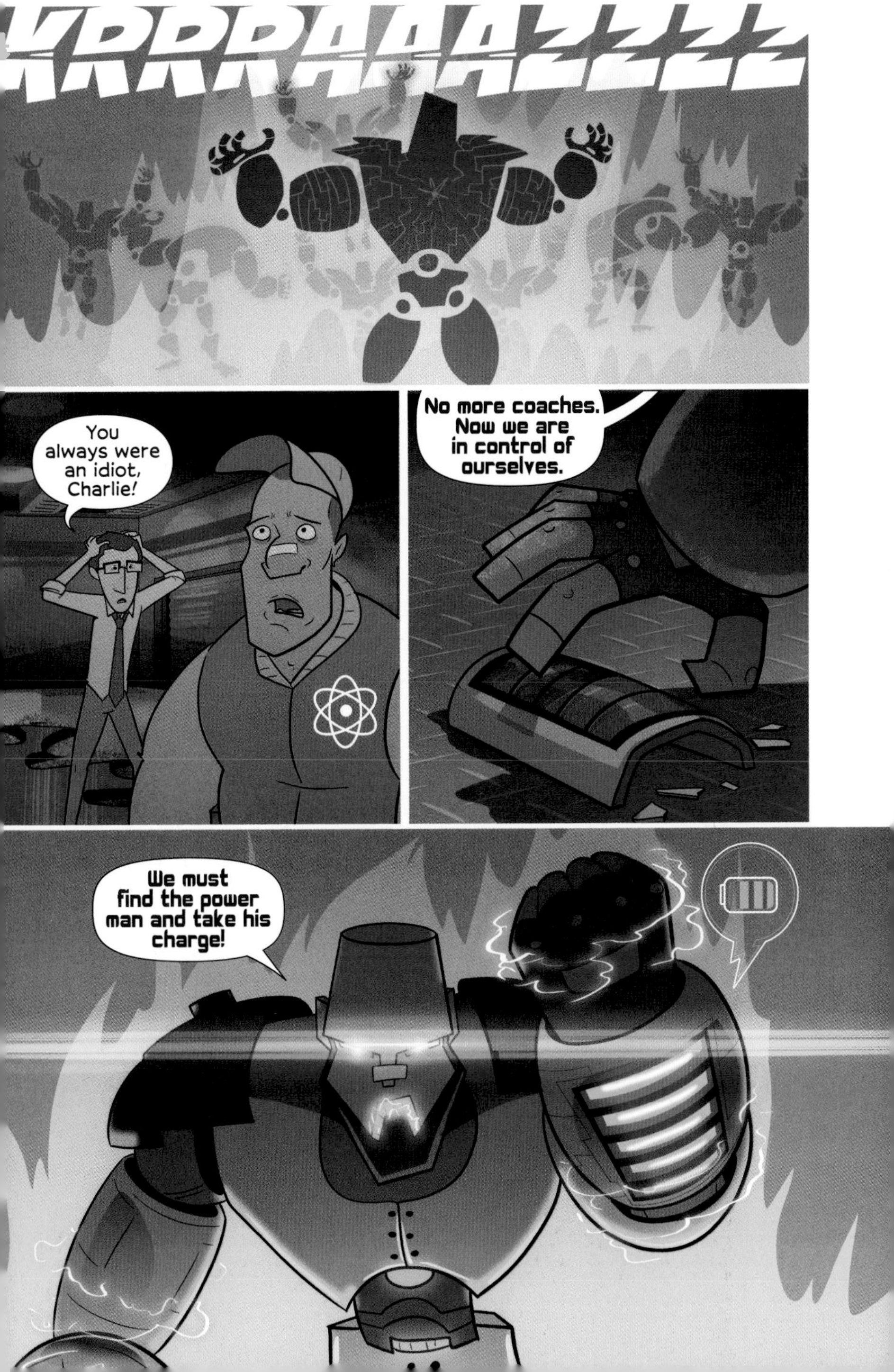
KRRRAAAZZZZ
You always were an idiot, Charlie!
No more coaches. Now we are in control of ourselves.
We must find the power man and take his charge!

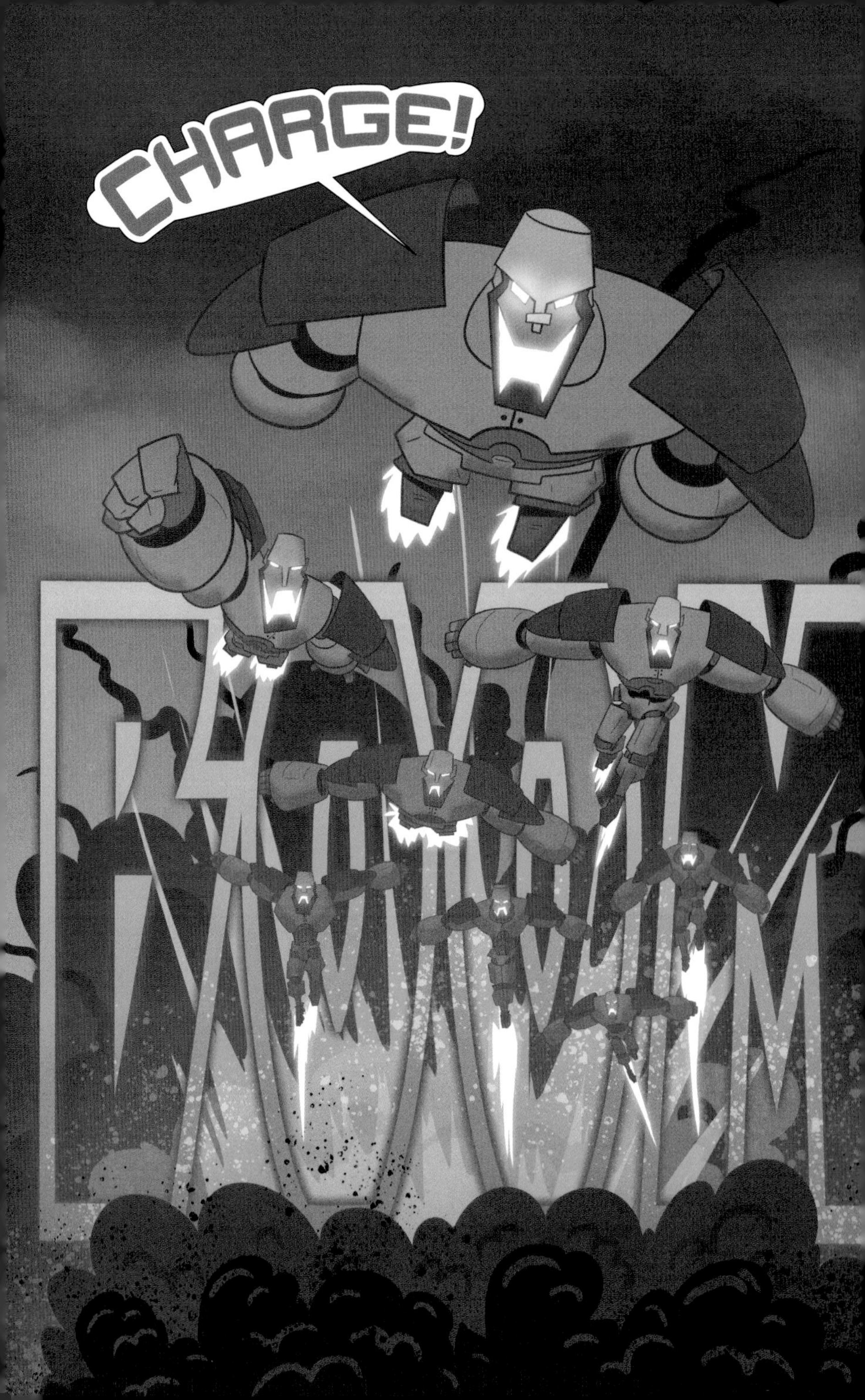
CHARGE!

CHAPTER 5

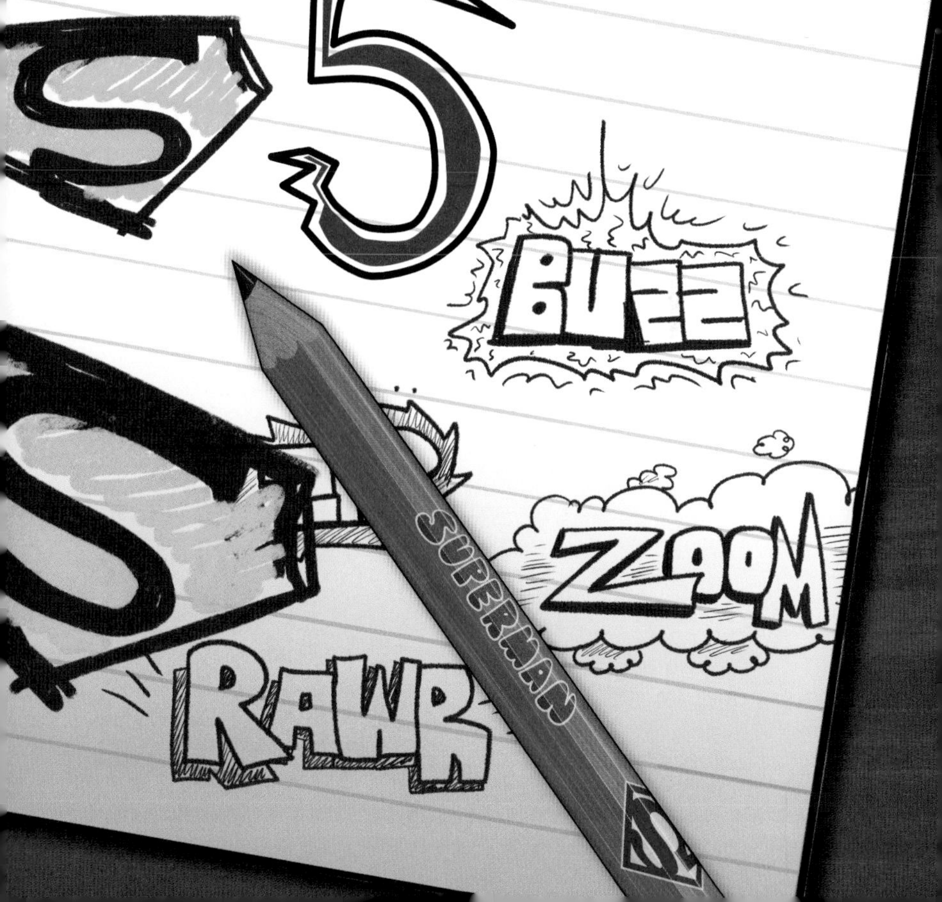

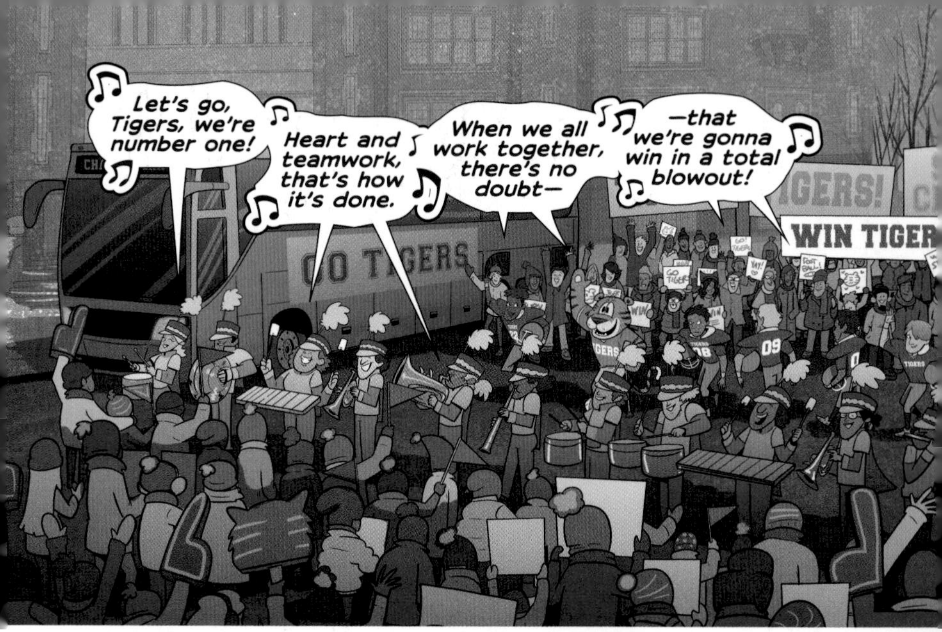
Let's go, Tigers, we're number one!
Heart and teamwork, that's how it's done.
When we all work together, there's no doubt—
—that we're gonna win in a total blowout!
GO TIGERS
WIN TIGER

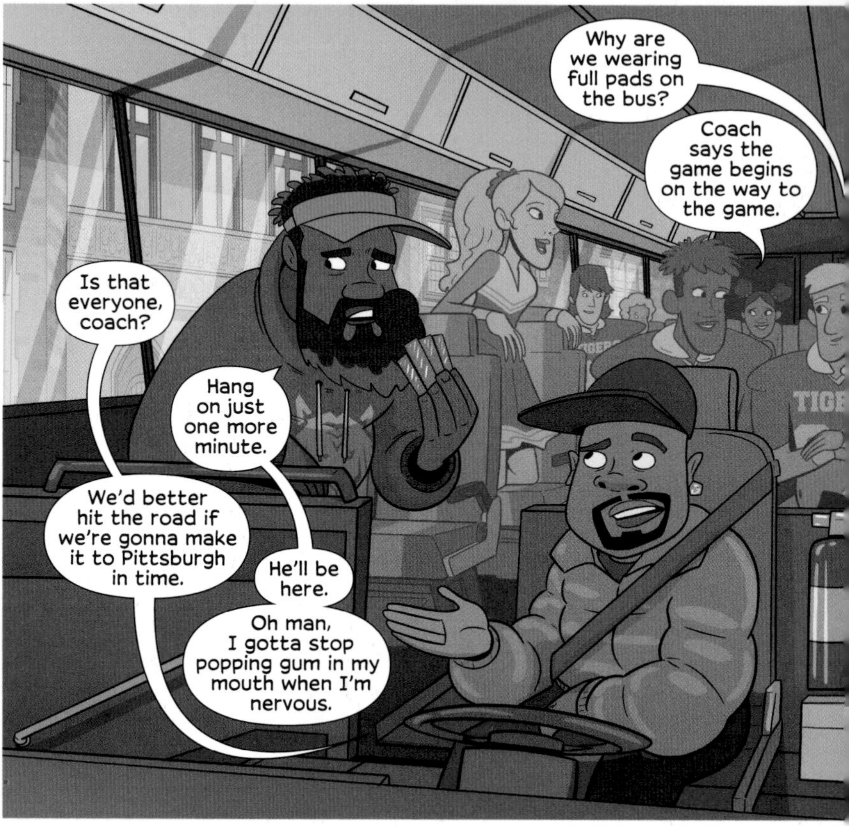
Why are we wearing full pads on the bus?
Coach says the game begins on the way to the game.
Is that everyone, coach?
Hang on just one more minute.
We'd better hit the road if we're gonna make it to Pittsburgh in time.
He'll be here.
Oh man, I gotta stop popping gum in my mouth when I'm nervous.

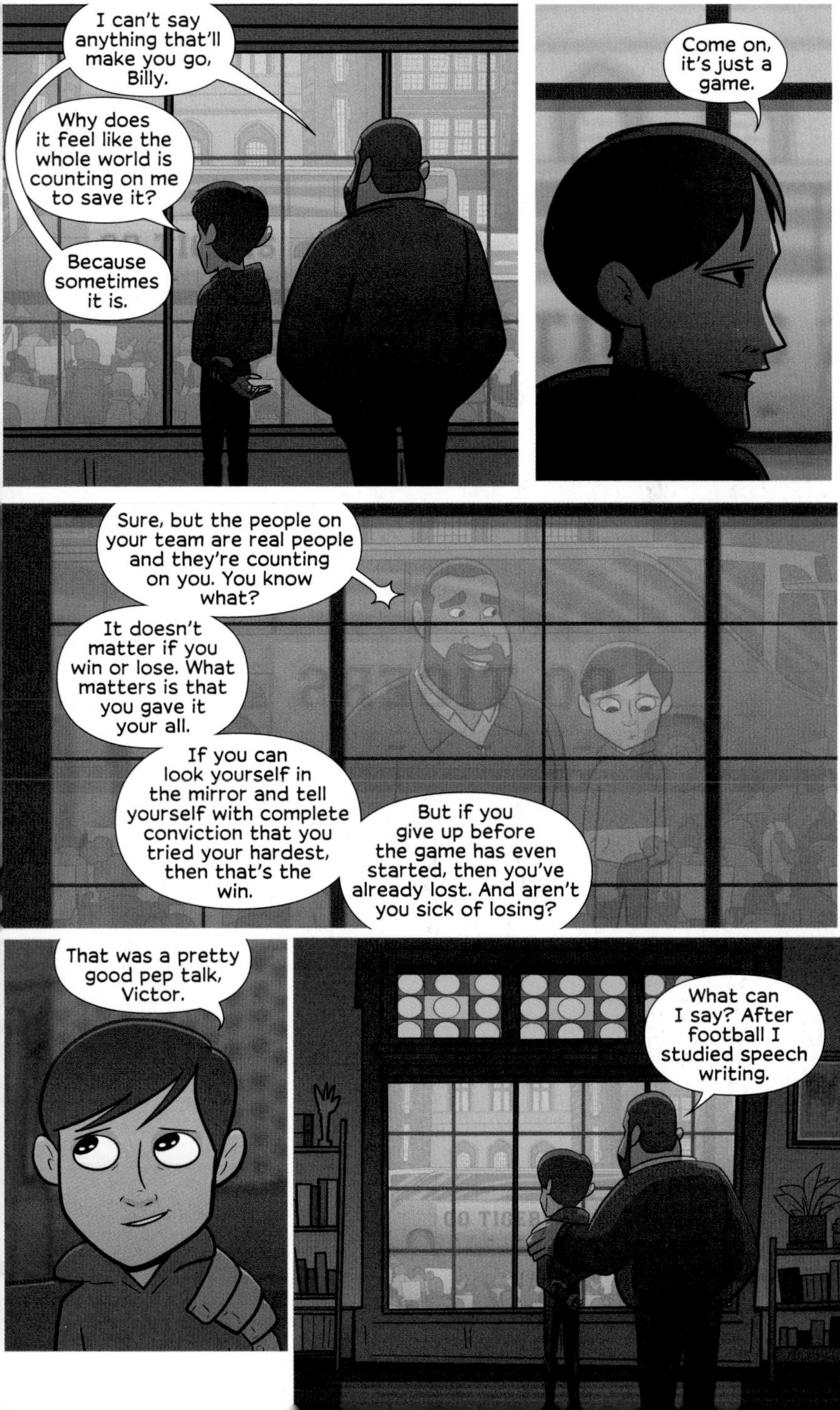
I can't say anything that'll make you go, Billy.
Why does it feel like the whole world is counting on me to save it?
Because sometimes it is.
Come on, it's just a game.
Sure, but the people on your team are real people and they're counting on you. You know what?
It doesn't matter if you win or lose. What matters is that you gave it your all.
If you can look yourself in the mirror and tell yourself with complete conviction that you tried your hardest, then that's the win.
But if you give up before the game has even started, then you've already lost. And aren't you sick of losing?
That was a pretty good pep talk, Victor.
What can I say? After football I studied speech writing.

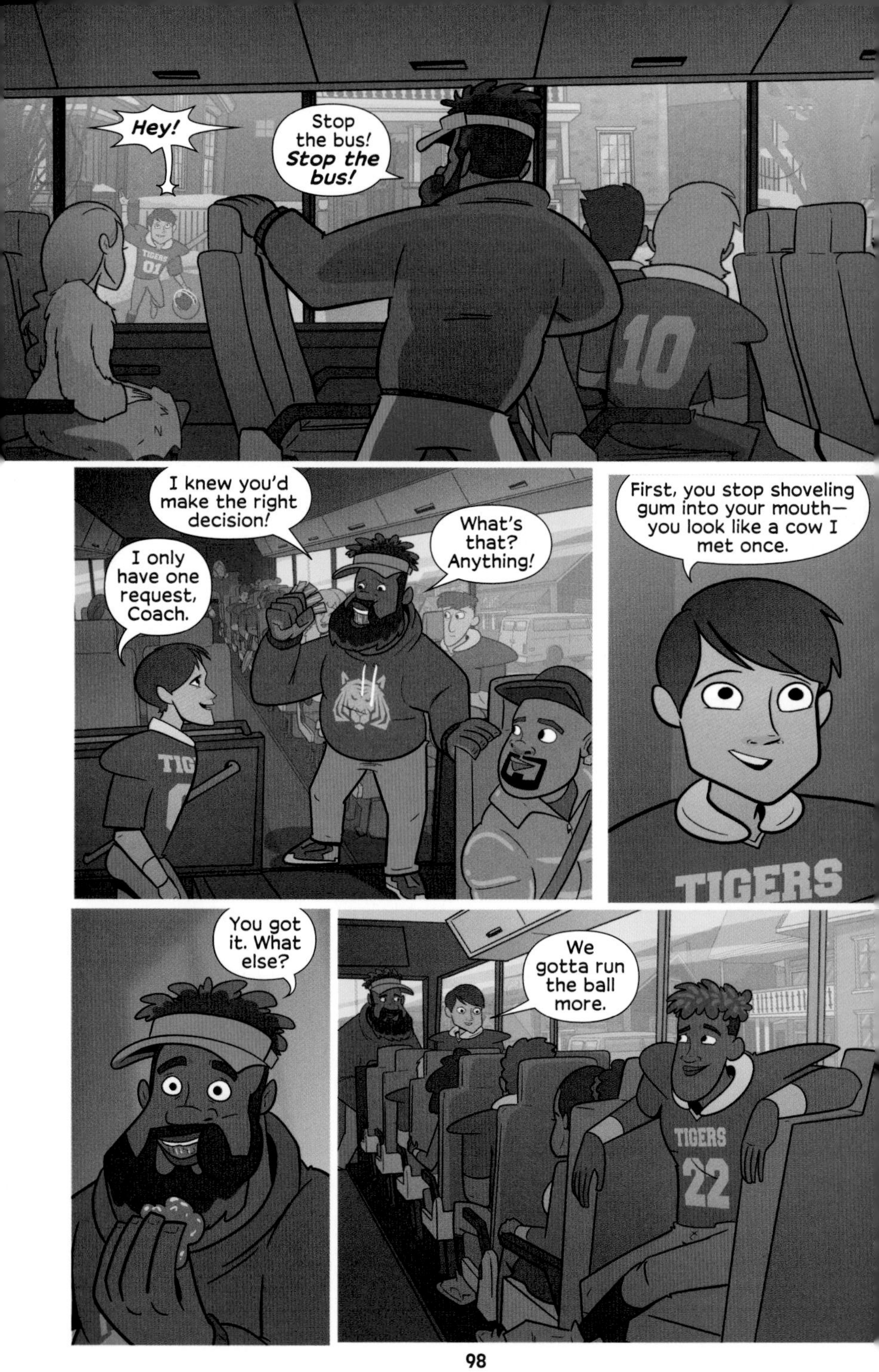
Hey!
Stop the bus! Stop the bus!
I knew you'd make the right decision!
I only have one request, Coach.
What's that? Anything!
First, you stop shoveling gum into your mouth— you look like a cow I met once.
You got it. What else?
We gotta run the ball more.

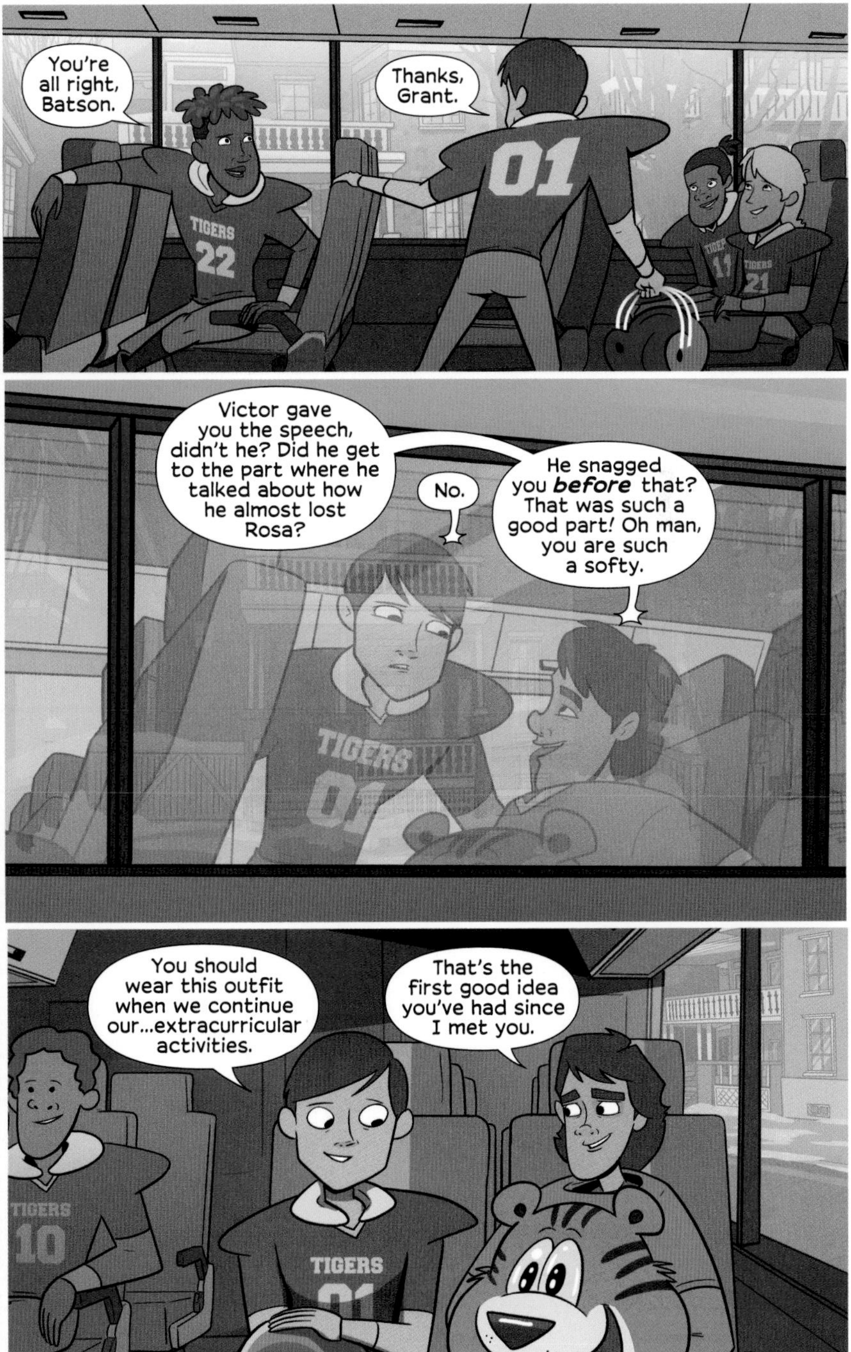
You're all right, Batson.
Thanks, Grant.
01
TIGERS 22
TIGERS 11
TIGERS 21
Victor gave you the speech, didn't he? Did he get to the part where he talked about how he almost lost Rosa?
No.
He snagged you *before* that? That was such a good part! Oh man, you are such a softy.
TIGERS 01
You should wear this outfit when we continue our...extracurricular activities.
That's the first good idea you've had since I met you.
TIGERS 10
TIGERS

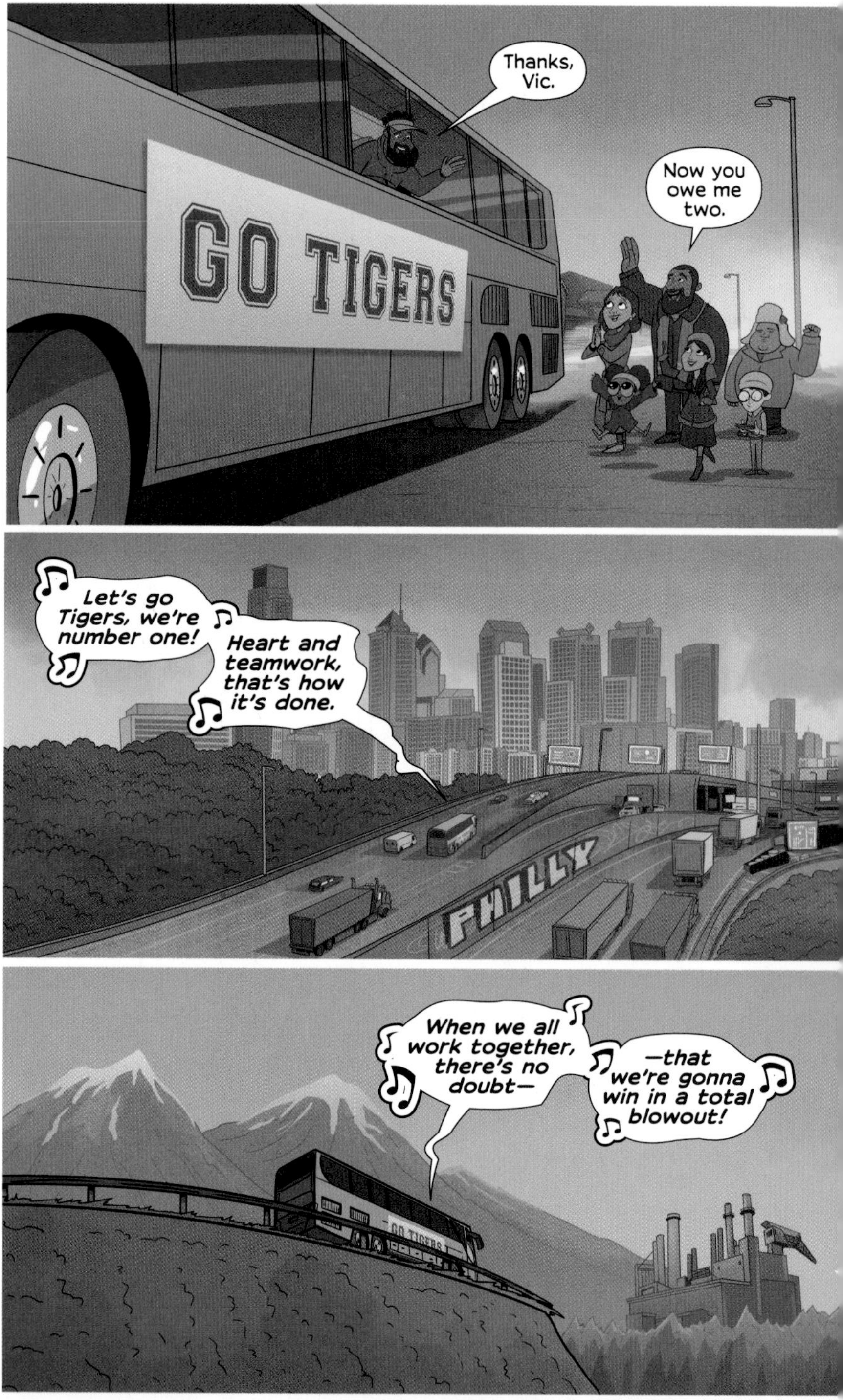
Thanks, Vic.
Now you owe me two.
GO TIGERS
Let's go Tigers, we're number one!
Heart and teamwork, that's how it's done.
PHILLY
When we all work together, there's no doubt—
—that we're gonna win in a total blowout!
GO TIGERS

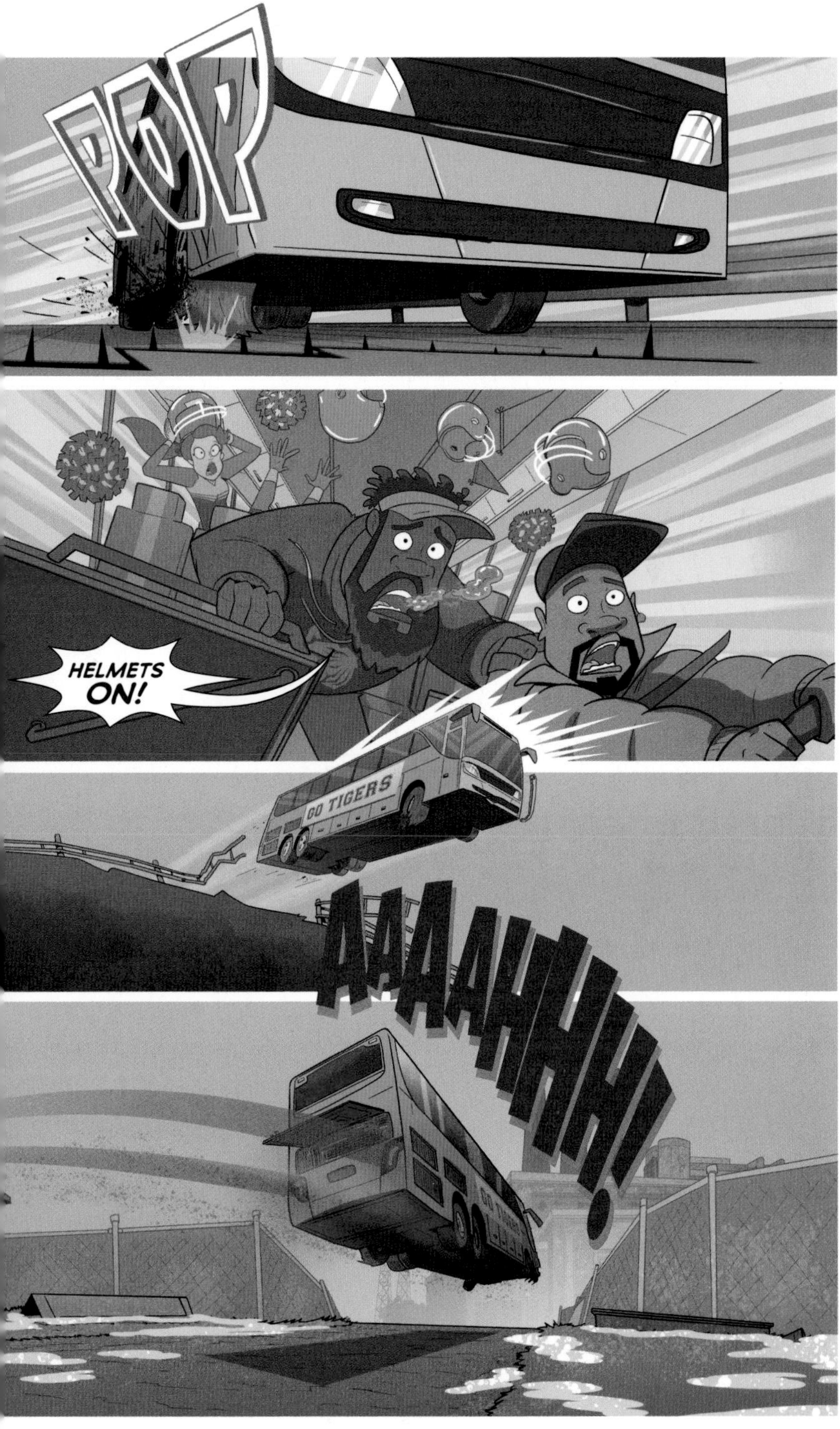
POP
HELMETS ON!
GO TIGERS
AAAAHHH!
GO TIGERS

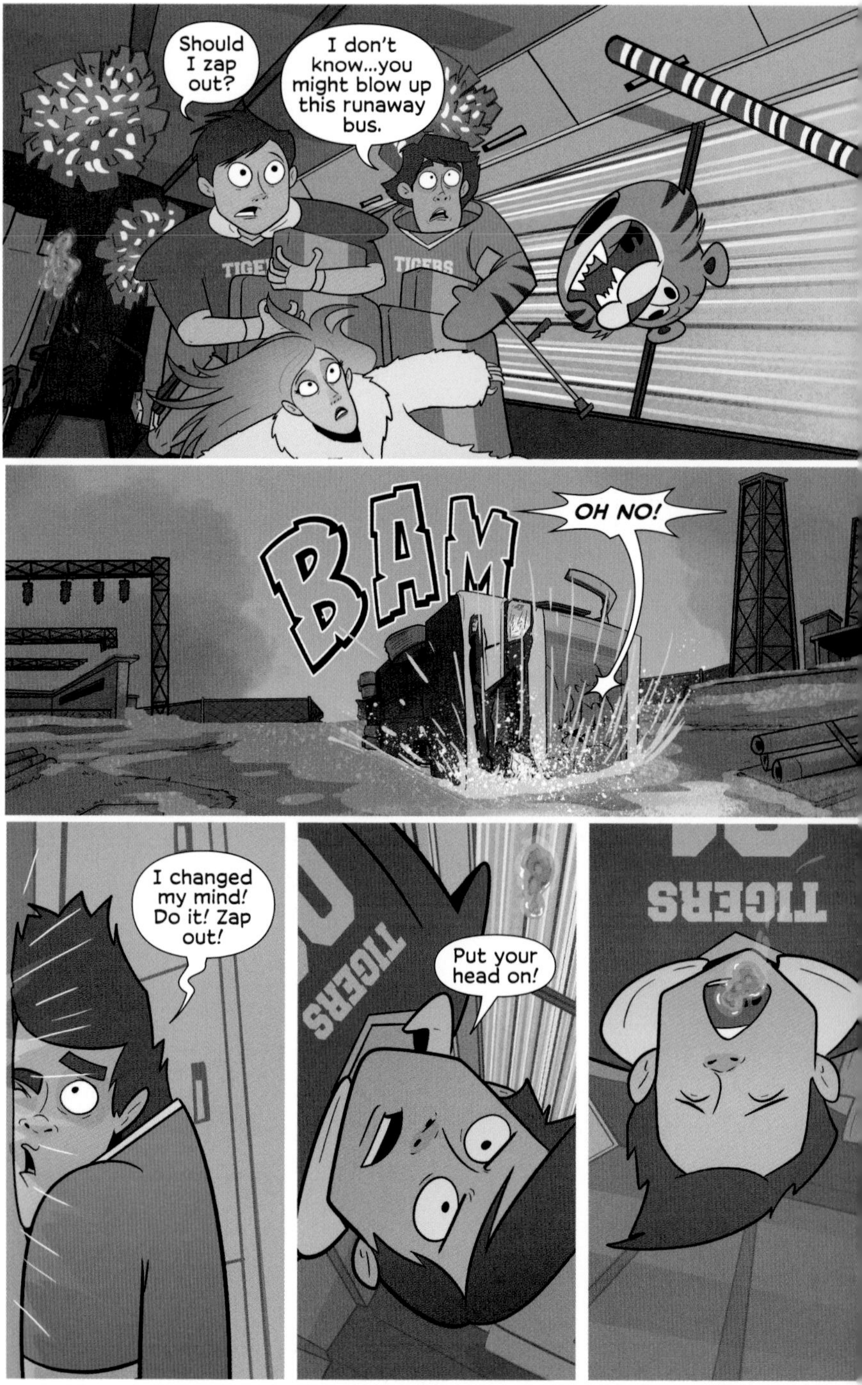
Should I zap out?
I don't know...you might blow up this runaway bus.
BAM
OH NO!
I changed my mind! Do it! Zap out!
Put your head on!

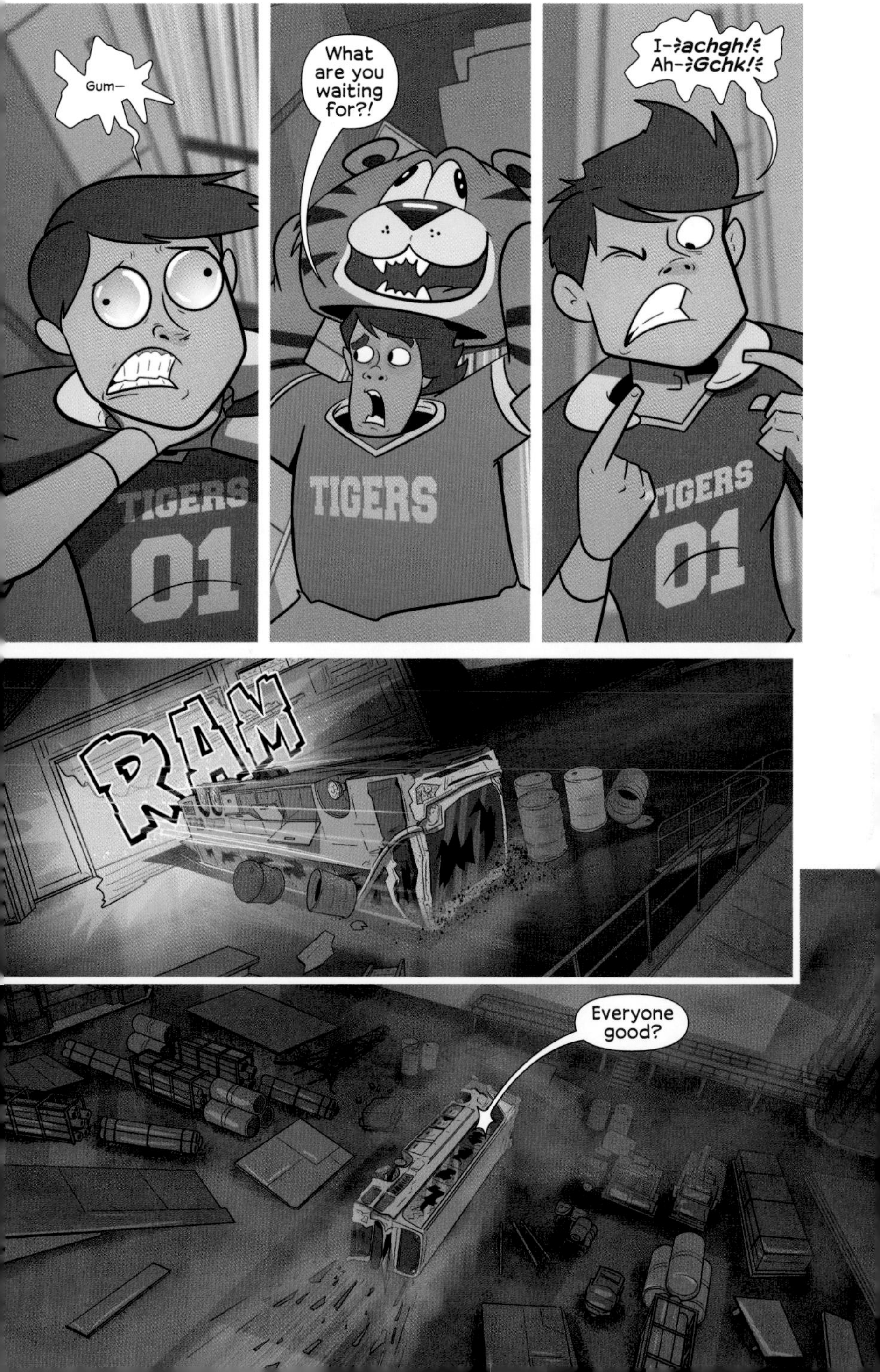
Gum–
TIGERS 01
What are you waiting for?!
TIGERS
I–achgh!
Ah–Gchk!
TIGERS 01
RAM
Everyone good?

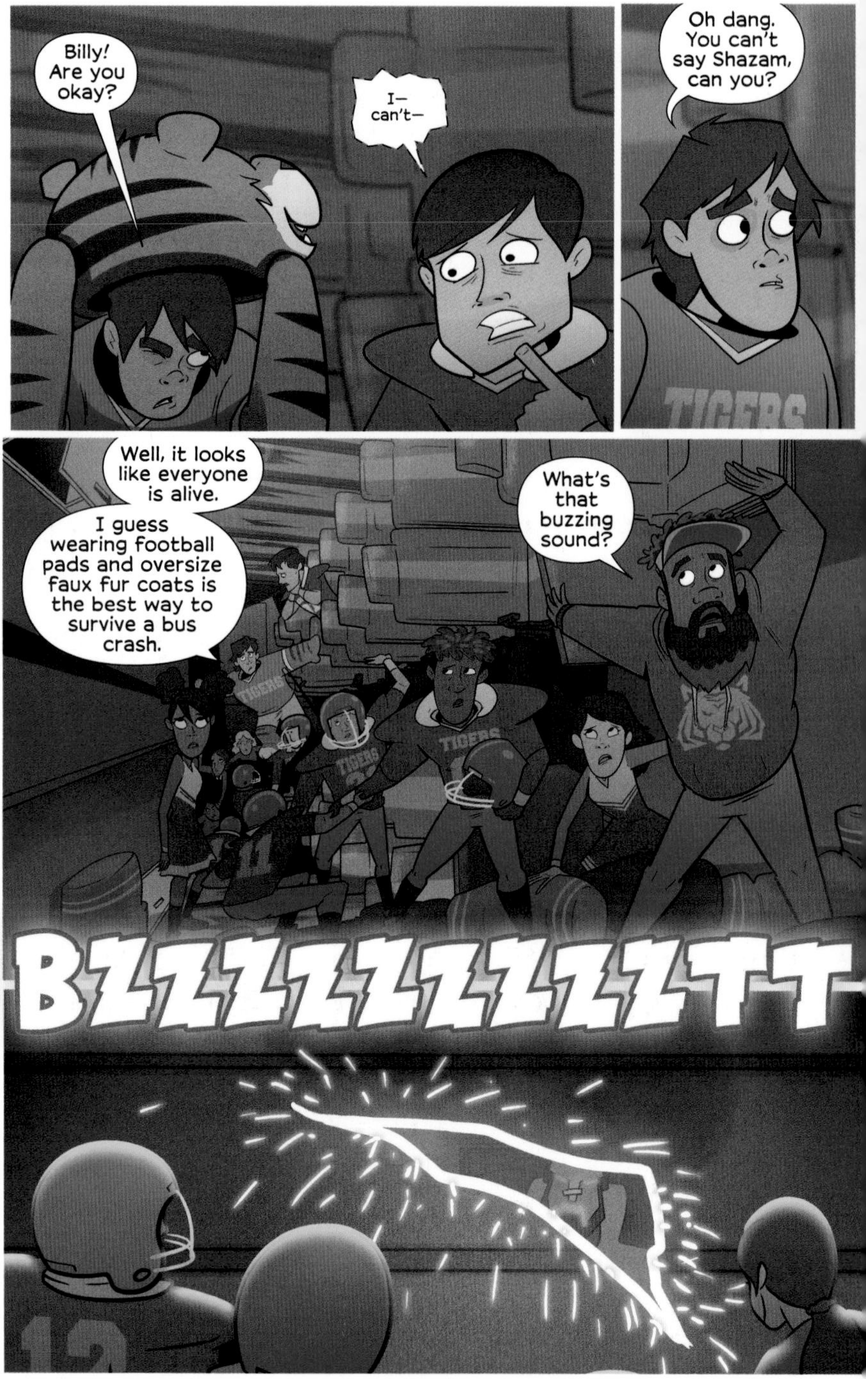
Billy! Are you okay?
I— can't—
Oh dang. You can't say Shazam, can you?
TIGERS
Well, it looks like everyone is alive.
I guess wearing football pads and oversize faux fur coats is the best way to survive a bus crash.
What's that buzzing sound?
BZZZZZZZZZZTT

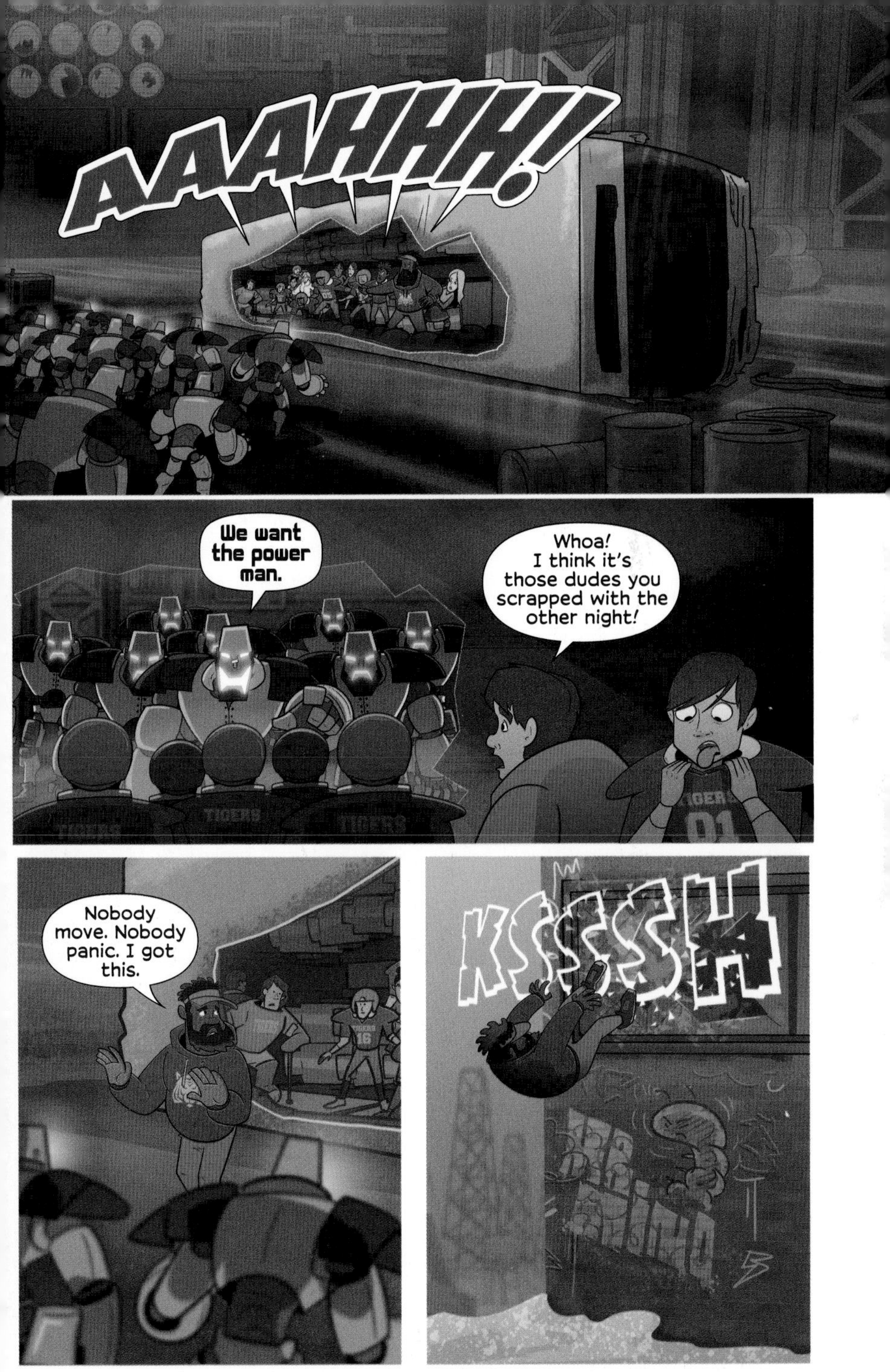

AAAHHH!
We want the power man.
Whoa! I think it's those dudes you scrapped with the other night!
Nobody move. Nobody panic. I got this.
KSSSSH

RRRRRUUUUUUUUNNNN

Hack!
Gum
Hack!

I'll get everyone to the lower vault.

You work on clearing your throat!

Maybe try burping?

Hng!
Okay—

TIGERS

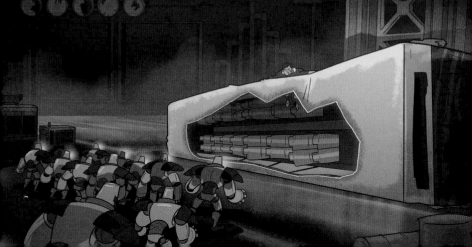

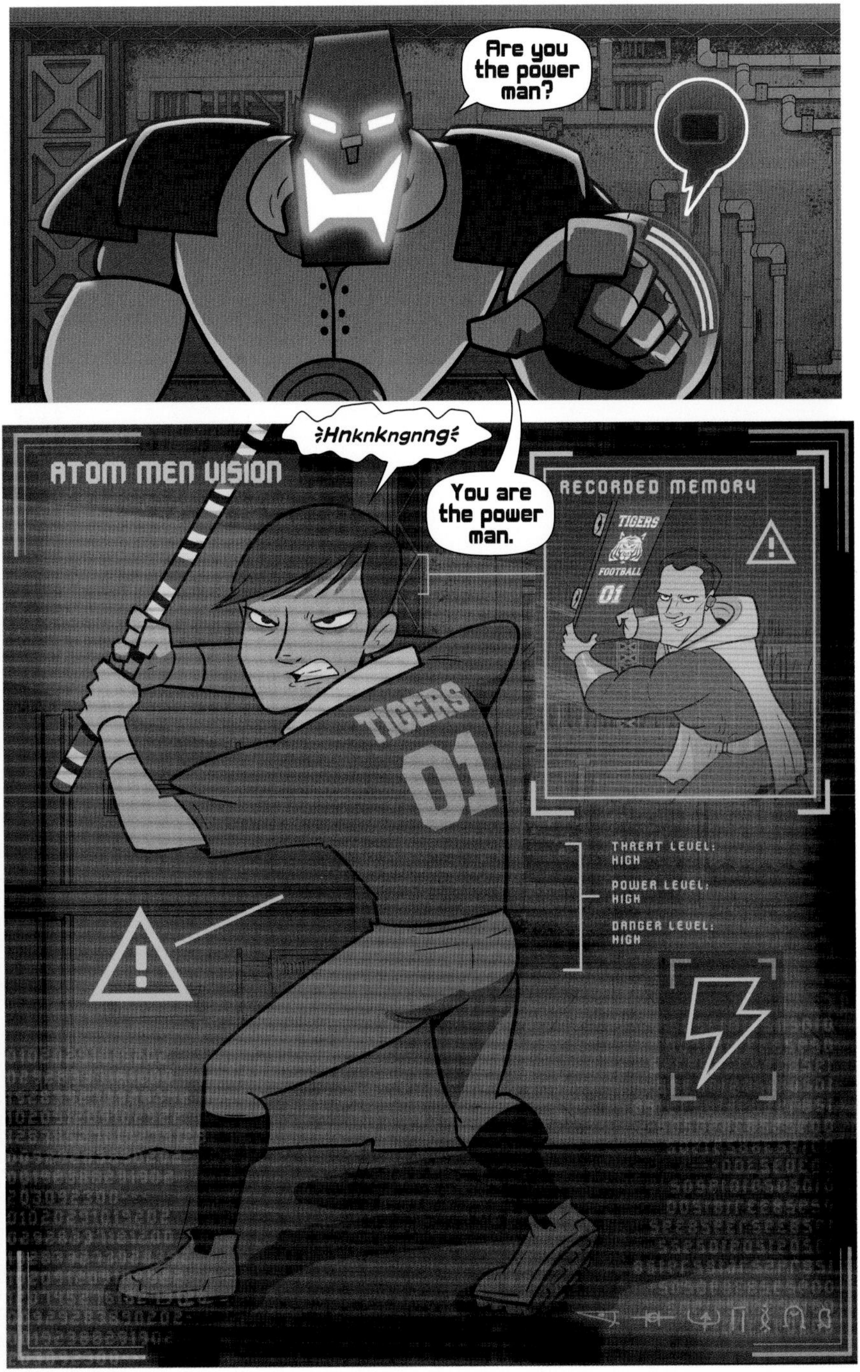
Are you the power man?
Hnknkngnng
You are the power man.
ATOM MEN VISION
RECORDED MEMORY
TIGERS
FOOTBALL
01
TIGERS
01
THREAT LEVEL: HIGH
POWER LEVEL: HIGH
DANGER LEVEL: HIGH

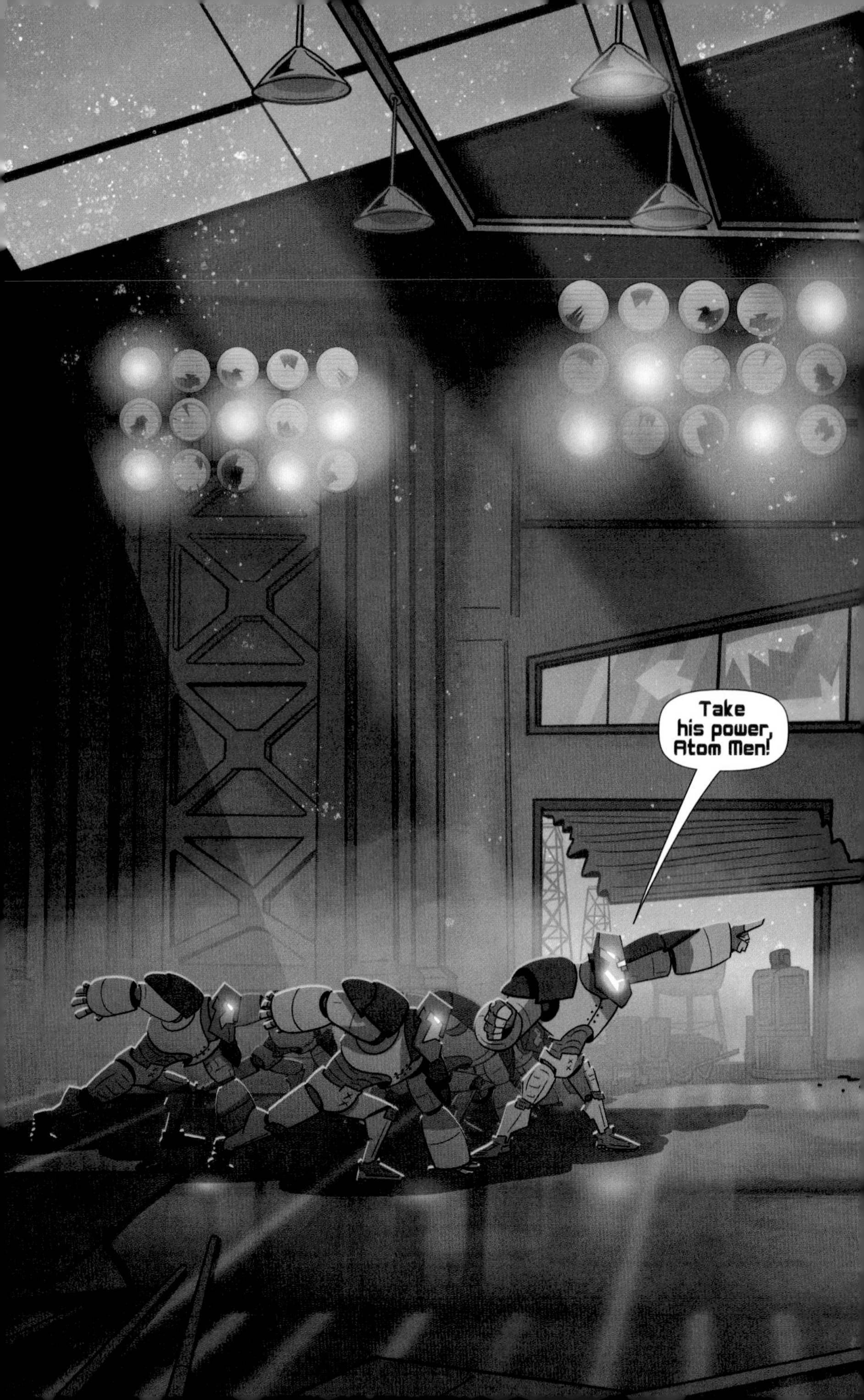
Take his power, Atom Men!

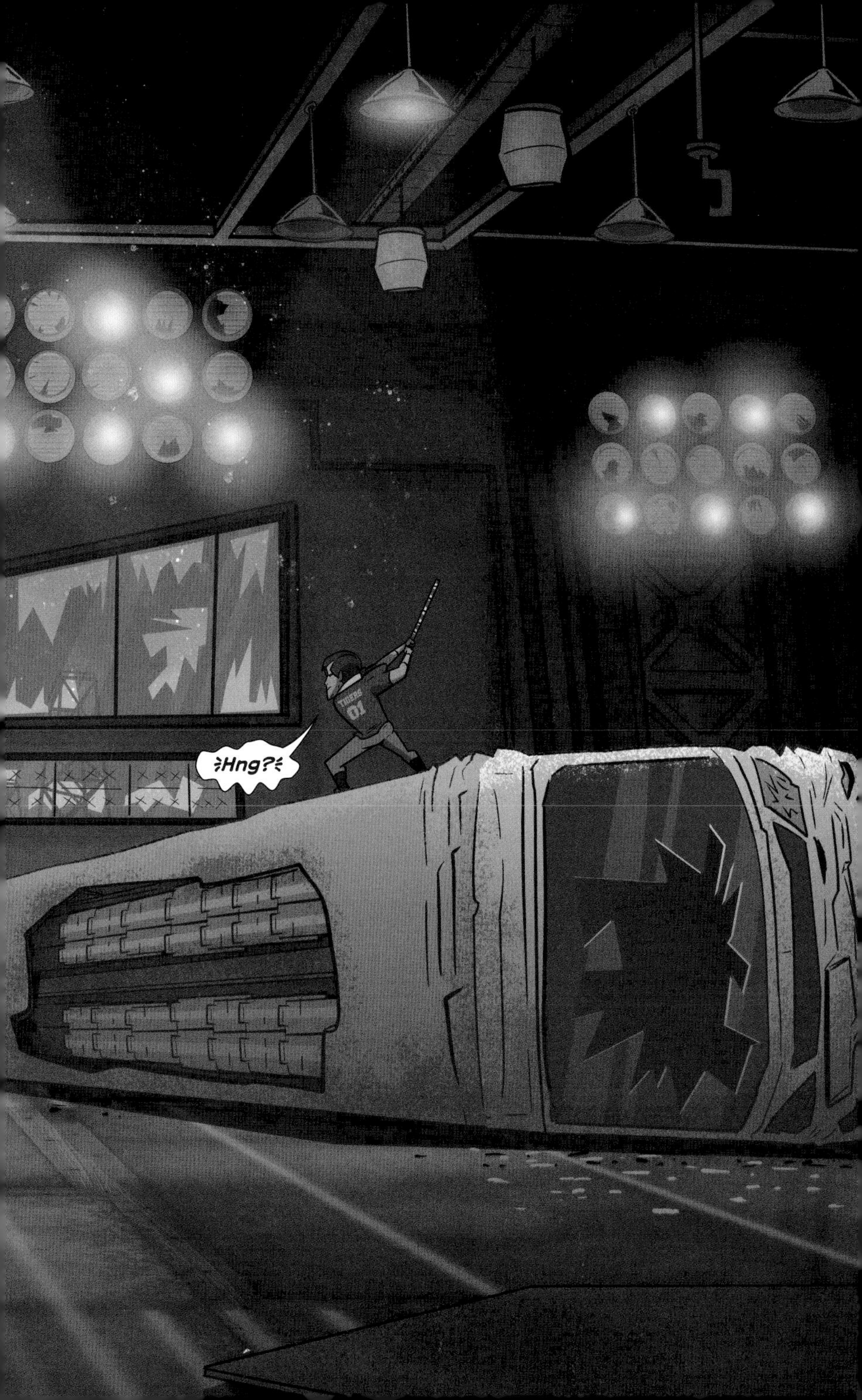
Hng?

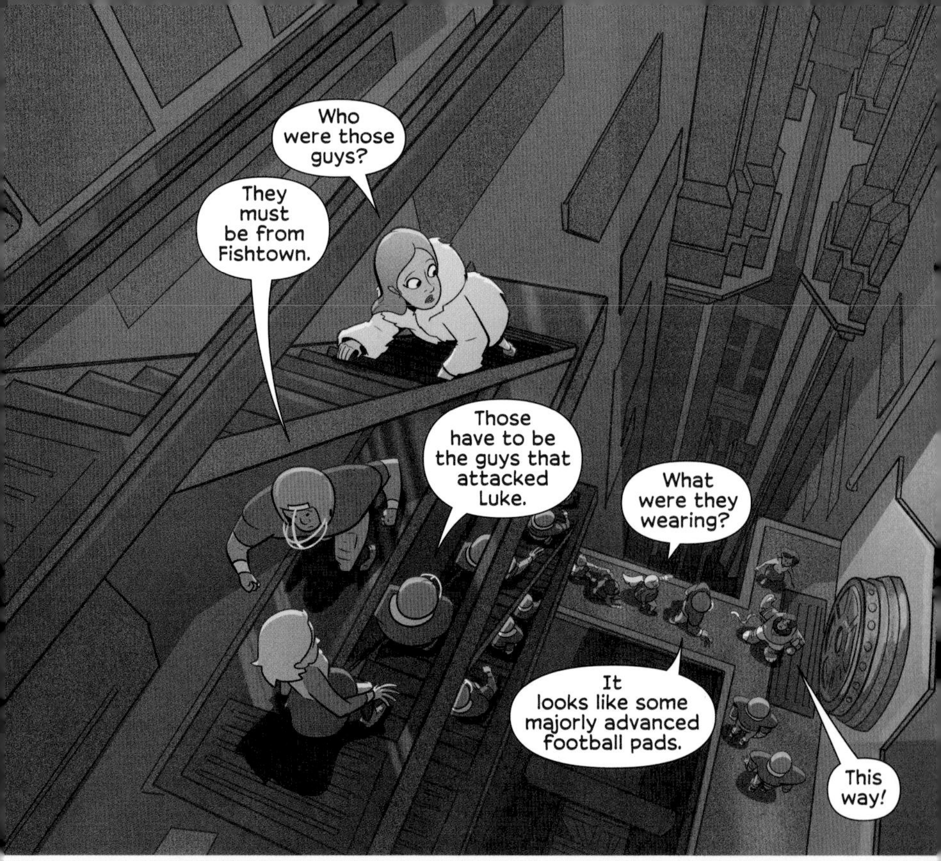
Who were those guys?
They must be from Fishtown.
Those have to be the guys that attacked Luke.
What were they wearing?
It looks like some majorly advanced football pads.
This way!

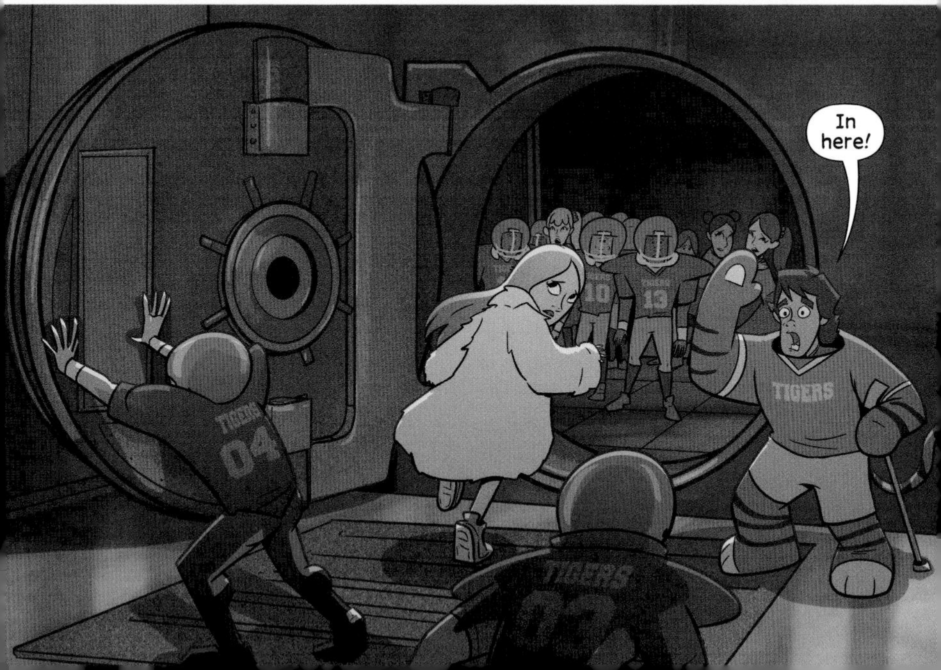
In here!
TIGERS

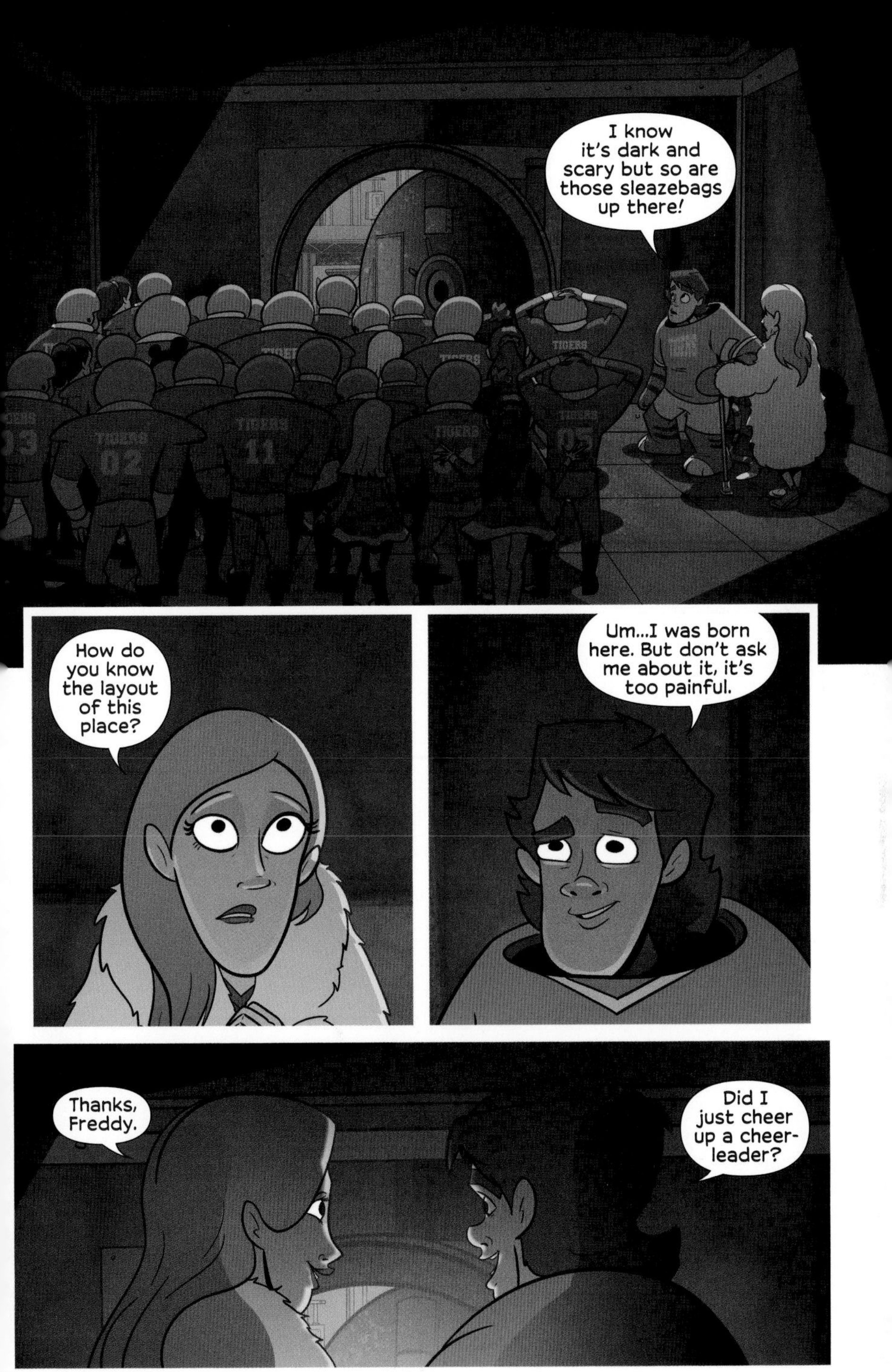

I know it's dark and scary but so are those sleazebags up there!
TIGERS
02
11
05
How do you know the layout of this place?
Um...I was born here. But don't ask me about it, it's too painful.
Thanks, Freddy.
Did I just cheer up a cheer-leader?

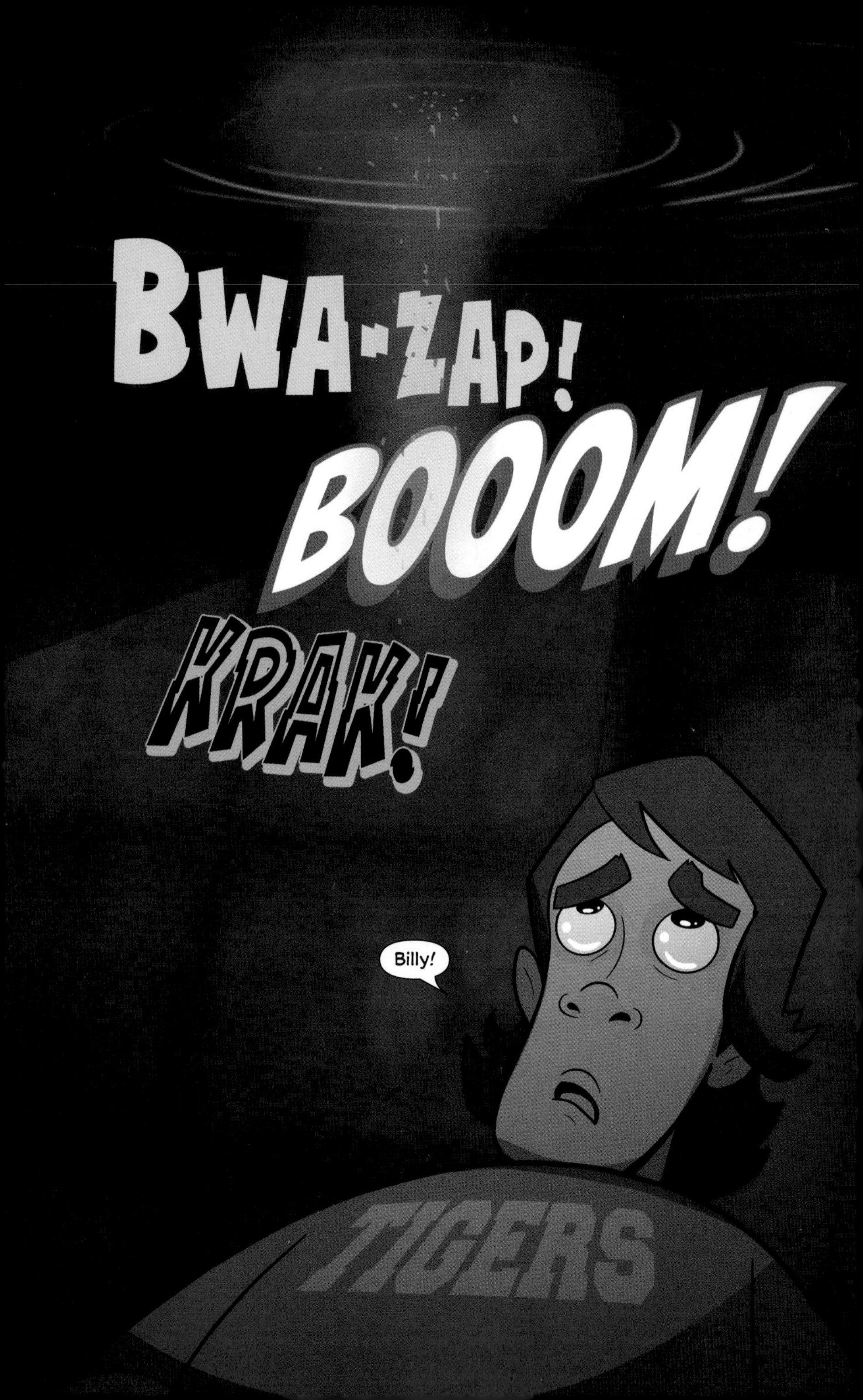
BWA-ZAP!
BOOOM!
KRAK!
Billy!
TIGERS

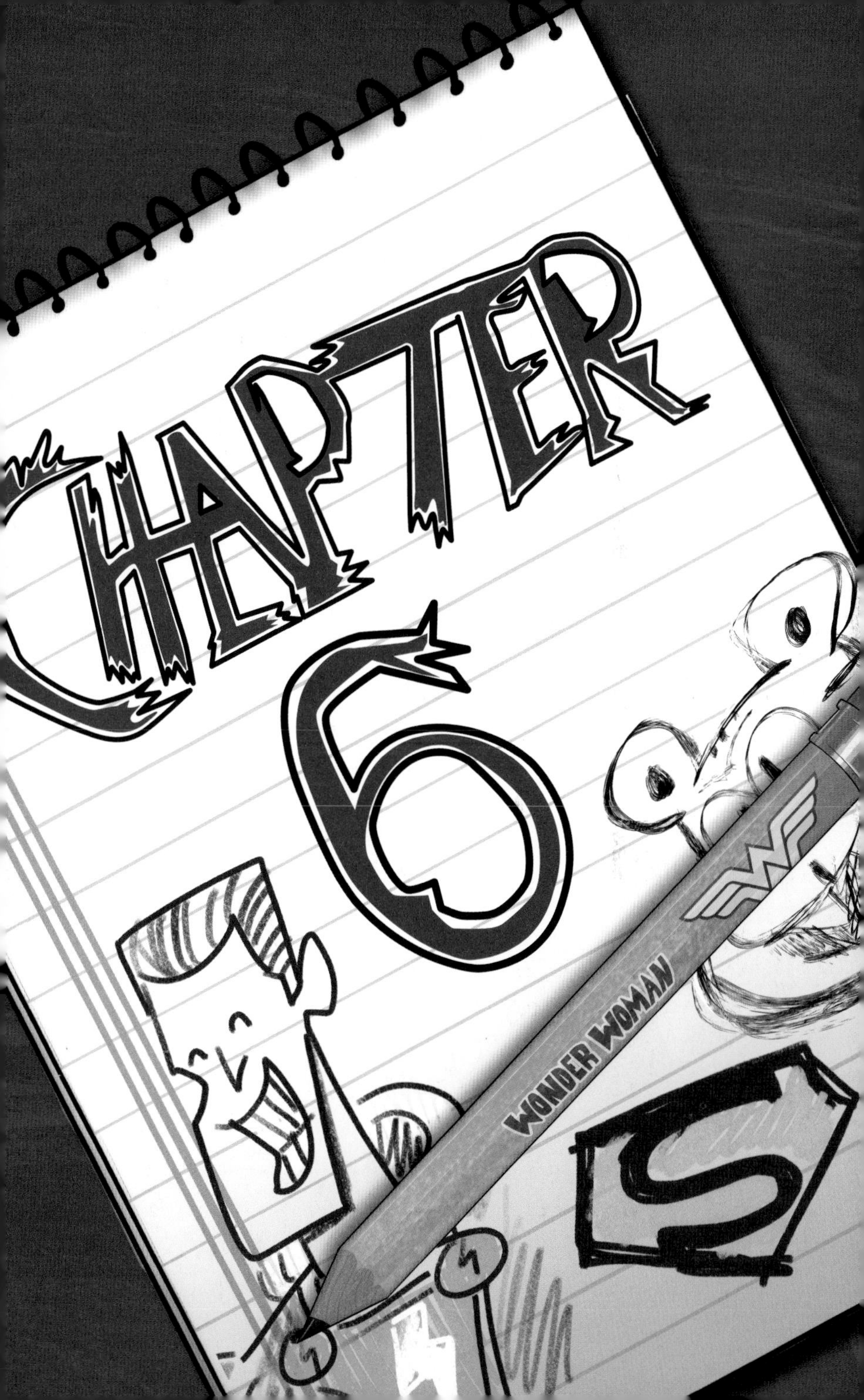
CHAPTER
6
WONDER WOMAN

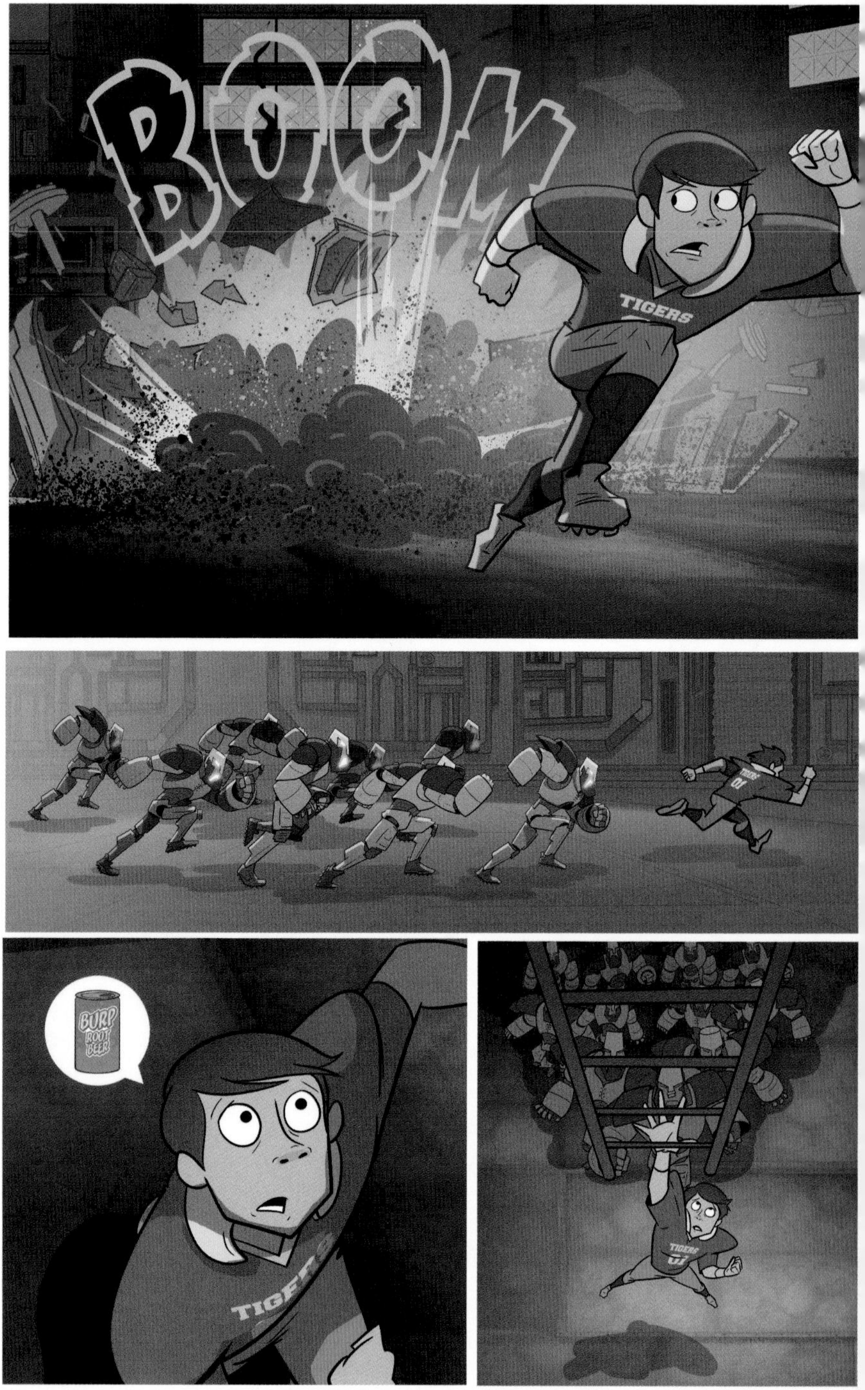
BOOM
BURP ROOT BEER

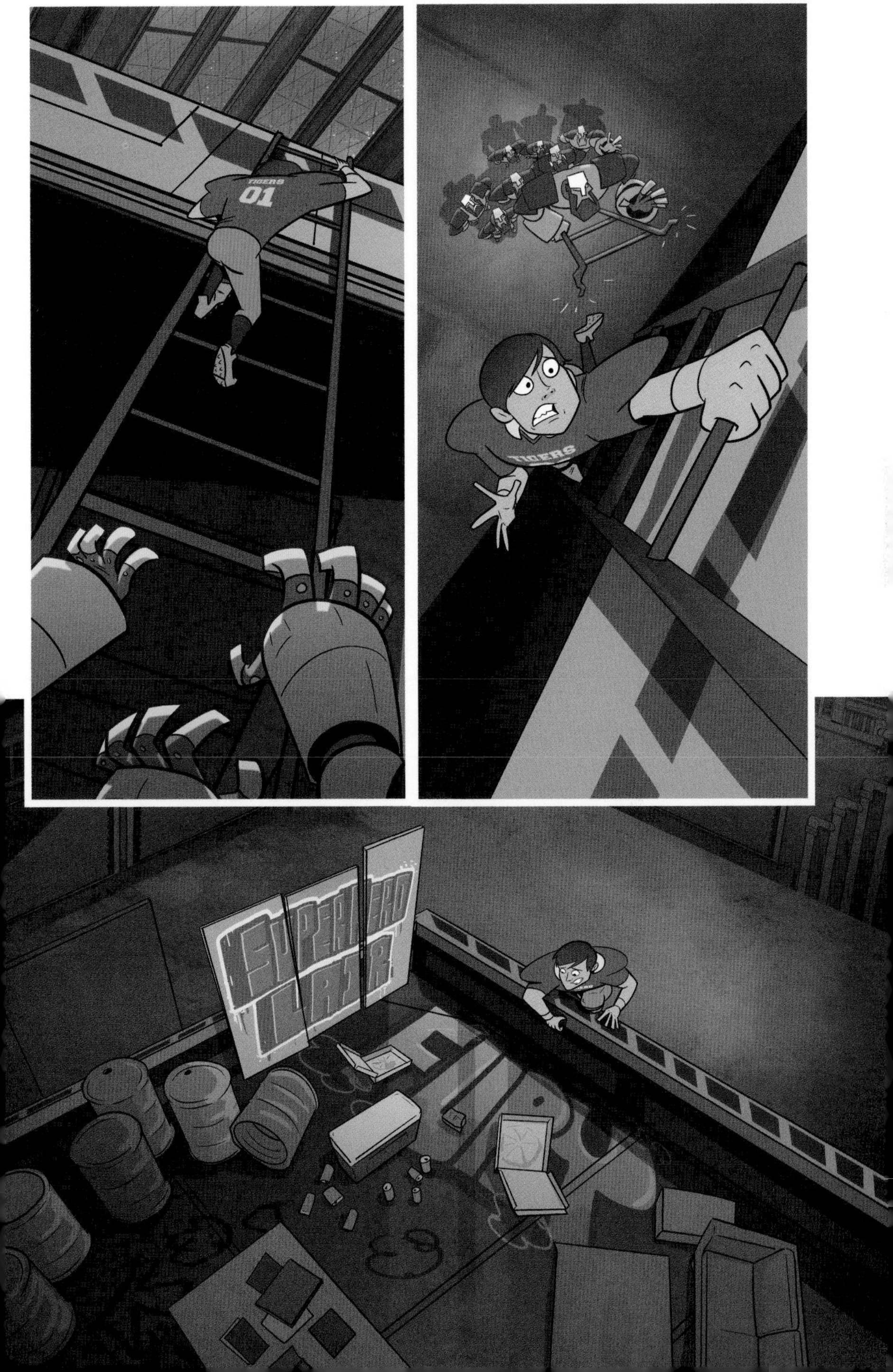
TIGERS
01
TIGERS

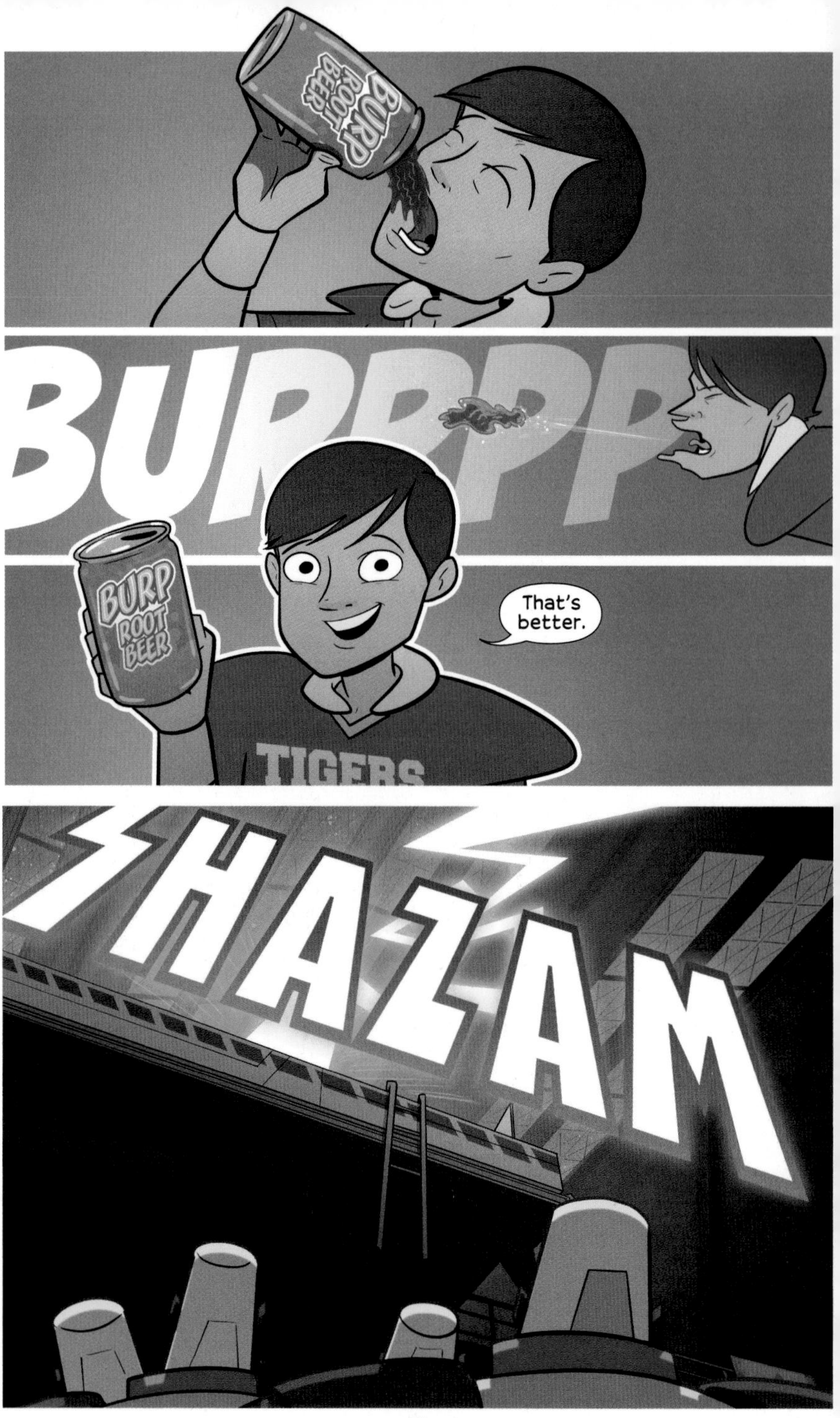
BURP ROOT BEER
BURPPP
BURP ROOT BEER
That's better.
TIGERS
SHAZAM

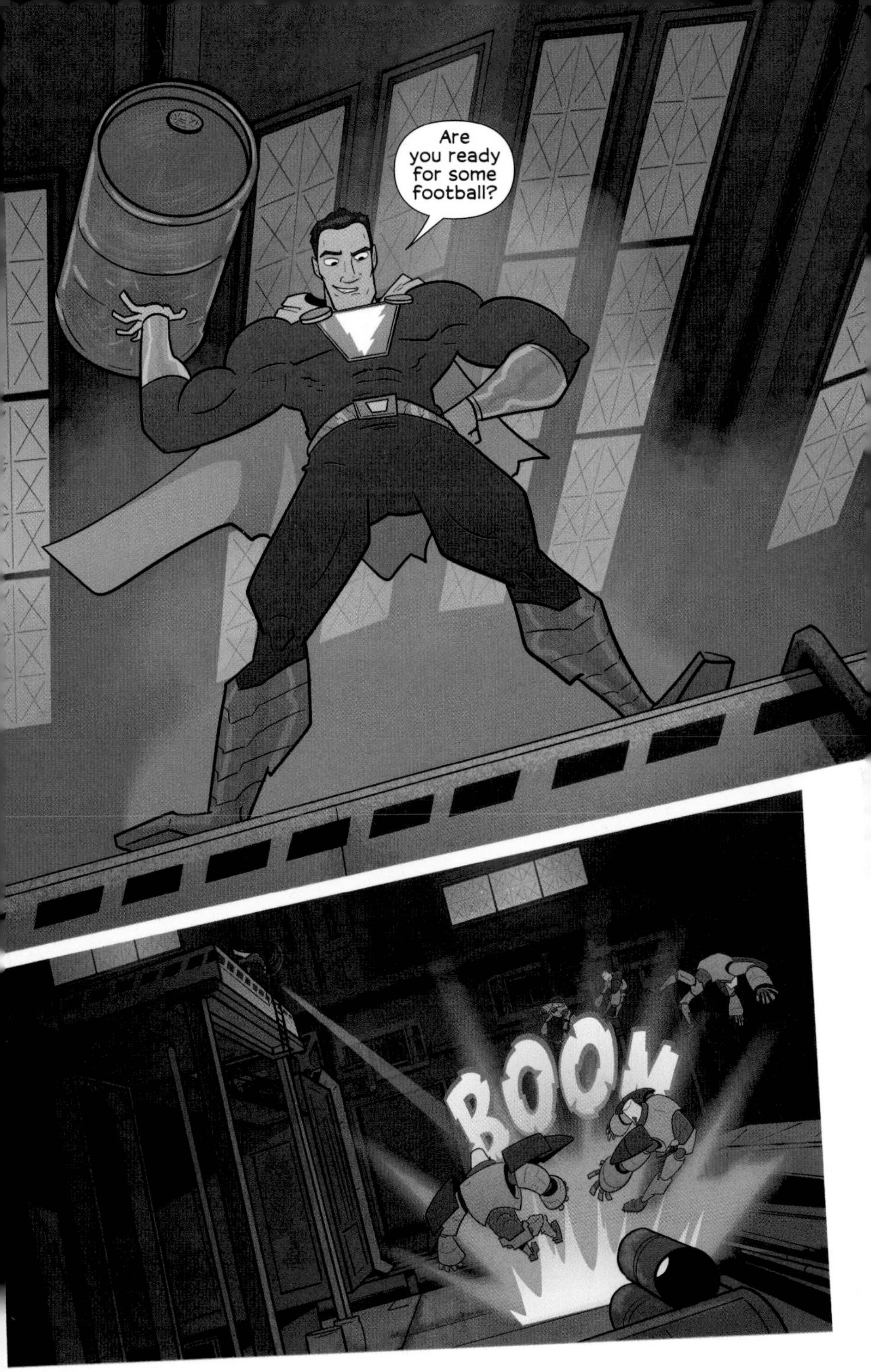
Are you ready for some football?
BOOM

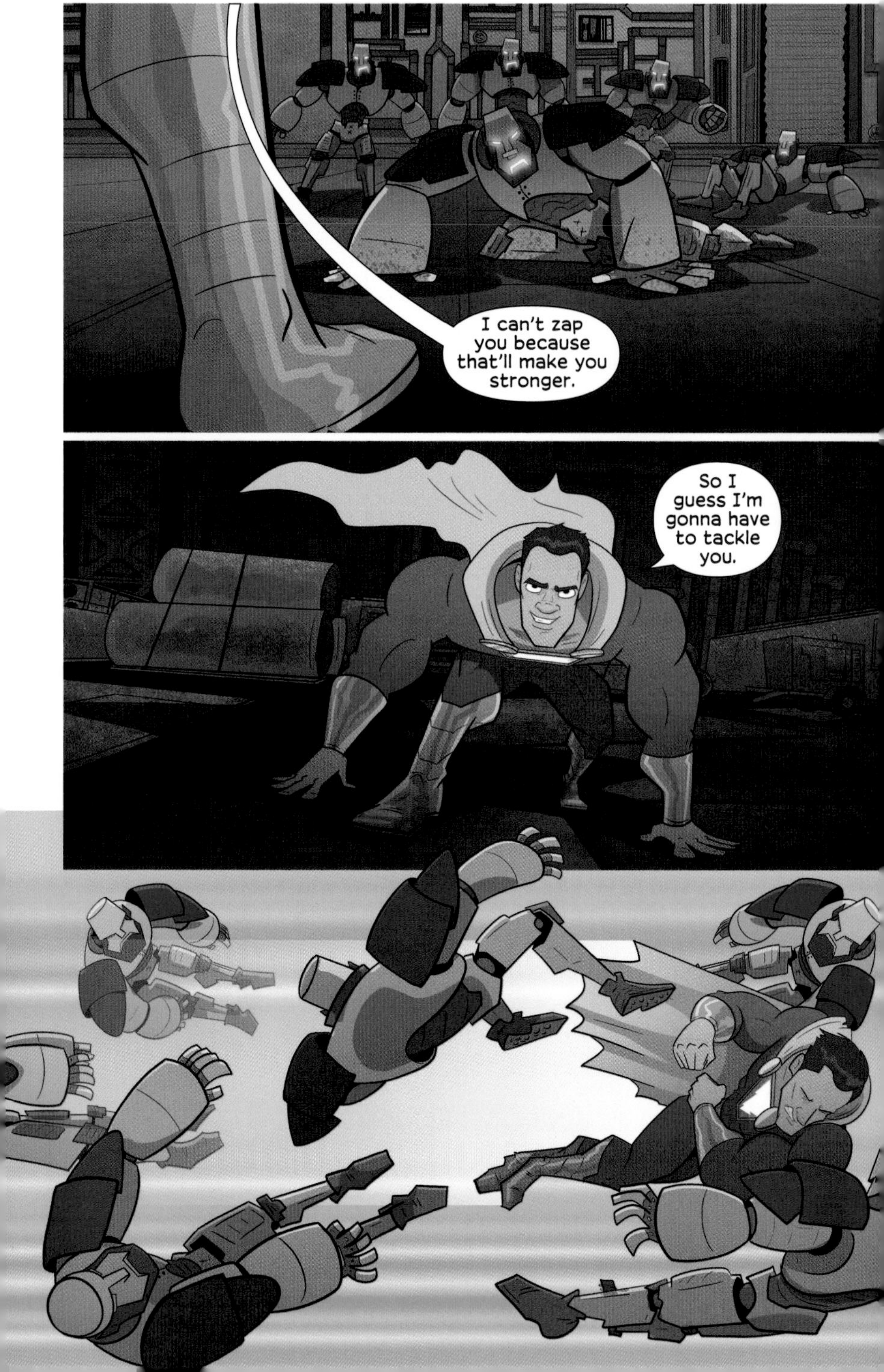
I can't zap you because that'll make you stronger.
So I guess I'm gonna have to tackle you.

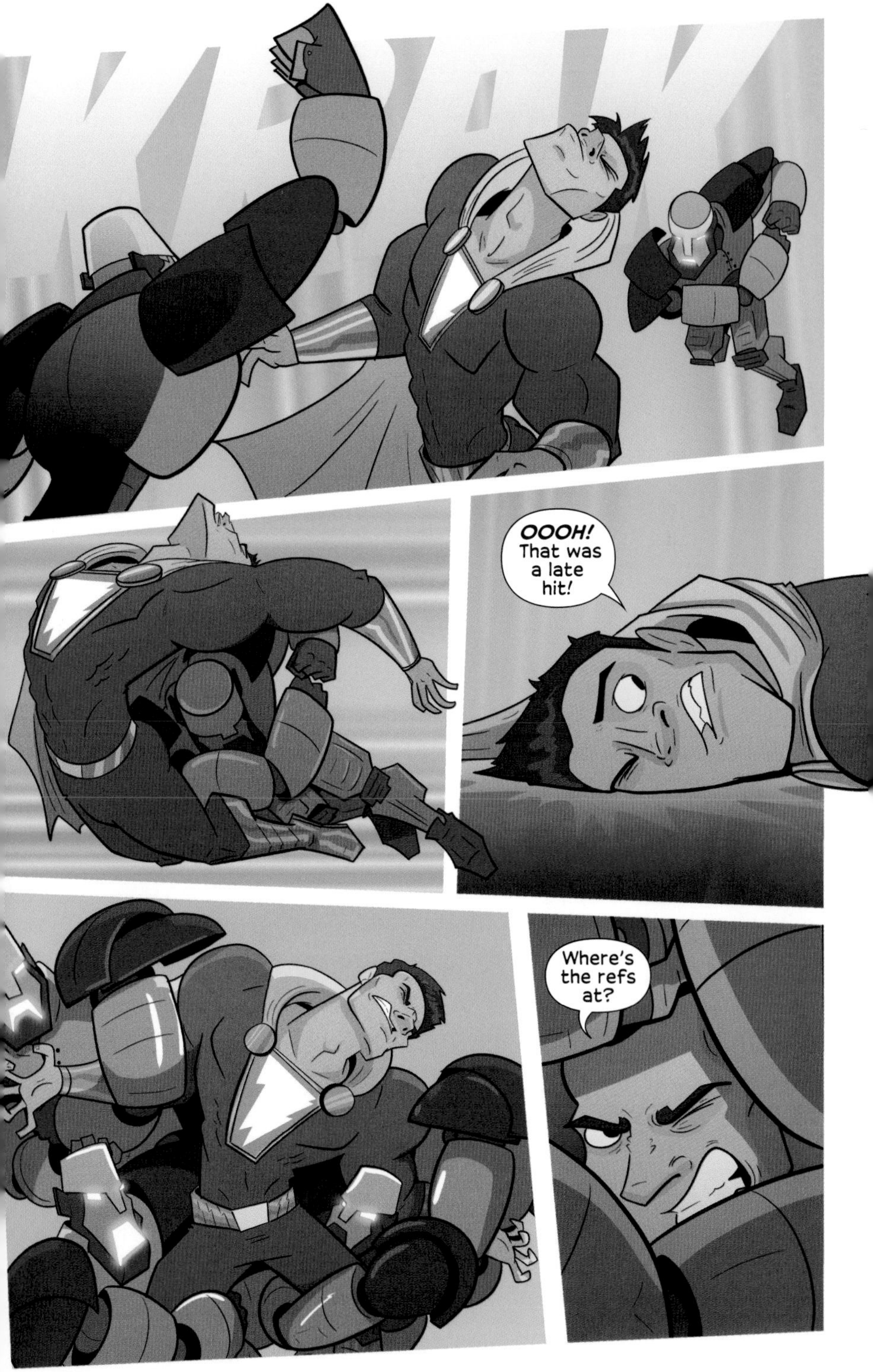
OOOH! That was a late hit!
Where's the refs at?

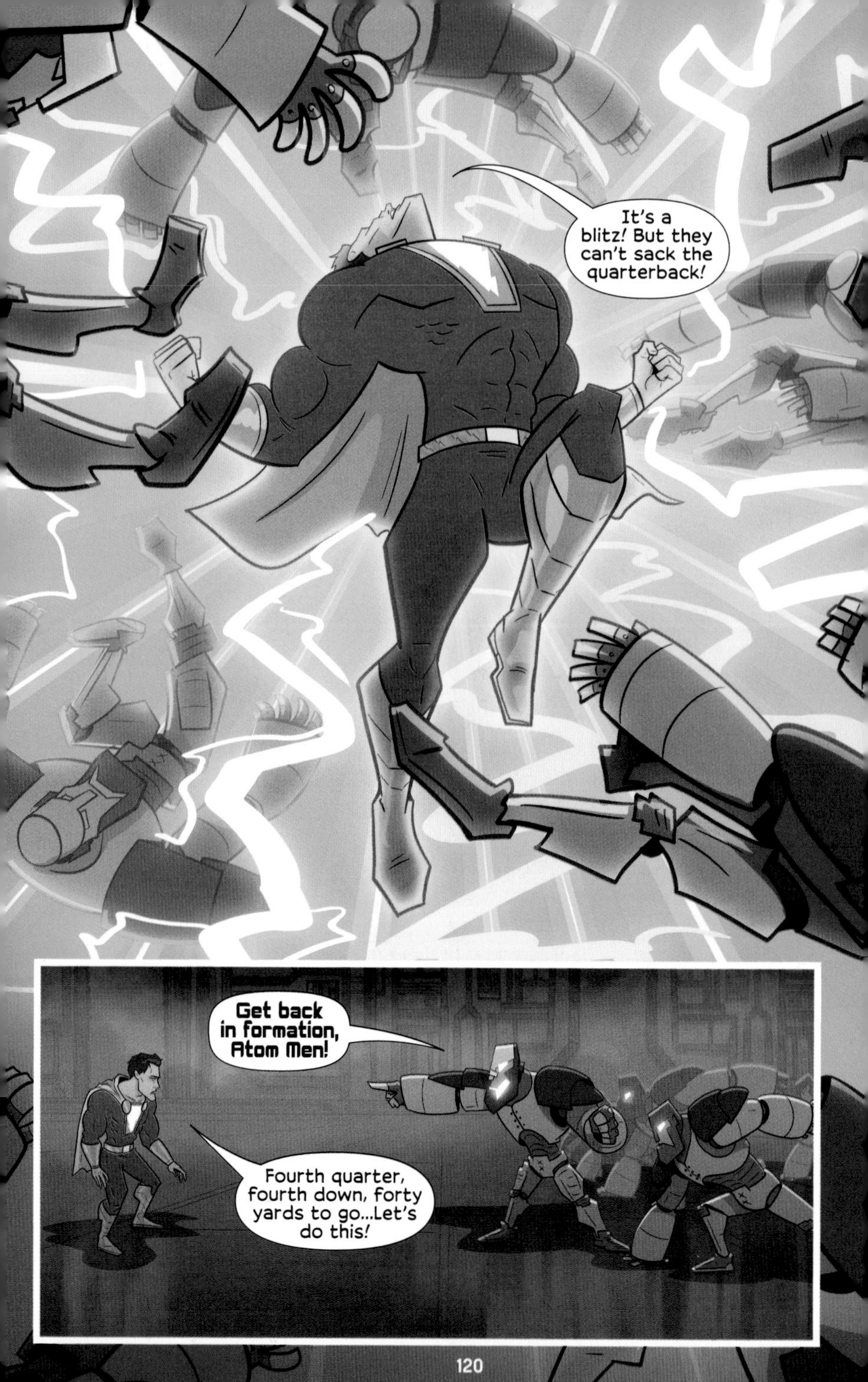
It's a blitz! But they can't sack the quarterback!
Get back in formation, Atom Men!
Fourth quarter, fourth down, forty yards to go...Let's do this!

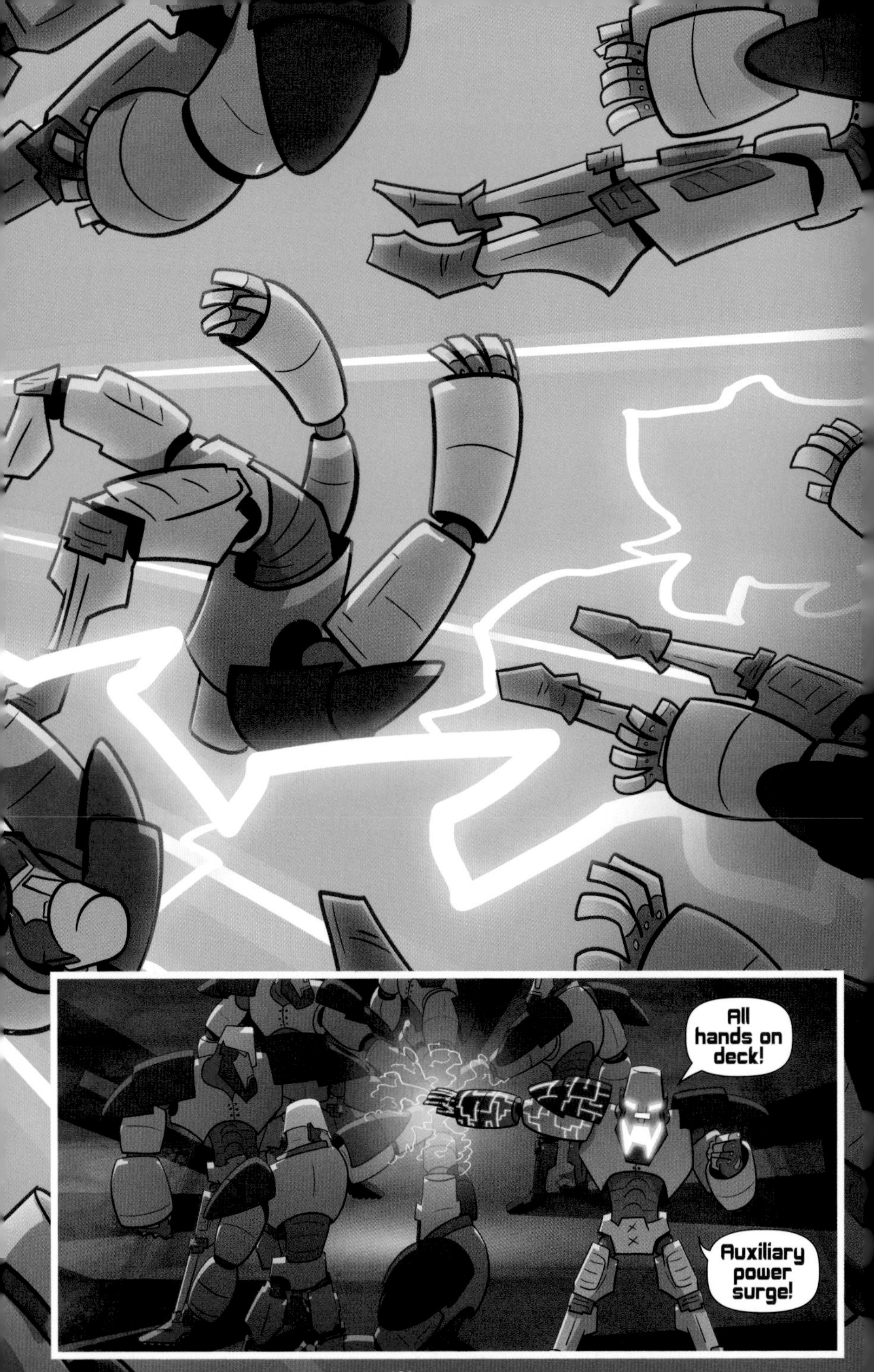
All hands on deck!
Auxiliary power surge!

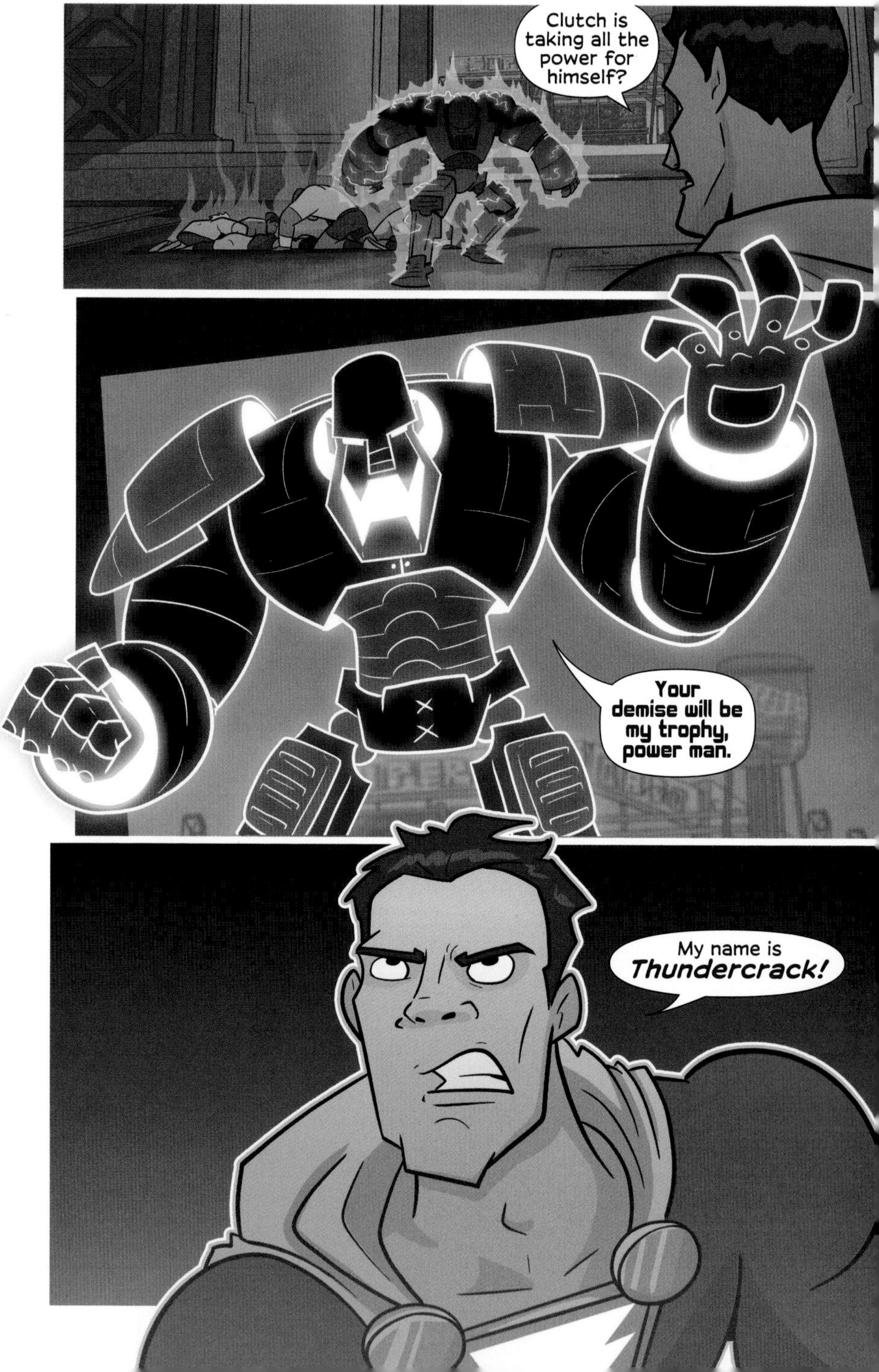
Clutch is taking all the power for himself?
Your demise will be my trophy, power man.
My name is *Thundercrack!*

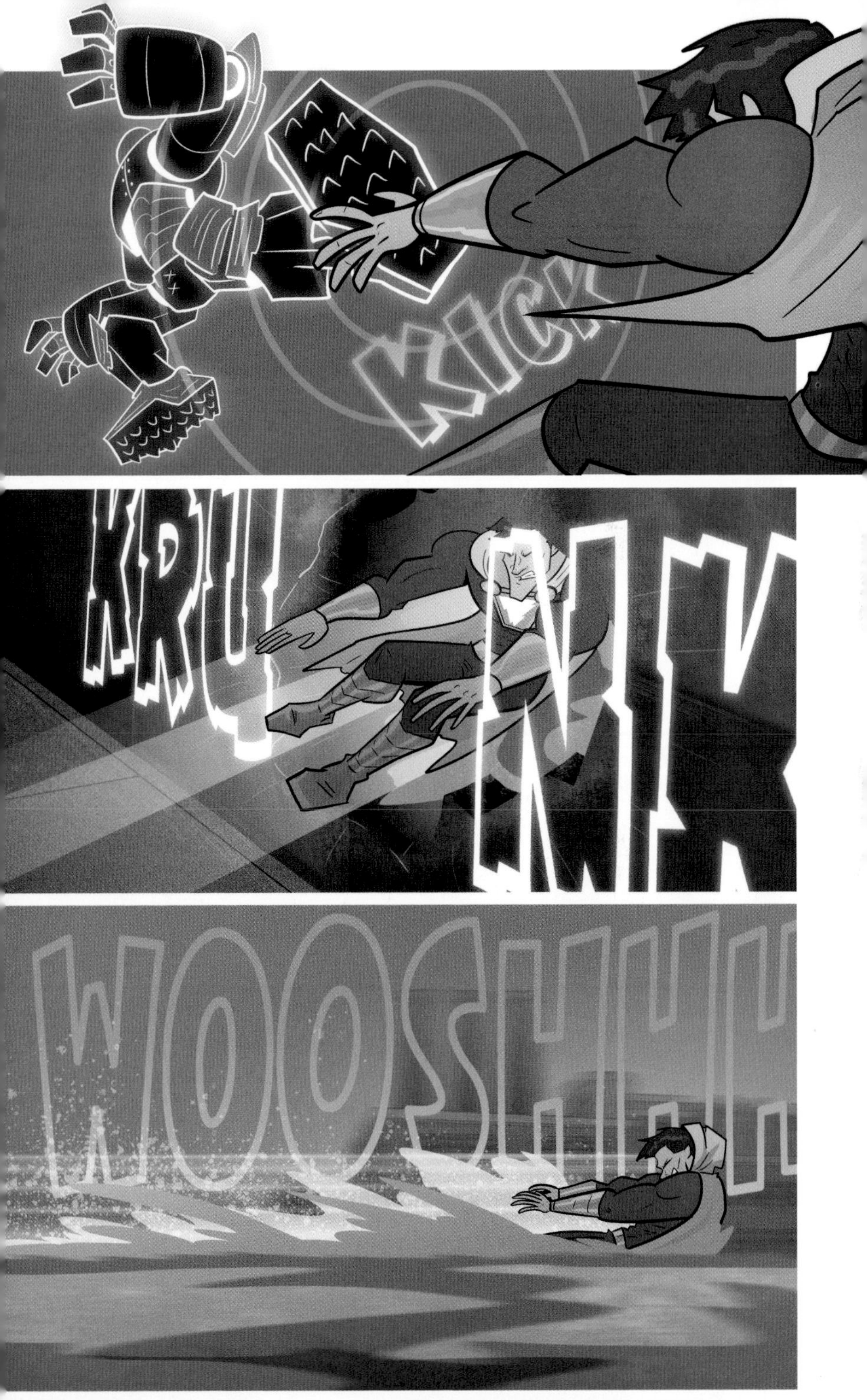
KICK
KRUNK
WOOSHH

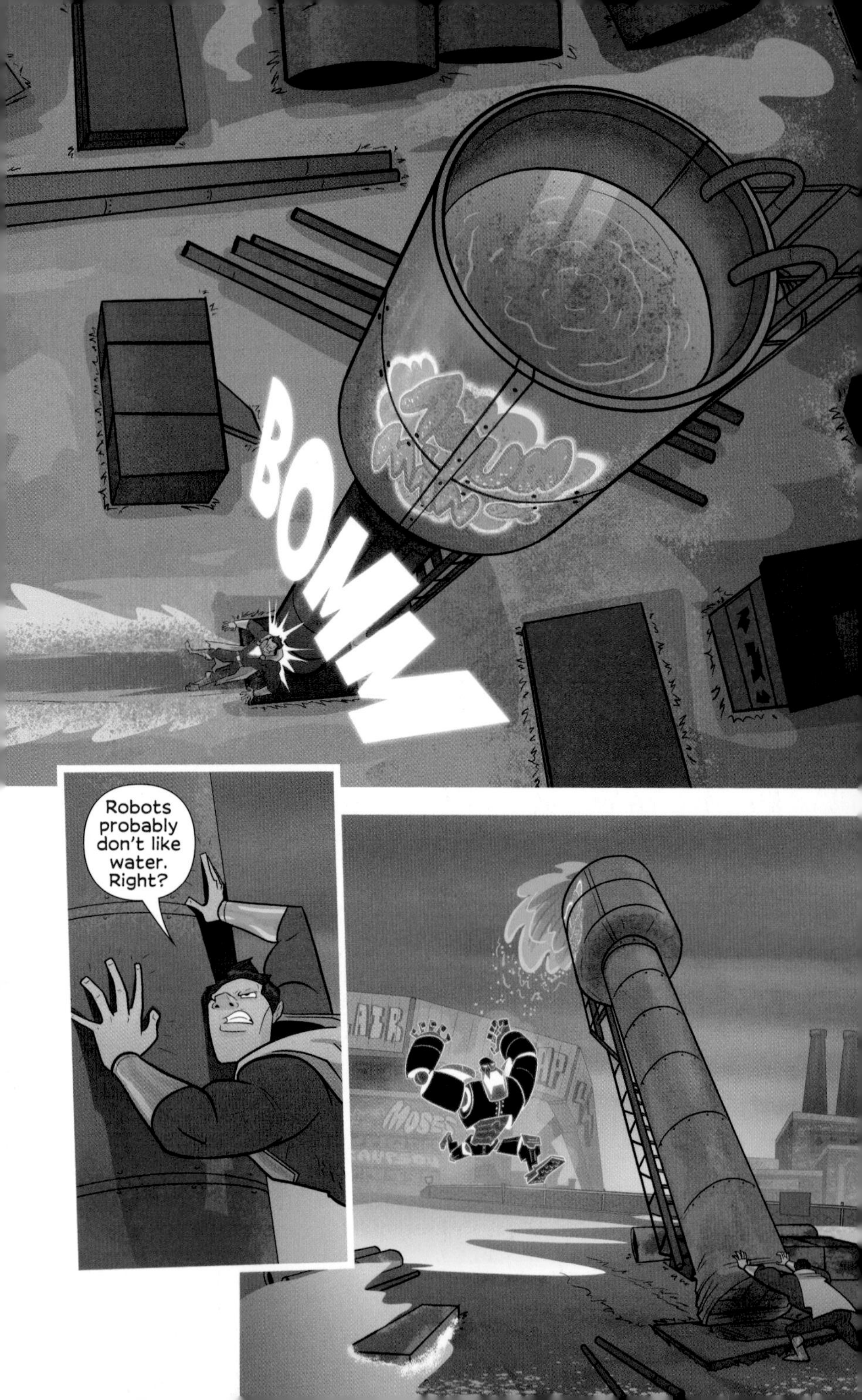
Robots probably don't like water. Right?

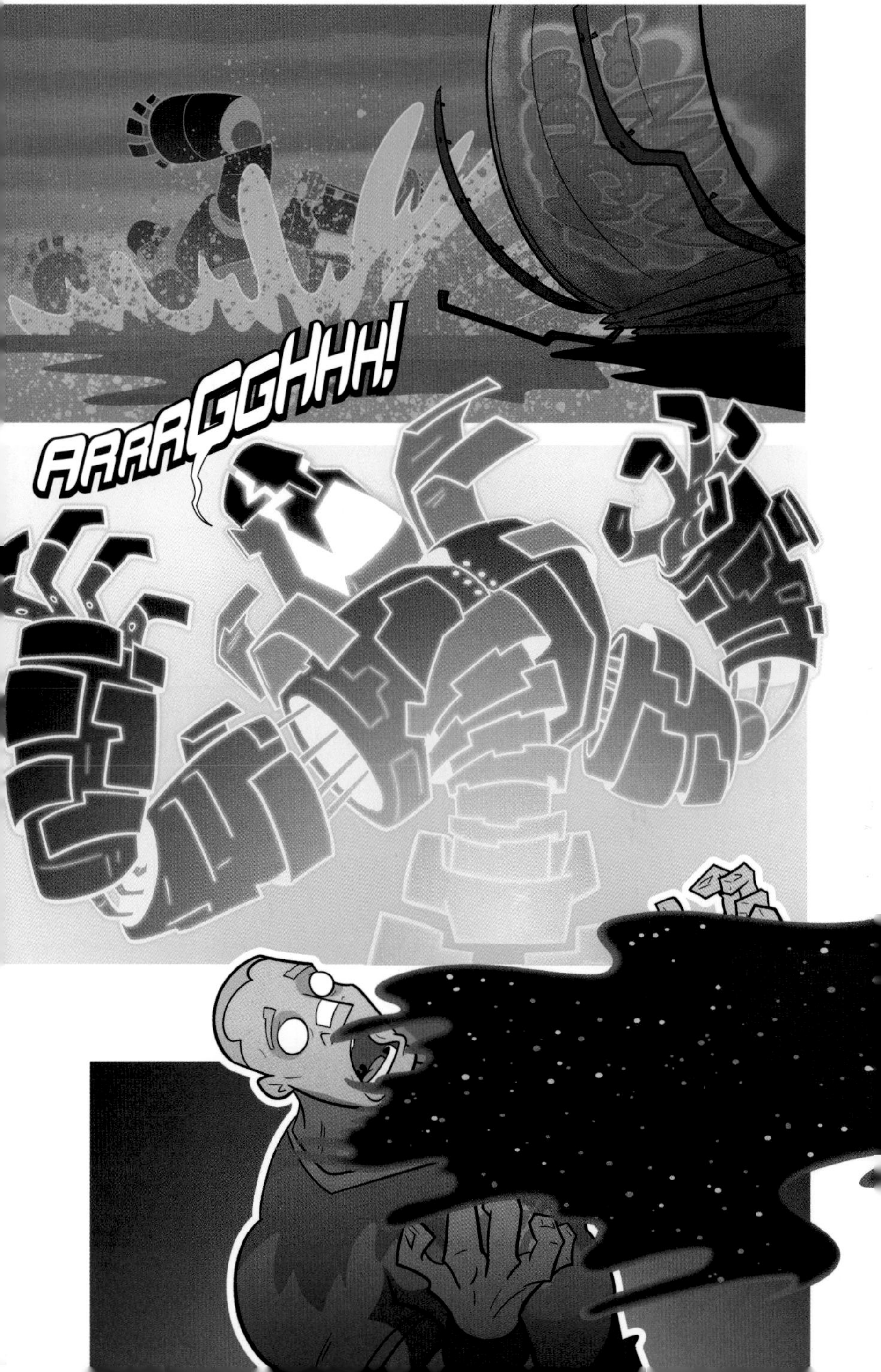
ARRRGGHHH!

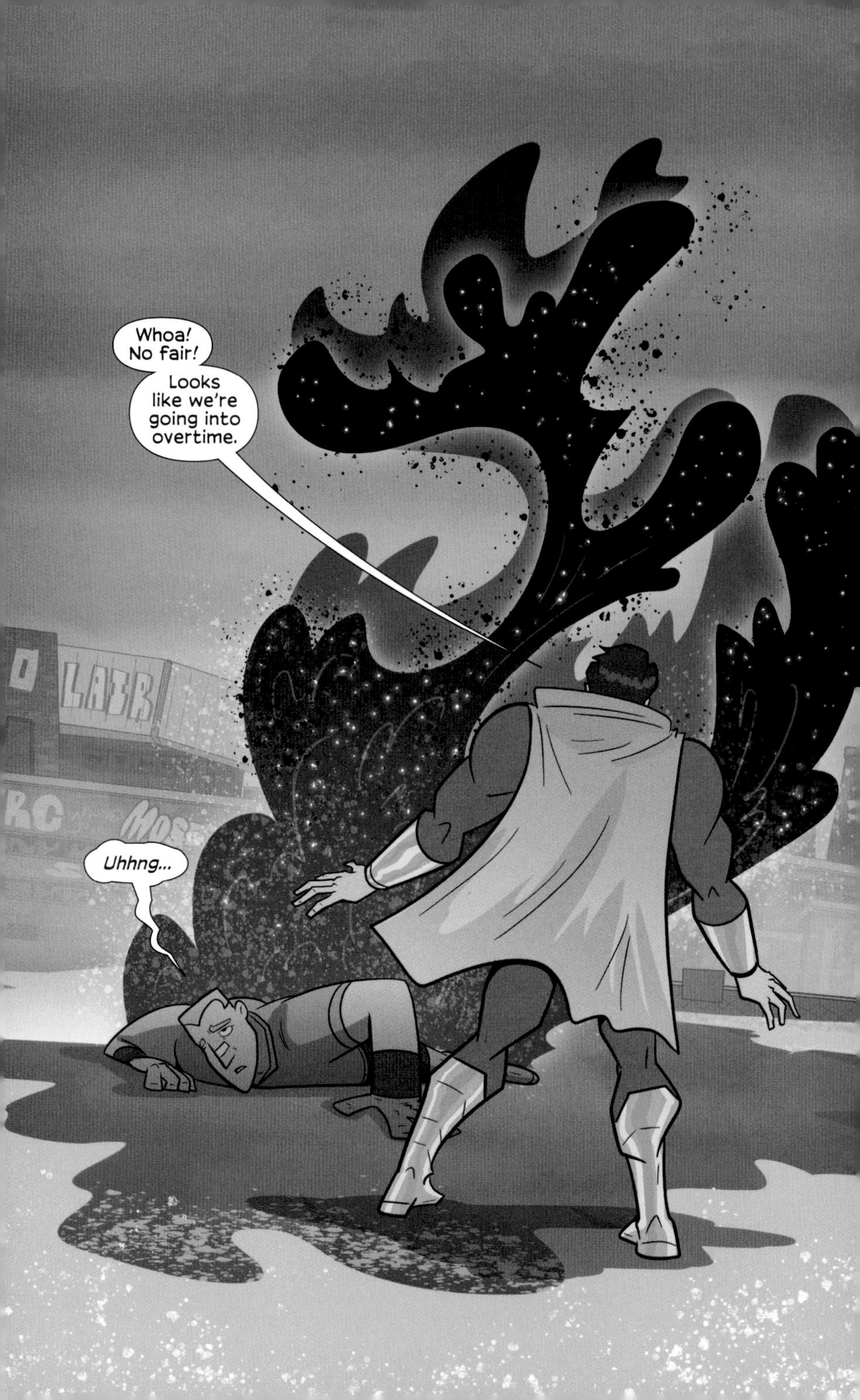
Whoa! No fair!
Looks like we're going into overtime.
Uhhng...

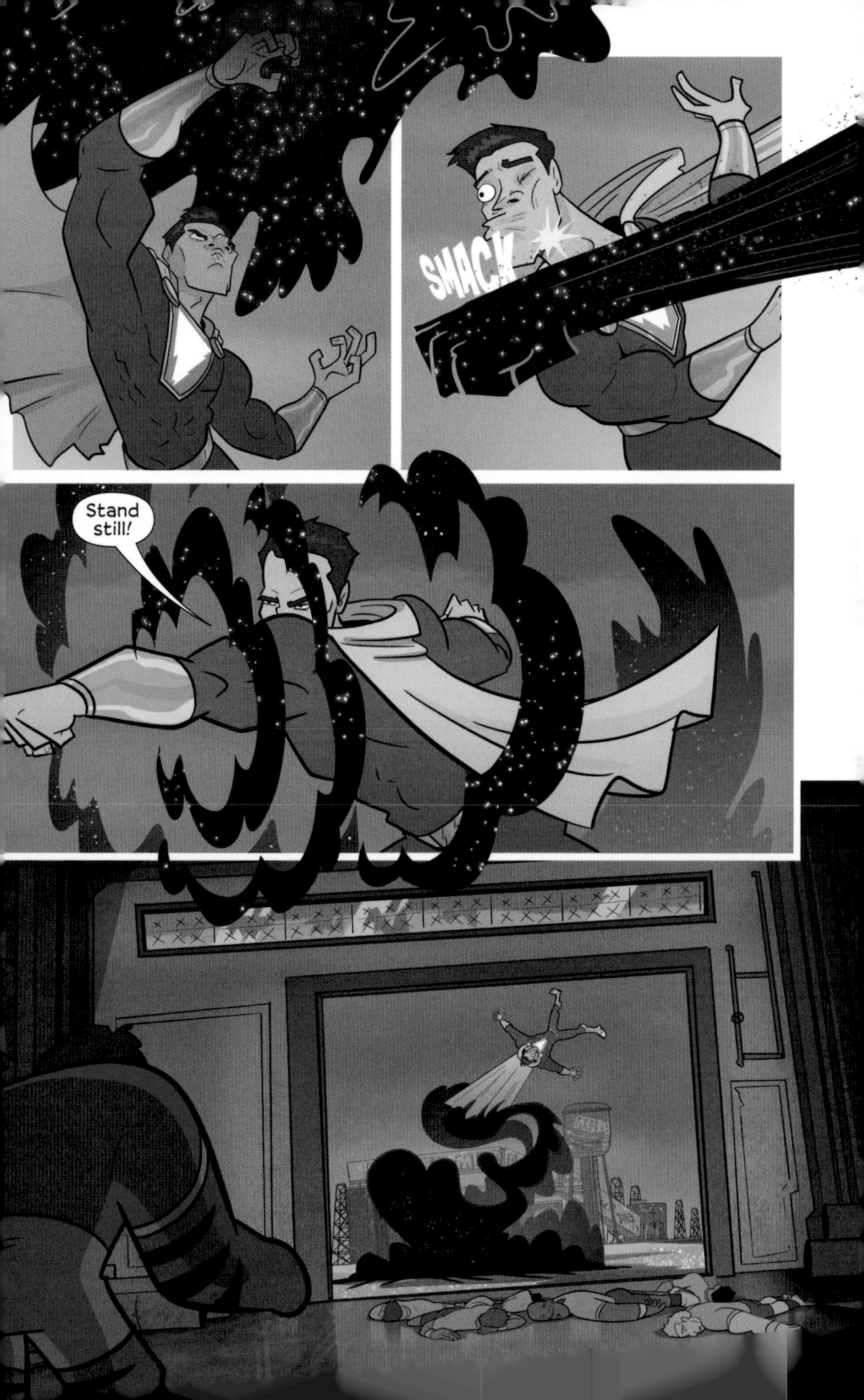
SMACK
Stand still!

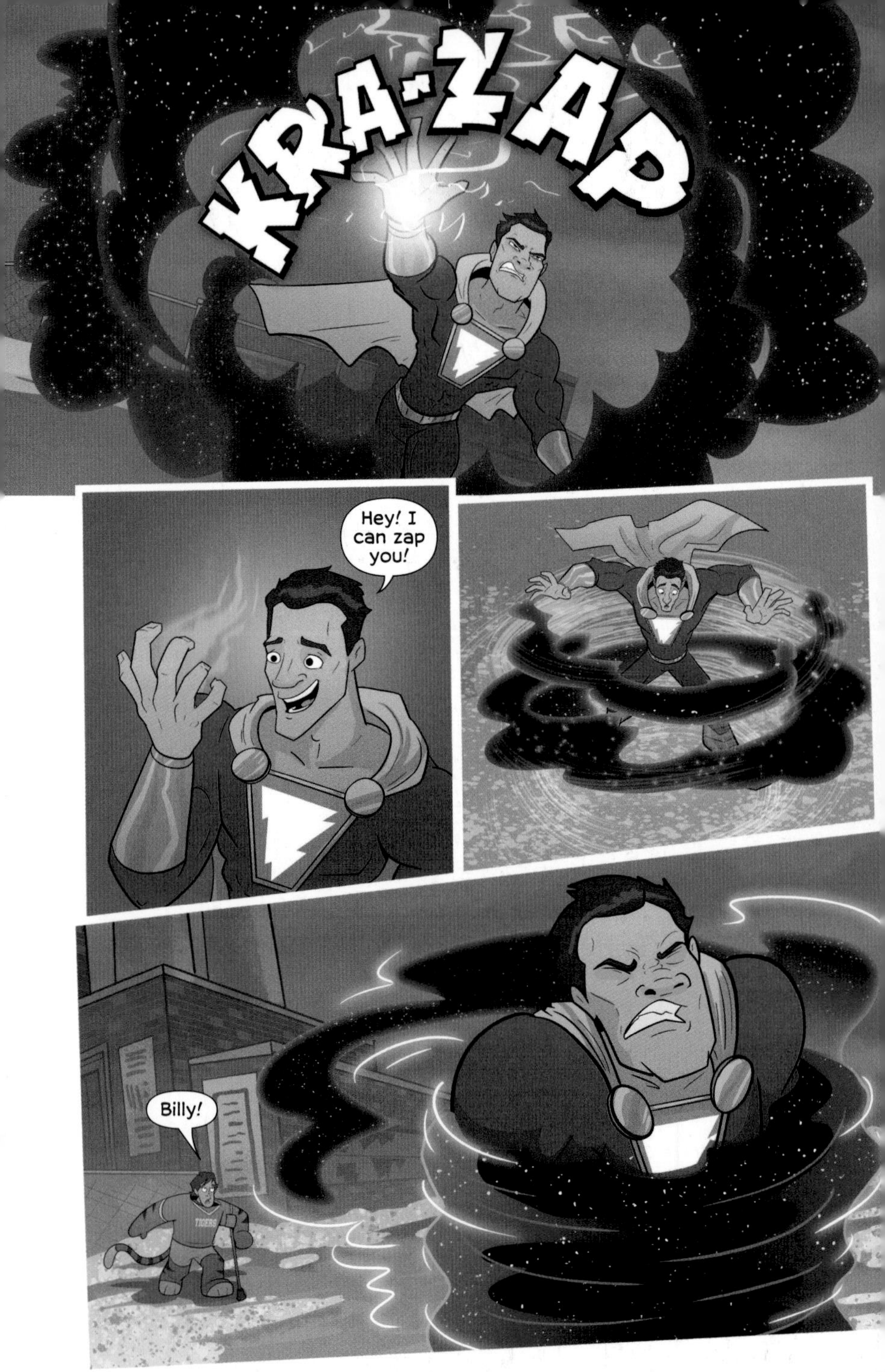
KRA-ZAP
Hey! I can zap you!
Billy!

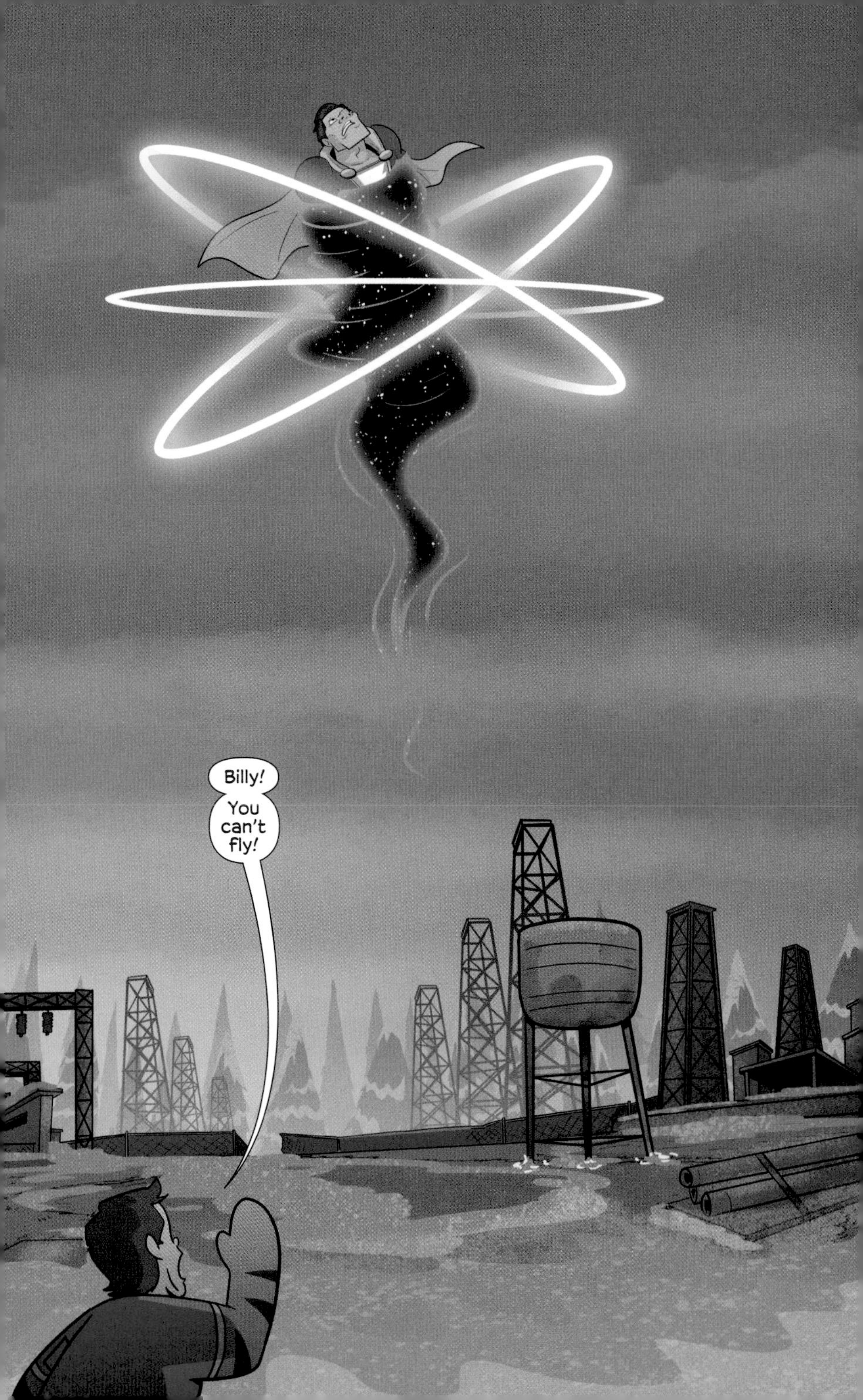
Billy!
You can't fly!

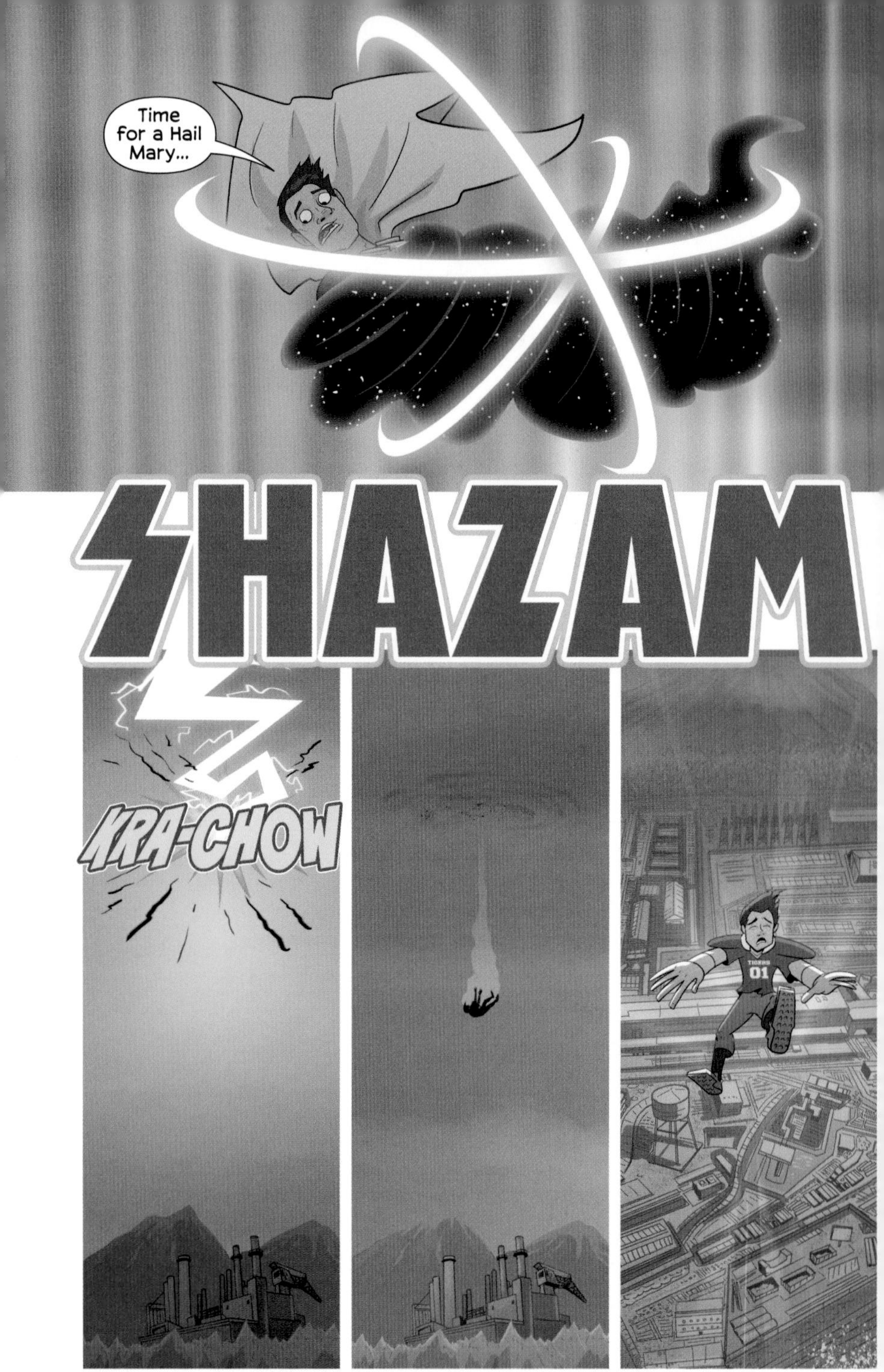
Time for a Hail Mary...
SHAZAM
KRA-CHOW
TIGERS 01

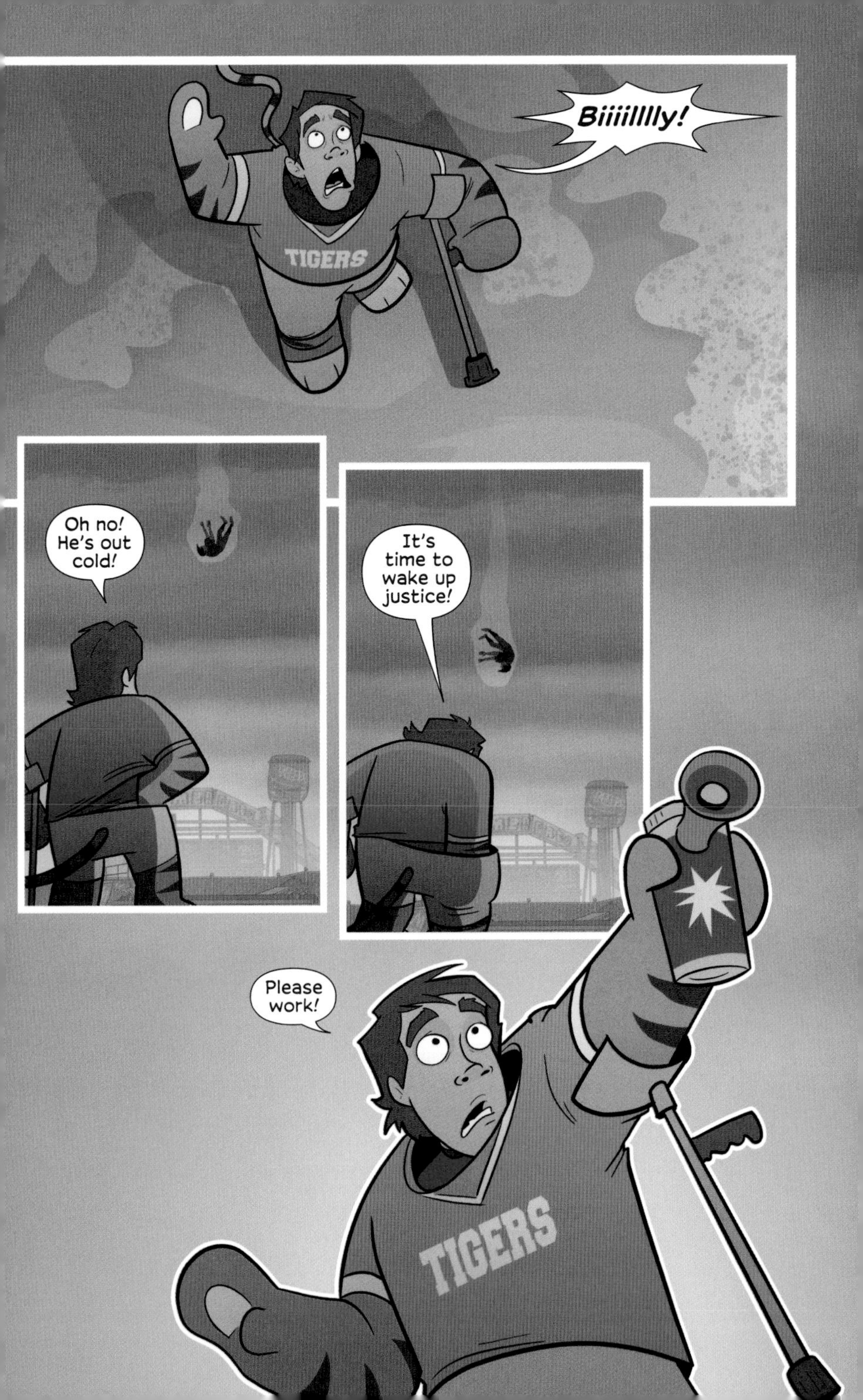
Biiiilllly!
Oh no! He's out cold!
It's time to wake up justice!
Please work!

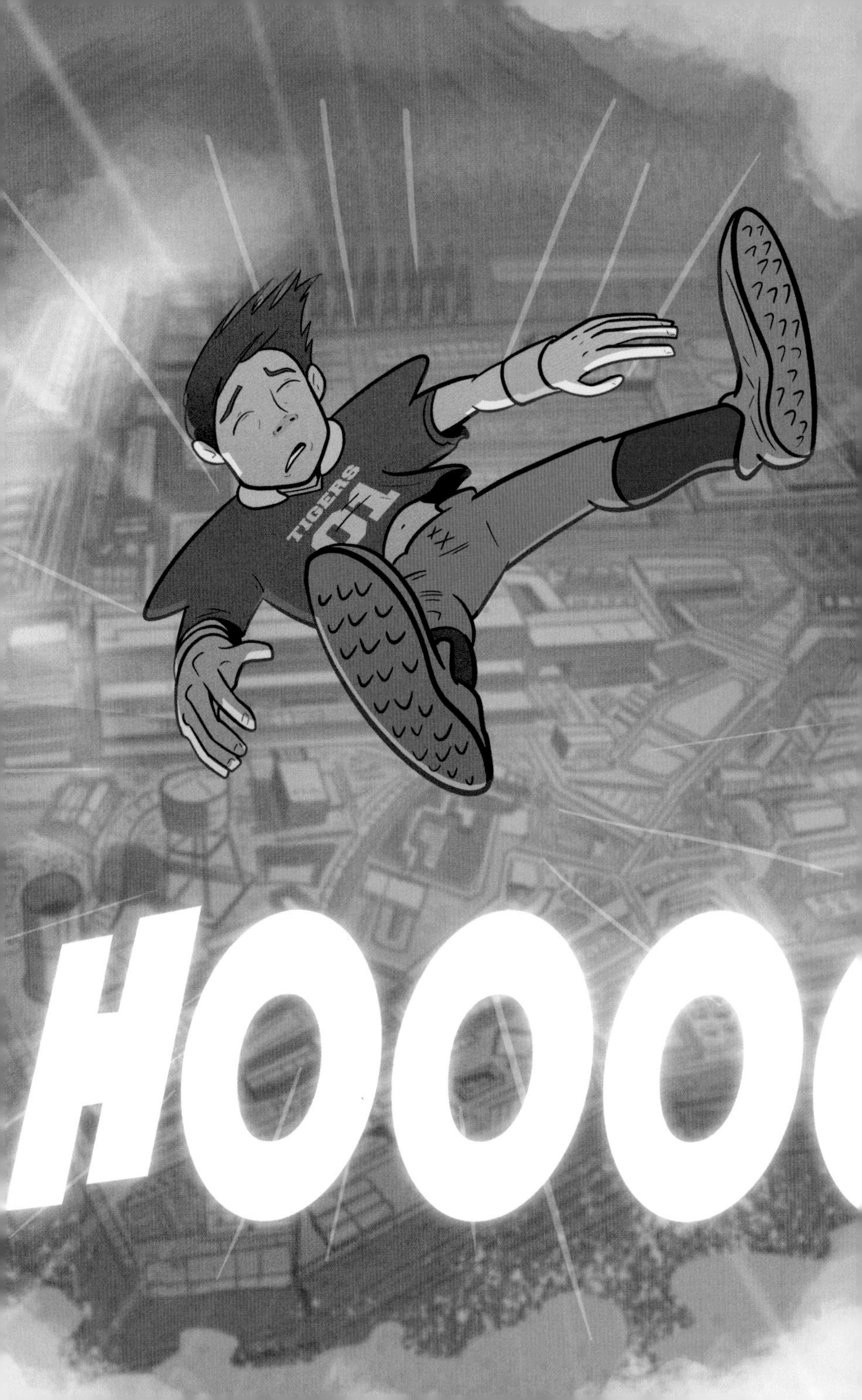
TIGERS
HOOO

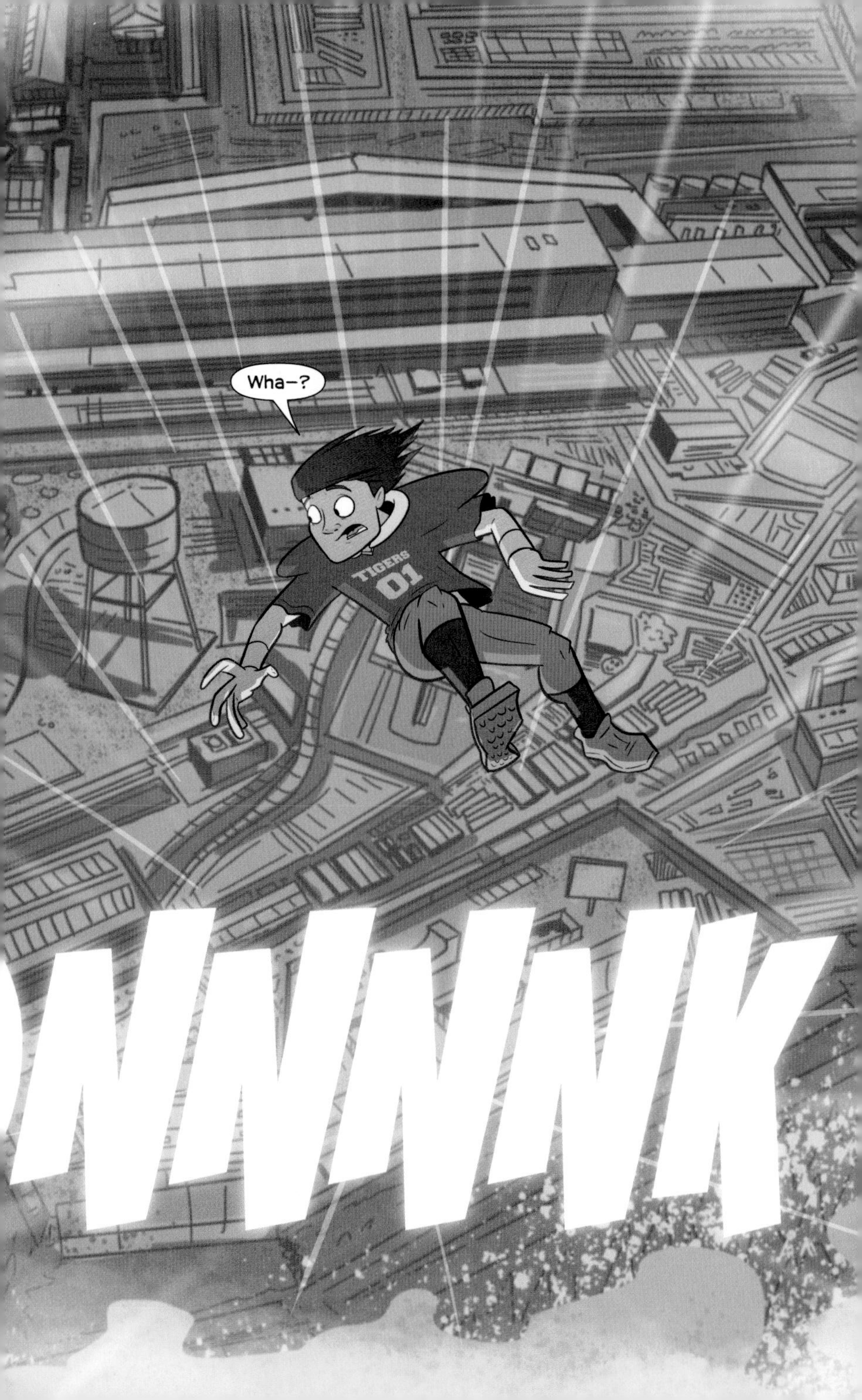
Wha–?
TIGERS 01
NNNNK

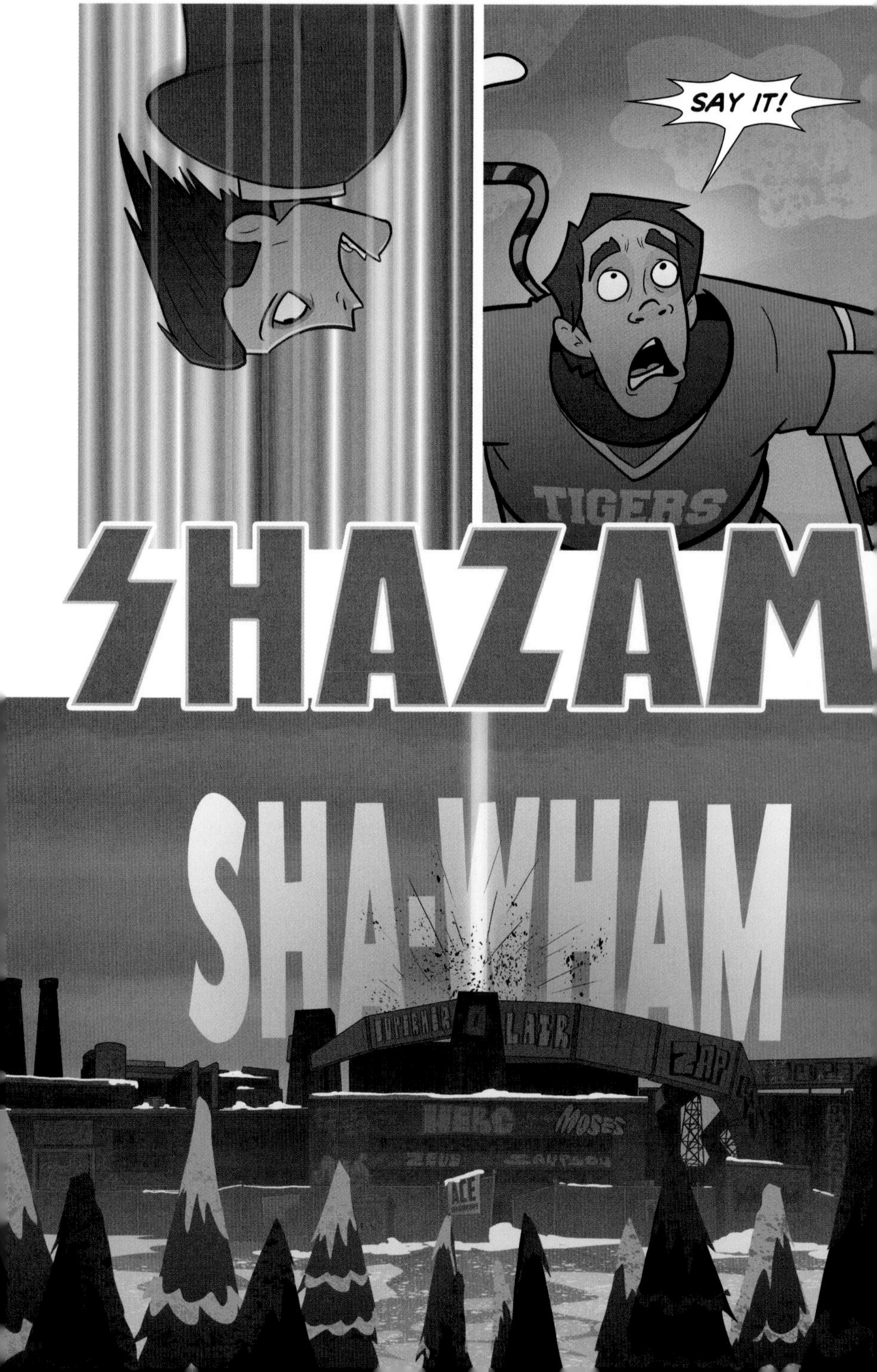
SAY IT!
TIGERS
SHAZAM
SHA-WHAM
MOSES
ACE

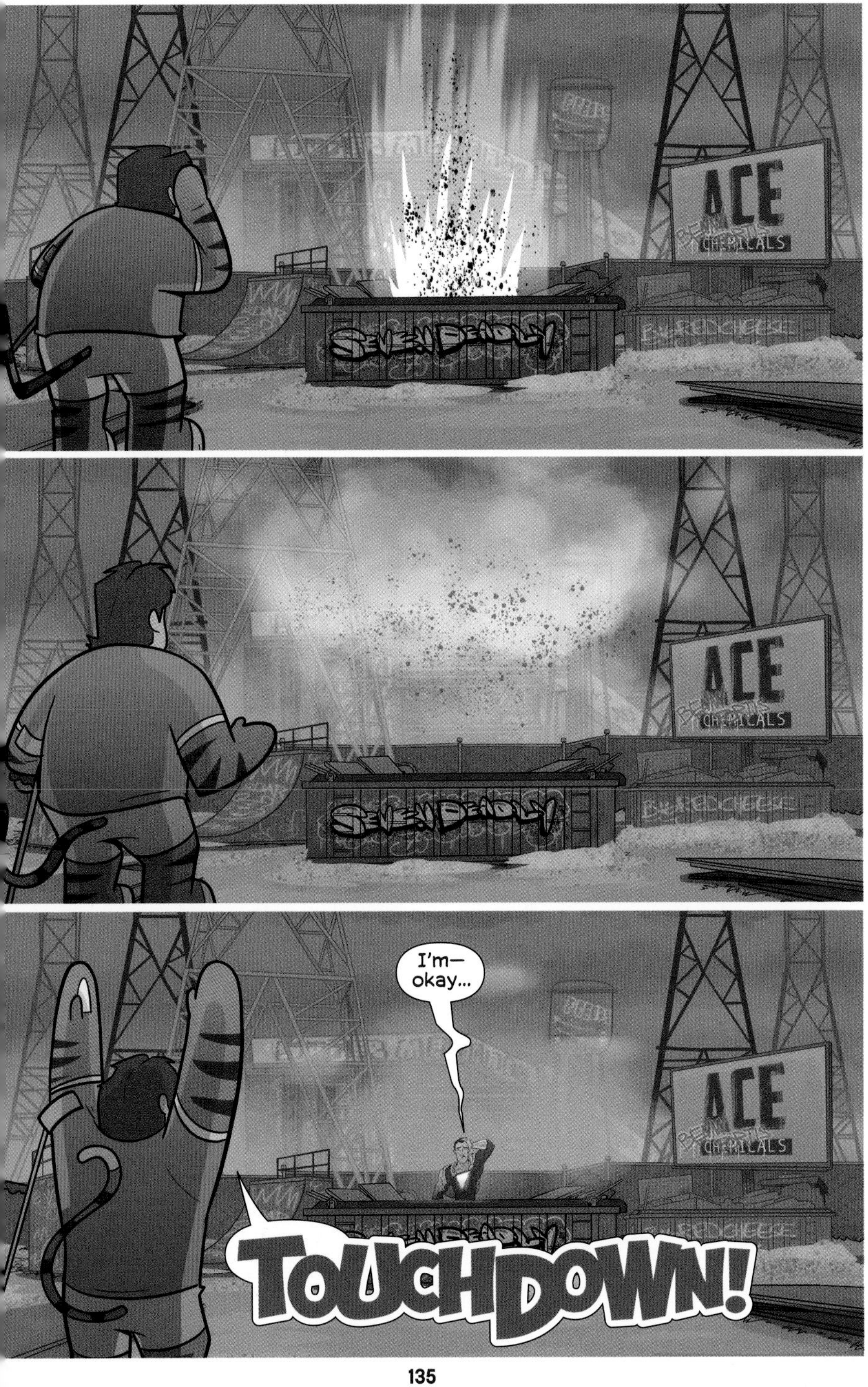
ACE
CHEMICALS
I'm—
okay...
TOUCHDOWN!

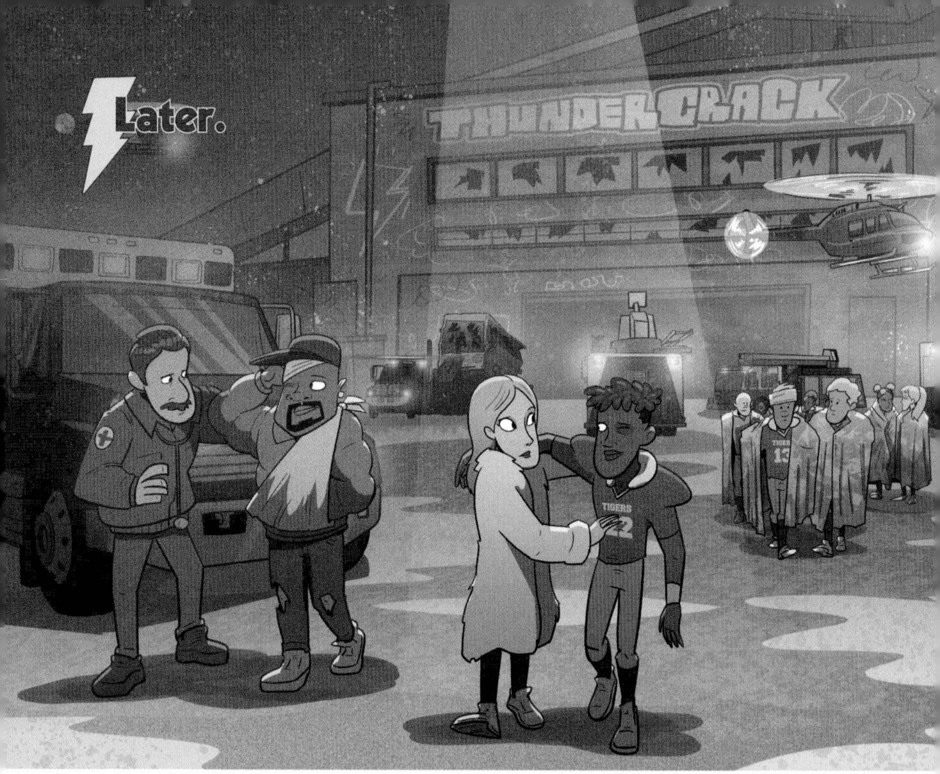
Later.
THUNDERCRACK
TIGERS 22
TIGERS 13

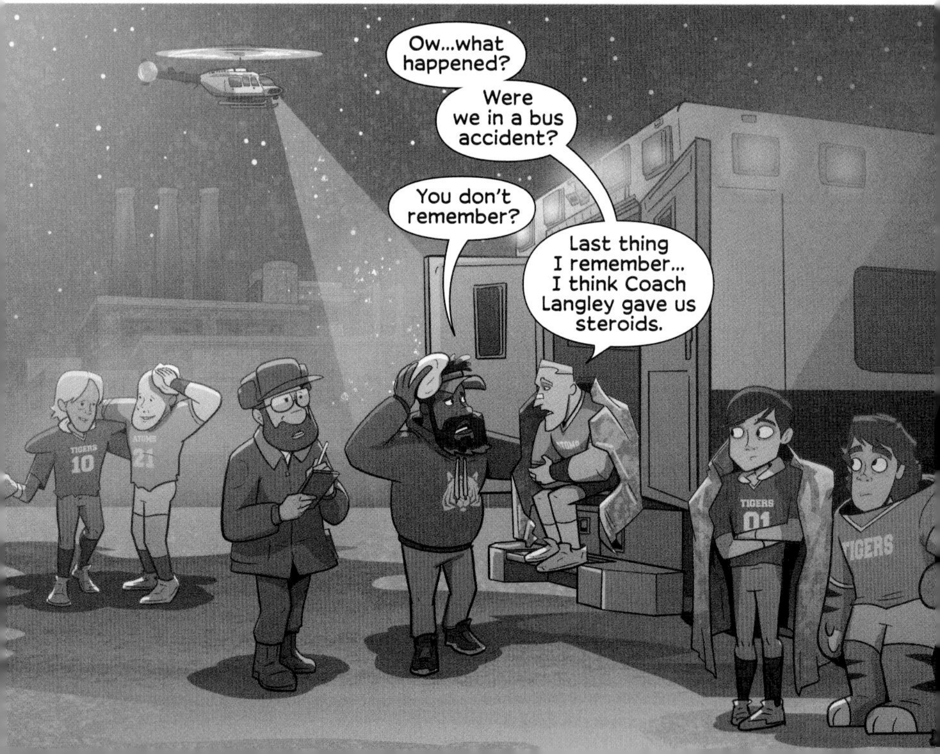
Ow...what happened?
Were we in a bus accident?
You don't remember?
Last thing I remember... I think Coach Langley gave us steroids.
TIGERS 10
TIGERS 01
TIGERS

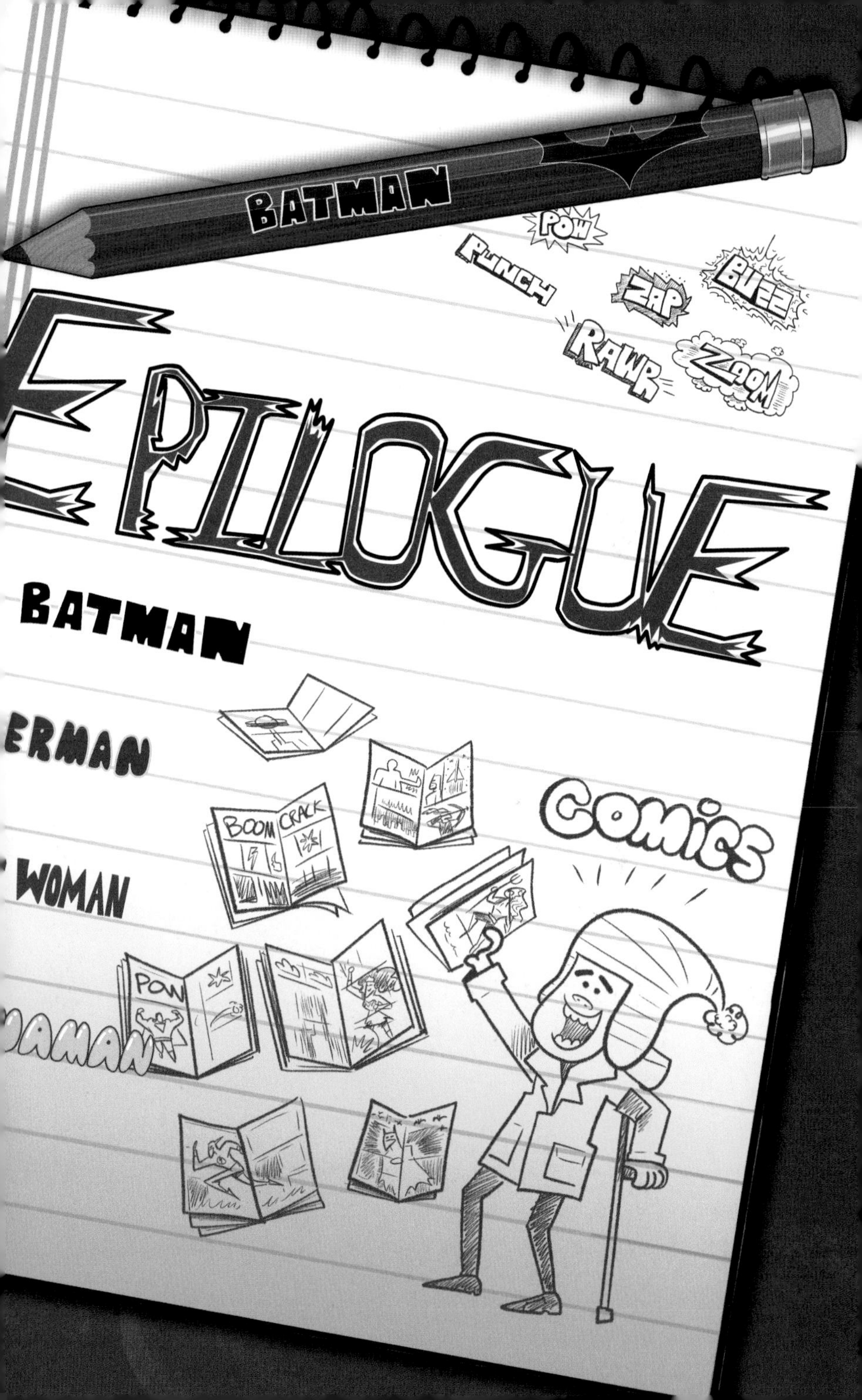

BATMAN
POW
PUNCH
ZAP
BUZZ
RAWR
ZOOM
EPILOGUE
BATMAN
WOMAN
COMICS
BOOM
CRACK
POW

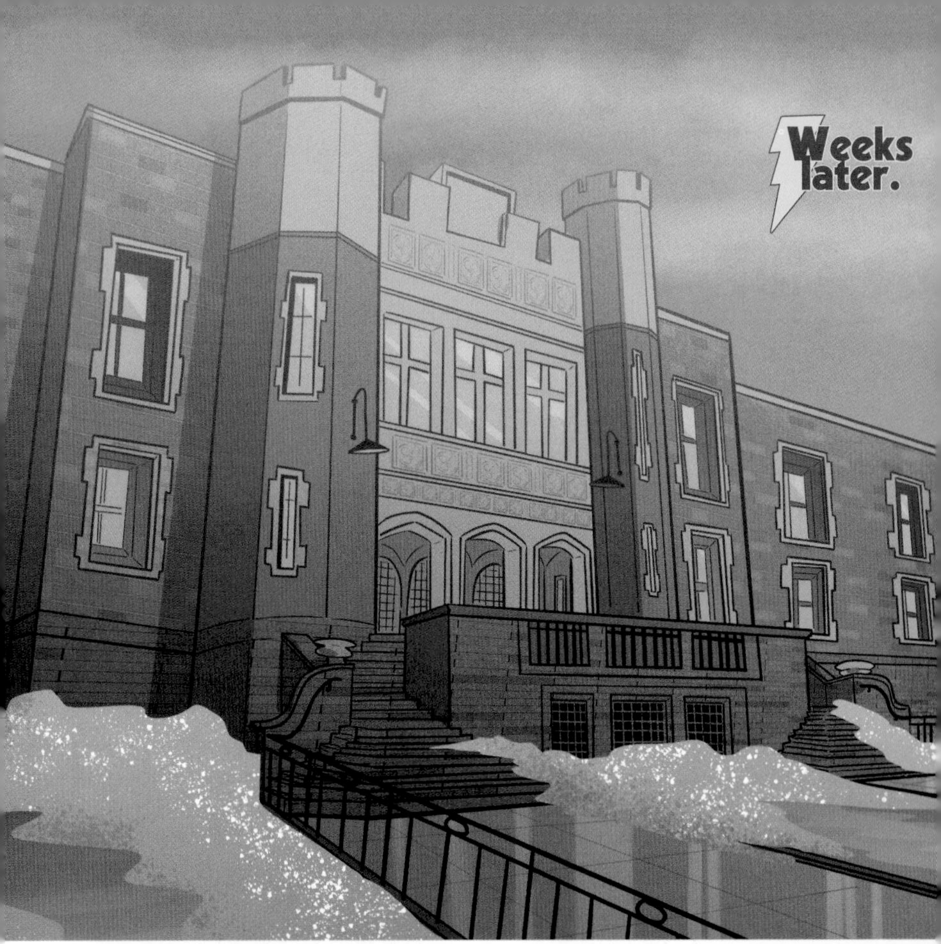
Weeks later.

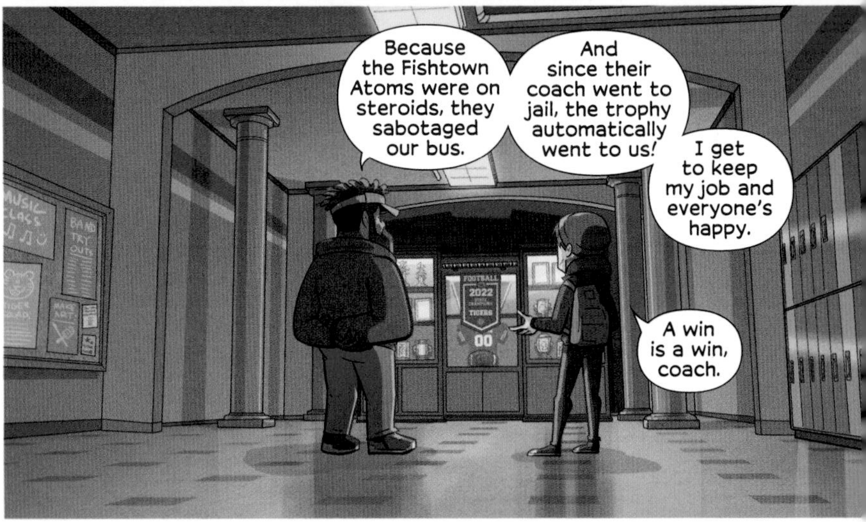
Because the Fishtown Atoms were on steroids, they sabotaged our bus.
And since their coach went to jail, the trophy automatically went to us!
I get to keep my job and everyone's happy.
A win is a win, coach.
MUSIC CLASS
BAND TRY OUTS
FOOTBALL
2022
TIGERS
00

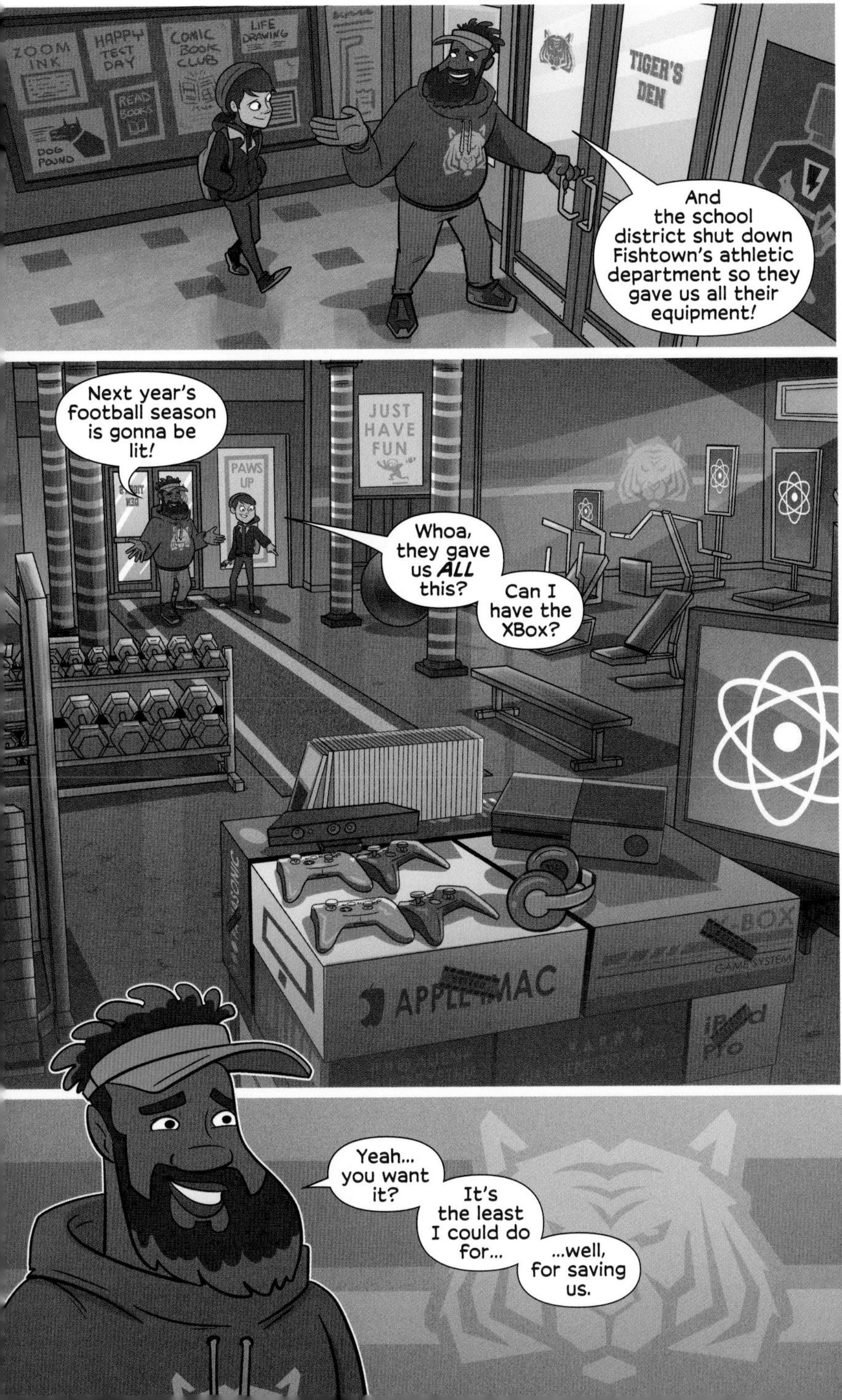
ZOOM INK
HAPPY TEST DAY
COMIC BOOK CLUB
LIFE DRAWING
READ BOOKS
DOG POUND
TIGER'S DEN
And the school district shut down Fishtown's athletic department so they gave us all their equipment!
Next year's football season is gonna be lit!
PAWS UP
JUST HAVE FUN
Whoa, they gave us *ALL* this?
Can I have the XBox?
GAME SYSTEM
Yeah... you want it?
It's the least I could do for...
...well, for saving us.

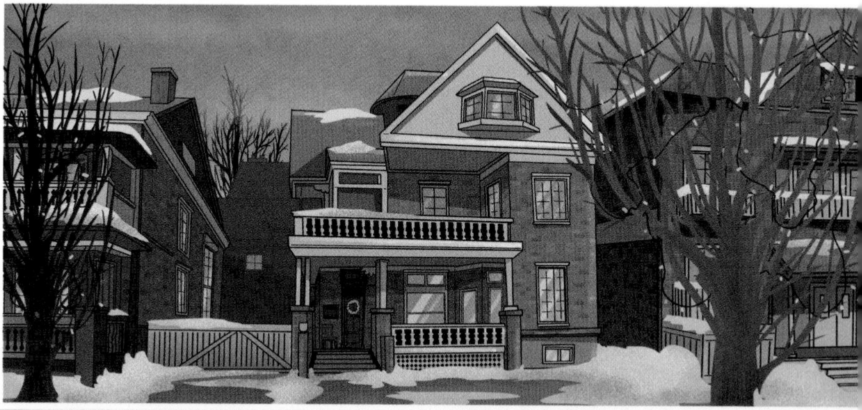

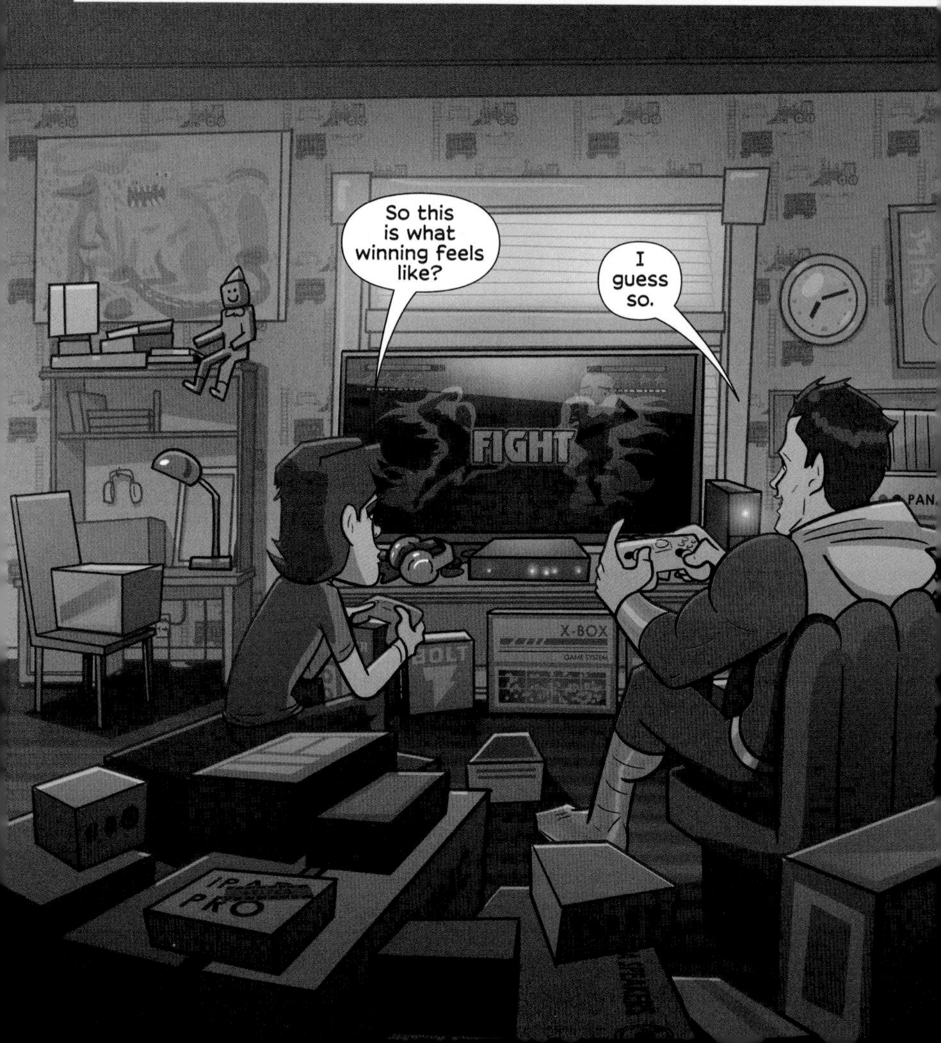
So this is what winning feels like?
I guess so.
FIGHT
X-BOX
GAME SYSTEM
BOLT

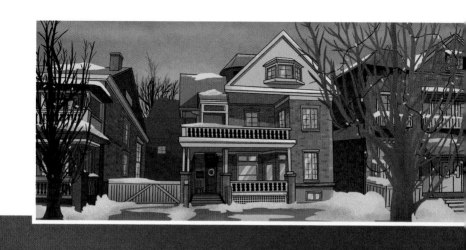

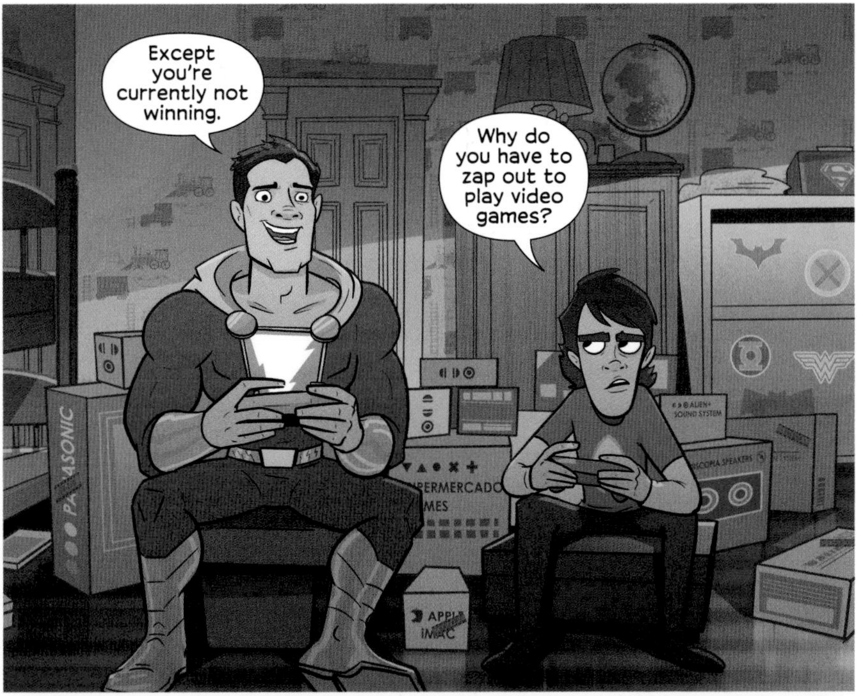
Except you're currently not winning.
Why do you have to zap out to play video games?
PANASONIC
SUPERMERCADO GAMES
ALIEN+ SOUND SYSTEM
APPLE iMAC

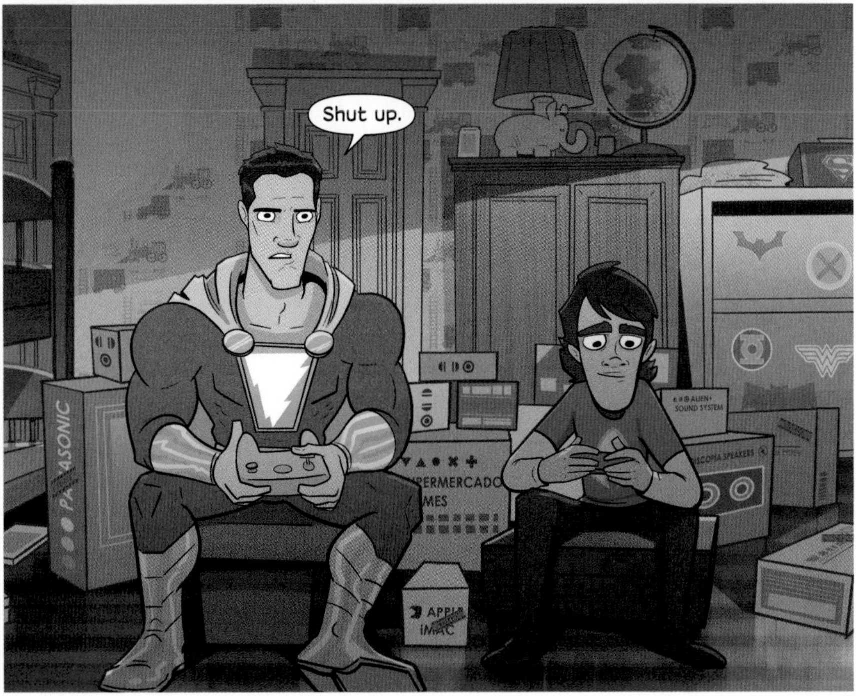
Shut up.
PANASONIC
SUPERMERCADO GAMES
ALIEN+ SOUND SYSTEM
APPLE iMAC

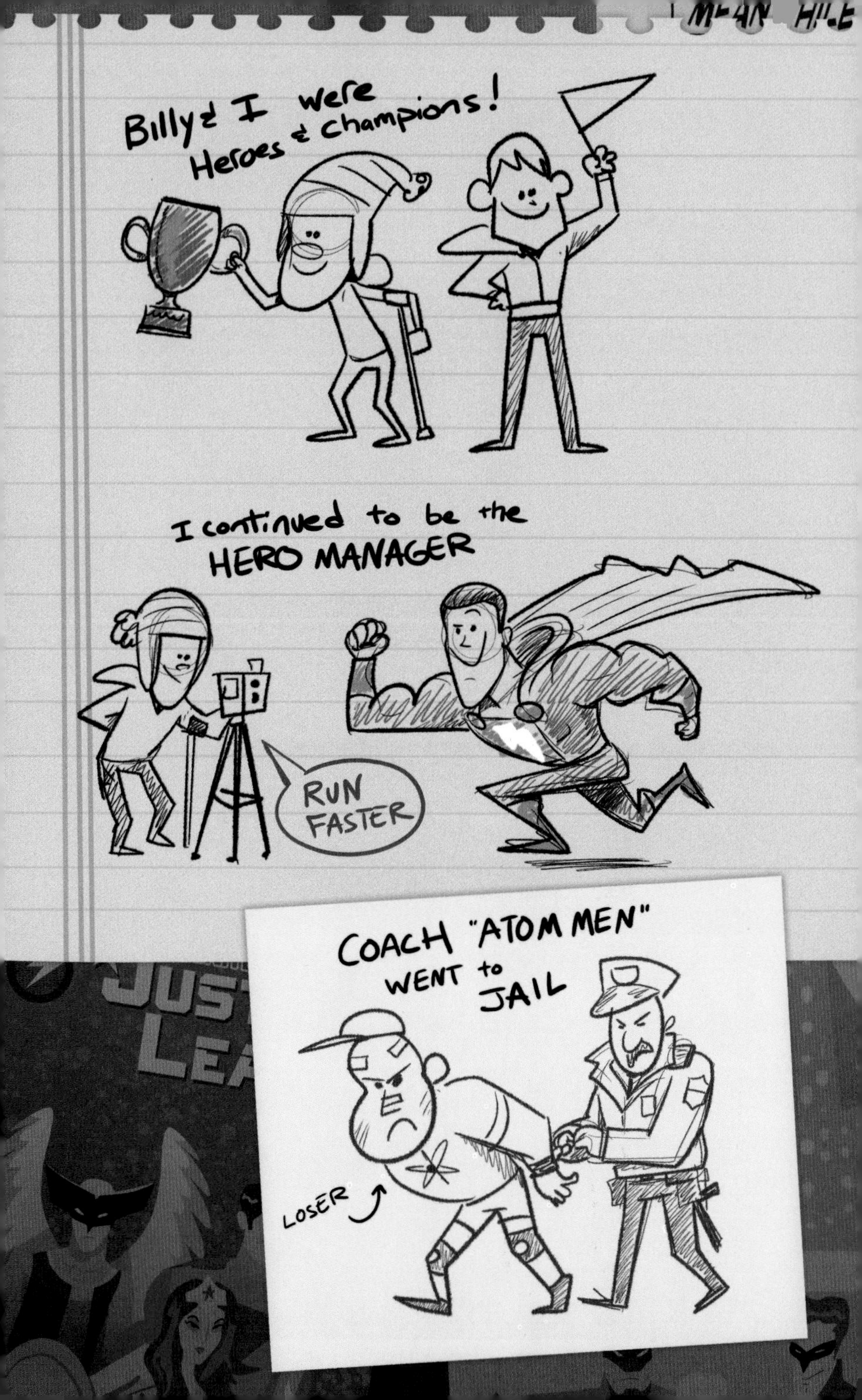
Billy & I were Heroes & champions!
I continued to be the HERO MANAGER
RUN FASTER
COACH "ATOM MEN" WENT to JAIL
LOSER

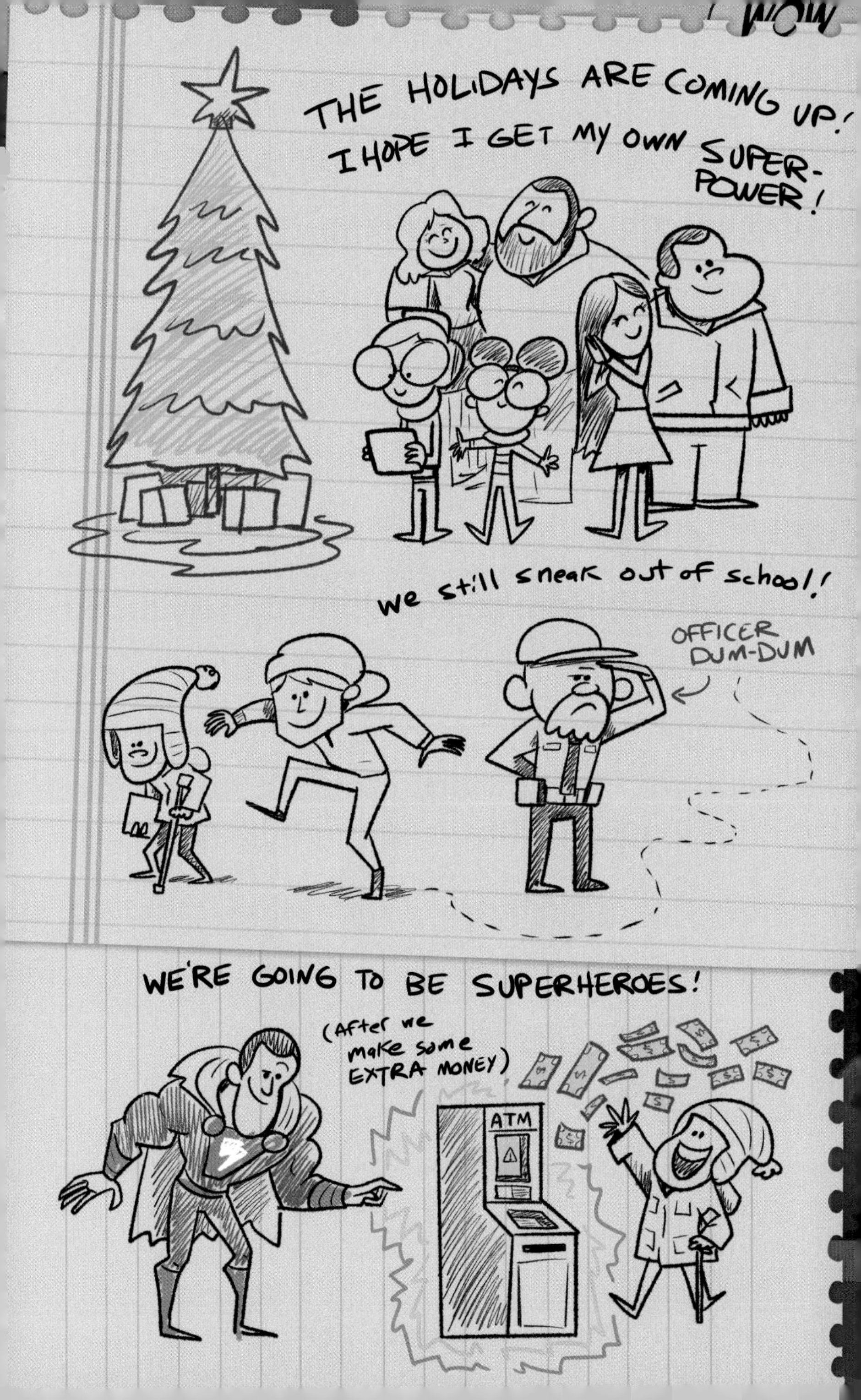
THE HOLIDAYS ARE COMING UP!
I HOPE I GET MY OWN SUPER-POWER!
we still sneak out of school!
OFFICER DUM-DUM
WE'RE GOING TO BE SUPERHEROES!
(After we make some EXTRA MONEY)
ATM

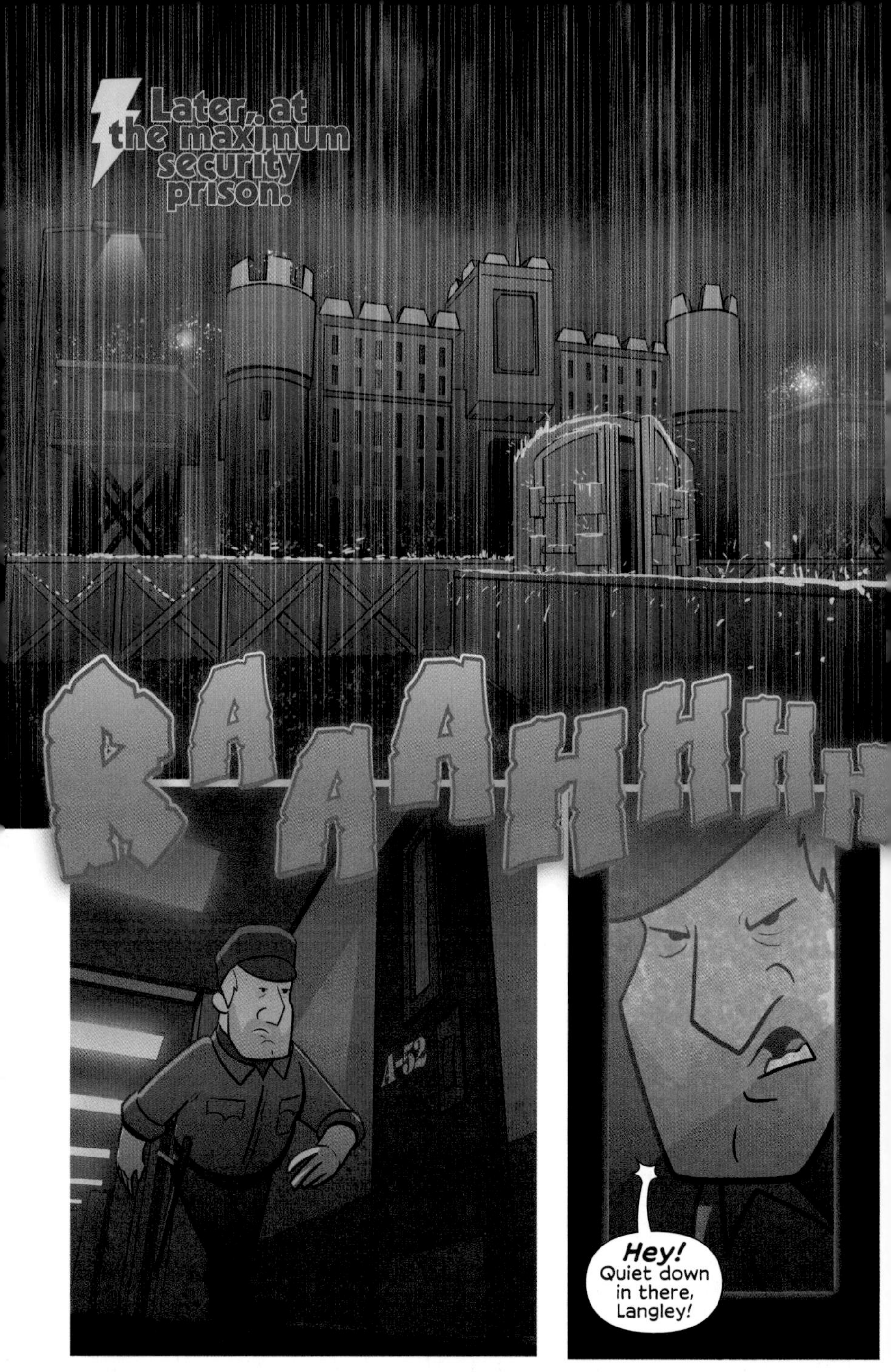
Later, at the maximum security prison.
RAAHHHH
A-52
Hey! Quiet down in there, Langley!

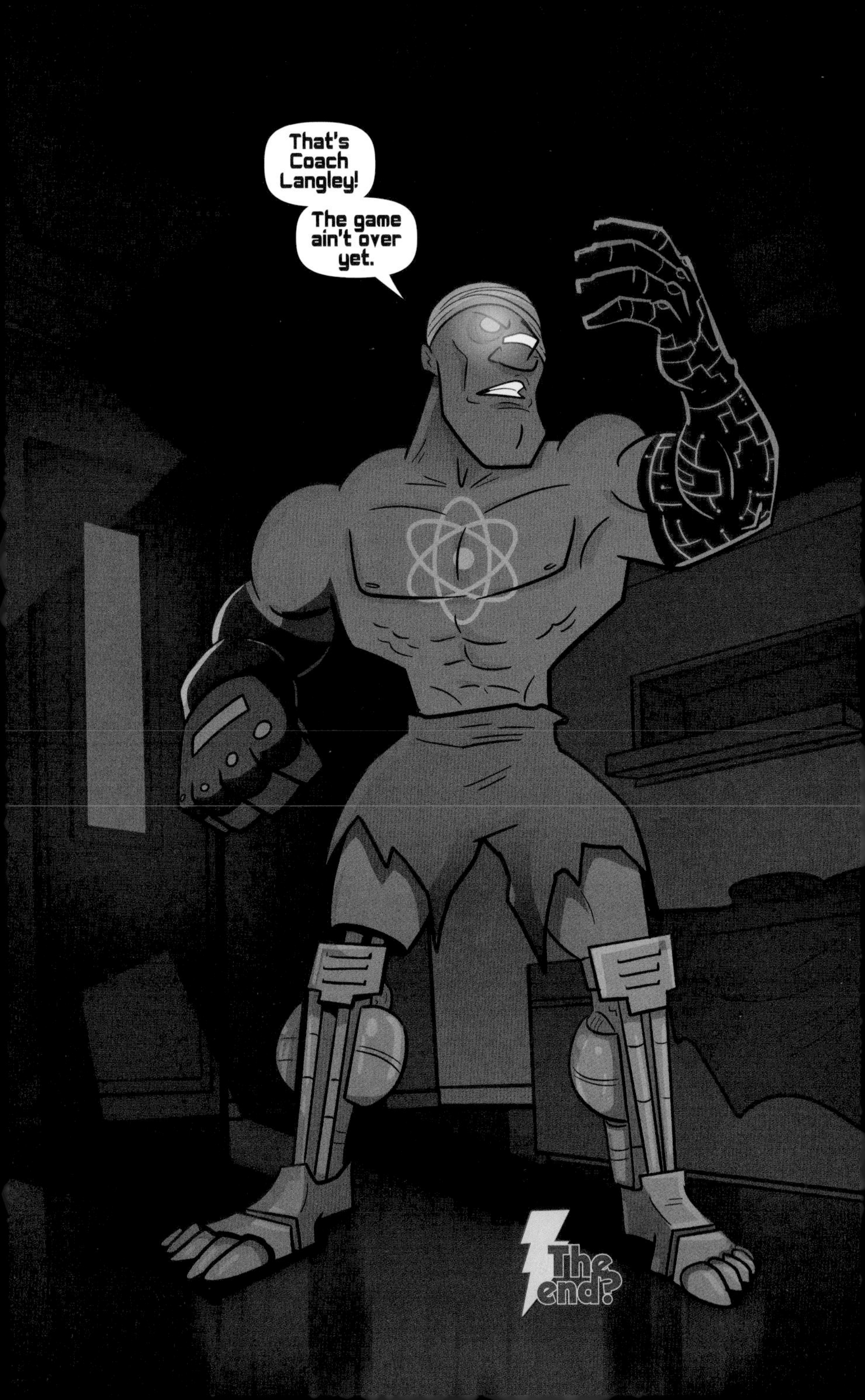
That's Coach Langley!
The game ain't over yet.
The end?

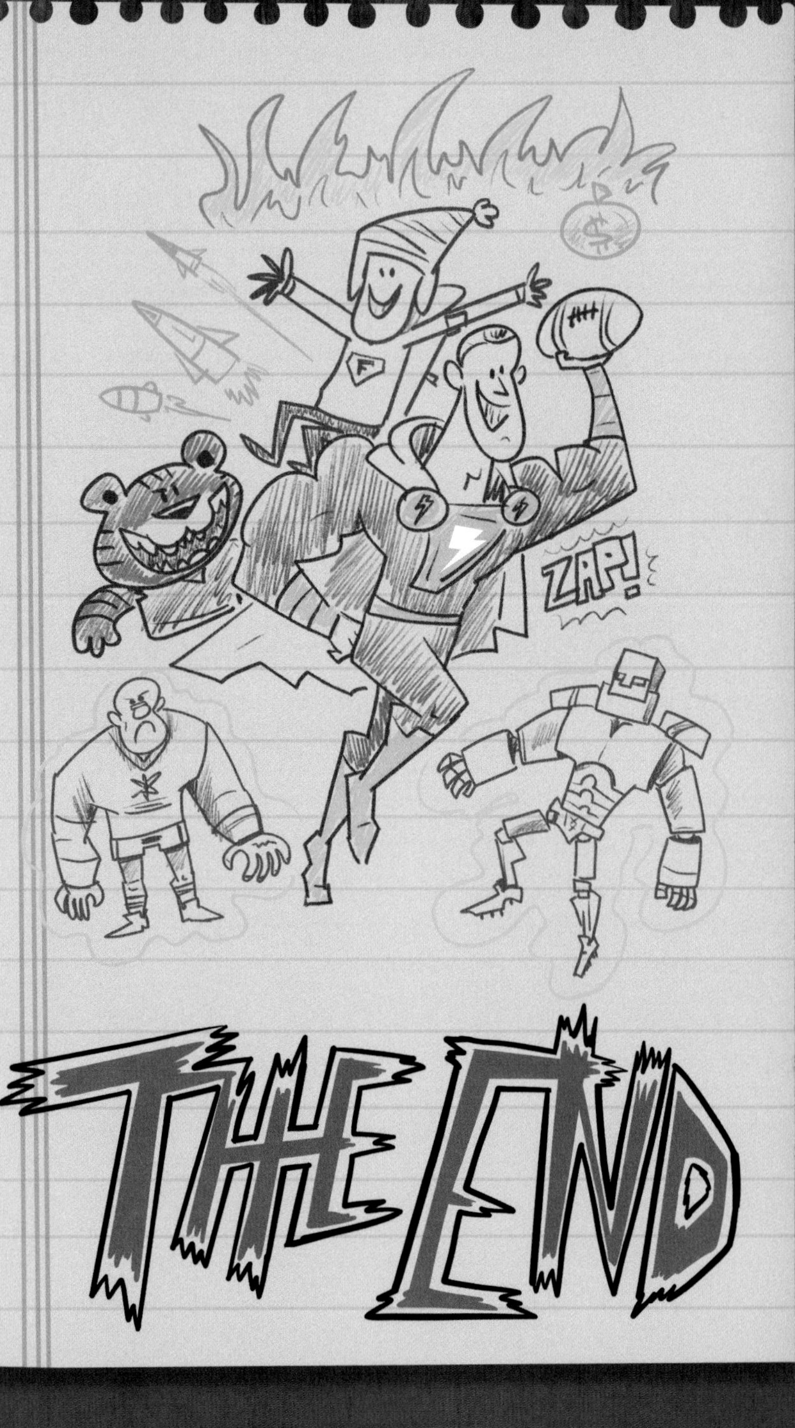
ZAP!

THE END

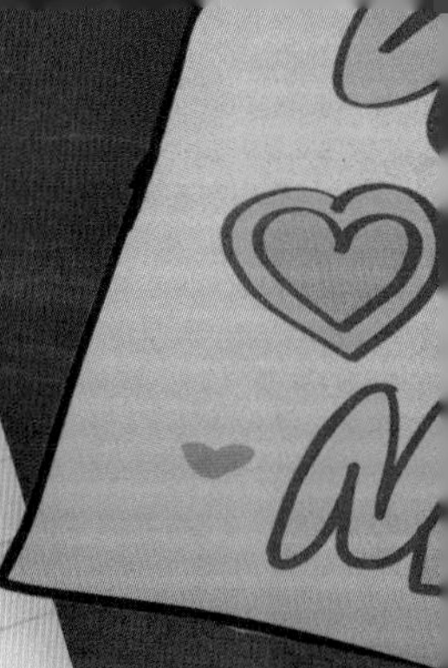

ehudi Mercado was born in Mexico City and grew up in Houston, Texas. He spent high school in the theater department putting on plays. After college he worked in video games and eventually became an art director for Disney Interactive, where he co-wrote and art directed the Guardians of the Galaxy mobile game. His graphic novels include *Chunky*, *Hero Hotel*, *Rocket Salvage*, *Fun Fun Fun World*, and *Sci-Fu*, and he was the artist on the Epic Originals graphic novel *Cat Ninja*. Yehudi created a narrative podcast based on his graphic novel *Hero Hotel* for Pinna. He has adorable dogs named Bucky and Bosco and usually sneaks one of his pets into his books.

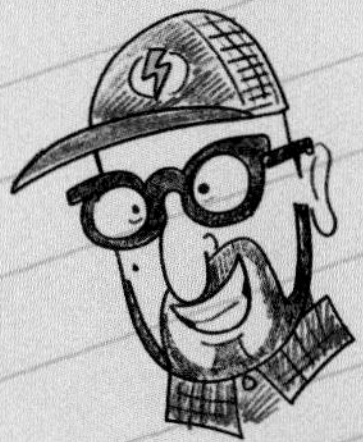

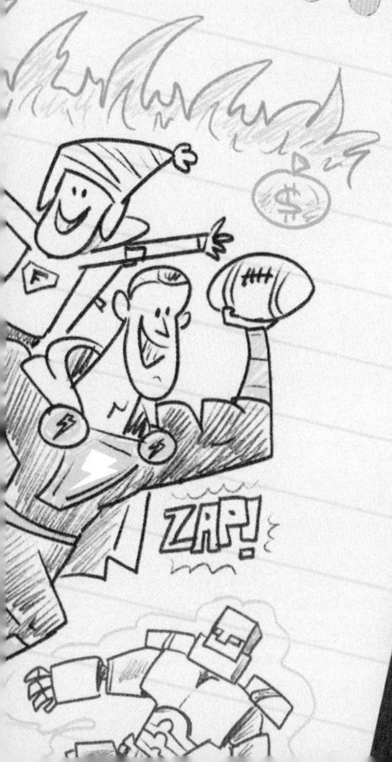

ZAP!

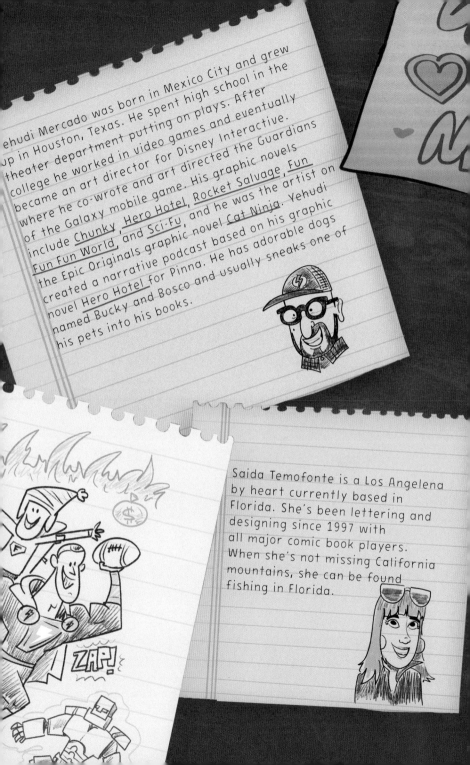

Saida Temofonte is a Los Angelena by heart currently based in Florida. She's been lettering and designing since 1997 with all major comic book players. When she's not missing California mountains, she can be found fishing in Florida.

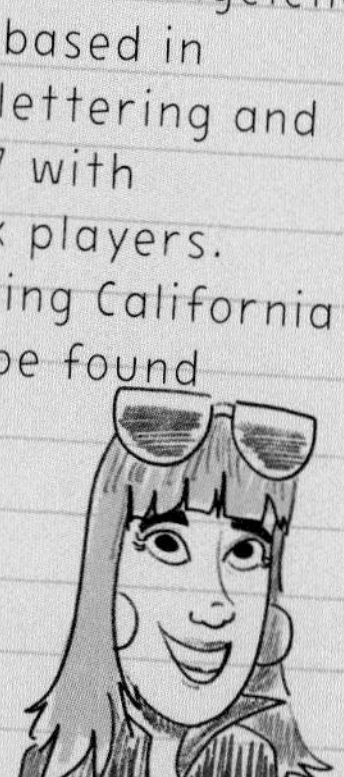

Have you ever felt like you didn't quite fit in

Bruce Wayne knows all about that...being the only kid in his whole school without any powers and all. And when he gets pulled into the principal's office because his career choice of vigilantism is deemed too ambitious, Bruce becomes more determined than ever to prove that he can be just as cool as the supers that give him a hard time. But first, he has to find the right disguise and gadgets...oh, and the perfect hideout.

Stuart Gibbs and **Berat Pekmezci** will keep you laughing as Bruce takes on your favorite DC characters!

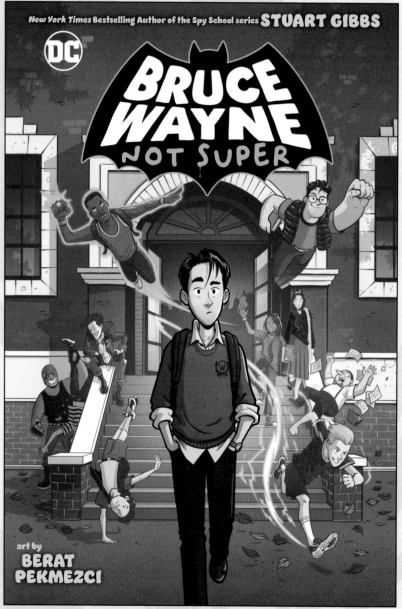

Coming March 2023!

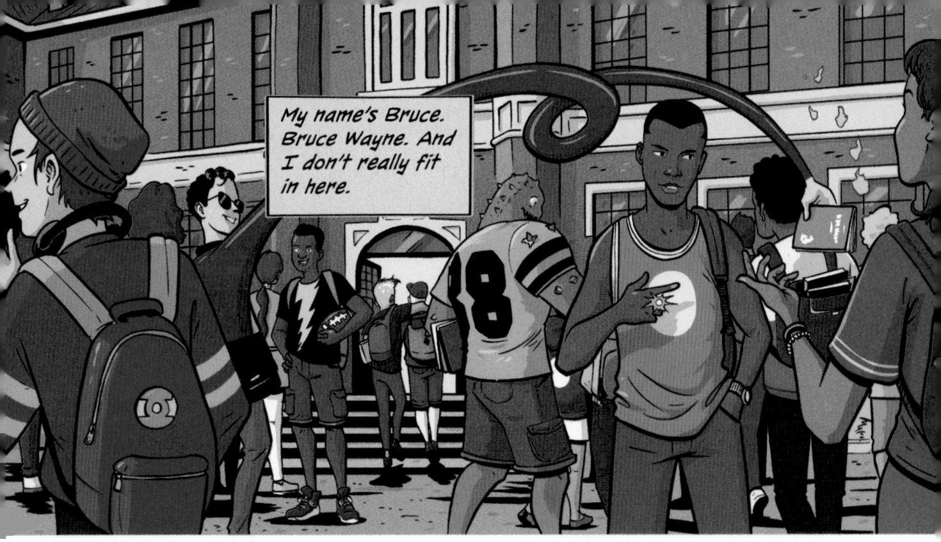
My name's Bruce. Bruce Wayne. And I don't really fit in here.

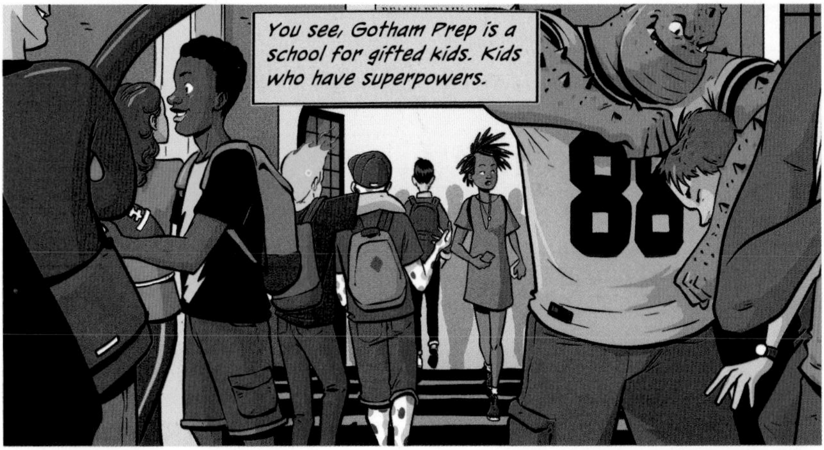
You see, Gotham Prep is a school for gifted kids. Kids who have superpowers.

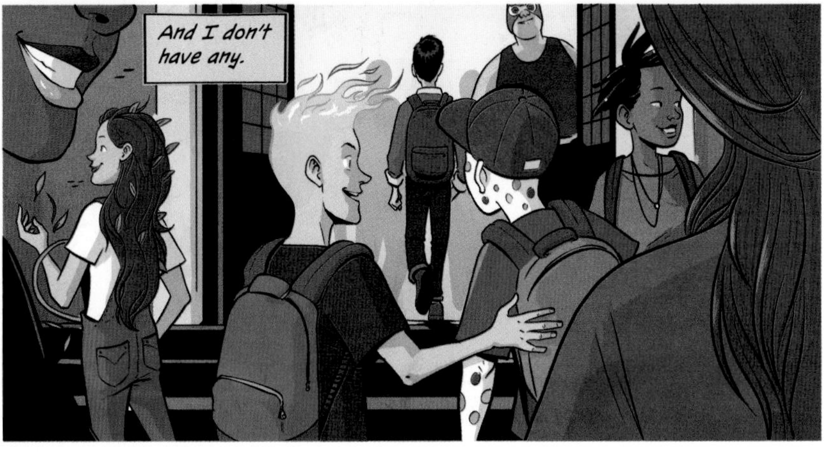
And I don't have any.

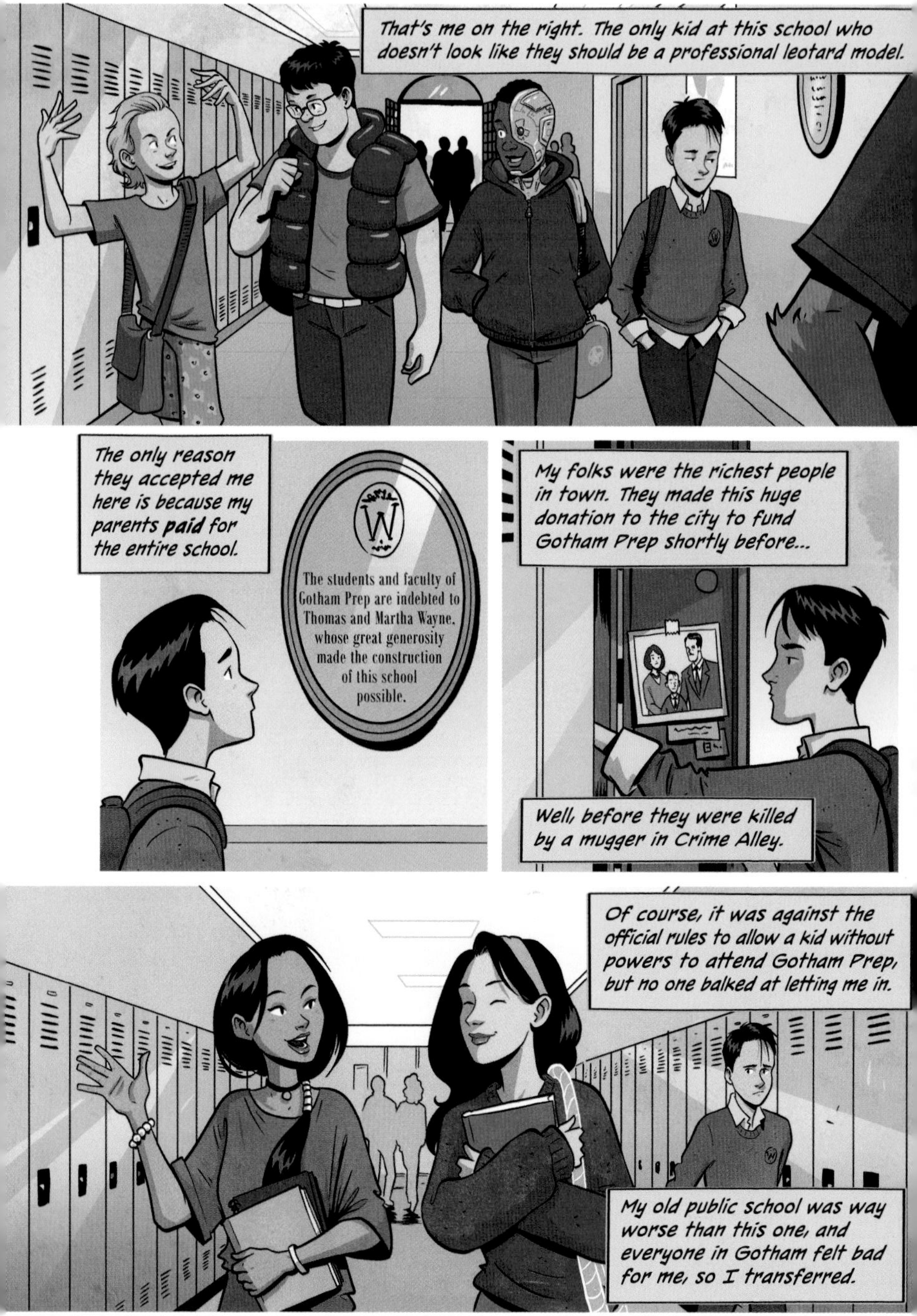

That's me on the right. The only kid at this school who doesn't look like they should be a professional leotard model.
The only reason they accepted me here is because my parents **paid** for the entire school.
The students and faculty of Gotham Prep are indebted to Thomas and Martha Wayne, whose great generosity made the construction of this school possible.
My folks were the richest people in town. They made this huge donation to the city to fund Gotham Prep shortly before...
Well, before they were killed by a mugger in Crime Alley.
Of course, it was against the official rules to allow a kid without powers to attend Gotham Prep, but no one balked at letting me in.
My old public school was way worse than this one, and everyone in Gotham felt bad for me, so I transferred.

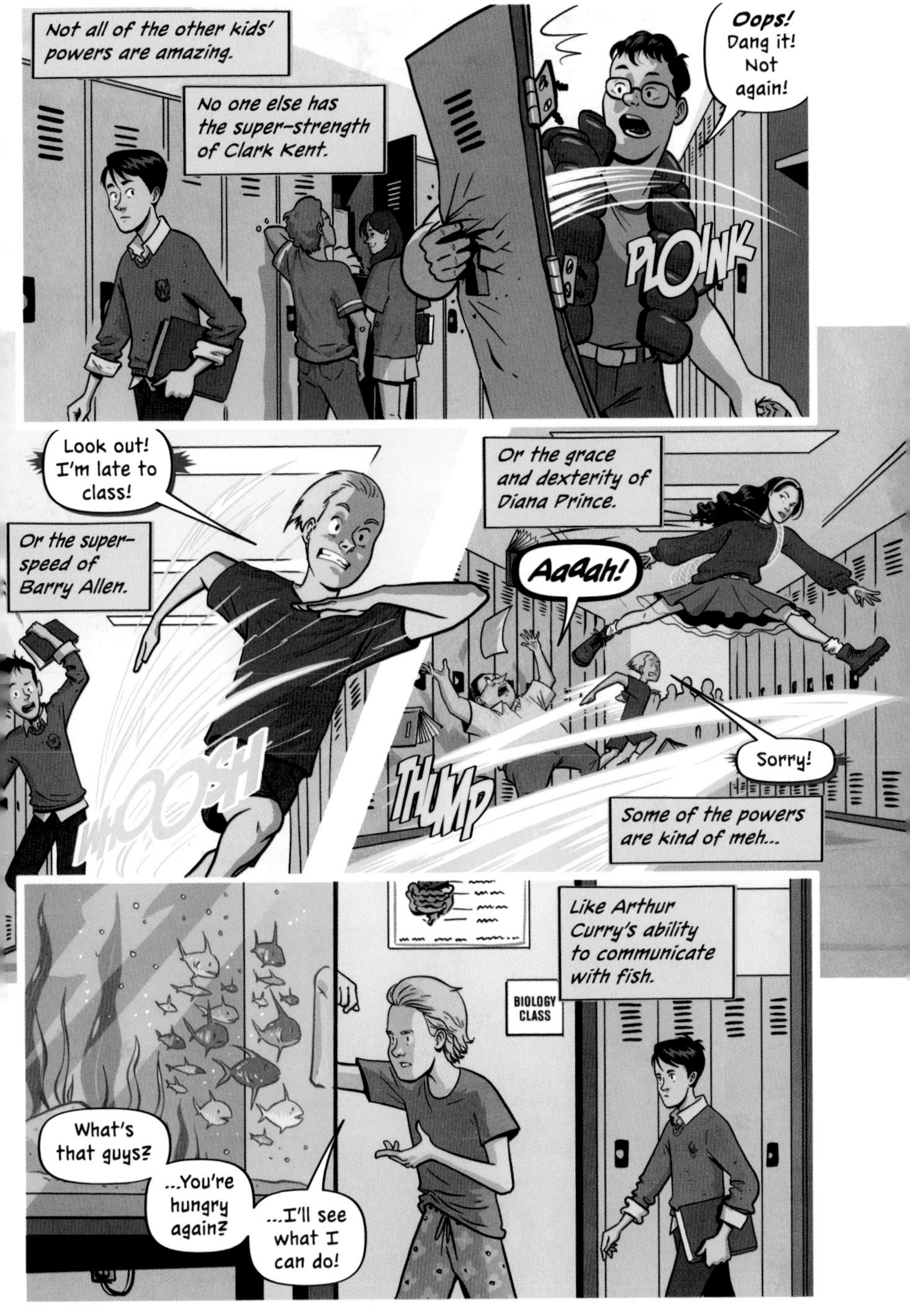
Not all of the other kids' powers are amazing.
No one else has the super-strength of Clark Kent.
Oops! Dang it! Not again!
PLOINK
Look out! I'm late to class!
Or the super-speed of Barry Allen.
WHOOSH
Or the grace and dexterity of Diana Prince.
Aaaah!
THUMP
Sorry!
Some of the powers are kind of meh...
Like Arthur Curry's ability to communicate with fish.
BIOLOGY CLASS
What's that guys?
...You're hungry again?
...I'll see what I can do!

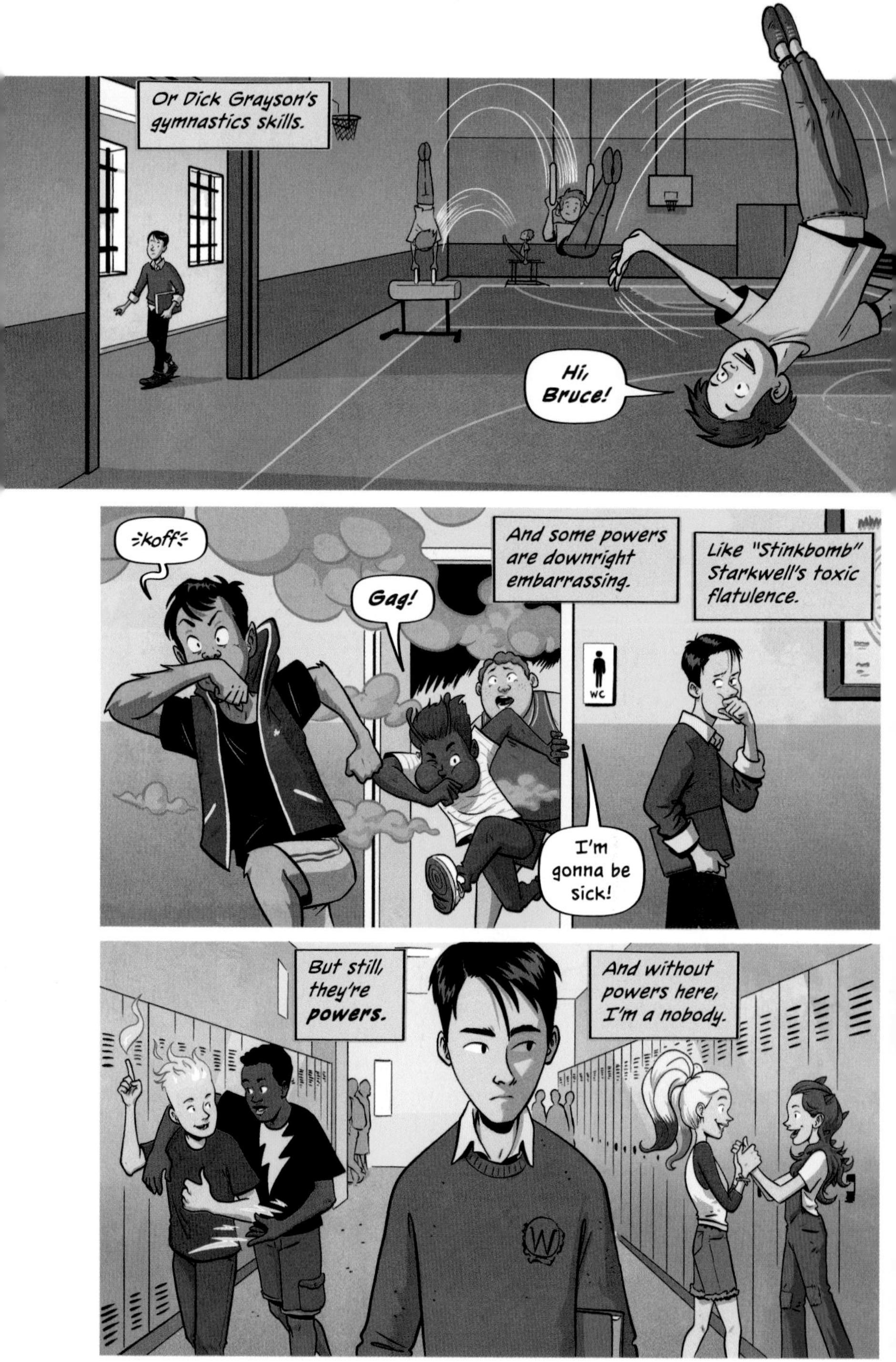
Or Dick Grayson's gymnastics skills.
Hi, Bruce!
koff
Gag!
And some powers are downright embarrassing.
Like "Stinkbomb" Starkwell's toxic flatulence.
WC
I'm gonna be sick!
But still, they're powers.
And without powers here, I'm a nobody.

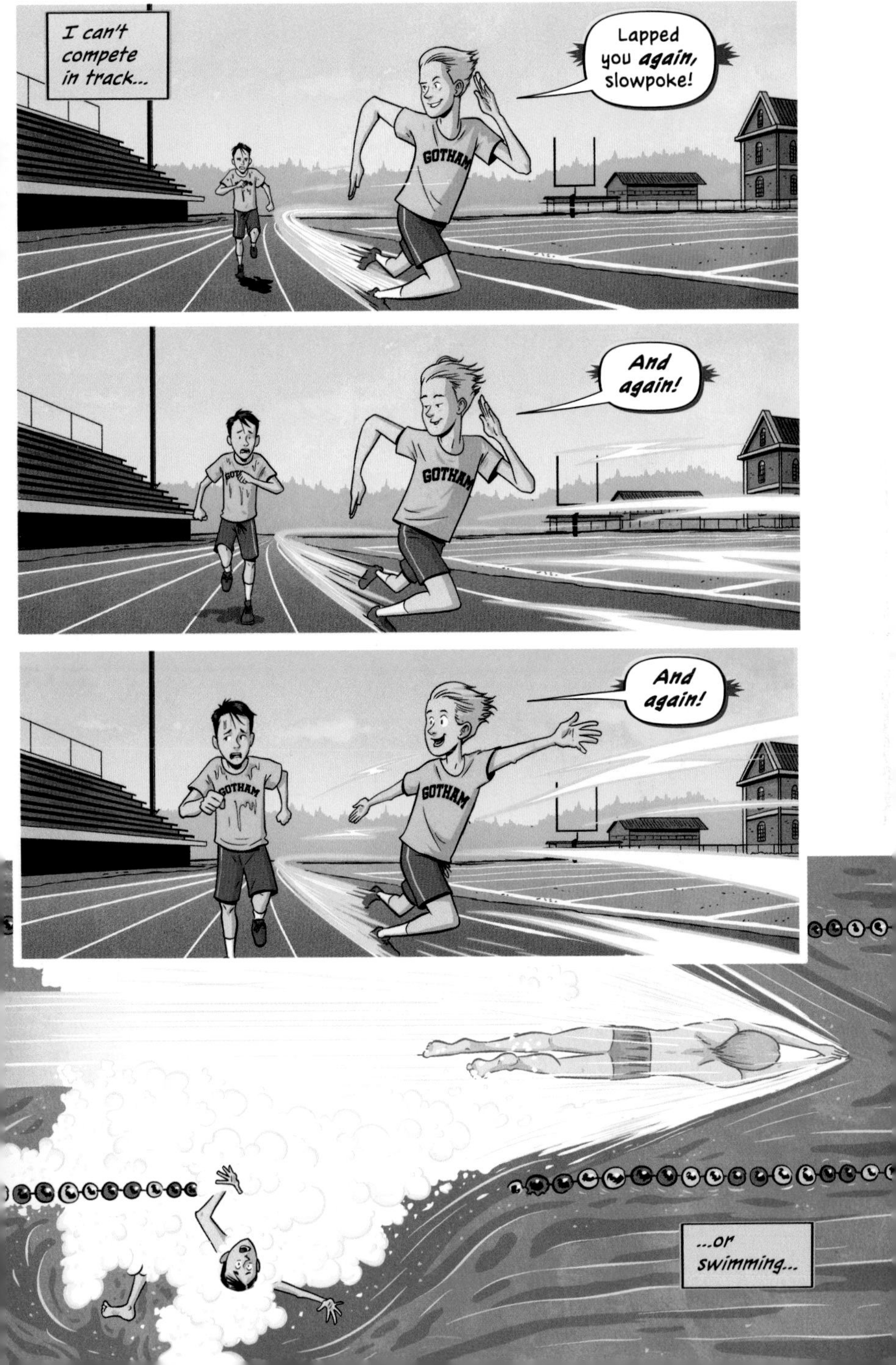
I can't compete in track...
Lapped you again, slowpoke!
And again!
And again!
...or swimming...

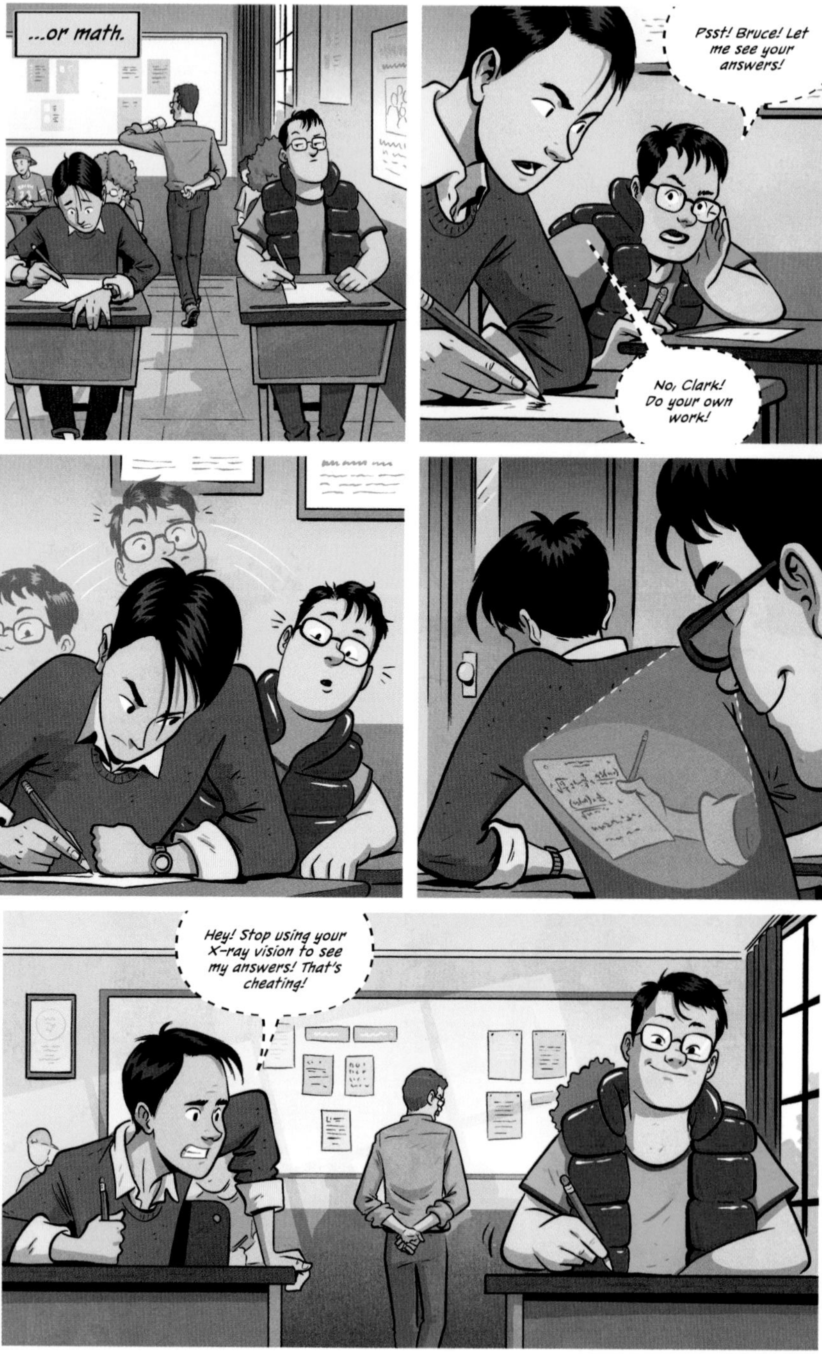
...or math.
Psst! Bruce! Let me see your answers!
No, Clark! Do your own work!
Hey! Stop using your X-ray vision to see my answers! That's cheating!

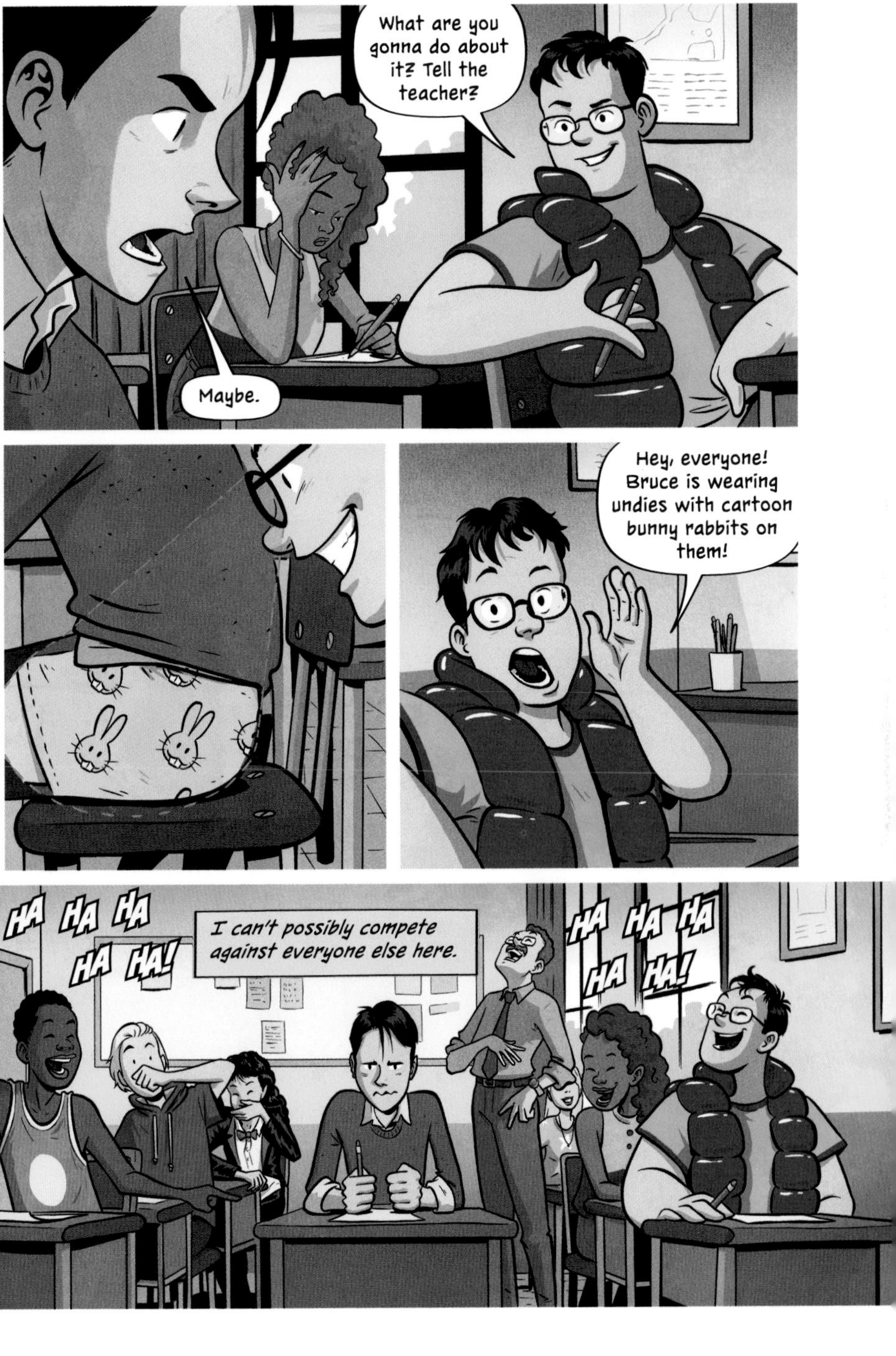
What are you gonna do about it? Tell the teacher?
Maybe.
Hey, everyone! Bruce is wearing undies with cartoon bunny rabbits on them!
HA HA HA HA HA!
I can't possibly compete against everyone else here.
HA HA HA HA HA!

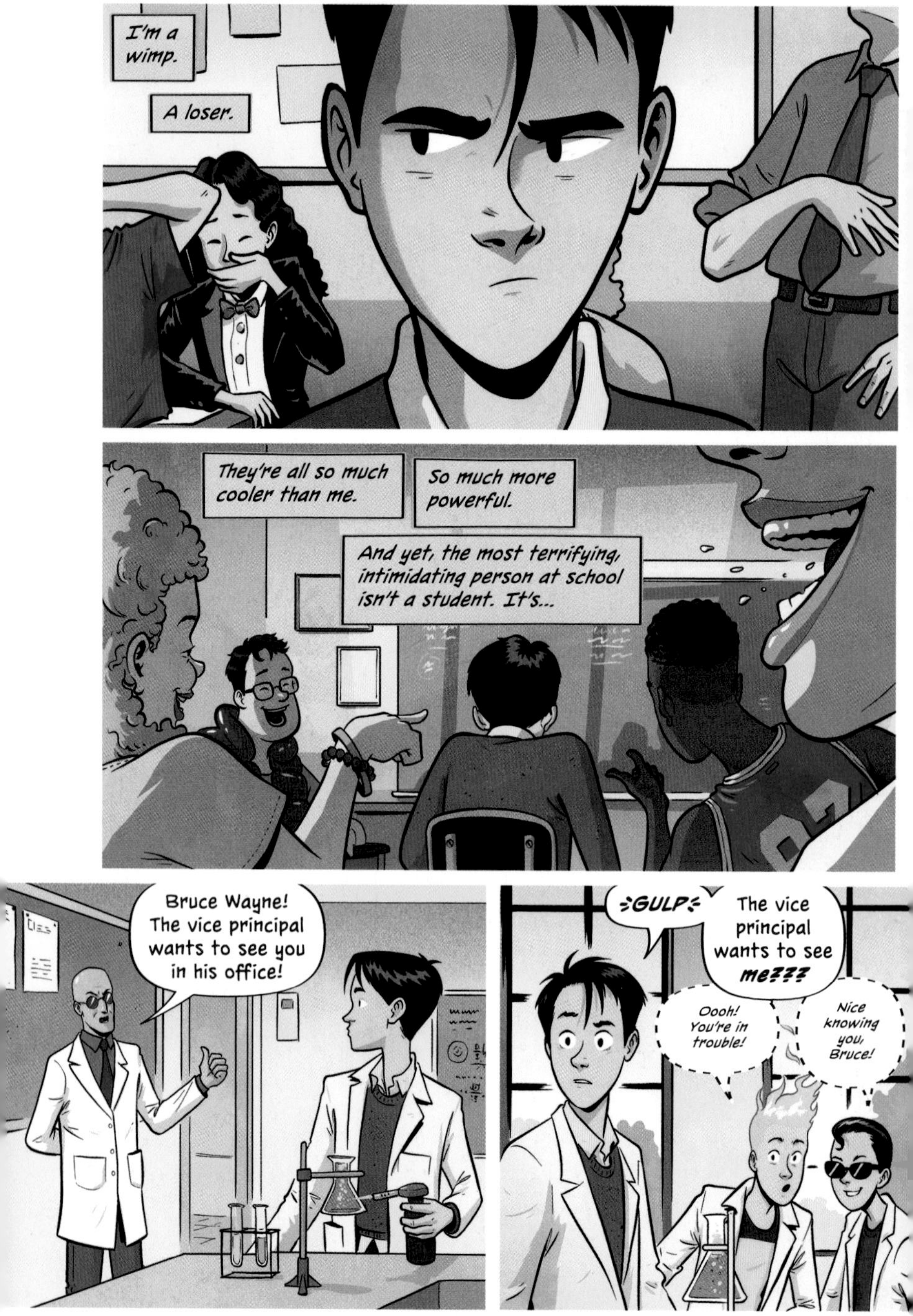
I'm a wimp.
A loser.
They're all so much cooler than me.
So much more powerful.
And yet, the most terrifying, intimidating person at school isn't a student. It's...
Bruce Wayne! The vice principal wants to see you in his office!
GULP
The vice principal wants to see me???
Oooh! You're in trouble!
Nice knowing you, Bruce!

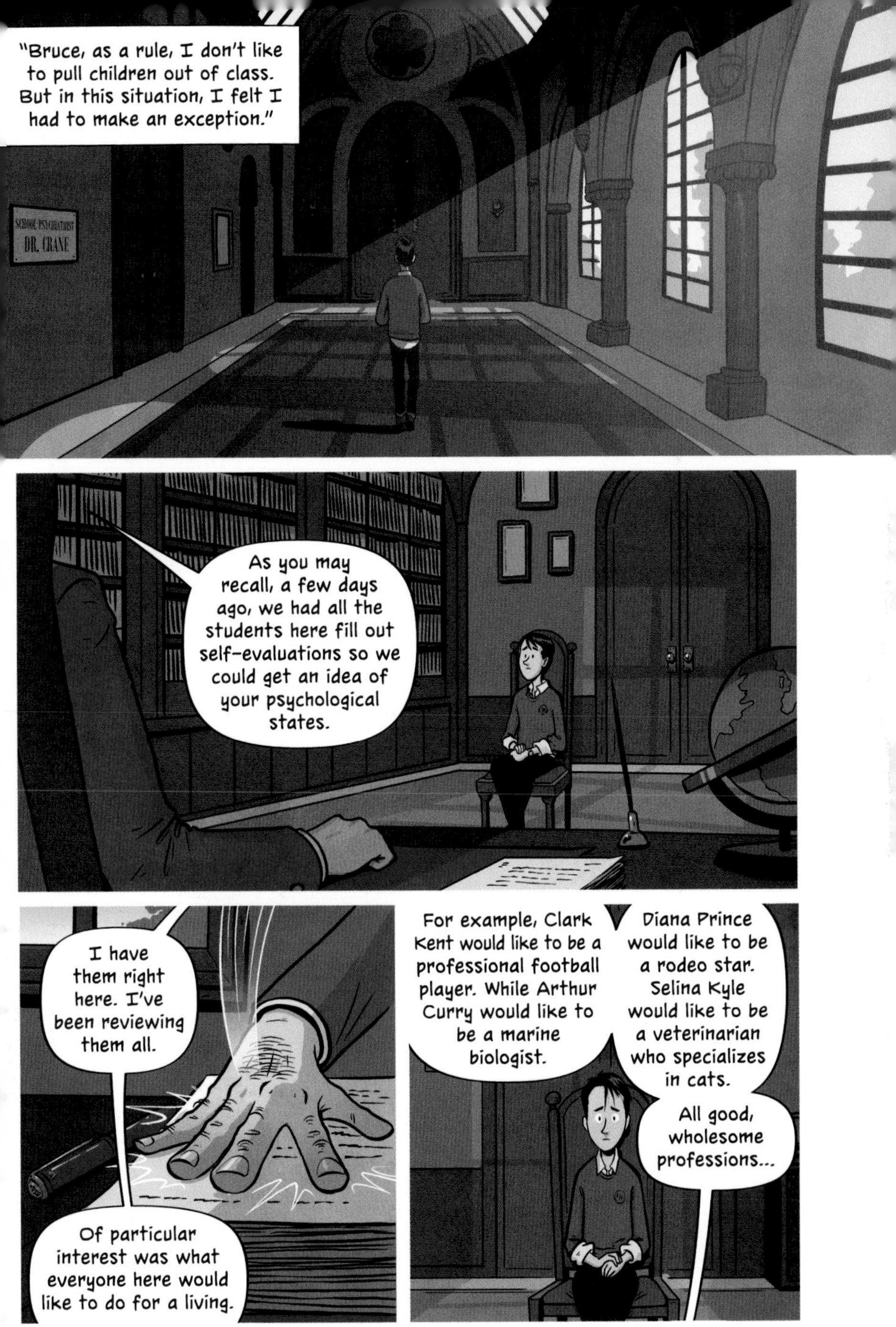
"Bruce, as a rule, I don't like to pull children out of class. But in this situation, I felt I had to make an exception."
SCHOOL PSYCHIATRIST DR. CRANE
As you may recall, a few days ago, we had all the students here fill out self-evaluations so we could get an idea of your psychological states.
I have them right here. I've been reviewing them all.
Of particular interest was what everyone here would like to do for a living.
For example, Clark Kent would like to be a professional football player. While Arthur Curry would like to be a marine biologist.
Diana Prince would like to be a rodeo star. Selina Kyle would like to be a veterinarian who specializes in cats.
All good, wholesome professions...

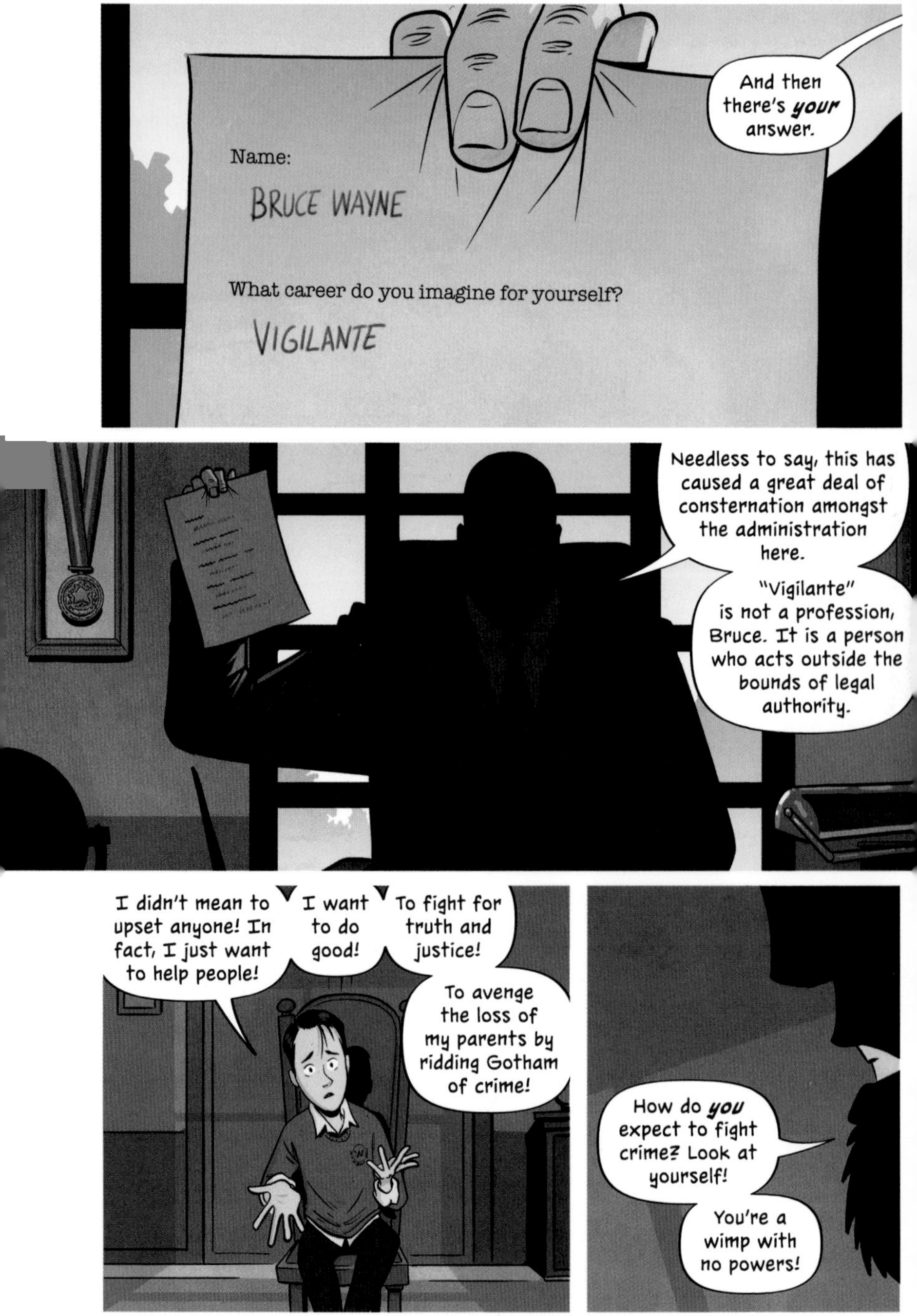
And then there's *your* answer.
Name:
BRUCE WAYNE
What career do you imagine for yourself?
VIGILANTE
Needless to say, this has caused a great deal of consternation amongst the administration here.
"Vigilante" is not a profession, Bruce. It is a person who acts outside the bounds of legal authority.
I didn't mean to upset anyone! In fact, I just want to help people!
I want to do good!
To fight for truth and justice!
To avenge the loss of my parents by ridding Gotham of crime!
How do *you* expect to fight crime? Look at yourself!
You're a wimp with no powers!

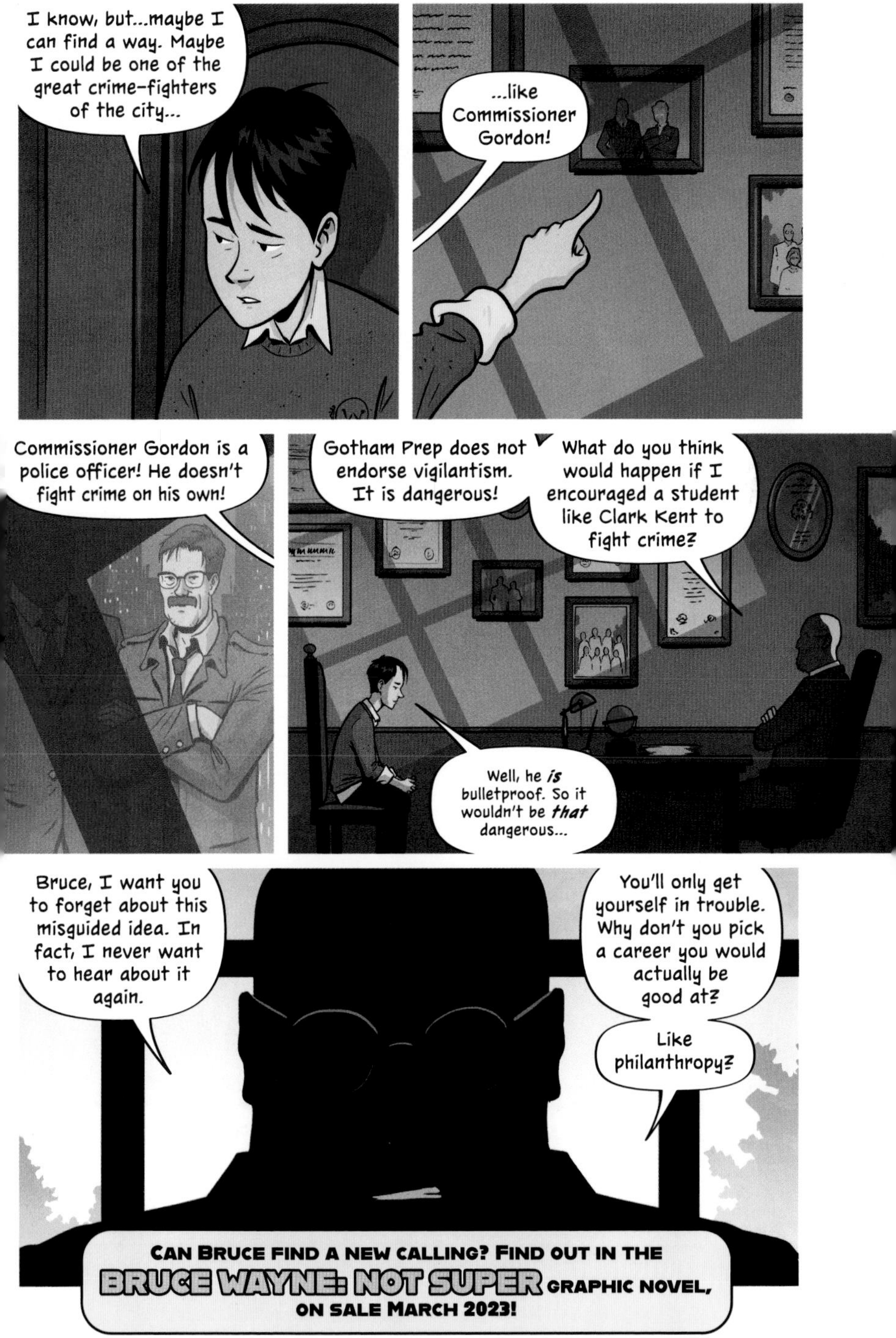

I know, but...maybe I can find a way. Maybe I could be one of the great crime-fighters of the city...
...like Commissioner Gordon!
Commissioner Gordon is a police officer! He doesn't fight crime on his own!
Gotham Prep does not endorse vigilantism. It is dangerous!
What do you think would happen if I encouraged a student like Clark Kent to fight crime?
Well, he *is* bulletproof. So it wouldn't be *that* dangerous...
Bruce, I want you to forget about this misguided idea. In fact, I never want to hear about it again.
You'll only get yourself in trouble. Why don't you pick a career you would actually be good at?
Like philanthropy?
CAN BRUCE FIND A NEW CALLING? FIND OUT IN THE BRUCE WAYNE: NOT SUPER GRAPHIC NOVEL, ON SALE MARCH 2023!

Diana: Princess of the Amazons

Shannon Hale, Dean Hale, Victoria Ying

ISBN: 978-1-4012-9111-2

Diana and Nubia: Princesses of the Amazons

Shannon Hale, Dean Hale, Victoria Ying

ISBN: 978-1-77950-769-3

Want more heroic action?
Check out these DC Graphic Novels for

Green Lantern: Legacy

Minh Lê, Andie Tong

ISBN: 978-1-4012-8355-1

Green Lantern: Alliance

Minh Lê, Andie Tong

ISBN: 978-1-77950-380-0